Jackie Ashenden writ[...] alpha heroes who've ju[...] only to have it blown [...] heroines. She lives in [...] her husband, the inimitable Dr Jax, two kids and two rats. When she's not torturing alpha males and their gutsy heroines she can be found drinking chocolate martinis, reading anything she can lay her hands on, wasting time on social media, or being forced to go mountain biking with her husband. To keep up to date with Jackie's new releases and other news sign up to her newsletter at jackieashenden.com.

Cara Lockwood is the *USA TODAY* bestselling author of more than eighteen books, including *I Do (But I Don't)*, which was made into a Lifetime Original movie. She's written the *Bard Academy* series for young adults, and has had her work translated into several languages around the world. Born and raised in Dallas, Cara now lives near Chicago with her husband and their five children. Find out more about her at caralockwood.com, 'friend' her on Facebook, facebook.com/authorcaralockwood, or follow her on Twitter, @caralockwood.

If you liked *King's Price* and *Look at Me*
why not try

Unleashed by Caitlin Crews
Play Thing by Nicola Marsh

Discover more at millsandboon.co.uk.

KING'S PRICE

JACKIE ASHENDEN

LOOK AT ME

CARA LOCKWOOD

MILLS & BOON

First Published in Great Britain 2018
by Mills & Boon, an imprint of HarperCollins*Publishers*
1 London Bridge Street, London, SE1 9GF

King's Price © 2018 Jackie Ashenden

Look at Me © 2018 Cara Lockwood

ISBN: 978-0-263-26654-2

Printed and bound in Spain
by CPI, Barcelona

KING'S PRICE

JACKIE ASHENDEN

MILLS & BOON

CHAPTER ONE

Leon

'IT'S VERY SIMPLE.' I kept my back to the office as I gazed out of the floor-to-ceiling windows that gave magnificent views of Sydney's impressive harbour. 'I want your daughter.'

There was silence behind me.

Clearly, I'd shocked Thomas Hamilton—one of Sydney's most beloved and lauded philanthropists—into silence.

Excellent. Keeping him off-balance until he'd agreed to my demands was half the battle.

'What do you mean you want my daughter?' he asked.

There was a hint of unsteadiness in his voice. It was very, very slight but I heard it, oh, yes, I did.

I said nothing, letting him stew, watching the yachts in the harbour and the ferry sailing towards Manly, the sunlight touching on the white curves of the iconic Opera House.

Christ, I loved Sydney. Bright and flashy and sexy, with a dark, dirty underbelly. My kind of town.

It was like looking at myself in the mirror.

Leon King. Second son of Augustus King, the erstwhile emperor of Sydney's crime scene, now answering for those crimes in a maximum security correctional facility…aka prison.

Yeah, the King is dead. Long live the King.

Or should I say 'Kings'?

The new Kings of Sydney were me and my two brothers, Ajax and Xander, and it wasn't our father's old empire we wanted to inherit, not when we were the ones who'd toppled it in the first place.

No, we were after redemption. Making good on the King name. Building something out of the ashes of the old empire. Going legit or some such bullshit.

At least that was what Xander and Ajax wanted.

Me, I was fine with going legit. Things were a hell of a lot easier if you didn't have the cops interfering with your business, but it wasn't redemption I needed.

I didn't even particularly care about the King name.

I'd been my father's lieutenant, the muscle at his back, and years of dealing out violence to other people had burned the fucks I had to give right out of me.

I'd been happy to be the bad guy back then and, five years after my father had gone to jail, I was still happy to be the bad guy.

It was a fresh start I wanted, in a city where no one knew who I was or who the Kings used to be. Where I didn't have a past. Where I could be whoever and whatever I wanted to be, master of my own destiny. Where I could escape.

But before all of that, I had one last order to obey. A debt I owed to my oldest brother. And I was prepared to do anything to make good on it.

I turned from the view to the sleek minimalist room that was my office. We were in the tower that housed King Enterprises, the hugely successful property development company my brothers and I had formed out of the rubble of Dad's empire.

Hamilton was sitting in the uncomfortable chair I'd positioned in front of my desk. He was an older man, silver-haired and blue-eyed, with that well-preserved look that only the very rich had.

Except he looked every bit of his sixty-plus years right now.

I tended to have that effect on people.

'What do you think I mean?' I gave him my very widest smile, the one that I was infamous for giving right before I was about to do some serious damage; nothing put someone off-balance like a smile right before you punched them in the face. 'I want to marry her.'

Hamilton paled. 'You can't be serious.'

'Of course I'm bloody serious. I'd never joke about the sanctity of marriage.'

He stared at me, confused by my sarcasm and my smile.

Good. Let him stay confused. It would make it easier to close the deal.

'But…why do you want to marry my daughter?'

'I thought I explained.' I adjusted the cuffs of my white cotton shirt, admiring the contrast with the dark blue of my suit and taking my time about it. Small movements right before the gut punch. Another way to play with an opponent, and I did love to play with my opponents. It was such a power trip. 'My brother wants to expand the King portfolio into the luxury apartment market and we're having difficulty getting investors.'

Hamilton nodded. 'I understand that. But I still fail to see why marriage is necessary for that kind of expansion.'

'It's the name,' I said. 'No one wants to put money behind a King. Not with our past.'

A muscle twitched in the side of Hamilton's jaw. 'But you don't need my daughter for that. Simply pay me the money you said you would, and I'll mention to my friends that you're a good bet and—'

'If only it were that simple,' I interrupted with a heavy sigh. 'But sadly it isn't. I need an…insurance policy, you see. In case you decide to renege on the deal or change it, or alter the terms.'

'I would never do that!' Hamilton looked incensed.

I didn't give a shit. He wasn't the do-gooding pillar of the community everyone thought he was, not when he was up to his eyeballs in debts from a gambling addiction he'd tried to keep secret.

Unfortunately for him, it was no longer a secret. At least not to me. I was good at finding dirt on people and I'd found plenty of it on him.

'I don't care what you would or wouldn't do,' I said

coldly. 'I need an insurance policy and your daughter is it. Plus, a few "introductions" to your friends is not enough. We need a total image overhaul.' I paused to make sure he was with me. 'Having Sydney's biggest charity donor as my father-in-law will silence anyone who still has doubts about us. And hopefully set a few minds at ease about investing with King Enterprises.'

It had only been five years since our father had gone to jail but people's memories could be long. Ajax, Xander and I had done very well to get where we were in that time, yet many viewed us and our intentions with suspicion.

We'd gone straight, but in some people's minds we were still criminals.

A past like ours was difficult to escape—and I never would—but I'd do my bit to help my brothers escape.

Hamilton shook his head, but I continued. 'You'll put the word around that we can be trusted. Invite us to all the best charity parties, talk us up to your cronies, tell them the past is in the past, et cetera.'

'You can't possibly think that I'd—'

'And in return,' I interrupted, 'I'll pay your gambling debts.'

Hamilton's mouth closed with a snap, his expression becoming sharper, more predatory. 'Gambling debts?'

'Come now, Tommy,' I murmured, enjoying the spark of anger in his eyes at my patronising tone. 'You're neck-deep in the red at the moment. All those investments you thought would pay off that didn't, all that tax evasion with those wonderful charities that isn't as effective as it used to be. Or maybe you're simply living beyond your means? Whatever it is, I can help.' I gave him another smile. 'All you have to do in return is give King Enterprises the big thumbs-up to your friends. Oh, yes, and your daughter as an insurance policy.'

This time Hamilton's stare was much more assessing, as if he was weighing up a business decision. Which it was: my help in clearing his debts in return for assistance in the image department for the whole King family.

It was a win-win for everyone.

'I have two daughters,' Hamilton said at last, eyeing me.

Interesting. I only knew of the one who featured in all the society pages. Clara Hamilton. A pretty little socialite with a wealth of honey-blonde hair, big blue eyes and gorgeous tits. In other words, exactly my type, and I did like a society girl. It was funny how all their socialite ways would vanish once their clothes were off and I was inside them. How their dignity would crumble as they begged, as I made them scream my name.

On the outside they made a fuss about my past, about my links to my father's crime empire, about all that nasty violence.

But on the inside, in the darkness of the bedroom, they loved it. That past thrilled them, got them off. Those girls loved a bad boy and I was as bad as it got.

Apart from Ajax. He was worse.

'Give me the pretty one,' I said.

Hamilton's mouth twisted. 'Clara isn't—'

'I can't promise I won't touch her, but I can promise I won't hurt her.' I didn't mind a bit of pain with my sex, but I wasn't a fan of forcing myself on anyone. Where was the fun in that?

But Hamilton didn't like it. At all. 'And if she says she doesn't want to marry you?'

'That's your problem, not mine.' I put my hands in my pockets, my posture relaxed. 'Look, it's not a life sentence. Tell her all I want from her is to pretend we've had a whirlwind romance and that she's desperately in love with me. Then we'll have a nice big society wedding and afterwards she can have my Darling Point mansion. I'll be leaving the country so she'll get it all to herself. In six months, once we've got some solid financial backing, she can send me the divorce papers and we'll both go our separate ways, no harm, no foul.'

Hamilton's eyes narrowed. 'Why the pretence?'

'Appearances matter, Tommy,' I pointed out. 'Which you, of all people, should know. Wouldn't do for it to look like a marriage of convenience now, would it? It's a bit too mercenary. Not at all the image we want for the King name.'

'Divorce so soon afterwards wouldn't exactly project the right image either.'

'It's long enough to convince enough people it's legit and, like I said, bag some investment dollars.' I gave him a conspiratorial look. 'It'll be our little secret, hmm?'

Hamilton leaned an elbow on the arm of his chair and stroked his chin, acting like he was thinking carefully about it. But that gleam in his eye told a different story. He wanted my money and he wanted it desperately.

Perfect.

I remained standing, staying casual. Strange how being relaxed could put people on edge, but it did.

It was putting Hamilton on edge right now. I could see it in the tension in his shoulders and the way he was tapping one foot against the carpet.

I said nothing, letting the silence sit there, because silence could be a useful weapon to someone who knew how to use it. And I did. I was very good with weapons in general.

The silence lengthened, became oppressive.

Eventually, Hamilton shifted then said, 'I'll put the idea to Clara and see what she says.'

I shook my head. 'You do want the money, don't you? I mean, without it, you'll lose everything. And think of the scandal if word got out about your little gambling problem. I don't think you want that, do you?'

He shifted again. 'Fine. I'll make sure she's onboard with the idea then.'

I was conscious of a slight loosening inside my chest, one that couldn't and shouldn't be relief, not when I'd been confident he'd agree to my request, yet felt like it all the same.

Ajax had given me responsibility for securing the King Enterprises' potential expansion and I wanted to make sure I fulfilled that responsibility, especially given what I owed him.

Now it looked like that debt would be paid.

It was satisfying, I couldn't deny it.

What a good little soldier you are.

But not for much longer. Once I was away from Sydney I'd get something I'd always been denied: the luxury of choice.

'You do that,' I said to Hamilton. 'And if she has any issues with the marriage remind her that my house has a pool. Girls love pools.'

Slowly, Hamilton pushed himself out of the uncomfortable chair. 'I do have a condition.'

My smile froze. 'I'm not sure you're in any position to demand conditions.'

'Nevertheless, I have one.' His gaze was very direct and very certain; he wasn't going to back down on this. 'You're not to make contact with her before the wedding. And you're not to touch her after it. It will be a marriage in name only.'

I almost laughed. 'What? You don't want my filthy King hands all over your precious daughter?'

He said nothing, but the look in his eyes was clear. No. He didn't.

I raised a brow, playing with him because that was the fun part and I could never resist a show of power. 'But what if she wants to put her hands on me?'

He flushed. 'She won't. She abhors you.'

'Sure she does. When she doesn't know me from Adam.' I lifted a shoulder. 'Not that I care. Like I told you, if she doesn't want me I won't force myself on her. But if she does…well…' I grinned, just to mess with him '… I can make no guarantees.'

Hamilton's expression became fixed. 'She won't. I can guarantee that.'

It was sweet how protective this pillar of the community was of his daughter. Except, again, I knew it was a sham. It was himself and the reputation of his family that he cared about, like all men of that sort. That and money. I'm sure if I'd offered him more cash he'd have had no problem with me claiming a wedding night from his precious daughter.

Unfortunately, though, telling me not to touch the girl only made me want to touch her even more.

I was perverse like that. Or a cliché—take your pick.

'Sadly for you, not making contact with your daughter negates my need for a public love affair, which means I'm going to have to refuse your condition,' I said, letting my grin fade, showing him steel instead. 'You want my money then you give me the girl. That's all.'

He didn't like that, naturally enough, but, since he didn't have the leverage, all he could do was bluster empty threats as I got Security to usher him out of my office.

As soon as the office door shut behind him I reached for my phone and hit Ajax's number.

He answered with a curt, 'Yeah, what?'

'You'll be pleased to know that Hamilton will give us his backing when it comes to finding investors for the new King Enterprises expansion,' I said.

He grunted. 'How? That prick didn't want anything to do with us.'

'Let's just say I offered him a big incentive.'

'What did you—? On second thoughts, I don't want to know.'

'You don't,' I agreed. 'There's one other thing.'

'What?'

'You need to offer me your congratulations, brother.'

'Why?'

I turned to the view once more, my reflection staring back at me, the predatory smile on my face a reflection of the monster beneath the handsome prince. It didn't scare me, that monster, not any more.

Your bride is going to get one hell of a shock, though.

Yes, she might.

I smiled wider. 'Why? Because I'm getting married.'

CHAPTER TWO

Vita

'YOU'VE GOT TO be kidding.' I stared at my father in shock. 'You want me to marry who?'

Dad had that hard expression on his face, the one he always got when he wanted his own way. 'Leon King, of King Enterprises. The one who—'

'I know who he is,' I interrupted, folding my hands in my lap so he wouldn't see them shake. 'The whole city knows the King brothers.'

Property developers who'd made a lot of money in a very short space of time. Ex-criminals, some would say. Still criminals, said others.

I had no opinion on the subject since it didn't interest me. At least, it hadn't interested me. Not until my father had called me—a shock in itself since I hadn't had contact with either of my parents for about six months—and asked me to come to his downtown office for a meeting.

I hadn't wanted to—I had a report I had to write for my job as a research assistant at Sydney University and the last thing I felt like doing was trying to pretend I still had a relationship with my family. But he'd insisted. Told me it was important. That it concerned my sister.

That I owed them.

He wasn't wrong. I did owe them. In fact, I'd been waiting ten years for him to call in that debt, because I'd had no doubt at all that he would. And now he had it was a relief in many ways.

Except that he wanted me to marry some total stranger in place of my sister.

'Why me?' I tried to keep my voice calm and level because there was no point getting emotional. I'd learned that the hard way. 'Did Clara say no?'

Dad moved around behind his massive oak desk and sat down, giving me the cold judgemental look he'd perfected over the years. 'Not exactly. I haven't told her about it.'

I blinked. This whole thing was getting weirder and weirder.

Odd enough that Dad had called me out of the blue to ask me to take Clara's place and marry some criminal, but that he hadn't even told Clara about it...?

'You're going to have to explain,' I said carefully. 'Because I don't understand how you can not tell Clara. Or even why you're asking me, for that matter.'

Dad was silent, staring at me as if weighing up what he wanted to say.

I stared back. If he thought I was going to fall in line, like Mum and Clara always did, he could think again. Years ago, he'd sent me away to an aunt up north and I'd gone without protest, finishing my schooling away from Sydney society and its far-too-bright lights, burying myself in the relative obscurity of a tiny town and concerning myself only with my studies.

But I wasn't the same person now as I'd been back then. I wasn't seventeen for a start, and I was happy out of the spotlight. In fact, out of the spotlight was where I wanted to stay.

I had a nice, quiet, comfortable life in the labs at the university, completely separate from my family. A life I didn't particularly want to change.

'Fine,' he said after a moment. 'I have some…debts that need to be paid and King has offered to pay them for me. In return, he wants my help with legitimising the King name.' Dad paused. 'And to do that he wants to marry Clara.'

Debts? I shoved that question aside for the moment.

'Why?' I asked. 'How is marrying Clara going to legitimise the King name?'

Anger burned in my father's blue eyes. 'He and his brothers are looking to break into the luxury apartment market and they need investors. So he wants me to get the business community on his side—allay fears about their past, that kind of thing.' Dad said the words as if they tasted bad in his mouth. 'He thinks marrying Clara will help.'

I understood. Though their father had been imprisoned for his crimes years ago, the association still followed his sons around. Not that I knew much about them, aside from the fact that they were notorious for their cut-throat business practices as property developers.

The business world wasn't my world anyway. I preferred science, the quiet atmosphere of the lab I worked in and the comparatively small power plays that were university politics. Not that I involved myself with those either. I kept to myself and I liked it that way.

'I see,' I said carefully. 'It seems an extreme move to marry Clara in order to get a few investors. You can't refuse?'

'No.' The word was flat. 'I need that bastard's money.' He paused. 'It's either that or bankruptcy.'

I stared, shocked. 'Bankruptcy? Seriously? Dad, what did you—?'

'That's not important,' he interrupted. 'The important thing is that he's not going to get his dirty hands on Clara.'

The implication bolted like a small pulse of electricity down my spine, reactivating old hurts, making them echo.

Of course he'd never give up his precious Clara. He's going to sacrifice you instead, the less important one…

I ignored the thoughts. I was over that now. My older sister led a life of parties and social gatherings and shopping, all funded by Dad, but it wasn't a life I wanted. I'd found my place in the lab and I was perfectly happy there. I didn't need him or anyone else to validate me.

'Yet you're okay with him getting his dirty hands all over me,' I commented dryly.

Dad's gaze flickered. 'You're stronger than she is, Vita. You always have been. You'll be able to handle him. She won't.'

Ten years ago I would have lapped up his praise. Nowadays, I knew better. He wasn't praising me—he was manipulating me.

'You're assuming I'm going to say yes.'

His expression hardened. 'You are. These debts must be paid. Including yours.'

It stung, no point in pretending otherwise. He'd always blamed me for what had happened all those years ago, even though, at seventeen, I'd had no idea what I was doing. I'd thought Simon had loved me. I hadn't known he would film himself taking my virginity and put it up on the Internet, with commentary, for his friends to laugh at.

I hadn't known that it would go viral and that soon everyone in the entire world would see it too—including my parents. There had been a media storm and some of the charities Dad did fundraising for and who sponsored Dad's various business activities had withdrawn their sponsorship. Our family had been shamed and embarrassed socially, and it had taken at least six months before people had moved on to the next scandal.

The damage had been done, though. Dad's business empire had teetered on the brink of bankruptcy and it had taken years for him to drag it back.

All because I'd been a seventeen-year-old girl who'd stupidly thought she was in love.

My fault. And Dad never let me forget it.

I looked down at my hands, clasped tightly in my lap. I had no answer to that and he knew it.

'He won't touch you,' Dad said when I stayed quiet. 'All you have to do is go through with the ceremony and live in his Darling Point mansion afterwards. He won't even be there. He'll be leaving the country. And in six months he'll give you a divorce.'

And once you've done it your debt to the family will be paid.

That at least was true. If I did this for my father he couldn't ask anything more of me, surely? I could go back to the private life I'd built for myself. Where I was good at what I did and I was confident in myself. Where I was the one in control.

'You'll get to keep the house, by the way,' Dad added.

I kept my gaze on my hands. The dark blue polish I'd painted on them was chipping at the ends where I'd bitten them, a nervous habit I was trying to break.

I didn't need a house. I lived in a terrace apartment near the university that Dad had bought for me and I insisted on paying the mortgage. My assistant wages were meagre and I was barely able to pay that and cover my living expenses at the same time, but I didn't want any more debts than I had already.

A house in Darling Point, though. You could sell it. Pay Dad back with the proceeds…

No. I would pay my debts myself. My way. With

my own money. I wasn't going to depend on anyone else's, no matter how much it was.

Money was never the answer anyway, even though lots of people thought it was. People like Dad.

'I don't want a house,' I said flatly. 'And I don't want money. What I want is my debt to be cleared and never spoken of again.'

Dad sat back in his big black leather office chair and I thought I saw a flicker of surprise in his gaze, as if he'd been expecting me to say something different. 'Okay,' he said. 'If you do this, consider it cleared.'

'You'll stop holding it over my head for good?'

He gave a sharp nod. 'We'll never speak of it again.'

That was something.

You're seriously considering this?

With an effort I managed to stop myself from shifting nervously in my chair, even though fear was winding tight inside me.

No. No fear. No emotion. Marrying a stranger was nothing. Merely a business proposition or an experiment. Or even trying out a new recipe. Sometimes it worked out and sometimes it didn't, but it was nothing to get emotional about.

Nothing I needed to care about.

'Does he know he'll be getting me instead?' I curled my fingers in tight to my palm to stop from lifting them to my mouth and nibbling on the ends.

Slowly, Dad shook his head.

We both knew why that was. No self-respecting playboy would choose me when he could have Clara.

'He'll be angry,' I said.

'He'll have to deal with it.'

Dad's expression had hardened, making the fear inside me tighten, no matter how much I tried to ignore it.

Leon King would be angry. He thought he'd be getting curvaceous and beautiful Clara and he'd end up with…me.

Vita Hamilton. Tall and bony. No curves to speak of. Two aspirins on an ironing board. And those were the kinder things Simon had said about me in his commentary on the video. Other people had rushed in with worse comments about my thick gingery hair. My freckles. And…other things.

I shoved the memories away. My physical appearance wasn't important and I'd been stupid to let all those comments get to me. It was my mind, my intellect that made me stand out and that, at least, I was proud of.

'He might refuse to go ahead with it,' I said.

'He wants those investors, Vita.' Dad's expression was nothing but sure. 'He'll go through with it. Don't worry about that.'

That…wasn't exactly what I was worried about, though I wasn't sure what I was worried about or why I was afraid.

I didn't know Leon King so his opinion of me—if he had one at all—didn't count. All I had to do was say the words, get the ring, live in his stupid house and then it would be done.

No big deal.

Except Leon King was newsworthy, and no doubt the media would be very interested if he suddenly turned up with a fiancée. Especially a fiancée like me.

There goes your nice quiet life.

My heart was suddenly beating fast and my palms were damp and sweaty. I gritted my teeth, reining in my flailing emotions and shoving them aside.

I needed to be cool about this. Logical. Practical. I was a scientist now, not a shamed and humiliated teenager that the entire world had seen naked.

I was stronger than that—much stronger.

There is a way out of this.

An idea opened up inside me like an elegant solution to a difficult research question, or the missing ingredient in a recipe I hadn't managed to perfect.

Leon King wasn't a man who'd appreciate being played the way my father was intending to play him. And he certainly wouldn't be pleased to find out he'd be getting me, not Clara.

But what if I approached him myself and told him what my father was planning? What if I gave him a heads-up? He'd probably take one look at me, realise I was no Clara and decide he didn't want to get married after all. There was the issue of Dad's debts, but maybe he'd simply be happy to have Dad talk him up in return for paying those off. He didn't need to marry me.

It might not work. Leon King was, after all, a notoriously ruthless businessman and I was simply a research assistant. But I was sure I could make him see reason. Once I explained it all logically, he'd understand.

'Well?' Dad said sharply. 'Think of your sister. Are you going to do this for us or not?'

I lifted my gaze from my hands and met Dad's. 'Okay,' I said. 'So, what do I need to do?'

He looked away. 'Nothing at the moment. Just keep your head down until the big day.'

Of course I would.

After I'd let Leon King know exactly what was going on.

CHAPTER THREE

Leon

'SHE'S NOT HERE,' Xander said, his clear, cold voice cutting through the hard beat of the nightclub's music.

I ignored him, looking out over the heaving crowd and trying to figure out which of the blondes on the dance floor was Clara Hamilton. It was difficult to tell since there were a lot of blondes and the dim lighting made their faces hard to recognise.

We were sitting in the VIP area of Red Door, the city's current nightclub du jour, and pretty little Clara was supposed to be here—at least that was what Hamilton had assured me. But, as my younger brother had so eloquently pointed out, she wasn't.

Annoying.

I'd sent Hamilton an email detailing the number of dates Clara and I were to go on, the locations and what would be expected of her in order to make this look real. And he'd sent me a response letting me know that Clara had agreed to my terms and that she'd be there for the first date, tonight, at Red Door.

But I'd been here a good hour already and there was no sign of her.

I was beginning to wonder if good old Tommy Hamilton had lied and hidden his daughter from me. If so, there would be words to be had. A great many fucking words and none of them to his liking.

Xander sat opposite me, stone-faced as usual, his dark eyes glittering as the club's lights flashed. It wasn't his scene—he spent most nights holed up in his office since he was a total workaholic—so I was surprised he'd decided to come with me tonight.

'Do you have a reason for being here?' I asked. 'Or is it to sit around pointing out stuff I'm already aware of?'

'I wanted to meet her.' He didn't look at me, too busy studying the dance floor. 'Make sure she's no threat to us.'

'She's a pretty socialite, Xan. How much threat could she possibly be?'

His gaze met mine. 'Some women are dangerous.'

He would say that since he was currently having issues with our stepsister, Poppy. As in he hated her and she hated him.

I grinned. 'Relax, brother. She's my beautiful bride. Of course she's not dangerous.'

I'd given him the run-down of my plan, along with Ajax, and both of them were on board with it, though Ajax more than Xander. Ajax liked the idea of rubbing our status in the noses of those who'd once been our enemies, while Xander didn't much care. He was all about the money and protecting our investments.

Xander snorted and looked away, studying the dance floor again.

'Have a drink,' I said. 'In fact, have two. Maybe they'll dissolve that stick currently jammed up your ass.'

Ajax would have told me to fuck off. Xander merely ignored me, then, without a word, pushed himself up off the couch and disappeared through the crowd, heading towards the bar.

Good. I could use some time to myself to figure out what to do about Clara's non-appearance.

I sat back on the couch, reaching for the glass of very expensive single malt I preferred and, as I did so, I caught the gaze of a woman sitting at a table near the stairs to the VIP area.

She was staring very hard at me.

Stares weren't unusual—I got them a lot, especially from women—but I never looked back unless the woman was worth a second glance. And this one wasn't.

Yet I found myself looking back now, unable to put my finger on why. She definitely wasn't my type. At all. She wore a close-fitting black dress, more suited to a funeral dinner than a nightclub, that highlighted a body that was all angles and no curves. Her dark hair had been drawn back unflatteringly tight against her skull, making her plain, sharp face seem even more disapproving than it already was.

She looked like an offended nun.

Why the hell was I staring at her?

Christ, I had no idea. Maybe it was the way she

was staring at me: intense, direct. No blushing and looking away like some women did, or lowering her lashes and shooting me flirtatious glances from underneath them. No come-and-get-me smiles or looking past me, pretending she hadn't been staring.

No, she simply stared. Then she slid off her stool and headed towards the stairs to the VIP area.

Shit. She was coming up here?

Intrigued despite myself, I watched her make her way to the top of the stairs and talk to the bouncer who was guarding the area. She pointed at me as she did so, an earnest expression on her face and, sure enough, the bouncer glanced at me then headed in my direction.

Interesting. What could this woman possibly want? Other than the usual. But then there hadn't been anything flirtatious or sexual in her gaze. No, it wasn't sex she wanted, I was sure.

'Mr King?' The bouncer came to a stop in front of my table. 'There's a woman here who wants to talk to you. She says it's about Clara Hamilton.'

I stilled. Looked like my evening was about to get even more interesting.

'Send her over.' I glanced past him to where she stood, looking in my direction. There was a crease between her brows that disappeared as the bouncer signalled to her, then she started forward without hesitation.

Keen little thing, wasn't she?

Though, as she got closer, it soon became clear she wasn't little. Tall. Taller even than I'd thought at first and her heels weren't exactly high. She moved with purpose too, as if she knew exactly where she was going and why.

'Mr King.' She came to a stop in front of my table. 'Thanks for seeing me.' Without waiting for me to reply, she held out her hand. 'I'm Vita Hamilton.'

I made no move to get up or take her hand, settling for staring at her instead.

She had dark eyes, almost as dark as Xander's yet without the black hole effect his had. Hers were very bright, as if there were tiny stars dancing in the depths. And she didn't smile, merely pinned me with those dark, bright eyes, her hand held out steadily.

People didn't hold my gaze for long. They didn't like what they saw in it, especially when I smiled.

I stared right back. And grinned.

There was a tiny flicker of response, but that was it. She didn't look away or drop her gaze. Or her hand.

Hell, that was…intriguing.

A woman of determination, obviously.

I leaned back in my seat, raising my glass and sipping again, pointedly ignoring her hand just to be a prick.

A flash of irritation crossed her face. Again, intriguing. People were too afraid to get irritated with me. Instead, they either got embarrassed or pretended whatever I'd said or done hadn't happened.

Vita Hamilton didn't pretend.

'Well.' Her voice was clear and bright like her eyes. 'I was only trying to be polite. You don't have to be rude.'

Was she reprimanding me?

Holy shit, she was.

Without waiting for a reply, she dropped her hand then sat down on the seat that Xander had vacated, opposite me, leaning forward and once again pinning me with that dark, starlit stare. 'Now,' she said seriously. 'Like I said, my name is Vita Hamilton and I—'

'I heard the first time, sweetheart,' I interrupted. 'You don't have to say it again.'

She bristled, her mouth thinning in annoyance. 'I'm not your sweetheart.'

That mouth… If the rest of her was sharp and angular, that mouth was not. It was full and very red and, like a particularly juicy apple, I wanted to take a bite out of it.

Maybe I would. Later.

I lifted my gaze to hers. 'Since you're only here with my permission, you're whoever I want you to be.'

She sniffed, annoyance glittering in her eyes. That was different. Fear was the usual response to me, either that or sexual hunger. But I wasn't getting either of those from her.

How fun. I hadn't had a prim girl to play with in a long time.

'Whatever,' she said, clearly uninterested in flirting or any other kind of chit-chat. 'I'm here to talk to you about Clara. I'm her sister.'

Well, that got me.

I gave her another once-over, trying to see the resemblance. Around the mouth maybe, but that was the only thing about her similar to Clara. The rest of her… She wasn't at all like her pretty, curvy, sexy sister.

I took another long sip of my Scotch. 'Perhaps you could tell me where she is then? She's supposed to be here. With me,' I added, just in case things needed clarifying.

Little Miss Vita didn't blink or look away, which was strange when most people sensed what was beneath the mask I wore of the handsome, charming playboy. They could sense the predator, the shark beneath the surface of the beautiful blue sea. And, whether or not they knew what I truly was, they certainly feared it.

But not this woman. She either couldn't see or sense my true self or…she wasn't afraid.

A bolt of something electric, like lightning, went through me, making me go very, very still.

'I don't know where she is,' Vita said, holding my gaze and not even flinching. 'You're supposed to be marrying her, though, aren't you?'

Was she afraid? Did she really not see me?

I smiled wider, giving her a glimpse. 'And?'

Again, not a blink. All I got back was another flicker of irritation. 'Well, I'm here to warn you that you're not.' She hesitated only a fraction. 'My father is planning on making you marry me instead.'

CHAPTER FOUR

Vita

HE WAS LIKE a big cat about to pounce, and my heart started beating very loud and very fast in my ears.

Leon King was dangerous, that much I'd known from the moment I'd laid eyes on him. Very, very dangerous. And right now he was radiating that danger so intensely I could almost taste it.

It made me want to cower away like a frightened rabbit, but I was a professional woman of twenty-six and there was no way I was going to run so I kept staring at him instead, refusing to look away.

He was probably the most beautiful man I'd ever seen.

His features were strong, with a high forehead, chiselled jaw and cheekbones to die for. His eyes were a smoky amber, framed by thick dark lashes and straight dark brows and his hair was tawny, threads of gold and caramel gleaming in the nightclub's dim lighting. Those flashes of gold looked like someone had taken a paintbrush to him and gilded his features.

He wore a white business shirt beneath his dark blue suit and it was open at the neck, exposing golden skin. And he sat there, all sprawled and lazy like a lion sunning himself on a rock.

A predator pretending not to notice its prey, as it readied itself to lunge.

That amber gaze was on mine and the air of danger around him was so thick I could barely breathe. The primitive fight or flight response was kicking in now, urging me to run, but I ignored it.

It was simply a chemical reaction and, as a chemist, I knew all about those. The danger wasn't real so I stayed exactly where I was, determined to show this rude asshole I wasn't intimidated.

'I think you'd better explain, sweetheart.' His voice was deep and rich and vaguely hypnotic. 'Why is your father planning a bait and switch?'

I ignored the sweetheart thing. He was only doing it to get a rise out of me, I was sure. 'Because he doesn't want you to marry her.' I didn't add the fact that it was because I was more expendable. It certainly wasn't about me being stronger than Clara, that was for sure.

'Uh-huh.' Leon King's stare was absolutely relentless and completely terrifying. The smile that curved his beautiful, sensual mouth even more so. 'You're telling me this, why?'

That caught me off-balance. I thought he'd be angry about it and yet... I didn't see anger in his dark golden eyes. No, it was worse. There was nothing in his eyes at all. Absolutely nothing.

I tried to get my thoughts together. 'I'm telling you because I thought you'd want to know. And because…' I steeled myself '… I thought that if you knew, maybe you'd change your mind about this marriage business.'

'Right.' He said the word slowly, drawing it out. 'This marriage business…' Raising his glass, he took another sip of the liquid, his movements unhurried, as if he had all the time in the world. 'And why would I change my mind?'

I blinked, nonplussed and not sure what to say. 'You wanted Clara. And instead you'll get me.' Surely he'd see he wasn't exactly getting a bargain? 'You can't be happy with that. Anyway, I know you're only marrying her to get what you want for your company.' I leaned forward, keen to make him see reason. 'Which makes it pretty simple. All you have to do is pay Dad the money you were going to and he'll make his friends invest or whatever it is you want them to do. There's no real need to marry her or anyone, in fact.'

'You're assuming that's the only reason I wanted to marry her.' He smiled that terrifying smile. 'But it's not.'

A kind of foreboding settled in my gut.

Maybe I didn't want to know his real reason. Before I'd ventured into the city to find him I'd done a bit of research into him and his background, and what I'd found was every bit as terrifying as his smile.

His father had once run the biggest crime network in Sydney. Guns, prostitutes, drugs… You name it, Augustus King had been into it. And Leon had been part of that network, enforcing his father's word as law. At least until he and his two brothers had taken their father down. They'd been granted immunity from prosecution—likely in return for testifying against their father—and had spent the last five years building up King Enterprises, their property development firm.

He was supposed to be going straight, but that smile of his told another story. A story I probably wouldn't like.

'Go on,' he murmured when I didn't say anything, watching me from over the rim of his glass. 'Ask me what my other reason is.'

I wanted to refuse, but the scientist in me wouldn't let it go. 'Okay, so what's your other reason, then?'

'I don't trust your father, sweetheart. I need an insurance policy. Something to make sure he keeps his word, if you understand me.' He smiled yet again. I wished he'd stop doing that. 'Clara was supposed to be my insurance policy. Sure, I would have preferred her but…' His gaze dropped, running over me. 'You'll do. Yes, you'll do very nicely indeed.'

At first, I didn't know what he was talking about. Since the sex tape crap had hit the media and I'd hidden myself away, I'd cut men out of my life for good. I'd had less than no interest in them or dating, or any kind of relationship at all in fact.

I had good working relationships with my male colleagues, but I made sure to keep them at a distance. All my colleagues. I didn't want anyone knowing about me. I didn't want anyone interested in me. And for ten years that had worked well.

Yet the way Leon King was looking at me, so blatantly sexual… No one had looked at me like that in a long time, if ever. But what was even worse was the sudden wave of heat that licked over my skin in response. Like I'd been caught in the backdraught of a wildfire.

It was so intense I looked away despite all my determination not to, my cheeks getting hot.

Hell. I was blushing. When was the last time that had happened?

Pretending I was studying the crowd and not avoiding his gaze, I said, 'I don't want to marry you. Insurance policy or not.'

'Why not?'

The question irritated me. Was he stupid? Did he really not know?

I steeled myself yet again to meet his dark golden eyes. 'Why do you think? I don't even know you.'

He gave an elegant shrug. 'So?'

'What do you mean "so"? You're a complete stranger.'

'Why does that matter? Complete strangers marry each other every day.' He tilted his head, the lights striking deep gold from his hair, his gaze gleaming. 'I presume your father told you that you'll get my house. Plus I can throw in some more money to sweeten the deal.'

'I don't want your house and I don't want your money,' I said flatly.

'Sex then. You can have me.' That smile lost its edge, became warmer, which somehow made it seem even more terrifying than before. 'I assure you I'm worth it.'

He was so damn arrogant that I should have laughed. If he'd been another man, I would have. But again that strange heat licked up inside me at the words, a pull deep inside.

Yes, and remember what happened last time you felt that?

Shame. Humiliation. Pain.

No, I shouldn't think of that. Chemicals, that was all this reaction was. Serotonin. Adrenaline. Dopamine. Nothing more.

'No.' I put every ounce of denial I could into the word, sitting up straight and tall to show him I meant business. 'I don't want you either.'

He laughed, a soft sound that made me shiver. 'Then maybe your poor father doesn't get his money.'

'Why not? You'd really pull out just because I won't marry you?'

He gave another shrug as if it wasn't a big deal. 'I'm not risking my money to your father's promises, not without some guarantee.'

Dammit.

I shifted on the chair then rubbed my temples with one hand. The relentless beat of the music was giving me a headache and this was…not going like I'd planned. I'd thought he'd be a typical man, only concerned with having the beautiful trophy woman on his arm. But apparently he was different for some reason. Which was irritating.

Tell him it's all off. Leave Dad to get out of this one himself.

I could. Except then the debt I owed Dad would still be there, hanging over my head. He'd got me away during the media storm, tried to cover my tracks and get rid of that recording. All the while facing the bankruptcy that I'd caused. I did owe him something.

Leon watched me, his gaze a searchlight uncovering all kinds of things I'd prefer to keep hidden.

'What, exactly, is your problem?' he asked. 'I won't touch you if you don't want me to, and at the end of six months you can have my house and a divorce. I'll be leaving the country after that anyway. You'll barely see me.'

He made it sound so reasonable. Why was I balking? I didn't have any particular beliefs around marriage and love wasn't real anyway. So what did it matter?

'I don't like…the attention,' I said lamely, settling on the most logical reason for my reluctance. 'I'm not comfortable being in the spotlight. And marrying you will draw attention.'

'Of course it will. I want it to.' His gaze wandered over me again and I felt my skin prickle in response. 'I want people to think we're in love, not that I married you purely to get an in with your father.'

Well, Dad had not mentioned anything about a love affair.

'But that's why you are marrying me,' I pointed out.

'Well, yes. I just don't want other people to know that.'

'Why not? Why should you care?'

He gave another of those soft laughs, his eyes gleaming. 'The King family has changed, Miss Hamilton. We're not the criminals everyone seems to think we are, not any more. And what better way to illustrate that than for one of us to fall desperately in love and marry a good woman from a very good family?'

'Not to mention getting investors for your company's expansion,' I said dryly.

'That too.' He swirled the liquid in his glass. 'It's a multi-layered, complicated problem. I wouldn't think too hard about it if I were you.'

Was that a not-so-subtle dig at my intelligence? 'Not to worry my pretty little head, you mean?'

He shrugged, his gaze guileless, and didn't answer. 'Did you know I was supposed to be meeting Clara for our first public date tonight?' he asked instead. 'She didn't turn up, but you did.'

Public dates? Dad hadn't mentioned anything about public dates.

Because he knew you'd refuse.

'I didn't know Clara was supposed to be here,' I snapped, freshly annoyed at my father all over again. 'Dad didn't mention it to me. And I'm certainly not here to be her stand-in either.'

'Clearly not.' He tilted his head. 'What have you got against a bit of attention, though?'

Great. That was all I needed. To drag up what had happened to me ten years ago. I didn't want to talk about it and I especially didn't want to talk about it to him.

'I just don't like it,' I said.

'Bullshit. Must be something pretty bad for it to involve coming to talk to me personally.'

Dammit. My options were either lying or simply not answering the question, but I was hopeless at lying and I had a feeling he wasn't the type to simply drop a subject.

Hiding it wasn't an option either, not when a quick search on my name would bring up the video. No matter how hard Dad had tried to scour it from the Internet, he hadn't been able to. The Internet was for ever and so was my video.

He'll see it if you tell him.

My jaw tightened. Well, everyone in creation had seen it, so why should I care if he did? Possibly he already had.

'Google my name and you'll find out.' I lifted my chin and folded my hands in my lap so I wouldn't be tempted to bite on my nails.

He gave me a long, silent, assessing look. Then he put down his glass and reached into his pocket, bringing out his phone.

I opened my mouth to tell him that he should wait until I wasn't around at least. But his long fingers were already moving over the screen and a moment or two later he lifted his gaze from the phone and looked at me.

I blushed again, the old feelings of humiliation and shame washing over me, but I shoved them away. I wasn't that girl in the video, not any more.

Instead, I stared, daring him to say a single word.

He merely lifted one dark brow. 'So you had a sex tape drama. Who hasn't?'

Was he being flippant? I couldn't tell.

'But you can see why I don't want any kind of public attention. I don't want anyone dragging that up again.'

'You're thinking about this all wrong, sweetheart.' Casually, he dumped his phone on the table then sat back against the couch, lifting his arms along the back. 'You could hide away for ever, afraid of all that coming back up again. Or you could go for a little revenge.'

It was not what I'd expected him to say.

'Revenge? What do you mean revenge?'

'A hot guy slept with you and humiliated you. And millions saw it. What better revenge than to show those millions of people another guy falling for you? Incredibly handsome, sickeningly rich.' He gave another smile, utterly and completely charming, and not at all modest. 'Notorious. Not a man anyone would mess with. Yet you'd have him wrapped around your little finger.'

The words slid under my skin in a way I wasn't comfortable with. Revenge wasn't what I wanted. Oblivion was, and I didn't want anything to disrupt that. And yet…

'I'd already planned some dates with Clara,' he went on, that rich, deep voice of his winding around me. 'Nothing major, just a few public outings to show people we're in love. And then a big wedding to top it all off.' His voice deepened, became softer. 'Yes, it's attention. But this time you get to call the shots. And it ends with you getting everything. The wedding, the mansion, the money.' He paused, gold glimmering in his eyes, his smile making me feel hot, even though I wasn't. 'And, of course, you get the man.'

My instant response was to tell him no, that I didn't care. I'd got past what had happened to me and what I wanted was to go back to my obscure life and carry on as if none of this had ever happened.

You could do that. Or you could rewrite your own story. And this time with the ending you want.

The thought hit me hard.

Back when I was seventeen, being Clara's tall, gangly stick of a sister had been tough, and I'd longed to be like her. Pretty and curvy, popular with all the boys. I'd been an easy mark for Simon. Desperate for attention, insecure, a prime target for his manipulation. And he had manipulated me. He'd made me think he wanted me, that he loved me.

Then he'd used me, humiliated me, and all because he'd wanted my sister and she'd refused him. I'd been his revenge on her, too naive and stupid to understand what he was doing.

So, in a way, Leon King was right. This would be

a perfect kind of revenge. And it would be my choice. Something I could do for myself.

Slowly, I let out a breath and looked at him. 'So… when you say a few public dates, how many are we talking here?'

CHAPTER FIVE

Leon

I HAD HER. Definitely I had her and a good thing too.

Satisfaction swept through me. Yes, Clara would have been preferable and I was pissed off at Hamilton for trying to pull a bait and switch, but fundamentally I didn't much care which sister I married.

It was the marriage itself, the connection to the Hamiltons and the image it projected that I was concerned about.

Vita Hamilton wasn't beautiful. But she'd do.

Besides, the way she'd kept looking at me intrigued me. How she hadn't been afraid and how she'd refused me—and no one ever refused me. Or at least they didn't without risking the consequences.

But she had. And it had been a challenge I hadn't been able to resist.

Five years ago I would have answered that challenge with force. Not physical—not with a woman—but I'd have considered that sex tape information the perfect way to blackmail her into doing what I wanted.

Maybe I would have had to resort to that if she hadn't agreed, but she had. And I had to admit that there was something sweet about her choosing me without the need for coercion.

She sat on the edge of the chair, her head tilted slightly, watching me with those bright eyes. Like a cautious bird or a curious fox. No, definitely more fox than bird with that undercurrent of auburn in her brown hair.

That was fine. She could be a little fox. But there was no doubt as to who the dominant predator here was. Me. And she knew it. I hadn't missed how she'd looked away earlier when I'd let my gaze run over her, or how she'd blushed. And it didn't take a genius to figure out that she wasn't as immune to me as she acted.

'How many dates?' I took another long, slow look at her body to see if I'd get the same reaction. 'I had three or four planned so far.'

The swell of her breasts was tantalising beneath the black fabric of her dress. They were small and round, a perfect fit for my hand. The rest of her was difficult to see from the way she sat, but her legs would be long and no doubt they'd wrap perfectly around my waist. Or drape over my shoulders...

'But they'd be in public?' She held my gaze, determined to show me how unbothered she was by the way I was looking at her.

She didn't fool me, however. Even in the dim light

of the nightclub I could see how she was blushing. Christ, did she really think I wouldn't notice?

I watched as the stain of red crept down the delicate arch of her throat to the neckline of her boring black dress. 'Not much point otherwise.'

She shifted on the edge of her chair and at last dragged her gaze from mine. Her hand half lifted, her finger nearly at her mouth before she put it back down in her lap again. Her nail polish was chipped. A nail-biter perhaps?

'What kind of dates are we talking about?' She gave the crowd a leisurely survey before glancing back to me again. 'Going to the movies? That sort of thing?'

I grinned, letting her know that I'd caught her small nervous movement and how she'd had to look away. That I knew I was getting to her. 'The movies? No, sweetheart. Think bigger.'

Her dark reddish brows arrowed down, the lights in her eyes flickering with irritation. 'Don't call me sweetheart.'

I was definitely getting to her. How satisfying.

'You don't like sweetheart?' I asked mildly.

'Not when my name is Vita.'

'Sure, but you'll be my fiancée. You need a pet name.'

Her mouth tightened. 'I don't want a pet name.'

'Too bad, you're getting one.' I was being a prick, but I hadn't had anyone this delicious to play with for years and I was going to enjoy the hell out of it. 'You can choose which, though. If you don't like sweetheart, your other choices are "baby", "little girl", "honey", "darling" or "sweet cheeks".'

She glared. 'I don't want you to call me any of those things.'

'Hey, I'm all for equal opportunities. I don't mind a pet name for myself. "Stud" or "big boy" is fine. I don't mind "hot stuff". My preference, though, is for "sir".'

Her frown deepened. 'Stop playing with me. I don't like it.'

So. A woman who didn't play games and had no interest in playing them either.

Disappointing. Still, her honesty and directness were refreshing. And, being the perverse bastard I was, they made me want to play with her even more.

Maybe I'd save that for later, though. Now I'd got her agreement to the marriage there was no point risking that for a bit of fun.

'Fine,' I said. 'No games. As to the dates, I'll send you the details later. But fair warning. There will be press involved. My aim is to show the entire world we're in love.'

Another flicker of emotion crossed her face at the mention of the press and it looked like trepidation. Not that I could blame her. I'd only had a cursory look at the first couple of results of that search on her name, but that sex tape looked like it had been a major scandal. Seventeen was a hell of an age for that sort of attention, especially when that attention was the wrong kind.

'But I get to say what happens on them, right?' The

trepidation had vanished, her expression becoming more concentrated, fierce almost.

Ah, yes. I had said something like that, hadn't I?

A thread of unease wound through me. I wasn't good at taking orders, never had been, even when my father had been the one giving them. Plus, I hated the thought of relinquishing control of a situation to someone else.

Then again, there were ways around that. Topping from the bottom, and all that.

'Revenge,' Vita said suddenly, as if she could sense my discomfort and was hoping to exploit it. 'That's what you told me. I could rewrite my own story, this time with me calling the shots.'

Shit. Little vixen was good at sniffing out a weakness, wasn't she?

Not that it mattered. It was only a couple of dates, holding hands and some kissing. Maybe more than kissing depending on the situation. And if she didn't want that, then so what? I wasn't attracted to her anyway.

Yet... The devil inside me found her fascinating. It wanted a reaction from her, some kind of response, and I didn't care that she wasn't my type.

I was a predator who wanted the chase and who knew she'd put up one hell of a fight in the end.

'Yes,' I said, already thinking about how I could turn this to my advantage. 'You get to call the shots.'

She gave a nod as if she'd been expecting me to okay it all along. 'All right then. I agree to marry you.

But only on the condition that whatever happens in public is directed by me.'

I waved a hand. 'Be my guest.'

'So what happens after the wedding?'

'We'll have a couple of months of blissfully happy marriage so my brothers and I can get as many investors on board as we can, and then I leave the country.'

Her hand lifted to her mouth again, and I was pretty sure it was an unconscious thing because she didn't seem to be aware of it. 'So, I have to live with you?'

'Yes, you'll stay with me at my house—don't worry, it's massive; you can have your own wing. You won't even see me if you don't want to.'

'And then?' She nibbled absently on the end of her nail.

Holy Christ, that mouth. I stared at the full, red shape of it. What if she had those lips wrapped around my cock instead of her own finger? Would she use her teeth? Dear God, I hoped so.

Why are you having fantasies about Vita Hamilton's mouth?

I had no fucking idea.

'Then, like I said, I leave the country.' My voice sounded rough. Jesus.

She tilted her head, dark eyes on mine. 'Why?'

I shifted, uncomfortably aware that my suit trousers were tighter than they'd been two seconds ago. 'Why am I leaving the country? Because I am.'

'Will you come back?'

'No. Hence you getting the house. We'll leave it

six months, then sign the divorce papers and you'll be free to go.'

She continued to nibble on her nail, frowning at me, as if she was working out a tricky problem in her head. 'I won't have to do anything I don't want to do, right?'

'Right.' Though I could think of a couple of things I could convince her that she did want to do. Things involving that mouth. I was, after all, very good at convincing people.

'Okay.' Abruptly, she took her finger out of her mouth, much to my relief. 'That's all the questions I have for now.' She reached for the small handbag she'd put down on the seat next to her, obviously getting ready to go.

Except I hadn't finished.

We were in a nightclub and there were a lot of people around and, if I wasn't much mistaken, a couple of columnists from the local gossip websites were propping up the bar. Which made right here, right now a prime opportunity to make our so-called relationship public. Plus, there was a small experiment I wanted to run. Just a test to…confirm something.

'Excellent.' I sat forward. 'Give me your hand.'

She turned her head, giving me a wary sidelong look. 'Why?'

'You're full of questions.'

'I'm a scientist. Asking questions is what I do.'

'A scientist?' Diverted, I gave her another once-over. 'You don't look like one.'

'Really?' Her expression was scornful. 'And what does a scientist look like?'

'Blonde.' I couldn't resist playing with her. 'Big tits. Glasses. Short white coat.'

'No,' she said flatly, refusing the bait. 'Some scientists might look like that, but not the ones I know.'

'Where do you work?'

'In the university, in the labs. I'm a research assistant.' The scorn faded from her voice, a note of pride entering it. 'I have a PhD.' She stared at me as she said it, like she was throwing down a challenge, though what she expected me to say I had no idea.

'Smart, huh?' I refused her bait as she'd refused mine. 'I like a smart woman. You'll have to tell me more on our next date.'

'What do you mean next date? We haven't even had one yet.'

'Sure we have. This is our first.' I reached out towards her. 'Your hand, honey.'

'Not honey.'

'Sweetheart, then.'

'I don't want—'

'Scared?'

Irritation rippled over her sharp little face. 'I'm not falling for that.'

'You know what they say, darling. You have to stand for something or else you'll fall for anything.'

If she could have growled at me she would have, I'm sure.

Instead, she let out an annoyed breath. 'Don't make me regret this.' Then she stuck out her hand.

I didn't hesitate to take it or expect to feel anything when I did. Sure, I'd been fixated on her mouth and had thought about how her legs would feel wrapped around me, but I often thought those things about women. I was a man, after all, and not a very good one at that.

So I wasn't prepared for the shock of raw electricity that jolted me the moment her long slender fingers touched mine. Or to see the same shock mirrored in the wide dark of her eyes.

She went still, the muscles in her arm tightening in preparation to jerk her hand away.

And I had one crystal-clear thought.

No. She wasn't going to do that. Not here, not in full view of everyone. Not when this was the moment I'd chosen to reveal our relationship to the world.

So I closed my fingers around hers and held on.

She took a sharp breath.

Her skin was cool but it warmed against mine, and I didn't think it was my imagination that the lights in her eyes flared briefly.

Yes, she felt this too.

I held her gaze in silent challenge. Then slowly I rose to my feet.

Her gaze was wary, watching me as if I was a dangerous animal she had to keep an eye on. It nearly made me smile.

Yes, keep watching, little vixen. You never know what I might do to you.

Keeping my fingers wrapped around hers, I moved

towards the stairs that led out of the VIP area and down to the dance floor, tugging her with me.

She resisted at first but I didn't pause, drawing her down the stairs and into the crowd.

'What are you doing?' she snapped as I stopped on the dance floor, a small space opening up around us, then turned to face her.

'What does it look like?' I gave her another tug, drawing her closer. 'I'm going to dance with you.'

She blinked. 'What? But I… I don't know how to dance.'

Her wariness had been replaced with an adorable mixture of shock and confusion. And that was perhaps why she didn't resist as I put my hands on her hips and drew her even closer, our bodies almost touching.

She was tall enough that I didn't have to tilt my head to look down into her eyes.

'Don't worry,' I said softly, staring into her bright, black gaze. 'Just follow my lead.'

She blinked again and something hot and raw sizzled between us.

We were mere inches apart, the soft curve of her breasts nearly brushing my chest, the heat of her soaking into my palms where they rested on her hips. She wasn't wearing any kind of perfume but I could smell her, a delicate musky scent with a floral hint.

It was delicious. It sent a bolt of pure lust straight to my cock.

Oh, pretending to be in love with her was going to be no hardship. No hardship at all.

I firmed my grip on her and a spark flared bright and brilliant in her eyes, making everything in me harden in anticipation.

I could kiss her right here, right now, and she wouldn't protest. That beautiful mouth would open under mine and she'd taste so sweet, I just knew it.

But…perhaps not yet. It would be better to give her some time to get used to the idea of marrying me, not to mention get used to me getting close. It wouldn't do to come on strong and frighten her away.

We were supposed to be madly in love after all.

So I didn't kiss her. Instead, I let her go. 'Perhaps we'll leave it tonight then,' I murmured, not bothering to explain. 'I'll be in touch.'

I smiled at her. Then I walked away.

CHAPTER SIX

Vita

LEON KING WAS a Grade A bastard.

The day after I'd met him in the nightclub and he'd forced me to dance he sent me a schedule of the dates he'd be taking me on, with times, not to mention the name of the wedding planner who'd be handling the wedding itself. There were dates attached to that too—he wanted the marriage to happen as soon as possible while at the same time generating the maximum amount of publicity.

Four weeks was enough time apparently.

And he hadn't only sent the schedule to me; he'd sent it to my father as well. So now Dad knew that not only had I met with Leon King without telling him, I'd tipped Leon off about me being Clara's stand-in.

Yet that wasn't the worst part.

The worst part was the link Leon had included with the schedule. A link that went to a page on some awful gossip website where there was a terrible write-up about Leon King's new 'love'. A photo accompanied it. A photo of him holding me on the dance floor just before he'd walked away.

I'd tried very hard to forget about the moment he'd held me close, his predator's eyes watching me all the while. And I still didn't know what had happened to me in that second. Why I'd let those big, warm hands of his rest on my hips and that tall, muscled body get close to mine.

It had been like I'd gone deaf, the beat of the music fading away, the crowds disappearing, everything lost in the dark gold of his eyes.

I'd just…forgotten I could move.

I'd forgotten I could breathe.

His nearness had been electric, my skin prickling all over, a strange restlessness coiling deep inside me, a heat that seemed to pool right down between my thighs.

It was as if he'd hypnotised me.

I didn't know what it was in the end that made him walk away, but I was glad of it. Even more glad to get out of that damn club as quickly as I could.

What would you have done if he hadn't let you go?

Nothing, of course. All that physical reaction was simply oestrogen reacting to testosterone, or pheromones or adrenaline, take your pick. None of that meant anything, and I should know since I still had the scars to prove it.

Anyway, the upshot was Dad not being pleased and I had to endure a speech down the phone about how irresponsible I'd been and how I'd put the whole plan at risk. I decided not to bother telling him I'd been trying to get Leon to drop the marriage thing to save us both, listening to him in silence instead then disconnecting the call without a word.

He wanted me to marry Leon King and I would.

But not for him or my sister. I was going to do it for me.

For the last ten years I'd been the one in charge of my life and now that I had the chance to right a wrong that had been done to me, I'd take it. I'd marry Leon, slay a few personal demons and then return to the peace of the lab.

My father could take my so-called 'debt' and go screw himself.

The next date was in a couple of days, which unfortunately left some time for the media to find out where I was and how to contact me, and it wasn't long before the phone calls and emails started.

Dread coiled in my stomach every time I looked at my phone and all the notifications and missed calls, but fear was just another chemical reaction and that made it easy to ignore.

I spent the day of the next date head down in the lab, experimenting with a few new compounds. Concentrating only on that and not on the fact that I would be entering the arena again, the media circling me like wolves, while the lion I had to defeat waited in the centre for me, a hungry look in his eyes.

Luckily it didn't seem like my colleagues had noticed any of the websites carrying the story, so I was able to go about my day with relative ease. But naturally Leon wouldn't let me forget and I received a text in the afternoon from him, reminding me of the date and time I would be picked up.

How he'd got hold of my number I didn't know, but it annoyed me.

That night I put on my black dress again—it was the only halfway decent thing in my wardrobe and I couldn't be bothered dressing up anyway—and did a quick make-up job. I hated spending too much time on my appearance and didn't see why I should take more time on it now.

Leon might want us to look like we were in love— as real as love ever got—but we weren't. It was all fake, all pretend. A show for the cameras. Except that I wasn't very good at pretend.

Leon would be, though, I'd have laid money on it. After all, he was a man with a very dark past, though you'd never know to look at him. On the surface he was all beauty and charm, while underneath lurked something else. Something much darker.

Something that makes you curious…

No. Most definitely not. Curious was the last thing I was about him. The very last.

A car came to pick me up at eight and I got in, re-fusing to give in to my trepidation about the evening by thinking about a new muffin recipe I wanted to try. I loved baking in my spare time since it was basi-cally chemistry with delicious results. And it worked. Kind of.

But what I really should have been thinking about was how I was going to handle this date. I was sup-

posed to be calling the shots yet I had no idea what
kind of shots I wanted to call.

It had been ten years since I'd been on a date and
I could hardly remember what one was like. Dinner,
a movie and awkward conversation were the only
things I could recall. That and the desperate desire
to be more like my sister and not the gangly girl that
nobody liked.

Hideous in other words.

I forced aside the memory and stared out into the
city as the car moved through the streets. We were
supposed to be going to some expensive restaurant
down by the waterfront and he was going to meet
me there.

I wondered what on earth I'd talk to him about because we'd have nothing in common, and then what
I'd do if he tried to touch me again. It was discon-
certing to realise I had no idea about either of those
things.

At that moment the driver unexpectedly pulled the
car over to the kerb and I was about to ask him what
was happening when the back door opened.

And Leon King got in beside me.

I was so surprised that for a second I could only
stare at him.

Back in the nightclub, he'd seemed tall—over six
two at least—but now, in the close confines of the car,
there was no escaping the sheer size of him. He took
up all the space with his long legs and broad shoulders, making me feel dwarfed even though I had to
be only a couple of inches shorter than he was.

And it wasn't only to do with his height. His physical presence pushed at me, making me want to squeeze myself into the corner of the seat and get as far away from him as possible.

He was so...hot. I could feel the warmth of his body even though he wasn't touching me, and I could smell his scent too. Spicy, like a cedar forest. And I had a weird urge to get close and inhale it, touch his skin to test his heat.

You wanted to do that with Simon too. Remember?

How could I forget? Handsome, attractive Simon. The first man to pay attention to me. The first man I fell in love with. The man who recorded himself taking my virginity then uploaded it onto the Net, complete with commentary.

The memory was enough to banish the urge to touch Leon King completely, but not quite enough to make me shift away. No way was I going to let him know that he affected me.

'Good evening, sweetheart,' he said, grinning as he pulled the door closed after him. 'Hope you don't mind me dropping in like this, but I thought we should arrive together. Plus, I wanted to give you something.' His smoky golden gaze flashed over me then narrowed as he took in what I was wearing, his grin fading. 'Please don't tell me you're wearing the same dress that you wore to the nightclub.'

Irritated by the effect of his physical presence and unexpectedly stung by the disapproving look on his face, I folded my hands in my lap and lifted my chin. 'Okay. I won't tell you.'

'You couldn't have worn something different?'

'I don't have anything different. Anyway, it's a perfectly nice dress.'

'For a funeral.' He shifted, reaching into his back pocket to take something out of it. 'We need to have a little talk about clothing.'

'No, we don't,' I said firmly. 'I'm the one calling the shots, remember? And if I want to wear this, I will. Besides…' I sniffed '…you're my fiancé and you're supposed to love me no matter what I wear.'

His mouth curled and for a second genuine amusement gleamed in his eyes. It made something in my chest shift and I had to look away, pretending I was smoothing a crease in the material over my knees instead.

'I stand corrected.' There was a note I couldn't place in his rich voice. 'But you need to work on being more convincing when you mention the word love. Especially since we're supposed to be in it.'

'Love isn't real,' I informed him, keeping my attention on my dress. 'Feelings are simply chemicals.'

'Is that so?' He really did sound amused now. 'Well, you might not want to say that where people can hear us.'

'I suppose not.'

'Excellent. Well, keep the dress, but for the love of God, could you not wear your hair like that?'

I bristled. 'What's wrong with my hair?'

'It's a bit…' He stopped, frowning. Then, before I could protest, he leaned towards me, reaching around behind my head and neatly pulling off the band I'd used to secure my hair.

I blinked in surprise, feeling the heavy weight of it begin to uncoil and slide down over my shoulders. 'What on earth do you think you're doing?' I demanded. 'I didn't say you could touch me.'

'You didn't say I couldn't either.' A look of satisfaction crossed his ridiculously handsome face. 'But that's better. Much better.'

'You can't touch me.' I had to fight not to slap him, which only rattled me further since I had no idea why. 'That's my first rule for the evening.'

He only stared at me, perfectly composed, taking up all the space the way arrogant men often did. He wore another beautifully tailored suit, in dark charcoal this time, with a black shirt open at the neck, revealing smooth golden skin.

He was gorgeous, and rationally I knew it. But he didn't affect me physically. To admit that would be stupid.

Testosterone. Dopamine. Serotonin. That was all it was.

'Well,' he said on a long sigh, 'I suppose if you insist. But if I can't touch you, how am I going to give you this?' He lifted the box he'd taken out of his pocket. It was small and black—a ring box.

I glanced at it. 'An engagement ring?'

'Of course. I organised one this week.' He flipped open the lid, revealing a massive diamond gleaming on a platinum band. 'You're going to need to wear something.'

It wasn't just 'something'. It was a ring that must have cost him thousands. And all for a pretence.

'I hope you can return that,' I muttered, staring at the diamond.

'No. It's yours.' He took the ring out, discarding the box then holding out his other hand imperiously. 'Your hand, sweetheart.'

Oh, no. Not again.

I kept my hands firmly in my lap. 'I can put my own ring on, thank you.'

His eyes gleamed and suddenly I knew I'd said the wrong thing. 'Of course you can. But I want to do it.'

'Why?'

'Because I said so.'

My heart began to beat a little faster. 'I thought I got to call the shots.' I had no idea why I was arguing since it would only make things worse. I just… didn't want him to touch me again.

'And you do,' he said easily. 'While we're on the date. But we're not on the date yet.'

'Yes, we are.'

'We're not in public. And we're not at the restaurant. Therefore we're not on a date.' His mouth curved into the same lazy, dangerous smile he'd given me at the nightclub. 'Your hand, sweetheart.'

Protesting more would only make this into a big deal and it was already a bigger deal than I'd intended it to be.

I was being stupid. He was simply going to put the ring on, nothing more. So there was no reason for my heartbeat to speed up, or my lungs to feel like they couldn't get enough air. No reason for a prickle of excitement to race down my spine.

A streetlight shining through the window of the car highlighted the exquisite bone structure of his face, picking up the brilliant gold threads in his dark tawny hair. The same gold that gleamed deep in his eyes as he stared at me.

A challenge.

'Can't handle it?' His velvety voice slid over me. 'Don't worry, I won't bite.' He paused and his smile widened. 'Much.'

Now he's playing with you again. And you're letting him. Idiot.

Annoyed with myself, I shoved my hand at him, inwardly bracing myself for his touch. And, sure enough, I felt it as his fingers closed around mine, a shock of heat, a burst of wild electricity that made me nearly shiver.

I remembered that electricity. I'd felt it with Simon. Only with Leon it was ten thousand times more intense. Which made it ten thousand times more dangerous.

With an effort I managed to repress the shiver and simply stared back as he studied me, clearly looking for a reaction.

I didn't give it to him.

His smile deepened, as if he knew what I was feeling anyway. As if he could tell how hot the tips of his fingers felt against my skin and how badly I wanted to pull away. And how much his touch frightened me.

And not because you don't like it.

Testosterone. Dopamine. Serotonin.

Maybe if you keep telling yourself that you'll believe it.

I ignored the voice in my head, keeping my gaze on his as he slid the diamond onto my ring finger, his fingertips brushing my skin all the way. It felt like I'd been stroked with a flame and it was all I could do not to jerk away.

But I didn't.

He continued to hold my hand, turning it this way and that, admiring the sparkle of the diamond. 'What do you think?' he asked. 'Beautiful, isn't it?'

'It's too big.' My voice sounded thick. 'And it's too expensive.'

'Yes. That's what I wanted. Big, flashy and expensive.' A gleam of gold as he looked at me. 'Like me.'

'I'm not keeping it,' I said flatly. 'I can't.'

He shrugged. 'I don't care what you do with it. It's yours now.' He released my hand, turning his attention to the driver. 'Let's go.'

I felt relieved that he wasn't touching me any more, but the heat of it lingered on my skin like a burn.

And that disturbed me more than anything else the entire evening.

CHAPTER SEVEN

Leon

I TOOK HER to Ocean, one of the most exclusive restaurants in Sydney, with views over the harbour that included the Opera House and the Sydney Harbour Bridge.

I'd wanted us to enter together, holding hands, but she balked at the last minute, making sure those long slender fingers were occupied with smoothing her hair and her dress and fussing with her handbag.

She was nervous and I knew why.

I'd watched her video.

I'd thought I'd better see it since I was marrying her, plus I was curious. So I'd watched it the night I'd got back from the nightclub. The video itself was difficult to find—her father must have paid someone a lot of money to get rid of it—but sure enough, I found it lurking on a dodgy pirate site.

It had been shot on someone's phone, the whole thing grainy and badly lit. But the sound was clear and even though the face of the man was obscured most of the time, the face of the woman was not.

A very young Vita, slender and pale, swamped by her wealth of auburn hair.

The video wasn't long but it was cruel, her lover providing a running commentary about her narrow body and its failings. It was obvious she had no idea she was being filmed. She took off her clothes awkwardly, but her hands were shaking as she did so and not from fear, not when her excitement and passion were obvious. He made rude comments about that too.

The sex itself looked perfunctory and not at all titillating, and her lover made it clear he didn't enjoy it, all the while mocking her painfully honest responses to him in the commentary.

I didn't like that. Didn't like the way he made fun of her, which was strange because since when did I give a shit about anything? Then again, maybe not so strange. I knew what it was like to be at the mercy of someone else.

I should have turned it off then as there wasn't anything else about it that interested me. Except I couldn't.

Her face caught my attention and held it fast.

As her lover touched her, she looked up at him like he was the only thing in the world worth looking at, the only thing in the entire universe worth looking at. Her heart showed in her face, the contents of her soul incandescent in her dark eyes.

When she looked at him she was…beautiful. There was no other word for it.

'I love you,' she whispered to the fucker who'd

filmed her, who'd stopped narrating just so every-one could hear her confession. 'I love you so much.'

The video ended there, with him laughing as if that was the punchline to some extended joke.

So I played it again. And again. Wishing I still had a gun so I could shoot the prick in the face, because I didn't like bullies.

It stuck in my head. Made me wonder what it would feel like to have someone look at me like that. As if I was their entire world and nothing existed for them but me.

I wasn't sure why that mattered to me, not when for the last eighteen years it wasn't adoration I had sought but fear. Being dangerous was better than being loved or adored. Being dangerous made you powerful, and when you were powerful you were the one in control.

So by rights that expression on Vita's face should have made my lip curl.

But it didn't. It got to me. Hit me in a place I hadn't realised I was vulnerable. Which was a worry, yet it didn't stop me wondering about it all the same.

I glanced at Vita now as she fussed with her hair, still thinking about that goddamn video. Thinking about that expression on her face, the passion in her gaze. All of that was now hidden away behind those guarded dark eyes. Banished maybe but not excised, I was sure.

Maybe you could uncover it. Maybe you could get her to look at you the way she looked at the prick who filmed her.

The thought came out of nowhere, sending a thrill shooting down my spine.

Arrested, I went still, studying her face.

I could do it. I could make her look at me like that, make her want me so badly she'd think of nothing else. Sure, she'd been less than impressed with me a few nights earlier, but seduction hadn't been top of my list of things to do then.

To be honest, I wasn't sure why I was thinking about it now.

It wasn't like this marriage would be real in any way, shape or form, so there wasn't much point. Then again, it would annoy the hell out of her father. Plus, there was something about the woman that got under my skin.

I definitely hadn't liked my response to her video, not when I'd been expecting to be mildly titillated. Instead, I'd had what could only be deemed an emotional response and I did not appreciate that.

It felt too much like caring—and caring was a great way to lose control of a situation. And once you lost that control you were fucked.

Not that I would. No matter what I'd told her about her calling the shots, ultimately I had the power here. And maybe seducing her would be a great demonstration of that power.

The idea was attractive. Seducing a woman was one of life's pleasures, especially when she threw down a challenge.

Besides, we were supposed to be in love. She might think it was only chemicals, but some chemistry couldn't be denied. Hell, the glow of a well-fucked woman was often mistaken for love.

What if she doesn't want you?

Ah, but she did want me; I'd seen her response to our physical chemistry in her eyes. She might not like that she wanted me, but she did all the same.

Noticing me staring at her, she flashed me a wary look. 'What?'

I gave her a wolfish grin, turning over thoughts of seduction in my head and not bothering to hide it. 'Don't think I don't know what you're doing.'

'I'm not doing anything.' She turned towards the entrance to the restaurant. 'Come on. Let's get this over with.' Without waiting for me to respond, she strode purposefully towards the doors.

She was definitely avoiding getting close to me.

I followed along behind her, not minding one bit since it gave me the opportunity to examine her figure in greater detail than I had in the nightclub.

Not that the unflattering black dress she wore allowed me to see it, but enough to get an impression of a narrow waist and a slight flaring of hips and thighs. I remembered the feel of those hips under my palms that night in the club, their slight roundness and heat. She didn't have the abundant curves of her sister, but there was no hiding the fact that she was all woman.

The maître d' greeted us as we entered the restaurant and it amused me that Vita didn't wait for me to speak. She gave the man my name and booking time as if she was the one who'd made the reservation.

'Of course,' the maître d' said gracefully. 'Come

right this way. We have Mr King's table already set up for him.'

I'd requested the best table, one right in front of the big windows that looked out over the harbour. It was in full view of the rest of the restaurant too, so we'd be seen by the other diners. And, hopefully, the press.

I'd put it out discreetly to various different contacts that we would be dining at Ocean tonight and with any luck that would get us a few pictures. Certainly we would once it became known I was having dinner with the 'I Love You Girl'.

That was the name the press had given her.

After the maître d' had showed us to our table he went to pull Vita's chair out for her, but I waved him away and went to stand behind it myself.

She gave me one of her wary looks, radiating discomfort at my nearness, but I ignored her, smiling and pulling the chair out, gesturing at her to sit.

There was a moment's hesitation then she visibly steeled herself and came to sit down.

I looked down at her as I pushed her chair back in, the lights glossing the auburn in her thick, dark hair and making it gleam. I wanted to stroke it, see if it was as soft as it looked, and why not? She was my fiancée. I had every right to touch her.

So I did, letting my fingertips brush the silky-looking strands. I was right—it was as soft as it looked.

Vita stiffened, jerking her head around sharply and giving me a glare. 'What are you doing?'

I put my hands on the back of her chair and bent

so our faces were close, an intimate posture. 'We're supposed to be madly in love,' I reminded her quietly. 'Which means you not jerking away from my touch and glaring at me.'

Her dark gaze flickered. 'You're not supposed to touch me.'

'You're my fiancée. It's going to look weird if I don't.'

She seemed to consider that. 'I…guess so.'

I paused, conscious of the people watching us. 'You're going to have to make it up to me.'

'What do you mean?'

'I mean, you need to show the rest of the nice people watching that you welcome your fiancé's touch and definitely didn't mean to snap at him the way you did.'

Again, her gaze flickered. Wariness combined with irritation, and perhaps a bit of fear.

'I watched your video.' I kept my voice low, looking into her eyes. 'I watched the whole thing.'

A tide of red moved over her pale cheeks and the brightness in the depths of her gaze dimmed. But there was no flicker this time. She was brave, I had to give her that.

'Did you?' Her voice was level, though I heard a faint wobble in it. 'Well, thanks for that, but I didn't need to know.'

'There's nothing in that video you need to be ashamed of. You were beautiful.' I didn't know why I was telling her this. Maybe it was all manipulation, to get her to do what I wanted. Or maybe it was simply that I didn't like the fear in her eyes, because I knew what it felt like to be afraid.

Her cheeks went scarlet and she looked down, silky reddish lashes veiling her gaze. 'I don't want to talk about it.'

'So don't. But remember, you were going to show them someone different this time around. You were going to be the one in charge.'

She still didn't look at me. 'I am in charge.'

'No, you're not. You're afraid.'

That got a response.

Her lashes flicked up, her dark eyes meeting mine. 'I'm not afraid.'

'Aren't you?' I stared back. 'If you're not scared, then why did you jerk away from me just now? And why aren't you hell-bent on showing this whole fucking restaurant how wrapped around your little finger I am?'

Anger gleamed in her expression, which was very satisfying, and that lovely, lovely mouth of hers went tight. She knew I was right and that pissed her off.

Excellent. I'd take anger over fear any day.

But I'd underestimated her.

The next second she reached up, pushed her fingers through my hair and pulled my lips down on hers.

CHAPTER EIGHT

Vita

KISSING LEON KING was a stupid idea and I didn't know what possessed me.

But the moment he'd mentioned that he'd seen that horrible video, where I'd been at my most vulnerable, something inside me had…changed. Hardened.

Naturally he would have watched it. Why wouldn't he? Everyone else in the history of creation had, so the fact that he'd seen it shouldn't make any difference. Yet it did.

He was so powerful, so dangerous, and so very beautiful. Everything that I wasn't. And that made me feel vulnerable.

My physical responses to him made me feel vulnerable too.

I'd been telling myself it was all about the chemicals, but no amount of rationalising made any difference to the feelings that had swept through me as he'd touched my hair. I'd been achingly conscious of his nearness, of his scent and his heat. Of how long it had been since anyone had touched me and how I'd wanted him more than my next breath.

I thought I'd got rid of desire long ago, but it was clear I hadn't. It had only been sleeping. And now he'd woken it.

And his challenge to show everyone in the restaurant how I'd wrapped him around my finger had been the perfect opportunity to show him that I wasn't afraid.

It had also been the perfect opportunity to prove to myself that this really was just a stupid chemical reaction, nothing more.

So I'd reached for him, pushed my fingers into his hair and pulled his mouth down. But the last man I'd kissed had been Simon and that had been ten years ago, and kissing Leon King was nothing like that. Nothing like it at all.

The second his lips touched mine, electricity coursed the length of my body, earthing through the soles of my feet. Intense, powerful and shockingly hot. The heat of his lips a flame brushing me. Scorching me.

I was conscious of everything: his scent and how soft his mouth was compared to how hard and dangerous he appeared; how silky his hair felt between my fingers and how tall he was, bending over my chair.

The kiss had been meant as an answer to his challenge and as proof to myself that this…chemistry was nothing. That it didn't affect me in the slightest.

But it did. And suddenly I was seventeen again. Nervous and excited, and desperate to touch the man

I wanted. The man whom I wanted to touch me in return.

A lie.

Remembered shame and humiliation flooded through me and I pulled away, turning to face the table once again, folding my shaking hands in my lap.

My mouth was tingling, the echoes of that electricity pulsing through me, my heart beating wildly in my chest.

It's not just chemicals, is it?

No, it had to be. Chemicals I understood and could manipulate. I did it every day in my lab. But these... feelings? I didn't understand them and I didn't want them. I hated them.

I sensed him behind me, his presence a hot, muscular wall at my back, and I thought he might say something. But I didn't turn and he remained silent.

Slowly, I raised my gaze from my lap.

His dark gold eyes were watching me from across the table.

Electricity sparked again, a current that raised all the hairs on my body. But this time I pushed the feeling to one side and didn't look away.

The expression on his perfect face was difficult to interpret so I didn't try. I didn't want to know what he was thinking anyway.

'So,' I said acidly, 'are we supposed to sit here and pretend we're having a lovely time?'

His beautiful mouth curled and I felt another spark light up inside me. I'd kissed that mouth. Me. Gangly, ginger, two-tablets-on-an-ironing-board Vita.

'Yes,' he said. 'That's exactly what we're supposed to do. Why don't you tell me about your job at the university? You said you were a research assistant. What are you researching?'

Ugh.

I tried to think of an alternative topic, but my mind had gone blank and I couldn't think of a single thing.

I fiddled with my napkin to stop myself from lifting a finger to my mouth and nibbling on it. 'It's difficult to explain to a layperson.'

'Try me.' His voice was level yet I had the impression that he hadn't much liked being called a layperson.

I frowned at him, trying to work out why he wanted to know. 'Do you have a postgraduate chemistry background?'

Once again that smile flicked. 'No.'

'Did you study science at university?'

'I didn't go to university, sweetheart.'

'What about high school? Did you do any science at high school?'

'My schooling was…patchy, let's say.'

A hint of curiosity caught at me. Did members of crime families even go to school? Not that I wanted to know. I wasn't interested in him in the slightest.

'I'm not sure I can explain it to you in that case,' I said firmly. 'You need a science background to understand it.' Then, before he could argue the point, I asked, because men did like to talk about themselves, 'Why don't you tell me more about why the Kings are expanding into luxury apartments?'

He stared at me for a long moment. Then he gave a soft laugh and sat back in his seat. 'Fine. We can talk about me if you like, though it's my brother Ajax who heads King Enterprises, and the luxury apartment market is his idea.'

'So what exactly is your role?' I asked, curious.

A glitter of some emotion I couldn't interpret flickered in his eyes as another of those dark, dangerous smiles curved his mouth. 'I'm the PR boy. I get people to see things Ajax's way. It's not so different from what I used to do five years ago, but nowadays I do it with a lot less blood.'

I could see he'd meant it as a joke, but the reminder of his past caught at me, hooked into my curiosity at the same time as it made me uncomfortable. What exactly did he mean by 'a lot less blood'?

I wasn't sure what to say, but luckily the waiter arrived with menus so I was granted a brief respite.

Leon decided on some wine and then there was a brief discussion about food. I wasn't hungry, but I picked something at random from the menu.

A few minutes later, the wine brought and served, we were alone again.

'You're curious, aren't you?' Leon's voice was soft. 'About my past.' He was looking at me with that lion's stare, a silent challenge. 'You can ask. I don't mind talking about it.'

'No, thank you,' I said firmly. 'I'm not curious.'

'Liar.' He lifted his wine glass in his long, tanned fingers and idly swirled the liquid around in it. 'Of course you are. But you don't want to ask about it, do you? Why? Does the thought make you uncomfortable? Does violence make you squeamish?'

I watched that dark gleam in his eyes. It looked like anger, which was odd. Did he really want to talk about that? Or was he simply pushing to get a reaction out of me?

'Not really.' I kept my tone neutral. 'Maybe we should spend more time getting to know one another before we talk about your criminal past.'

The gleam in his eyes became molten and for a second I wondered if I'd said the wrong thing, my heart squeezing in my chest as the tension pulled tight between us.

I saw a movement out of the corner of my eye and a flash.

A camera. Which meant there were press. Which meant people had noticed us. They'd noticed me.

I don't know why I hadn't thought about it earlier—perhaps I'd been too busy worrying about Leon. Now I was all too aware of the purpose of this date: to show the world that we were a newly engaged couple who were deeply in love.

The thought made my entire body go cold.

It was all going to get dragged up again, wasn't it? They knew my name and soon the media interest would intensify. And no doubt my video would start doing the rounds again. I could see the headlines now: The Return of the 'I Love You Girl'!

'Hey.' Leon's quiet voice somehow cut through the icy panic that was winding slow fingers through me. 'Look at me.'

It was a command, the note of absolute authority in the words making me obey him before I realised what I was doing.

I met his gaze, felt the jolt as his focus zeroed in on me.

'Don't give them anything.' The words were low, fierce. 'Don't give them your fear or your anger. Don't let them see it. They don't deserve it. This is your story, remember? You get to decide how it goes, not them. You're the "I Love You Girl" and this time you're getting your happy ending.'

How he knew what I was thinking I had no idea.

I had no idea why looking into his amber gaze or hearing the insistent note in his dark, rich voice felt reassuring either.

Yet it was.

And he was right. This was my story and rewriting it was why I'd chosen to do this in the first place. And all those people watching, all the media waiting, would have to follow my lead.

I reached out across the table towards him, not really knowing what I was doing. But he seemed to, his fingers twining with mine on the white tablecloth.

Electricity seared me at his touch, but I didn't let go. The gold in his eyes felt strangely like a lifeline, as if with one moment's inattention I'd drown in the panic that ran like an icy current through my veins.

His thumb found my palm and he began to stroke it, a slow back and forth that made my breath catch and the light glitter on the flashy diamond on my finger. 'So,' he said softly, 'you've got a very rich, very dangerous and possibly criminal man at your mercy. How does the rest of the story go, sweetheart?'

CHAPTER NINE

Leon

IT WAS THE FEAR in her bright eyes that got to me, because I knew what that felt like. It had been years, yet I could still remember the bitter taste of it on my tongue. To be afraid, to be someone's target.

To be powerless.

I didn't want that for her. Not now, not here. And definitely not when her focus should be on me.

Her palm was very soft where I stroked it, her skin warm. And her gaze was pinned to mine as if I was the only thing standing between her and certain death.

It was…intoxicating.

People usually looked at me with either fear or, depending on who they were and what kind of emotion I wanted from them, longing.

No one looked at me as if I could save them.

Unwanted emotion shifted in my chest and I knew I should let go of her hand, ignore the need to help her. But I couldn't do it.

She was bringing back memories I thought I'd left behind long ago. Memories of being terrified and powerless and utterly at someone else's mercy.

I'd only been fifteen when Thompson, an enemy of my father's, had taken me. I'd been a kid, caught up in my father's shitty, dirty world, and I'd paid the price for it. In blood. Christ, I even had the scars to prove it.

This wasn't the same situation, obviously, but I'd learned how to protect myself. Ajax had shown me. He'd taught me how to be the predator rather than the prey, the hunter not the hunted.

Looked like Vita could have done with the same lessons.

'How does the story go?' Her voice was faint and husky-sounding. 'I don't know how to—'

'Keep looking at me.' I ran my thumb over her palm again, making sure I had her attention. 'Don't think about them. Think about the fact that I'm sitting opposite you, desperately in love with you. You have the power this time. You get to control what they see. So what are you going to do? How are you going to show them that the "I Love You Girl" has moved on?'

She took a breath, her gaze searching mine as if I had the answers she was looking for.

Luckily for her, I did.

'Put your other hand under the table,' I murmured.

'What?'

'Do it.'

Slowly, she did so and I reached for it with my free hand. I kept stroking her palm where it rested on top

of the table, while underneath I twined my fingers
with hers and drew them to rest on my thigh. Then
I held them down.

The table wasn't very wide so she didn't have to
lean far, but she stiffened as she touched me.

'What are you doing?' She sounded shocked.

'I'm going to show you something.' I began easing her hand further up my thigh. 'I'm going to show
you exactly how much power you have.'

'But I—' She broke off as I pressed her palm down
over my fly, her eyes going wide.

The heat of her hand seeped through the wool of
my trousers, her touch electric, making my pulse race.

Tension held her arm rigid, but I didn't let her go
and I didn't look away.

'Feel that?' I pressed her palm down harder. Fuck,
I liked her touching me and apparently so did my
cock. 'That's me getting hard for you.'

Colour crept into her cheeks, which was better
than the pale look that had been there before.

'No one can see,' I went on. 'No one knows you've
got your hand on my dick and that you're making me
hard, but you know. You've got the power, sweetheart.
You've got the power to make me lose my mind right
here in front of all these people.'

She said nothing, her eyes dark as a midnight sky
and studded with stars.

I knew I was overstepping the mark here and had
no idea what she'd do in response. But then boundaries had never been my thing and I did like to live
dangerously.

It was risky to give her the control like this too—something I always kept hold of, both in the bedroom and out of it. But she needed some guidance. And it wasn't like I'd actually lose it.

No other woman had managed that so there was no reason this one should.

Then again, her palm was very warm and I was getting harder. Christ, I hadn't got laid in over a week and my damn dick was desperate for some action.

I considered unzipping my fly and dragging her hand inside my boxers, getting her to wrap those slender fingers around my cock. But me being insistent wasn't the point. Showing her what kind of power she had was.

So instead, I removed my hand from over hers, making it plain to her that she had a choice. She could choose to pull back or she could choose to keep her palm right where it was. The power was with her.

It was disturbing how much I hoped she'd leave it where it was.

A second passed. Neither of us spoke, and I was ready for her to jerk her hand from my crotch.

But she didn't.

And, just like that, I couldn't breathe, all my awareness narrowing to the warmth of her palm over my fly, the slight pressure of it settling on my aching dick.

Our other hands were still linked on the table-top but I'd stopped stroking her palm and was now gripping her fingers with more force.

Jesus, the feel of her hand and the wide-eyed

way she was looking at me were affecting me more than I'd expected. And I wasn't sure I liked it. Yet I couldn't be the one to pull away, not now. Not after I'd made such a fucking performance of giving her the power.

Her cheeks were a deep rose and her hand on my crotch moved. But not away. Instead, she began to carefully explore my hard-on through the wool of my trousers.

The lightness of her touch and the hesitant way she touched me, all cautious and wary, was so fucking hot it stole the remaining breath from my lungs.

She was looking very serious, a crease between her reddish brows, as if my cock was a problem she needed to solve or a puzzle she couldn't quite figure out.

I'd never had a woman touch me the way she was touching me and I had no idea why that was the hottest fucking thing I'd ever experienced, but it was.

'How is this going to go, sweetheart?' My voice had got rougher but I made no effort to smooth it out or hide the hunger I knew had to be burning in my gaze. She had to keep her attention on me and only seeing what she was doing to me was going to do it. 'You want to jerk me off right here? Make me come in front of everyone in this restaurant?'

The bright lights in her eyes flared. Under the table, her thumb brushed slowly over the head of my dick and I jerked in my chair, the sensation electric.

She noticed and her mouth opened in surprise. 'That's…me?'

Of course it was her. Did she really have no idea?

Stupid question. She was gazing at me with amazement, even a touch of wonder. So no, she had no idea. No idea at all.

The desire inside me changed, became something thicker, hotter.

Women looked at me with lust, but never with wonder. As if I was a brand-new discovery they'd made and were excited and curious about. Or a puzzle they couldn't wait to solve.

No, women loved the orgasms I gave them, but it wasn't me they were interested in. Which was fine and exactly what I wanted. Yet this, now, with Vita…

You need her to stop touching you.

Ridiculous thought. I wasn't so far gone that a hand job under the table and the look on a woman's face would undo me. Sure, I'd given her the control, but I was still master of myself.

'Yes,' I said through gritted teeth. 'That's all you.'

The contained, slightly stern look had gone from her expression and the stars in her eyes were dancing. She looked amazed. Christ, the way she was looking at me, the way she was touching me… It was hot. Fucking hot.

'But I…' She stopped, frowning. Then made another cautious pass over the head of my cock with her thumb, watching me intently as she did so.

I hissed as a bright flare of pleasure licked up my spine and, for the briefest moment, one corner of her mouth curled. As if she was pleased with herself.

And immediately I knew that if she didn't take

her hand off me I was going to go over, haul her out of her seat and find somewhere private where I could show her exactly how pleased with herself I could make her.

'Sweetheart,' I forced out. 'In about five seconds this particular story is going to end with me coming all over your hand. So, if you don't want that, I suggest you stop touching me.'

Her eyes went round, the colour in her cheeks creeping down her neck. 'But what if…? What if I wanted to keep touching you?' Her voice got lower, huskier. 'In front of all these people?'

Fuck. She'd taken the control I'd given her and she was bloody running with it.

Little vixen.

But that was my fault. I had given it to her, after all. I simply hadn't realised how it would affect me. How she would affect me.

'Then you'd better be prepared for the consequences, hadn't you?' I didn't bother to hide my own hunger. 'I hope you're ready for them.'

She didn't look the least bit chastened. Instead, the crease between her brows deepened. Then she ran that goddamn teasing thumb down the length of my increasingly desperate dick and I had to jerk my hand away from hers on the table-top before I crushed it, slamming my palm down as another burst of pleasure shot through me.

The glasses jumped, the cutlery rattling.

Fucking hell. She was killing me.

'Vita.' Her name came out in a growl, my fingers

gripping onto the tablecloth. 'Seriously, darling. I'm not joking.'

Neither was she, that was obvious. The pale, scared look had vanished from her face, the darkness of her eyes intensifying, studying me as if she had me under a microscope.

I brought my hands to the arms of my chair, ready to push myself out of it. Ready to do what I'd promised and haul her out of there.

But then the waiter returned with our food and Vita snatched her hand from my crotch, her cheeks going from rosy to scarlet.

I didn't know whether to be relieved or order her to put her hand back where it had been.

She didn't look at me as the waiter presented her with her food, her attention on her plate while I tried to slow my heartbeat and subdue my raging hard-on.

An impossible task.

I couldn't stop thinking about pushing her up against the nearest wall, ripping that awful dress off her and burying my cock deep inside her. Thoughts that weren't exactly conducive to entertaining dinner conversation.

Christ, I'd never not been able to think of something to say, yet now I couldn't think of a single thing. It was like the damn woman hadn't only stolen my breath, she'd stolen half my fucking brain too.

Vita picked up her cutlery, not saying a goddamn word. And I was still so fucking hard I ached.

It made me furious.

How dare she get under my skin? How dare she

play with me, get me hard, nearly make me lose it in public? How dare she take the control from me so completely I didn't know how to fucking breathe, let alone what to do with myself?

So I did what I normally did in these situations. I took back the control.

Shoving my chair back, I got to my feet.

Her head jerked up, her fork lowering, surprise crossing her face. 'Where are you going?'

I was already moving around the table, grabbing her elbow and pulling her to her feet. Her fork clattered onto her plate. 'Leon,' she said breathlessly. 'Wait. What are you—?'

I looked down into her flushed face, making no effort to hide my anger or the desire that was eating me alive. 'I told you there would be consequences.'

Then, without waiting for her to reply, I strode from the restaurant, dragging her along with me.

CHAPTER TEN

Vita

I STUMBLED HELPLESSLY after Leon, his grip on my arm firm enough to make pulling away difficult.

Not that I could have anyway.

My brain wasn't working right. I was still struggling to process what had happened when he'd drawn my hand beneath the table and got me to touch him. What I'd felt when he'd put my fingers on his fly. Long, thick…

He'd looked at me as he held my hand down, the hungry gold glitter in his eyes making it plain he hadn't been lying when he'd said I was making him hard.

The skinny, unattractive 'I Love You Girl'. Gangly, ginger Vita.

Me. Me.

I knew I should have taken my hand off him when he'd released it, but the shock of discovery had held me fast. I'd wanted to feel for myself whether it was actually true, whether it was really me doing this to him or…

But there couldn't have been anyone else. He'd looked at me the entire time and when I'd moved my hand on him I'd seen the flare in his eyes; felt him shudder and jerk; felt him get even harder.

He hadn't been lying. It was me doing that to him. And in that moment all I'd felt was amazement. That my touch could affect him, could make him want me.

He's a man. Any woman's hand on his crotch would have made him hard. It's not you.

Doubt whispered in my head, making me stumble, but Leon didn't pause. He didn't even slow. He pulled me out into the foyer and around a corner to where a short corridor led to the bathrooms.

Then he shoved me up against the wall.

I struggled to breathe, my heartbeat thudding, an unfamiliar excitement coiling in my veins. Strange. Shouldn't I be furious at the way he was handling me?

Yet it wasn't fury I felt as he put his hands on the wall on either side of my head and leaned down so we were nose to nose, his eyes burning into mine.

No, definitely not fury. Or even fear.

I was thrilled.

Simon had never looked at me like that. His interest had been entirely feigned and I'd been too young, too naive to understand the difference. But gazing up into Leon's handsome face, I understood now.

He was staring at me as if he wanted to eat me alive.

It's not you.

But it was so difficult to think about that when he was that close, the coiled threat of his tall, hard, muscled body making my knees go weak, surrounding me in his scent and his heat.

'You,' he growled, his rich voice roughened and deep, 'have been a very naughty girl.'

Adrenaline flooded my veins; my pulse was going wild.

I lifted my chin. 'Why? I didn't do anything.'

'Yes, you did. You got me hard. You nearly made me lose my goddamn mind.'

Wonder curled through me. I'd really done that to him?

You idiot. Most men get hard when you touch their dick.

Of course. It hadn't been me in particular, had it?

I couldn't have said why that felt like such a disappointment, not when it wasn't supposed to matter. I wasn't the desperate seventeen-year-old who only wanted to be beautiful and as loved as her sister. Not any more.

I tried to calm my raging heartbeat. 'You would have been hard regardless of who was touching you, Leon. It wasn't anything I did.'

He leaned closer, our noses almost touching, so close I could see the light brown of his irises and the seams of gold running through them. 'You think that happens with every woman I take out on a date? That I get her to touch me under the table then have to stop and drag her out of the restaurant because I'm so fucking desperate?' The raw heat in his eyes shocked me. 'No, little vixen. No, that doesn't happen to me, not unless I let it. And I wasn't planning on letting it.' He shifted even closer, surrounding me. 'Except you did something, and I don't know what it was, but you need to understand one thing. I'm in charge now, sweetheart, and I get to say what happens next. And since you nearly made me lose my mind out there, I'm going to make you lose yours.'

It couldn't be true, could it? Could I have really made this impossibly gorgeous man lose his mind? Simply by touching him?

It was dangerous to believe him, but... I didn't think he was lying.

Excitement hit me, shivering over my skin, and then I finally took in the last part of his sentence. He was going to make me lose my mind?

'No, you won't,' I shot back. 'No one makes me lose my mind if I don't want them to.'

He smiled, slowly and devastatingly sexily, with a feral edge that made my breath catch. 'We'll see about that. I told you there'd be consequences, didn't I? Time to show you what they are.'

I blinked, realising something that I should have before I'd opened my stupid mouth: I'd just issued him with a challenge. And he wasn't the type of man who let a challenge go unanswered.

Helpless anticipation coiled in my gut.

What had I done? I didn't actually want him to touch me, did I?

Leon moved, taking my wrist and raising it to his mouth, his lips brushing over the sensitive skin on the underside of it.

And all I could do was shudder, his kiss burning like a brand, raising goosebumps all over my body.

You should stop him. You don't want to do this. Not again.

I knew that. I knew what the terrible excitement and the ache that began to pulse between my thighs meant. I knew where it led. And yes, if I'd been thinking straight I would have stopped him.

But I wasn't thinking straight. Had a man ever looked at me this way? Like he was desperate? Like he couldn't wait to touch me?

Desire was rising inside me, a desire I thought I'd cut from my life, buried beneath compounds and test tubes and microscopes. Dizzying, intoxicating.

My breath came shorter, faster, my skin prickling and sensitive.

It had been so long since anyone had touched me. So long. And he was so beautiful, everything I'd once craved.

That's why he's dangerous.

Slowly, Leon raised my wrist above my head and pinned it to the wall, shifting his body in closer, making me so very aware of the bare inches that separated us. 'Well?' he demanded. 'Are you ready to answer for what you did to me out there?'

Another shudder shook me. I didn't know why, but I loved the dominant way he was holding me. Loved how caged and crowded I was by all that hard, hot muscle.

I tested his grip on my wrist and his fingers closed tighter. A thrill bolted the length of my spine.

'Yes,' I said huskily. 'But it won't work. A bunch of chemicals won't make me lose my mind.'

Fire leapt in his eyes. Fire that was burning for me.

'You think that's all this is? Chemicals?' His voice was low and rough and soft as velvet.

'Yes, of course. Testosterone. Oestrogen—' I broke off, a shocked gasp escaping me as he lifted his free hand from beside my head and lowered it, his fingertips brushing over my skin just above the neckline of my dress.

It felt like he'd trailed fire over my bare flesh.

'You were saying?' His hand brushed lower, following the swell of my breast, his fingertips finding the hardened tip of my nipple and stroking it through the fabric.

I gasped again as a bolt of what felt like lightning arrowed the length of my body, grounding between my thighs and coiling there in a pulsing, aching kind of heat. 'Oe-oestrogen,' I forced out, struggling to remember what I'd been saying. Something about chemicals… 'Dopamine. N-norepinephrine…'

'That's very interesting.' His finger brushed over my nipple again, sending another electric bolt of sensation down my spine. 'So all you're feeling now is just a few chemicals, huh?'

I could barely make my voice work. 'Y-yes.'

'Easy to resist then, hmm?'

That maddening finger circled my nipple yet again and I inhaled sharply.

God, we were in public. Someone might have heard me and even now be coming to investigate.

They'd find us standing here, see his hand on my breast, doing…things to me.

'D-don't,' I said, panting. 'Anyone could come.'

'They might,' he agreed, lazily circling again with his finger, drawing another helpless sound from me. 'But the only person coming will be you.'

'Leon—'

He bent, his mouth near my ear. 'I want to watch you. I want to see you come apart under my hand, little scientist. And you will, understand?'

Pure excitement shot through me, though I had no idea why the thought of him watching was quite so thrilling.

'Why do you want to see that?' I managed to ask.

'Because I do.' His fingers closed on my nipple through the fabric of my dress and pinched lightly. 'Because I want you to lose your mind for me.'

The breath rushed out of my lungs, both at the sharp jolt of sensation and at the ferocity in his voice. I wanted to ask him why that was so important to him but he pinched me again and only a choked sound of helpless pleasure escaped me.

He gave a low, satisfied growl, obviously pleased with my response, and did it again. Sparks scattered everywhere, all over my skin, lighting up every nerve ending I had, making me tremble.

'Do you want to know what it felt like to have you touch me?' He pinched my nipple harder, and I stiffened as a shock of the most intense pleasure streaked from my breast down to my sex. 'I'll give you a hint.' He slid his hand from my breast down my torso, then further, between my thighs. 'It felt like…this.' And he pressed down with his fingertips, unerringly finding my clit through the material of my dress.

It felt so good. Like I'd gone weeks without food and had finally been fed the most delicious meal I'd ever tasted.

'Leon…' My voice didn't sound like mine and I wasn't sure why I was saying his name. Whether it was to get him to stop or to tell him not to, I had no idea. 'I… Don't…'

'Hush.' His fingers circled and stroked, then slid further down as he pressed the heel of his hand against me, the look in his eyes burning me alive. 'It's just chemicals, little vixen. And they're making you wet for me, aren't they? I bet if I touched your pussy right now it would be all slick and hot.'

The raw way Leon said the words, with an undercurrent of rough heat, wound around me and pulled tight.

He was right. I was wet for him and if he pressed any more firmly between my legs he'd soon find out exactly how wet I was.

His hand rocked against me, an exquisite pressure, and I couldn't stop my hips from moving with him, trying to chase the friction.

Voices drifted from out in the foyer, people either arriving or leaving the restaurant. So close.

'Ignore them,' he ordered, soft and dark, as if he could read my mind. 'Pay attention to me.'

'But I…' I faltered as the heel of his hand found a

new rhythm, grinding against my clit, a white flash of pleasure nearly stopping my breath.

Pressure was building, relentless and inescapable.

You're going to lose it.

I said his name again, oddly panicked, as it built and built and built, reaching down with my free hand to pull his away, but he grabbed it and brought it up over my head, pinning both my wrists there with powerful fingers. Then he went back to touching me, stroking me, grinding against my sensitive clit until I was panting and writhing against the wall, helpless against the rising pleasure.

His head dipped further, his mouth brushing over mine. A light, agonisingly gentle kiss.

I was shaking now, the pleasure impossible to resist or contain.

It was going to happen. He was going to make me come, right here, right now.

There were people so close, but they didn't seem important any more. Because he lifted his head, his golden eyes filling my vision, letting me see the hunger burning in them.

Hunger for me.

'Come, Vita,' he said very quietly, pressing his thumb down on my clit. 'Come now.'

And the pleasure detonated like the sun going nova, bright and blinding, an explosion of heat and flame. Searing me. Burning me to ash.

A cry burst from me but Leon bent and covered my mouth with his, silencing me. Then he stood there, his body both blocking me from sight and holding me up as the aftershocks tore through me. Preventing me from sliding down the wall in a boneless heap.

I didn't know how long I stood there, trembling against him as I recovered from the effects of the orgasm, the heat and scent of his body comforting for reasons I couldn't have named.

At last he took his hand away from between my thighs, smoothing down my dress then hooking a rogue lock of hair behind my ear. He stared down at me, the look on his face impenetrable. But gold smouldered in his eyes like a banked fire.

'Time to go,' he said roughly. 'Before I fuck you right here against the wall.'

Heat tore through me and for a moment all I could think about was what it would be like to have him push my dress up and take me with people only just around the corner.

He must have read my mind because he gave me another of those feral smiles. 'Look at me like that again and I might just do it.'

What if I want you to? my brain whispered silently.

And maybe he heard it because his smile deepened.

'Later,' he said. 'And that's not a threat. It's a promise.'

CHAPTER ELEVEN

Leon

'WHAT'S WITH ALL the dating bullshit, Leon?' Ajax's deep voice on the other end of the phone sounded pissed off. 'She's hardly your type.'

I surveyed the view from my seat in one of Sydney's most exclusive rooftop bars down on The Rocks. Yet another vista of the harbour, my favourite theme.

'It's not bullshit,' I said. 'And what would you know about my type?'

'Big tits. Beautiful. Blonde. Am I getting warm?'

An image from a couple of nights ago, of my date with Vita at the restaurant, flickered in my memory. Her, pressed against the wall, cheeks flushed with pleasure, shuddering under my hand. My stern little vixen had thought she could hold out against me, but I'd taken her apart all the same.

'You're not warm,' I told him. 'And she's exactly my type. Anyway, what the fuck do you care whether I'm dating or not?'

'I don't want you losing focus. We need this expansion to happen.'

'I realise that.' I kept my voice neutral. 'And it will happen. Hamilton's already organising something as a way to introduce us around. As to the dating, it's necessary to make this marriage look real. I told you that.'

'Remind me why the fuck that's necessary?'

'Because I don't want it getting around that the Kings are paying for legitimacy.' I leaned forward, picking up the tumbler of Scotch that was sitting on the low table in front of me. 'What the hell is the matter with you? You're grumpy as fuck.'

'Nothing,' he said. 'Just remember what you're doing this for.'

The call disconnected abruptly.

I sighed and tossed the phone down on the white couch cushions beside me.

Like I'd ever forget why I was doing this. It was for him. For what he'd done for me after I'd nearly been broken by the kidnap and torture that I'd gone through at fifteen. He'd taught me how to protect myself and for that I owed him.

He'd get the expansion he wanted, plus the redemption of the King name. All of which would be accomplished through Vita.

Anticipation tightened in my gut at the thought of her.

I'd planned this second date meticulously. We'd spend some time at the bar out in public, making sure we were seen enjoying each other's company. Then we'd go back to my city penthouse, where I'd deal with this insane sexual attraction once and for all.

Christ, at that restaurant I'd wanted to lift her up against the wall and fuck us both into insensibility regardless of who might have been watching. But that would have undermined the way she'd surrendered to me so beautifully.

Instead, I'd taken her back into the restaurant and forced myself to sit through the rest of our meal. I'd barely been able to concentrate on her awkward attempts at conversation, too busy trying to master my raging hard-on. And when I'd finally dropped her back home I'd never been so relieved to see the back of a woman.

Tonight, though, I'd deal with our sexual attraction where and when I chose. And one little scientist feeling her way around my dick and talking about chemicals was not going to get to me. I wouldn't let her.

I glanced down at my watch. She hadn't wanted a pick-up tonight, telling me she'd make her own way to the bar, and I'd let her have that little bit of control and distance. Because she sure as hell wasn't going to get any of either once she got here.

I was in the middle of looking through some of the gossip websites, noting the reports on the 'unexpected and scandalous' love affair between the notorious Leon King and the 'I Love You Girl'—aka Thomas Hamilton's forgotten daughter—when I heard a hesitant footstep near my table.

I knew it was her even before I caught her scent. She hadn't been wearing perfume the last couple of

times we'd met, and she wasn't now, but still I rec-
ognised the delicate hint of feminine musk that told
me she was near.

Lowering my phone, I looked up.

She stood near the table, holding a little black
leather handbag protectively in front of her like a
shield. She wasn't—thank Christ—wearing the black
dress tonight, but a green silky-looking one with narrow straps that wrapped deliciously around her narrow body, showing off her slender frame.

I stared openly at the way the fabric cupped her
small, round breasts and pulled in at her waist, cling-
ing to the slight roundness of her thighs.

Jesus, the more I saw of her, the gladder I was that
she and not her sister had been given to me. Because
Clara would never have looked at me the way Vita
did. Nervous, wary, yet deep in her dark eyes hunger
burned. Hunger that only I could feed.

I rose, slid my phone into my pocket and closed the
distance between us before she could move.

Her eyes went wide, her lovely mouth opening, but
by then I'd settled my hands on her hips and pulled
her towards me.

I didn't wait, lowering my head and taking her
mouth like I had every right to it. Because, as far as
the rest of the world was concerned, I did have every
right to it.

But I also wanted to let her know that I hadn't forgotten what had happened between us at the restaurant. And that this particular evening she would be
at my mercy.

She stiffened but I didn't stop. Lifting a hand, I ran my fingers along her delicate jaw before letting my thumb trace the underside of her soft bottom lip, then pressing it down, encouraging her to open for me.

She shuddered, a soft moan escaping. Her lips parted and I swept my tongue into her hot mouth, sliding my hand behind her head, pushing my fingers into the softness of her hair and holding her where I wanted her. Then I began to explore her, kissing her hot and deep and slow.

She'd given me a taste back in the restaurant, but that had been so brief it may as well not have happened.

Not this time. This time I wanted her to know she'd been kissed—and kissed thoroughly. By me.

I tightened my grip in her hair, tugging her head back so I could kiss her more deeply, her body arching into mine. She tasted like heaven, like strawberries on a summer's day. And her body was melting against me, all those sharp angles softening in surrender.

Little vixen was passionate and sensual, as I'd known she would be. She kept it all locked up inside her but it was there; I'd seen it in that video of hers. I'd seen it again as I'd held her up against the wall in the restaurant too, and now I wanted more.

My cock was getting hard, liking that idea, and I debated whisking her out of the bar and back to my penthouse immediately. But that would be giving in to my impatience, and right now I needed to be in control of it. We also really needed more time to cement our relationship in public.

I lifted my mouth from hers, relishing the flush in her cheeks and the way she leaned into me, as if she wanted more too. Her already dark brown eyes had gone even darker, making the brightness that glowed in the depths of them more apparent. She stared at me then took a sharp breath and stepped back, clutching her handbag, clearly trying to put some distance between us.

I didn't let her.

Grabbing her hand, I drew her towards the couch then pulled her down onto it with me.

'Smile, sweetheart,' I murmured as she stiffened yet again. 'Remember who you are.'

She blinked rapidly, her lovely mouth curving into a fake-looking smile. 'You could have warned me before you kissed me,' she said through gritted teeth. 'It took me by surprise.'

'We're engaged, which means you're not supposed to need a warning.'

'Yes, but—'

'You kissed me back, Vita,' I pointed out.

'I'm supposed to kiss you back.' She sounded exasperated. 'It was just for show.'

If that wasn't a challenge, I didn't know what was.

'That night in the restaurant, when you came up against the wall, was that just for show too?'

She went pink, the colour contrasting beautifully with her green dress. 'I'd hoped you'd forgotten about that,' she muttered.

'Forgotten?' I lifted a brow. 'Seriously? Sweetheart, all I've been thinking about for two days straight is your hand on my cock. That and making you come again. This time with me inside you.'

Her colour deepened. 'Why?'

'Why do you think?' I let her see the hunger in my stare. 'You started something back in that restaurant and I want you to finish it.'

The green silk across her breasts pulled tight as she inhaled. The colour was lovely on her, bringing out the creaminess of her skin and contrasting beautifully with the auburn of her hair. Tonight she had it falling in soft waves down her back, all shining and glossy in the light of the bar.

She swallowed and I found my gaze drawn to the movement of her throat. It was pale and graceful. I wanted to put my teeth on it, to mark it.

'You don't need me,' she said, looking away. 'There are plenty of other women who'd give you what you want.'

I frowned. She'd said something similar at the restaurant, hadn't she? 'There are,' I agreed. 'But I don't want them. I want you.'

'Why?' Her gaze came back to mine, sharp as a knife. 'I'm not my sister, if that's what you're thinking.'

I didn't quite understand. Of course she wasn't her sister; any fool could see that. 'I don't think you're your sister,' I said. 'And I don't care about her anyway.'

'You wanted to marry her, though. You asked for her.'

Understanding began to filter through. Was she…

jealous? It had to be something like that. And it made sense. Clara was beautiful, while Vita was…

Plain?

I'd thought that the first time I'd seen her, but that was before she'd had her hand on my cock; before she'd come so passionately under my hand; before I'd felt the jolt of electricity between us.

No, she wasn't plain. Different, but not plain in the slightest.

'I've changed my mind,' I said, taking her hand in mine and stroking her warm palm. 'I've decided I've got a thing for redheads instead.'

She looked down at where I was holding her hand. She'd remembered to put the diamond on like a good girl and it sparkled under the lights strung on the trellis above our heads.

'That doesn't mean I'm ready to sleep with you.'

'Who said anything about sleeping?'

'You know what I mean.'

I lifted our linked hands and tugged, pulling her forward against my chest, taking advantage of showing the rest of the bar how in love we were.

Her free hand came out, her palm against my chest, holding herself away. Then she frowned. 'What's that?' She was looking at my throat.

I'd ditched my tie for the evening and the collar of my black business shirt was open, which was normally not an issue. But the way her hand was resting on my chest had pulled the fabric aside, revealing the twisting length of one of my scars.

A jolt of an emotion I couldn't place hit me.

Women had seen my scars before—they were all over my chest and back—but it had never been a big deal. I kept intrusive questions at bay by making sure they were too busy screaming my name to ask about them. And the few that did ask… Well, I always had answers to give them. A car accident. Escape from a burning building. A plane crash.

No one had ever pushed for more.

Apparently, Vita hadn't got the memo.

I wanted to pull the fabric over the scars Thompson had left on my body, wanted to hide them. Strange, when I'd never been ashamed of them before.

Dad had left me to escape Thompson and his men on my own because he wouldn't pay the ransom they'd demanded, and eventually I'd dragged myself back home.

Those scars, though, were a reminder of what I'd made myself into, and I was proud of them. So why I should want to hide them from Vita was anyone's guess.

'It's a scar,' I said levelly, treating it as no big deal.

'I know, but…' She eased the fabric aside a little more. 'It's quite big. Where on earth did you—?'

'Fell off a mountain bike when I was a kid.' I pulled her hand away and brought her palm to my mouth, kissing it. 'You look beautiful, by the way. Did you dress up especially for me? I hope you're not wearing anything underneath that pretty dress.'

Her gaze flickered from my throat to where I held her hand against my mouth, then she met my gaze. 'Doesn't look like a mountain bike scar.'

Curious vixen.

Irritation needled me. I didn't want to go through the tedious business of telling her the truth, or of fielding all the questions she'd have. I didn't want to go through my past at all. That wasn't why we were here.

I opened my mouth and pressed my teeth into the soft flesh of her palm. A sensual warning.

She caught her breath.

'Do we really need to talk about childhood injuries?' I nipped her again. 'I'd much rather take you back to the penthouse and do something much more fun.'

'But I—'

'Did you think about what I did to you in the restaurant? Did you dream about it?' I brushed my mouth over her palm again, feeling the tremble in her arm as I did so. Suddenly I wanted to know that she'd thought about it. That she'd thought about me.

'Well?' I demanded, getting impatient. 'Did you think about me? Yes or no?'

Something in Vita's gaze sparked.

It made me catch my breath.

'No,' she said.

CHAPTER TWELVE

Vita

IT WAS A LIE and I shouldn't have said it, but I wanted to punish him for how badly he was getting under my skin.

Not only had he made me fall apart in that restaurant, but for the last two days I'd been able to think about nothing else. Second-guessing everything that had happened, second-guessing myself.

I didn't want to fall back into the same trap I'd fallen into with Simon. I didn't want to be obsessed or full of doubt.

I didn't want to want him.

Yet I did and it was the strength of it that was getting to me. I hadn't cared about where I was that night at Ocean. I'd let him do whatever he wanted in that hallway, overwhelmed by his intensity and by how much he'd wanted me.

It would be easy to get addicted to that. And if there was one thing I didn't want to ever do again it was to fall for someone who didn't really want me and who'd only hurt me in the end.

Simon had been handsome, like Leon. Charming, like Leon. He hadn't had Leon's hard edge, but he'd had a touch of badness in him that had made teenage girls' hearts beat faster.

Teenage girls like me.

I'd been in my second to last year of school while he'd been a year ahead, in Clara's year. He'd started paying attention to me for reasons I hadn't known at the time, but which had become clear later on; he'd wanted her and thought being friends with me would get him access to her. I'd stupidly fallen for his charm, not knowing that he was using me, and the night we finally slept together was the night he'd tried and failed to seduce Clara.

He'd taken his disappointment and bitterness out on me and I never knew it until that video had surfaced. Until it had started making the rounds at school and people had started talking and laughing. Humiliating me.

After that, I'd been wary of men, especially handsome men. Luckily, no one had shown interest in me since and I'd been more than okay with that. Until now.

Until Leon.

'No?' he echoed softly, a hard edge running through his voice.

I could barely keep from shivering. 'No,' I repeated, trying to keep the word even. 'I didn't think about you once. I had some results to write up.'

'Liar.' The hard edge was more pronounced now, a smile bordering on savage curving his mouth. 'You thought about me. You thought about my hands on your body and the way I touched you. You thought about how hard you came for me.'

I had. I'd thought about all those things even though I'd tried not to. They'd made me ache, made me burn, made me want the things I'd told myself I'd never want again: to be desired; to be touched; to feel special; not to feel like an ugly duckling grown up into an ugly duck.

But admitting that felt like giving up some of my power and I didn't want to do that.

My palm pressed against the hard muscle of his chest, trying to get some distance. 'I didn't. Like I said, I was too busy with my test results.'

'Fuck your test results.' His free hand was at the small of my back, not giving me an inch of the distance I wanted. 'No, on second thoughts, fuck me instead.'

My heartbeat thudded even faster, the rough heat in his voice sending chills through me. He was so raw and demanding, leaving me in no doubt about what he wanted.

Me.

Dangerous. You like that too much.

It was and I did, and so I tried to resist.

'That wasn't in the deal,' I said. 'And anyway, I have some—'

Letting out a low growl, Leon shifted the hand holding me in place to the back of my head, fingers curling into my hair. Then he pulled me forward to claim my mouth.

The kiss was scorching and this time there was no
subtle invitation to open for him. He simply pushed
his tongue deep into my mouth as if he owned it.

The taste of him was devastating and I shuddered
as he explored me, achingly conscious of his body
resting under mine. I wanted to touch all that heat
and hard-packed muscle to see if it felt as perfect as
it looked. Yet I also didn't want to give in.

Helpless passion had hurt me before and I was
still afraid of it.

I shoved against his chest, panting as he broke the
kiss and stared at me.

'What?' His tawny brows pulled down. 'I know
you want me, Vita. You can't pretend otherwise, not
now.'

I didn't want to admit it but he was right. I opened
my mouth to tell him to let me go but, before I could
get the words out, he asked suddenly, 'What are you
afraid of?'

God, how had he seen my fear? I glanced away,
embarrassed.

But he took my chin in his fingers and turned me
to face him, his golden eyes unavoidable. 'Is it me?'
he asked bluntly.

'No,' I said, my denial instinctive. 'I'm not afraid
of you.'

He gave a bitter-sounding laugh. 'Then you're a
fool.'

'Why?' This time it was my turn to demand, my
attention momentarily diverted. 'Because of your
past?'

'We're not talking about me.' His fingers firmed on my chin. 'You're afraid of something and I want to know what it is.'

I didn't want to tell him, didn't want to make myself any more vulnerable than I was already, but the truth came out anyway. 'I'm afraid of…this.' I pushed against his chest for emphasis. 'This…chemistry between us.'

His frown deepened. 'Why? There's nothing wrong with sexual attraction.'

'There is if it's been used against you.'

Realisation dawned in his eyes and my face flamed. I tried to pull away but he only held me tighter.

'Listen to me,' he said, his voice quiet and fierce. 'There are many things you should be afraid of when it comes to me, Vita, but one thing you should never be afraid of is that I'll use your desire to hurt you.' His fingers were firm against my jaw and very warm, his gaze inescapable. 'I'm not so insecure that I need to film a woman and make fun of her in order to feel better about myself. You don't have to believe me, but that's the truth.'

His words dislodged something heavy in my chest, making it shift. 'So why, then?' I asked. 'What is it about me? No one else has ever wanted me. Why should you?'

Golden sparks flickered in his eyes. 'You really want to know?'

I couldn't pretend it wasn't important to me, not now. Not when I'd already given away so much. 'Yes.'

He smiled, an edge of savagery to it. 'I'll show you.'

Before I could respond, he got up off the couch, pulling me with him, and then we were moving to the bar's exit. He'd wound his fingers through mine, tugging me along as we threaded through the tables, and people turned to look at us as we left.

The attention normally would have made me want to run and hide, but tonight all I could think about was where he was leading me and what would happen when we got there. And whether I really wanted to see what it was he was going to show me.

Outside the bar was a long corridor that led to a lift.

Leon strode down it then hit the lift button. The doors opened instantly and he pulled me inside. I waited for him to press the ground floor button but, as the doors closed, it was the stop button he pressed instead.

My heart shuddered to a halt then resumed again, harder, faster. Thundering in my head.

The lift was small, the walls mirrored, Leon's tall, broad reflection filling the tiny space.

He turned to me, his hands on my hips, propelling me against the back wall of the lift.

The air around us had got thicker, his amber gaze burning into mine as the tension drew tighter.

I could feel his heat, see the flames of raw desire in his eyes. He wasn't hiding, he wasn't pretending. He was letting me see it—letting me see all of it.

Why did he want me so badly? What was it he saw in me?

My parents had always found me plain and uninteresting. My mother had never understood my lack of interest in clothes and parties; my father had never understood me, full stop. 'Be more like Clara,' he'd advised, and so I'd tried. But I hadn't been any good at that either.

Leon stared down at me, dark and intent, sliding his hands from my hips to my thighs then curling his fingers into the silky fabric of the new green dress a saleswoman had talked me into buying the day before.

'W-what are you going to show me?' I asked shakily, unable to bear the silence.

'You'll see.'

Then he began to ease the hem of my dress up slowly, taking his time, looking down into my face as the fabric rose higher and higher.

I began to tremble, both with inexplicable fear and a deep, thrilling excitement.

'Are you afraid?' he asked softly as the silk brushed over the tops of my thighs, cool air against my skin.

'Yes.' The word came out as a whisper.

One corner of his mouth quirked in a wicked smile. 'It's only chemicals, vixen. Remember?'

My own words come back to haunt me, but he was right.

'Besides,' he went on, easing my dress up to my waist. 'You can stop me whenever you like. But if you do you'll never get to see what I want to show you.'

My throat was dust-dry already, going even drier as his attention dropped from my face down to what he'd uncovered. Me, bare apart from my underwear, from the waist down.

He didn't move. 'Shall I stop?'

I wished I didn't have to make the decision. I wished he could make it for me because if I said yes I'd have no one to blame but myself if it went wrong. But I wasn't sure I could say no.

I ached. I burned. The desire he'd woken in me had been starved for too long and it needed to be fed.

I closed my eyes, shivering.

'Vita.' Impatience threaded his voice. 'Answer me.'

'Don't stop,' I croaked, keeping my eyes shut.

Silence fell.

'Then hold your knickers aside for me, sweetheart,' he murmured at last. 'I want to see that sweet little pussy.'

The blunt eroticism of the words made me blush at the same time as they sent a pulse of raw heat straight through me.

I couldn't do that, could I?

'Look at me,' he ordered.

My eyes flicked open, meeting the burning gold of his, and he leaned forward, resting his forearms on the mirrored surface of the wall on either side of my head, his face inches from mine.

'Do it.' He stared at me, his voice lower, rougher and taut with command. 'Show me what I have to be desperate about.'

The desire in his gaze was so compelling. I couldn't resist him, not any more.

My hands were shaking as I hooked my fingers in

the damp fabric of my underwear and pulled it aside, baring myself to him.

He pushed himself away and looked down.

'Fuck.' The word was hoarse, the intentness with which he studied me making my face flame. 'You're a natural redhead. I knew you would be.' He reached out and stroked the curls between my thighs, his fingertips brushing my sensitive flesh. 'I knew you'd be wet too.'

I shuddered, white heat streaking through me at his touch. He glanced up at me again, sliding a finger through my folds in a long, slow stroke that tore a gasp from my throat and sent an intense, brutal kind of pleasure licking up inside me.

His smile was dark as his hands dropped away from my sex, coming to rest on my hips. Then he turned me around so that I faced the back wall of the lift.

The mirrored back wall.

I stared at the woman reflected back at me, her hair all over her shoulders in glossy waves, her face flushed, her mouth full and red. Her eyes were very dark yet they glowed with heat.

A sensual woman. Maybe even a beautiful woman.

Behind her stood a beautiful man, tawny and gold like a lion. All command, all power. A faint line of colour stained his high cheekbones and a muscle leapt in the side of his hard jaw.

He looked like he wanted to eat the woman standing in front of him alive.

'I haven't…d-done this since that video,' I said

before I could stop myself, the last gasp of my fear. 'So…p-please go slow.'

His jaw seemed to harden, that muscle at the side of it leaping higher. And all he said was, 'Watch.'

CHAPTER THIRTEEN

Leon

I'D NEVER BEEN so hard in my entire fucking life.

Vita stood in front of me, her wide dark eyes looking at her own reflection in the mirrored wall of the lift then at me standing behind her.

I could see the arousal in her gaze and written all over her face. But there was apprehension there too, and no wonder. If she hadn't had sex since that video then this moment was going to be difficult.

The feelings of others had never bothered me; I simply didn't concern myself with them. But right now, right here, with Vita standing in front of me, I was concerned with her feelings.

She'd been cruelly manipulated and humiliated by some kid who should have known better, and I knew what that felt like. I knew how it messed with your head and how it made you see yourself differently.

Yet it had only been when she'd pushed me away a third time in the bar that I'd truly understood.

I'd automatically thought it had been me that she'd

been afraid of, but no, it was the sexual chemistry between us and, though she hadn't said it, I knew it was her own passion too that scared her.

But she didn't need to be afraid. I wouldn't use it to hurt her.

All I wanted to do was use it to give her a different vision of herself. One where she was desired—where she was beautiful, sexy and sensual. Everything that video had told her she wasn't.

I didn't know why it was important she saw that; I just didn't like that she'd been hurt. I didn't like that she'd been made to doubt herself and her desirability either.

I wanted to show her what I'd seen when she'd come apart under my touch at the restaurant.

She trembled as I reached into the back pocket of my trousers for my wallet and extracted the condom inside. I should have said something reassuring, but the scent of her arousal was everywhere and I was on a fucking knife-edge.

I could barely get the condom on, my hands were shaking so badly, let alone speak.

She'd asked me to go slowly but I wasn't going to have a choice. I'd have to go slowly simply to stay in control.

Christ, how had that even happened? How was it that Augustus King's most feared lieutenant was standing in a lift, shaking like a teenage boy seeing a bare pussy for the first time? And all because of one prickly little redhead.

I gripped my cock, staring at her in the reflective surface of the mirror. Correction, one beautiful little redhead.

Auburn hair everywhere, bright eyes, flushed with desire for me.

Couldn't she see what sheer fucking perfection she was?

'Hands on the rail,' I ordered, standing back from her. 'Then bend over. But keep your eyes on the mirror. Don't look away.'

She hesitated only for a moment before grabbing onto the rail that ran around the inside of the lift and bending over, giving me a fantastic view of her perfect ass.

Her dress was up around her waist, revealing the plain dark blue cotton knickers she wore. I wanted them gone, wanted to see more of what she'd shown me earlier, those beautiful reddish curls between her legs. So I hooked my fingers in the waistband and jerked them down her thighs.

She gave a gasp, her gaze meeting mine in the mirror.

I smiled then looked down beyond the white curve of her butt to where soft red curls guarded the slick wet flesh of her pussy.

'Gorgeous,' I said hoarsely, unable to stop looking. 'You're so fucking pretty.' I couldn't resist the urge to touch her, running my fingers over the soft skin of one butt cheek then squeezing it gently. I felt her tremble and when I ran my fingers down further to stroke those silky curls and slick folds, she trembled even harder.

I straightened, dragging my gaze from her pussy to meet her dark eyes in the mirror again. But I kept my fingers between her thighs, finding her hard little clit, circling it. 'Remember to watch. I want you to see how sexy you are.'

She shuddered, her face flushing red as she did as she was told, her knuckles white where she gripped the railing. A soft moan escaped her.

I took my hand away, my fingers covered in her wetness. Making sure she was watching me, I put them in my mouth, licking the salty sweet taste of her from my skin.

Her breath hitched, her expression mesmerised.

'You taste good, sweetheart,' I said. 'So very good. When I get you home I'm going to eat you out, make you scream. But before that happens…'

I moved closer, reaching down with one hand to grip my cock, my other hand on her hip, holding her steady. Then I positioned myself.

'Eyes on your reflection, little vixen.' I rubbed the head of my cock against her slick flesh, teasing her, teasing us both. 'I want you to watch yourself when I push inside you. So you can see what I see.'

She was panting, her breathing loud in the tiny space, and mine wasn't much better, though I was clearly more experienced at controlling it.

I had to do that now as I flexed my hips, pushing against her, easing the head of my dick into her pussy. The feel of her flesh parting around mine, then wet heat surrounding me, gripping me tightly, tore a growl from my throat.

Christ, she was tight. Slick. Hot. So fucking hot.

A long, low groan escaped her as I eased inside. Her gaze was pinned to her reflection, her mouth slightly open, her cheeks deeply flushed, little curls stuck to her forehead like tiny flames.

She looked wanton. Sensual. So desirable it was all I could do not to lose control completely and drive myself inside her until I passed out.

'See?' I gripped her hip, pushing in deeper, as deep as I could get. 'See how beautiful you are. How fucking sexy. And that look in your eyes… Christ, sweetheart. So much passion.' I drew myself out of her in a long, slow glide, pleasure making my fingers dig into the soft flesh of her hip. Then I pushed back in, deeper. Harder. She groaned, gripping tightly to the rail. 'That's what I see, Vita. That's what I want.' I drew back once more before thrusting into her slick heat again, gritting my teeth against the intense rush of pleasure. 'That's what I see in you. That is you.'

She gasped again as I pulled out then made another desperate sound as I thrust back in, her gaze fixed on her reflection in the mirror.

Watching her watch herself as I fucked her, as her pussy gripped me tight as a glove, was the most erotic experience I'd ever had in my life. Because there was wonder in her eyes. As if she was seeing herself for the first time.

I'd done that for her. I'd done that to her.

I'd made her look. I'd made her see how beautiful she was. How passionate.

Me, who'd only ever given others pain.

A hot, possessive feeling uncoiled in my chest, making me growl. Making me slam my cock deeper into her tight sex.

Her gaze came to mine, her eyes black in the dim light, and yet with that paradoxical bright glow. Full of stars.

'Leon.' Her voice was husky and I could hear the desperation in it. 'Oh, God... Leon...'

The way she said my name, as if I was the only one who could give her what she needed, intensified the pleasure that licked up my spine by a million fucking degrees.

I'd wanted to hold her on the edge, fuck her until she was screaming, all the while staying in control myself. But as soon as my name left her mouth I knew that wasn't going to happen.

So I reached around her, slid one hand over her stomach and down, finding her slick little clit. 'Watch,' I said roughly, stroking her as I thrust deep. 'Watch yourself come, sweetheart.'

And she did, her gaze fixed to her own reflection as I slammed deep inside her, holding my finger down and circling, stroking. Then her mouth opened and her back arched and her pussy clamped down hard on my cock as the climax took her. At the last minute, though, it wasn't herself she looked at as she cried out in ecstasy.

It was me.

Staring at me with wonder. With awe. As if I was

more than a monster in an expensive suit, a criminal with a pretty face.

As if I was someone worth looking at.

I'd told her what I'd seen in her. But what did she see in me?

Ah, fuck, what did that matter? It didn't. Not when her pussy was rippling around my cock, wet silk and heat and the pleasure that was rapidly making me lose my bloody mind.

All it took was one last thrust and the orgasm took me like a fucking hammer, exploding in my head. And it wasn't her who ended up screaming and blind with pleasure. It was me, roaring her name, seeing nothing but those bright eyes watching me as I came.

Afterwards I couldn't move—could only stand there with my legs shaking as I tried to get myself the fuck together.

Her head was hanging down, her hands gripping white-knuckled onto the rail, her body trembling as much as mine with the aftershocks.

I pulled out of her slowly, relishing the shiver she gave as I did so, dealing with the condom to dispose of later. Then I turned back to her, pulling her underwear back up and tugging her dress down, smoothing it in place. Slipping an arm around her waist, I got her to straighten then drew her against me, enjoying her soft warmth as she leaned into me, her head tipping back against my shoulder.

She looked at me in the mirror from beneath her

lashes, the dark glitter of her eyes making my insatiable cock harden again.

I hadn't thought of what we'd do after I'd been inside her. But now, as I met her gaze, it all became very, very clear.

'I'm taking you home,' I said, not caring how rough my voice sounded. 'To my place. You okay with that?'

She gave a nod.

'And screw whether sex was in our agreement or not,' I went on, because this was not going to be a one-off thing, no way in hell. 'It is now.'

She sighed. 'I suppose there's not much point arguing with you, is there?'

'No.' I spread my hand possessively on her stomach. 'Did you want to?'

'Not really.' She gave me a hesitant look. 'It's just sex, though?'

'Of course.' My gaze sharpened on hers. 'If you're wanting more—'

'I don't.' The words were emphatic. 'Just sex is fine with me. We let the chemical reaction burn itself out, right?'

Ah, yes. She was fond of her chemicals, wasn't she?

'Right,' I confirmed. Satisfaction spread through me, and I turned my head into her neck, nipping at her delicate skin possessively.

In the mirror her mouth curved. She had a lovely smile and the knowledge that I'd put it there made my heart beat hard.

'I owe you a thank you,' she said quietly.

'For what?'

'For showing me what you did. For making me see myself.'

The stark honesty in the words reached inside me, making my chest feel tight and uncomfortable.

Most people ended up cursing my name rather than thanking me and I'd never got any gratitude from my father for all the years of service I'd given him.

'Anyone could have done that for you, sweetheart,' I said, making light of it, because Christ knew I didn't want heavy. 'All you needed was some appreciation. Lots of guys can give you that.'

'Lots of guys might but you were the one who noticed and saw what I needed in the first place.' Her expression was serious, her gaze searching mine. 'And you were the one who cared enough to give it to me.'

That honesty again—fuck, it was a killer. Some part of me loved it, lapping that up and her gratitude along with it like a thirsty dog with a bowl of water. Yet at the same time another part of me hated it.

She shouldn't be grateful to a man who'd once used violence and blackmail the same way a builder used a hammer and nails. Not when she'd already been targeted by one bastard, and certainly not when I was an even bigger bastard than the man who'd filmed her.

I might have left my days of violence and blackmail behind me, but that didn't mean I was a good man.

'Why did you do that?' she asked when I didn't speak.

'You ask too many questions, sweetheart,' I murmured and, bending my head, I kissed her hard.

Before she could ask me anything else that I didn't have the answer to.

CHAPTER FOURTEEN

Vita

I woke up suddenly, not sure what had woken me. It might have been because I wasn't in my own bed in my little terrace house in Newtown, but in Leon's penthouse apartment overlooking Sydney Harbour.

The walls of the bedroom were nothing but windows and he didn't like obscuring the incredible view with something as mundane as blinds. Which meant I'd been woken at sunrise each morning after our last couple of dates with dawn flooding into the room and Leon's hands on my body, working his magic with his mouth and his fingers. And his cock.

But it wasn't dawn now and the bed beside me was empty.

In fact, it was full night, the lights of the harbour stretched out in front of me, with the Opera House below and beyond that the bridge in a shining arc.

No point in trying to go back to sleep. I probably wouldn't, not when Leon wasn't there.

I slipped out of bed, searching around for my

clothes before remembering they were out in the lounge, where Leon had ripped them off me after we'd got back from the nightclub.

Our fourth date and we hadn't even been there half an hour before Leon leaned in and whispered in my ear that the club could go fuck itself. He wanted to fuck me instead.

That had been the pattern after he'd taken me in the lift. We'd meet up in public, make a desultory attempt at conversation, then go back to his place where he'd have me naked and screaming his name within minutes.

Perhaps I should have been worried that every time he touched me I'd become putty in his hands. But I told myself that was simply due to the physical chemistry that we were burning out, and once that was gone it would be over.

Besides, in the mirrors of the lift that night, he'd shown me something in myself that I'd never seen before, a beauty and sensuality that I'd always thought was my sister's, never mine. But I'd seen it as he pushed into me and the pleasure had taken hold—as I watched myself come apart in the mirror right in front of me.

It should have been exposing but it wasn't.

With him behind me, the evidence of his desperation driving into me, his dark amber gaze pinned to our reflections, I'd felt beautiful for the first time in my life. Desirable. Wanted.

All the things I'd wanted to feel with Simon and hadn't.

It was the first time I'd ever felt any of those things and I couldn't give them up, not yet. Not while Leon could give them to me.

Anyway, I'd be careful to make sure only my body surrendered. Everything else remained my own and that was how it would stay.

Since my clothes weren't there, I found the dark blue shirt Leon had been wearing earlier that evening discarded over a low white chair opposite the bed and put it on.

I shivered as his warm scent enveloped me, making hunger turn over in my gut. I wanted him again, craved his touch and the way he made me feel.

He'd told me anyone could give me that, but he was wrong. No one had bothered looking past my façade for years, because no one had been interested enough.

But he had.

He hadn't given me an answer as to why, or what he got out of sleeping with me, not when there were plenty of women far more beautiful than I was to choose from, but unusually for me, I'd decided not to question further. Some things didn't stand up to scientific testing; you simply had to accept them for what they were. And I was sure that the sexual relationship I had with Leon wouldn't stand up to any kind of testing at all.

The thought made me uneasy. I wasn't used to not questioning things I didn't understand, but I didn't want anything to disturb the delicate balance between Leon and me so I ignored the feeling.

Moving out of the bedroom, I went down the long hallway that led to the lounge area.

It was a beautiful space, lots of windows to let in the brilliant sun and the amazing view. The walls were as pale as the carpet, the furniture upholstered in the same shades. It was clean, minimalist and very, very sophisticated.

I paused in the doorway, finding Leon sitting on the low white sofa, bare feet propped on the coffee table in front of him, laptop in his lap, staring down at it. He wore only his suit trousers, the light from the screen illuminating the cut muscles of his chest and abs and throwing shadows off his strong jaw and high cheekbones.

My heart squeezed at the sheer masculine beauty of him.

It seemed incredible that someone so breathtakingly beautiful should be mine. Or at least mine for a little while. And that he should find me just as beautiful and desirable as I found him.

Sometimes it felt like a dream. The secret fantasy of the 'I Love You Girl'. Where the ugly duckling didn't have to be a swan at all; she could be just a duck and be wanted all the same.

I leaned my head against the doorframe, staring at him, breathless. My fingers itched, longing to explore that hard-muscled body. Yet the nights we'd been together he'd strip me naked and spread me out on the floor of the lounge, or the couch or up against the window, and explore me with abandon, all the lights on so he could see me.

But when it came to me touching him, he'd be reticent. Not letting me until we were in the bedroom and the lights were off. It was another thing I hadn't questioned since he was good at distracting me. However, I was thinking about it now and it puzzled me.

Getting to know him hadn't seemed important before, not when our marriage wouldn't be a real one, yet it suddenly felt important to me now.

He'd shown me why he wanted me, healing a wound I hadn't known was still painful, yet what did he get out of sleeping with me? Physical pleasure, sure, but there had to be something else. Something he couldn't get from those other, more beautiful women.

I took the opportunity to study him while he wasn't aware of me, the scientist in me now firmly in control.

Faint lines tracked the golden skin of his torso, criss-crossing his abs and then, further up, his chest. Some of them were long and twisted, others merely small hollows. They were difficult to see in the pale light of the computer, but I knew what they were. Scars. Old ones.

I frowned. I'd felt them when I'd touched him in the darkness and in the rooftop bar that night I'd caught a glimpse of the one at his throat. He'd told me he'd got it from a mountain bike accident. But they didn't look like the kinds of scars you got in an accident.

Don't forget who he is.

A kernel of ice gathered in my gut. I had forgotten. He was the son of Augustus King, once Sydney's biggest crime boss. And not only that. Leon had been his lieutenant. I didn't know exactly what that meant, but he'd probably done some bad stuff and maybe those scars were evidence of that.

I shivered as reality crept into the bubble of happy sexual pleasure I'd surrounded myself with.

How could I have forgotten that there was always going to be more to him than the handsome, charming stranger who'd seduced me? That, although he might have made me feel good about myself, he'd done other things. Things that did not involve making people feel good about themselves.

You can't keep yourself in the dark. Not this time.

No, I couldn't. I was going to have to ask the hard questions. But at least with Leon, if I didn't like the answers I wouldn't lose anything.

'Miss me?' Leon said unexpectedly, not looking up from his screen.

'Yes.' Trying not to show my surprise that he'd spotted me, I pushed myself away from the doorway, forcing myself over to where he sat on the couch. Fear crept through me and I didn't know why. Was it him I was afraid of? Or was it what I might find out about him? Or was it simply that this affair might end and I didn't want it to? 'I woke up and you weren't there.'

'Just keeping track of what the media are saying about us.' His long fingers moved quickly over the touchpad, opening up the browser tab instead.

His hands weren't scarred, I couldn't help noting. Just his torso.

'What are they saying?' Not that I was interested.

I was more interested in the pattern of small round scars at the top of his six-pack instead. They looked like…cigarette burns.

'Mostly that it's a shocking scandal.' The wicked smile I'd come to know so well over the past few days curled his mouth. 'And they love it. Quite a few are on your side, believe it or not. They love the fact that the "I Love You Girl" has managed to snag Mr Tall, Blond and Dangerous. And that's a direct quote.'

Talk of the media momentarily distracted me from his scars. I'd had a few calls from various news outlets, wanting interviews and the inside story on how Leon and I had got together, as well as what I'd been doing for the past ten years since my video had gone viral.

I'd ignored them. Not because I was ashamed this time, but because I simply didn't care what the media said. I was too busy glorying in the pleasure he gave me every night to worry about it.

'Tall, blond and dangerous?' I echoed.

'Hey, is it my fault they find me irresistible?' He reached out and toyed with the hem of the shirt I wore, which ended mid-thigh. 'But what I really like is this. You wearing anything under that? No, wait, don't tell me. I want to find out for myself.' His tawny brows drew together all of a sudden, his dark amber gaze zeroing in on me in a way that made me uneasy. 'What's wrong?'

That stare pinned me, making my breath catch.

Did I really want to broach this topic? Did I really

want to test what was happening between us by asking him about his past?

You know the answer to that.

Of course. I was a scientist. And I needed answers.

I glanced down at the pattern of scars on his stomach and the ones slashing across his chest. I brushed my fingers over the small round scars that peppered his abs. 'You never did say where you got these.'

Leon closed the laptop with a snap, the light from the screen cutting off and plunging the room back into darkness. Then he grabbed my hand from his skin and moved it down to where I could feel him rapidly hardening under the fabric of his trousers.

'Yes, I did. But I think you should wonder about how you could fix this instead.' He flexed his hips in blatant invitation. 'I guarantee it'll be a lot more interesting.'

His face was shadowed in the dim light from the city outside the windows, his expression hidden. But I knew a distraction technique when I saw one.

He hadn't wanted to talk about those scars that night in the bar, and it seemed he didn't want to talk about them now either.

Are you sure you want to keep going?

No, I wasn't sure. But if we were going to continue to sleep together I needed to know just how dangerous this man truly was. Not that I was worried about my physical safety—I was sure he'd never hurt me. It was my peace of mind I was worried about.

'You said a mountain bike accident.' I shook his

hand off and reached out to touch him again. 'But these look like—'

His fingers closed around my wrist and it wasn't a playful hold this time. It was hard, his fingertips digging into my skin. 'They're not for you.' His voice had turned flat. 'If you want to touch me, put your hand on my cock instead.'

Okay, he definitely didn't want to talk about them. And maybe it wasn't any wonder since they must have been painful. But those round ones... Had someone ground out a cigarette on his skin?

The chill inside me deepened, horror rising as I stared at the scars. He'd been hurt. No, more than merely hurt. It looked like he'd been...

Tortured.

'No.' A low growl of warning cut into my thoughts. 'This is what you should be paying attention to.' And he shoved my palm insistently to the hard ridge beneath his fly.

But I couldn't drag my gaze from those scars—a stark reminder of who he was. What he was...

'I thought you weren't afraid of me.'

The sharp note in his voice made me look up and meet the laser-like intensity of his gaze. 'I—'

'But you are. I can see it in your eyes. Why? You weren't before.' His grip on my wrist tightened, though I'm sure he wasn't aware of it, not when he was too busy staring at me. 'What did I do?'

There wasn't any point denying my unease, not when he'd picked up on it. 'Nothing,' I said, being honest because he hadn't done anything. 'It's just...

those scars, Leon. They reminded me that I don't know anything about you. About your past...' I stopped, my throat dry. 'I think I need to know. Before this goes any further.'

'This?' The question sounded neutral but the grip on my wrist was not.

I gathered my courage. 'This being us, sleeping together.'

'I thought it was only sex. That's what you said.'

'I know. But—'

'But you don't want to sleep with a killer.'

The words were harsh, his voice harsher, but all I had to give him was honesty. 'No,' I said. 'I don't.

His grip loosened and he released me. 'So principled. I admire that, Vita.' Letting out a breath, he leaned back against the couch. 'Even if it pisses me off.'

'Leon, I—'

'I'm not a killer,' he interrupted flatly. 'Dad had other people who did that for him. But I did hurt people on Dad's orders. I punished them, made them see things his way.'

Was it relief I felt? I wasn't sure.

'Do you still do that? For your brothers?'

'No. That would make us criminals and we're not criminals.' He laughed without amusement. 'At least, not any more.'

Yet not exactly blameless either.

I should have left it then, taken those answers at face value and been satisfied. But it wasn't enough.

I had questions and the scientist in me couldn't leave them alone.

'And those scars?' I asked. 'Did you get those making people "see things his way"?'

'Why do you want to know? What difference does it make?'

'Why don't you want to tell me?'

'Because those scars mean nothing.' His eyes gleamed in the darkness. 'Maybe I simply got what I deserved.'

Bitterness laced the words and I studied him, trying to figure out why. 'Those scars look like you were...tortured.'

He lifted a shoulder as if bored of the conversation. 'Like I said, they mean nothing.'

But they did and I knew it. That bitterness gave it away.

'You can tell me,' I said before I could stop myself, wanting to give him something. 'You can tell me anything. I won't judge you. You can trust me.'

His whole body tensed, tight as a coiled spring, and danger thickened in the atmosphere around us. I couldn't tell his expression in the dim light, but there was no mistaking the menace glowing in his eyes.

He did not want to talk about this.

You need to stop pushing.

My pulse had sped up, my breath coming faster. Yes, I should, but he'd been hurt and I wanted to know why. He knew about my scars, the ones that weren't physical but were there all the same, the ones that had been inflicted by Simon and that video. He knew and had helped them hurt a little bit less, so why couldn't I do the same for him? At least I could try.

'Why should I trust you?' His tone was silky with menace. 'You're only the woman I'm sleeping with at the moment. Nothing else.'

An inexplicable hurt slid under my skin, though there was no reason it should. I was only the woman he was sleeping with and I didn't want to be anything more. Did I?

Yet…he sounded so bitter. Did he have anyone in his life he could trust? There were his brothers and I didn't know what kind of relationships he had with them, but he must trust them. He didn't need me poking at things that weren't my business.

'What?' he demanded. 'You want to say something?'

'Is there anyone you do trust?' The question was out before I could think better of it.

Instantly, his expression became shuttered and that was when I knew.

No. He didn't.

Determination shifted and turned inside me. When my video had hit, when everyone I'd trusted had betrayed me, the only person I'd had was my aunt. She hadn't been a warm person but she'd taught me to bake, and it had been in the moments when we were in the kitchen, just the two of us, measuring and weighing the ingredients, that I'd talked to her about my experience. She'd never said much in response, but she didn't judge, didn't blame. Simply let me talk.

Did Leon need someone to talk to? Did he have anyone he could talk to?

It hit me then—the reasons I was asking myself all these questions. I wanted him to talk to me. I wanted him to trust me.

But simply telling him he should wasn't going to work, and why should it? Given his past, he wouldn't be a man who trusted easily.

Which meant that if I wanted this I had to give him a reason.

I went with my instinct. Bending to pick up his laptop, I opened up the video programme that operated the camera. Then I put the computer down on the coffee table, angling it so the camera was directed at him and his whole body was in the shot.

Ignoring the frantic beat of my heart, I hit Record then turned back, moving to straddle his legs where they rested on the table in front of him.

A ripple of emotion crossed his face. He glanced at the computer, where the pair of us were on the screen, then back at me, surprised.

'What are you doing?'

I lifted my hands to the buttons of the shirt and slowly began to undo them. 'Giving you a reason to trust me.'

He glanced at the computer again and I saw realisation hit. Abruptly, he tried to grab my wrists. 'You don't need to—'

I shook his fingers off, letting the shirt slip from my shoulders.

A week ago, baring my body for a man like this,

let alone to yet another camera, would have filled me
with dread. But I couldn't think of any other way to
show him how serious I was. If I wanted his trust, I
had to show him he had mine.

'Don't turn it off,' I said fiercely. 'I want it to record us. I want to give you something I wouldn't ever
give anyone else. Because I trust you.'

Shock left his face momentarily blank and a small
spark of triumph went through me, pleased that I'd
surprised him so completely. But I didn't let myself
dwell on it. Instead, I took his hands and guided them
to my breasts, shivering at the contact of his warm
skin on mine.

'Why?' His voice was hoarse and he stared at me
like I was a stranger. 'I haven't done a single fucking
thing to deserve this.'

'You have.' I pressed his palms against my flesh,
letting him feel how my nipples hardened in response. 'You made me feel beautiful. You made me
feel wanted. You made me feel special.'

'Vita—'

'You need someone to talk to, Leon. You need
someone to trust. And you can trust me.' Then I
leaned forward, crushing his hands between our bodies as I brushed my mouth over his.

He was still for a second. Then he jerked his hands
from between us, the fingers of one hand burying
themselves in my hair while he wound his arm around
my waist, pulling me tight against him.

And he took control of the kiss.

His tongue swept into my mouth, the heat and taste

of him flooding my senses, so demanding that my fingers curled into his chest, trying to hold on to something—anything.

He was hard and hot beneath me, the wool of his suit trousers rubbing against the sensitive flesh of my bare sex and inner thighs. The feel of his chest against my nipples, smooth skin, firm muscle and the slight prickle of hair, was glorious.

I dug my nails into him, kissing him as desperately as he was kissing me, shivering as his teeth closed on my bottom lip in a short, hard nip.

Then I found myself flipped over onto my back on the couch, with him lying half on his side, half over me, golden eyes hot and possessive as he looked down at me.

'I'll tell you where my scars came from,' he said. 'On one condition. I want something pretty to look at and beautiful to touch when I do.'

I didn't understand what he meant at first. Then he cupped my breast in one large, warm palm and dragged his thumb with aching slowness over my nipple, making me gasp.

Pretty to look at and beautiful to touch…

He was talking about me.

My chest tightened and my eyes prickled. A ridiculously emotional reaction that I was powerless to stop. So, not only had he accepted my offer of trust, he was still making me feel beautiful with it.

I didn't know what I'd done to deserve it but this time I stayed quiet, not risking speaking in case he changed his mind.

'When I was fifteen,' Leon began, 'I was taken by some enemies of my father. They targeted me because my older brother Ajax was too dangerous and my younger brother was too well protected. But I wasn't. I was the middle child and pretty, a bookworm, easy prey.' He looked down to his hand on my breast, watching his thumb circle my nipple once more. 'They held me for a couple of days, trying to get money out of my father, but he wouldn't pay the ransom.'

His touch sent a lightning strike of pleasure from my breast straight to my sex, but through it I felt a deep foreboding settling down in my bones.

'They were...unhappy with my father's response,' he went on, his voice expressionless, his nail scraping gently against my sensitive nipple, making me tremble. 'So they took it out on me. With knives, cigarettes. One of them had a baseball bat and I got a few broken ribs from that.'

Despite the heat of pleasure, I felt cold. Oh, God, they had tortured him.

'Leon...' I began.

But he shook his head. 'No. Stay quiet.' His nail scraped over me again, making the pulse of pleasure between my thighs more intense. 'They would have killed me if I hadn't escaped. But I did.' His hand slid from my breast down my body, his gaze following it as his fingers grazed the curls between my thighs. 'They thought I was asleep, but I wasn't. I got out, got myself back home and demanded Dad tell me why he hadn't rescued me; why he wouldn't pay the ransom.' His fingers delicately parted my sensitive flesh and I couldn't stop the moan that escaped me as he found my clit, circling it gently. 'Do you know why he wouldn't? Because I was expendable. Because Ajax was the oldest and Xander was the clever one. But I was the pretty one, the useless one. I wasn't worth the time it would have taken for a rescue or the money for the ransom.'

He wasn't looking at me, watching his finger stroking my sex instead, which somehow made it that much hotter. So much so that it was difficult to focus on what he was saying and not get lost in the tide of pleasure slowly rising inside me. 'Dad only surrounded himself with people who were useful to him and apparently being his son wasn't enough. So I decided to make myself useful. I became his weapon, dangerous enough that no one would ever target me again.' He glanced at me at the same time as he eased one finger into me, going slow and deep, tearing a moan from my throat. His eyes were molten, glittering. 'And no one did, Vita. You know why? Because I made sure they were all too afraid of me.'

The pleasure was intense and I could barely hear him over the frantic beat of my heart and the overwhelming urge to lift my hips, ride that finger. But the hard note in his voice and the anger in his eyes stopped me from losing myself entirely.

So, he'd been tortured because his father hadn't thought he was worth rescuing. At fifteen.

Behind my ribs, my heart clenched tight.

That was so wrong. So awful. It had upset me that, after my video had hit, all my own father had thought about was the effect it was having on his business and the family's reputation rather than me. But at least he hadn't left me in the hands of people who'd hurt me, who'd possibly even kill me, just because I wasn't useful to him.

'Leon, stop.' I reached to pull his hand away because it felt wrong to be receiving such pleasure while he relived something so awful.

But he simply held my wrist down by my side and slid another finger into me, stretching me. 'I told you,' he said, rough and fierce. 'I want something beautiful to touch.'

I panted, unable to stop my back from arching or from lifting my hips in time with the movements of his fingers. 'But... I... I can't feel this while you... talk about t-torture.'

'Yes, you can. I'd rather you felt pleasure than pain. Or anything else for that matter.' He bent his head, his tongue finding my nipple and circling it as his fingers slid deep inside me. I groaned, the feel of his mouth incandescent. 'So don't feel sorry for me, vixen,' he murmured against my skin. 'Just scream my name when you come.'

But I didn't feel sorry for him. I felt nothing but a terrible sympathy while at the same time I was furious at the people who'd done this to him. His father, who hadn't even bothered looking for him, let alone rescuing him. While he'd had knives, cigarettes pressed against his skin, a baseball bat...

'Leon,' I whispered. 'You shouldn't…'

'Give me this, Vita.' A raw note had entered his voice. 'This is what I want to think about. The way you feel and the way you taste. Give me your pleasure. Give me something good that I can do for you. Please.'

He'd never said that word to me before. He'd never begged. And I couldn't deny him. I didn't have any advice or any words of wisdom. Nothing else to give him, apart from myself. My trust and my body.

So I gave him both.

'Okay,' I murmured.

He shifted, gripping my thigh and pushing it out, pressing it against the back of the couch, holding me open as he stared down at my exposed sex. Then he touched me with his free hand, stroking me, spreading my wet flesh, burying the terrible thing he'd told me under the delicate stroke of pleasure.

Holding me open, he bent his head and covered my sex with his mouth. I jerked in his grip, the slide of his tongue against my clit electric, lighting up every nerve ending I had.

I groaned, arching up into him as he licked and explored my slick flesh, as the hand on my thigh firmed, keeping me spread so he could sink his tongue deep inside me.

'Leon!' My hands groped for him, finding the softness of his hair. I wound my fingers in the thick silk of it, holding on tight as he brought his free hand into play, touching and stroking me as he licked me.

'Yes,' he murmured against me, his voice thick

with satisfaction. 'Tell me who's making you come. Tell me who's making you scream. Say my name, vixen.'

And I did, helplessly screaming it again as he pushed me off the edge of the world.

CHAPTER FIFTEEN

Leon

SHE WAS LAID out beneath me, naked and trembling, the sound of my name echoing in the room around us. Her eyes were fixed to mine, sweat beading her forehead and gathering in the hollow of her throat.

I was so hard I ached.

The salty sweet taste of her was in my mouth and I wanted to stay with my head buried between her legs, eating her out all night.

Forgetting everything I'd told her. Forgetting all about that fucking bastard Thompson and what he and his henchmen had done to me.

Forgetting about the note of desperation in my voice, the raw sound of pain. Of weakness.

I thought I'd put those memories behind me, thought they didn't matter any more, but telling her about Thompson had brought them all flooding back in vivid fucking Technicolor.

But I wasn't that sobbing, pathetic fifteen-year-old any more. I was someone much deadlier. Ajax had helped me craft myself into a weapon and, even though I no longer used violence, I was still lethal.

I was still fucking dangerous.

Fury burned in my veins and I wanted to punish her for making me tell her about my scars. For the mistake of giving me her trust.

I wanted to remind her who she was dealing with.

The angle of the laptop wouldn't have captured her face as I'd eaten her out, but I knew what to do so it would.

I leaned down and gathered her up in my arms, bringing her into my lap so she was facing me, straddling my thighs. She was panting, the heat of her pussy soaking through the wool of my trousers, making my cock ache. It would be so easy to unzip myself, slide into her welcoming heat, but that camera would only capture her back and I didn't want that.

I looked into her eyes, glazed and black with pleasure. 'Time to return the favour, sweetheart. Get on your knees.'

I should have known that Vita wouldn't do the expected thing and she didn't now. Instead of instantly obeying, she leaned forward and kissed me, her mouth hot and demanding, her tongue seeking, as if she wanted to taste herself on me.

I lifted my hand to her hair, intending to drag her mouth away and push her down to kneel in front of me, but I couldn't. Her kiss was such a sweet mix of inexperience and demand that I wound my fingers into her hair and held her there instead.

The lick of her tongue, the scrape of her teeth over my lip was electric, the taste of her like honey. I was desperate to devour her but the hungry way she kissed me did things to me, sucking away all my anger and giving me desire in its place.

She left me breathless.

Then suddenly her mouth was gone, trailing down over my jaw and my neck, her lips pressing against my throat. Going further, her tongue licking along the line of the scar Thompson's knife had left on me.

I didn't know why that made me feel like my heart was slowly being squeezed in a giant fist. And when her mouth moved down, tracing the line of each and every scar, the cigarettes they'd ground out on my chest and stomach, the twisted line where the base-ball bat had broken the skin, that fist squeezed tighter.

Making me weak. Leaving me vulnerable.

'Vita.' I gripped her hair, tugging her head away. 'No.'

But her black eyes were bright with determination. 'I want to give you better memories,' she said huskily. 'Let me, the way I let you.'

But I already had the taste and feel of her beautiful body, the sound of her screaming my name instead of the pain of the knife and the burn of the cigarettes. The scent of her arousal instead of the smell of my own flesh burning.

I didn't need her delicate tongue and her mouth tracing the reminders of how weak I'd been.

I gripped her hair tighter. 'No.'

'Please,' she said. 'You know you can trust me.'

Trust, fuck. I had no idea what that meant any more, if I ever had. Or why she offered it to me without guile or manipulation, her honesty laid bare in her eyes.

Such a mistake. She needed to protect herself better, especially from men like me.

I opened my mouth to tell her no, but she leaned forward again, giving me another of those sweet, soul-stealing kisses, and somehow I couldn't bring myself to pull her away again.

So I sat there, my fingers wound in the silkiness of her hair, letting her kiss her way down my body. Letting her lick and taste each mark, each scar. Tracing them then putting her mouth over them like she was sucking poison from a snakebite.

Thompson's knife had undone me with pain and now Vita was undoing me with pleasure. I should stop her, take control of the situation again, show her that she couldn't mess with me the way she was doing, but...

Christ. My pulse thundered in my head, my cock aching like a bastard, and I couldn't drag my gaze away from that little pink tongue, watching it on my skin as she went lower and lower.

And it struck me that I'd never been touched like this before. Oh, women had gone down on me—I liked a blow job; what man didn't? But I'd never let anyone run their tongue over my scars or trace them with their fingers. I'd never told anyone what they were or what they meant.

I'd never told anyone about them, full stop.

Yet I'd not only told Vita, I'd let her touch me too.

Vita, with her bright black eyes and her honesty, her trust and her passion.

Slipping between my thighs to kneel on the floor, she then reached to unzip me. I hadn't bothered with underwear when I'd got up earlier so there was nothing between her cool fingers and my rock-hard cock as she opened my trousers and drew me out.

My breath escaped in a hiss as she wrapped those fingers around me, her hair trailing silkily over my thighs and stomach as she bent forward. Then her lips brushed the head of my dick and a growl escaped my throat.

I reached down, gathering her hair in my fist and away from her face so I could watch that pretty tongue lick me.

'More,' I demanded, unable to help myself.

But she ignored me, licking, nipping, making me jerk and shiver under her touch, making me growl yet again.

I'd taught her what I liked in a blow job over the course of the past few days, and I liked it rough, with teeth and a firm touch. But she wasn't doing that now. She was being careful, delicate. Teasing me with gentleness. I wanted to push her head down on me, make her take me all the way to the back of her throat, yet...

I liked this. I liked the care she was taking with me and I had no bloody idea why.

Her tongue swirled, and I gritted my teeth, holding on to her hair as another electric jolt of pleasure hit.

'Put me in your mouth,' I ordered, though it sounded more like a plea. 'Fuck, Vita. Do it.'

Those perfect red lips closed around my cock and she watched me all the while, the heat of her mouth making me lose what little breath I had left.

'Jesus,' I forced out as her fingers tightened around my dick. 'Vixen...'

Then she sucked me. Slow and deep, fast and shallow. Hard then soft. Letting me see my own hard flesh disappearing into her mouth then sliding back out again.

I couldn't take my eyes off her.

The whole world shrank down to this moment. I forgot about Thompson and his fucking knives. I forgot about the scars marking me and how she'd undone me with her kisses. Forgot about the camera on the laptop recording us. I forgot about everything except her midnight gaze and the stars glittering in it. And her mouth surrounding me, taking me in so deep I could finally feel the back of her throat, her fingers squeezing me tight, pumping me.

I lifted my hips in time with the suction, the pleasure winding tighter and tighter, a hot ball of it at the base of my spine, ready to explode.

Then she lifted her lips a moment and whispered, 'Say my name,' before swallowing me down again, her fingers tight around my dick. She made a soft, satisfied sound that vibrated against my aching flesh and, just like that, the hot ball of pleasure detonated, a column of fire shooting straight up my spine, exploding like a bomb in my head.

My fingers tightened in her hair and I thrust help-lessly up into her mouth, roaring her name as I came.

Afterwards, my ears ringing, my body pulsing with the aftershocks, I hauled her up off the floor, putting her onto her back on the couch then shift-ing over her.

She put her arms around my neck, giving a deli-cious little shiver as I settled between her thighs. My cock brushed the wet folds of her pussy, already get-ting hard at the contact, but she gave no sign of notic-ing, her dark eyes serious as they searched my face.

'Leon, I—' she began.

But I'd said all I wanted to say about it for the night so I laid a finger over her mouth. 'No more,' I mur-mured. 'I gave you what you wanted. That's enough.'

Frustration flickered in her expression. 'But I want to talk about you. Why don't you tell me what you were like as a child?'

She was very warm under me and the smell of sex and feminine musk was heady. I could suddenly think of a million things I wanted to do more than talk about my childhood, and all of them included her naked body.

'Why?' I flexed my hips so my cock slid against her slick flesh. 'I'd rather fuck you senseless.'

She hissed, catching her bottom lip between her teeth. I wanted to bite it myself so I leaned down, but she jerked her head to the side, avoiding me. 'No, not yet.'

I growled, but she refused to be distracted. 'Come on, Leon. I'm curious.'

So she didn't want to play.

I debated trying to convince her, but then dismissed the idea. Clearly, she wasn't going to give up until I'd given her what she wanted. Bloody determined little vixen.

'What was I like as a kid?' I said, surrendering. 'I was quiet. I liked to read a lot. When I was about ten I got heavily into computers and computer games.'

Amusement glittered in her eyes. 'So, nerdy then?'

I thought about my younger self. Trying to escape the reality of his life any way he could, with books at first then in the glow of the computer screen and the roar of computer-generated gunfire.

'You could say that,' I agreed.

Amusement turned to mischief. 'Computer club at school?'

'Naturally. All the best people were in the computer club at school.'

'I know.' She grinned. 'I was in the computer club. And the science club. And the photography club. In fact, if there was a club you can pretty much guarantee that I was part of it.'

Curious, I searched for the teenager she'd once been in the sharp, lovely face of the controlled adult she'd become. She would have been bright. Intense. Passionate.

If I'd met her in high school I would have thought she was amazing, I realised. My childhood had been overshadowed by the reality of my father's business and his ruthlessness when it came to running it; Vita's intensity would have been a bright light shining in the darkness...

Christ, I wouldn't only have thought she was amazing. I would have fallen head over heels for her.

'I wish I'd known you then,' I said before I could stop myself. 'I think I would have liked you.'

Her smile became radiant. As if I'd given her a gift. 'I think I would have liked you too. Though you'd probably have intimidated the hell out of me.'

'Oh, really?'

She blushed. 'You're hot—and hot boys were always intimidating.'

'Why?'

'Only a very hot person would ask that question.' Ah.

I flexed my hips again, loving the feel of her against me. 'You shouldn't have been intimidated. Don't you know you're beautiful?'

She caught her breath but that smile still tugged at her mouth. 'That sounds like a song lyric.'

'All my best pick-up lines are song lyrics.' I stared down at her. 'Seriously, though, I mean it. You're lovely. I thought I showed you that in the mirror in the lift.'

'You did. But it's hard to accept sometimes, especially when it's always been made clear to you that you're not.'

I frowned, stroking the hair back from her forehead. 'That bastard Simon has a lot to answer for.'

'Not only Simon. My parents aren't exactly supportive types. Clara was the one with the looks in my family, which was pointed out to me a lot.'

Her insecurities made sense to me all of a sudden. A beautiful sister and parents who couldn't see what I saw—the passion, the honesty, the bright-eyed curiosity...

'Poor Clara,' I said. 'She only got looks. You got brains and beauty.'

Vita flushed. 'I wasn't fishing, if that's what you think.'

'I know you're not. I'm just giving you the truth.' And I let her see it in my gaze. 'Brains. Beauty. Honesty. Passion. You got it all, vixen.'

Her mouth curved, pleasure alight in her eyes. Then it faded, her expression turning serious. 'You're very good for me, Leon King. But you're also very bad. You probably need to stop.'

I didn't know what she meant by that.

Are you sure you don't?

Okay, maybe I did. And maybe I liked it. Especially the being good for her part.

I liked that very much.

'Do you really want me to stop?' I ran my hands down her sides then slid my palms beneath the curve of her butt. Gathering her flesh in my palms, I squeezed her lightly. 'Because I'm okay with being good for you.'

Her breath caught. 'Maybe...you don't need to stop that part.'

'What about the bad?' I slipped my fingers between her thighs, searching, exploring. 'I definitely don't want to be bad for you.'

She gave a soft gasp as my fingers found soft, wet flesh, then groaned. 'I think you should stop talking.'

I grinned. And stopped talking.

CHAPTER SIXTEEN

Vita

ALL THAT SEX should have knocked me out cold but I couldn't sleep. My head was too full of the terrible things Leon had told me and his understandable reluctance to talk about them.

Eventually, after tossing and turning, I slipped off the couch, leaving Leon fast asleep beside me, picking up his shirt again and putting it on. Then I got the throw that had been hung over the arm of the couch and covered him with it, being sure not to wake him.

As I drew the throw up around his bare shoulders I looked down at him, my heart aching.

His father must have been one hell of a bastard to have left him in the hands of the monsters who'd hurt him. No wonder he'd set about making himself dangerous. No wonder he'd turned himself into a weapon.

He'd done everything he could to protect himself.

Unsettled, I turned from him and, after a second's thought, went into the pristine minimalist stainless steel and white tile kitchen.

I loved kitchens. They were my laboratory for the wonderful chemistry that was baking, and Leon's kitchen was up there with the best. I wandered around it, checking out cupboards and poking my nose in drawers, opening up the oven to have a look.

Then, needing something to distract myself, I went over to the pantry to see what kind of baking ingredients he had. Not many, but the basics were there.

In the early days after I'd been sent to live with my aunt, when I couldn't sleep I would sometimes get up in the middle of the night and bake something. The focus it required had given me a break from my thoughts, plus I loved that it was chemistry without having to be in a lab.

I didn't think Leon would mind if I used his kitchen, so I set about whipping up a quick batch of scones. I'd been experimenting with an old recipe my aunt had given me, trying to get the best rise, but I hadn't had much luck. So now I pushed all thoughts of Leon's past out of my mind as I bustled about, getting the ingredients out.

Totally absorbed, I made two batches and was just getting the second batch out of the oven when a deep, husky male voice said from behind me, 'Do I want to know why you're baking scones in my kitchen at five-thirty in the morning?'

I turned around with my tray full of scones to find him standing on the other side of the kitchen island, his hands in his pockets and his trousers half zipped. The fabric sat low on his hips, revealing golden skin and a crisp glory trail of tawny hair that had my mouth watering.

'I couldn't sleep,' I said, clearing my throat as I put the tray down on the kitchen island counter.

'So you bake?'

I'd conditioned myself not to talk about the things that excited me, but there wasn't much point in pretending to be casual about my baking. Not now there were two batches of scones sitting there.

'Yes.' I took off the oven gloves and put them on the counter next to the tray. 'I like to. Especially when I can't sleep.'

His smoky golden gaze focused on the trays of scones. 'These look…amazing.'

The simple praise warmed me like the sun on a winter's day and I couldn't help smiling. 'Thanks. I've been messing around with a recipe of my aunt's, trying to get a better rise. I think the second batch is better.'

'They all look great to me, not to mention smell bloody delicious.' He lifted a brow. 'There's jam in the fridge. And butter.'

'Was that a subtle hint?'

'It was subtle?'

I laughed, turning to get what he'd suggested from the fridge. There was whipped cream in a spray can so I grabbed that too.

When I turned back, he was in the process of grinding beans and making coffee.

'It's tea and scones, you know,' I pointed out, putting the items down on the counter.

'Not here it isn't,' he said decisively. 'Coffee. Always.'

He filled the stovetop espresso maker and put it on the element, then came back over to the counter to stand beside me. 'Why baking?' He reached for a scone. 'Seems an odd thing for a scientist to do.'

'Not really. Baking is just chemistry.'

'It is?'

'Of course. It's all about mixing things to create chemical reactions. How one ingredient works with another, or doesn't work depending on the measurement. It's fascinating how they all work together.' I warmed to my favourite subject. 'Or don't if you mess up the proportions. Or how amazing it can turn out if you add something else.'

He smiled and it wasn't the manufactured smile of a man setting out to charm, but spontaneous and full of warmth. It turned him from hot to breathtaking in a matter of seconds. 'Where did you learn to bake? Did that get you into chemistry or vice versa?'

I blushed under the warmth of that smile. 'My aunt taught me. The one I got sent away to. She thought I needed something to do. And since it was like science, with all that precise measuring, I…' I faltered, feeling silly for no good reason.

'You liked it,' he finished, that gorgeous smile curling his mouth.

My cheeks felt hot. 'Yes.'

'And you're good at it too.' He pulled the scone in his hands apart and it steamed gently, the delicious smell filling the space between us. 'My mother died when I was young,' he went on. 'I don't remember her, but I do remember the various stepmothers I had. One of them used to bake. Not often and not well, but she did. Scones were her best recipe and, though they weren't as good as these, my brothers and I used to like them.' He looked down at the scone in his hand. 'When she baked, it was like… I had a normal family.'

My breath caught at the unexpected confession. He was looking down, golden lashes veiling his expression, but I heard the wistfulness in his voice.

Part of me didn't want to speak in case I ruined the moment, but I couldn't stop myself. He'd let me have another crumb of information about himself and I was hooked.

'Is that what you wanted?' I tried to sound casual. 'A normal family?'

'Yes. Christ, I would have given anything for Dad to be a builder or an accountant or, shit, a truck driver. But he wasn't.' There was a flash of gold as he glanced at me. 'I don't know why I'm telling you this.'

I tried to keep things light. 'Because you're hungry and you want a scone, and you'll do anything to get one?'

He smiled that breathtaking smile again. 'You shouldn't get comfortable with me, Vita. And you damn well shouldn't trust me.'

The words were offered so casually I almost didn't understand. And then I did.

'Why not?' I asked, even though I didn't want to know. 'Why shouldn't I trust you?'

'You know what kind of man I am.' His gaze didn't

flicker. 'I'm dangerous. I don't like being vulnerable and I hurt people who make me feel that way.'

My throat had gone dry, but I refused to admit it was fear. 'You won't hurt me.'

'Never physically, no. But you don't know me. And you don't know what I'm capable of. I might not use violence these days, but I use every other trick in the book to get people to do what my brothers and I want.' He paused, his gaze searching mine. 'I could use that video of us last night, for example.'

He won't.

The thought was instinctive and I accepted it without question. If he'd genuinely been going to use it he would have uploaded it first thing this morning, not threatened me with it first.

'But you won't.' I put all my certainty into the words. 'Because if I thought for a second you would, I wouldn't have given it to you.'

His smile faded. 'You don't know—'

This time it was my turn to put my finger over his beautiful mouth. 'You're trying very hard to convince me you're some kind of monster, Leon. And I don't know why.'

He put down the scone, gently wrapped his fingers around my wrist and tugged my finger from his mouth. 'As I was saying,' he went on as if I hadn't interrupted, 'I'll never willingly let anyone have power over me ever again.'

Again, the whisper of cold foreboding that I'd felt last night settled inside me, though I wasn't sure why.

'I understand that,' I said. 'After what happened to you, I wouldn't either.'

'No.' His voice was quiet. 'You don't understand. Once you've survived a world like my father's, protecting yourself becomes automatic. Instinctive. Because you can't ever let your guard down and you can't ever trust.'

'Yes, I get it.' I studied him. 'But you trust me, right?'

His golden gaze darkened. 'I can't, vixen. Not even you.'

CHAPTER SEVENTEEN

Leon

VITA STARED AT ME, her dark eyes wide. She was dressed only in my shirt and had a smear of flour on her cheek and a scattering of it in her hair. She looked like she'd wandered off the set of a feel-good movie starring an adorable baker heroine.

I had no idea what such a creature was doing in my kitchen, baking scones and getting flour everywhere, reminding me of happier times in my childhood and making me confess all kinds of ridiculous bullshit.

And the confessions kept on coming, things I'd never told anyone. Such as how all I'd wanted was a normal family. How I wasn't to be trusted, no matter what she thought of me.

How I would never—could never—trust her.

Her black eyes were very direct, very bright. 'Then why did you tell me all that stuff last night?'

'Because you wanted me to. Because you asked.'

She was silent for a long moment. 'You're trying to push me away, aren't you?'

She knew. She wasn't stupid.

'It's a warning,' I said. 'Don't get too close, sweetheart. And don't mess with me. I'm one experiment that might just blow up in your face.'

She bristled. 'I'm not messing with you. It's not my fault scones bring back memories you don't like.'

I'd offended her, as I'd meant to. As I'd intended. But I didn't feel pleased with myself. I felt ashamed.

All she'd done was bake her scones then shyly tell me about her love of baking, her eyes lighting up with pleasure as she'd done so.

'Baking is just chemistry', she'd said and I could see how that worked. It made me wish I'd woken earlier so I would have been able to watch her as she'd bustled about the kitchen I never used, mixing up her ingredients and creating those chemical reactions.

But that shouldn't be happening between us. She shouldn't be getting me to tell her things I'd never told anyone else. Things about myself that should stay buried. Sex was all it was, not whispered confessions and sweet kisses, and baking in the morning.

So yes, I wanted to push her away. I wanted some distance between us because it felt like she was cracking the armour I wore, putting little chinks in it, weakening it.

I couldn't let that happen but... I didn't like that I'd offended her. It made something deep inside me ache.

'I'm not a child,' she went on, her expression fierce. 'Yes, you did some bad things, and yes, you're ruthless. But I know that already. I mean, come on, Leon. Manipulating me into this marriage thing was kind of an indicator that you're not exactly pure as the driven snow.' A crease appeared between her brows as if something she hadn't thought of suddenly occurred to her. 'Actually, you were honest about that. And you didn't have to be.'

Christ. Next she'd be telling me what a hero I was.

I pushed the scone I'd pulled apart towards her. 'Why don't you put some butter and jam on this for me?'

One reddish brow rose imperiously. 'Excuse me?'

I met her gaze, steeling myself to do something I hardly ever did. 'I'm sorry,' I said and, possibly for the first time in years, I meant it. 'I know you're not a child. I just…don't want you to get hurt.'

Since when did you start caring about her feelings?

She blinked as if I'd said something unexpected. 'I won't get hurt. I can take care of myself.'

'Like you took care of yourself with Simon?'

She flushed. 'I was only seventeen. And I'm not seventeen now.' Reaching for the scone I'd pushed in her direction, she began to butter it. 'Anyway, you and me, it's just sex. That's what we agreed.' Carefully, she wiped the knife then began to spread the jam, then added, half to herself, 'A chemical reaction, that's all.'

She was right. That was exactly what we had. Nothing but chemicals.

So why do you still ache?

But I ignored that too. 'No more questions.'

'Okay, no more questions.' She lifted the scone

towards me. 'But that doesn't mean we can't talk, right?'

'We can talk,' I agreed then leaned forward and bit into the scone she held.

It was the most delicious thing I'd ever eaten in my life—apart from her.

She watched me as I chewed then swallowed, her gaze drifting to my mouth.

'You've got…' She reached out to swipe away the cream on my top lip.

I grabbed her wrist, licked the rest of the cream from her finger then drew it deep into my mouth, stroking it with my tongue.

Her lips parted, her dark gaze becoming even darker as she watched me lick her finger.

'The scone was delicious,' I murmured roughly against her skin. 'But you taste even better.' Taking her finger from my mouth, I pulled her towards me. 'And I'm done talking. Care to experiment with another kind of chemical reaction, vixen?'

CHAPTER EIGHTEEN

Leon

'DO I REALLY HAVE to try these on?' Vita's voice drifted from down the hallway, sounding exasperated. 'You've left this rather late.'

I smiled at her annoyed tone, settling back against the couch cushions and glancing towards the doorway.

I'd had some wedding gowns from an exclusive bridal salon sent to my penthouse for her to try on, and, yes, I'd left it late given that the wedding was only a couple of weeks away. The rest of the organisation was in the capable hands of the wedding planner and the King Enterprises corporate events team and I was confident they'd be able to pull it off to the specifications I'd given them.

Not that I'd given them many since I didn't really care how the wedding went. As long as it was big, that was all that mattered.

I'd planned the same thing for the wedding gowns, thinking to pick one at random for Vita to wear since, again, it didn't really matter what she wore.

Then I'd changed my mind, uncomfortable with the thought of her wearing something she might not like or that may not suit her.

I didn't think about why it was important to me that she liked her gown. I pushed that particular thought right to the back of my head.

I wanted her to like it, end of story.

A sigh came from the bedroom and I was very tempted to go in there and help her into the gown myself. Though that would probably end with us both naked and the gown on the floor. Which wasn't the point of the exercise.

I shifted on the couch, trying to ease the growing tightness in my trousers. The sweet scent of the chocolate chip cookies she'd baked earlier was still in the air, reminding me of how I'd laid her across the kitchen counter and licked melted chocolate off her body.

My cock liked that memory very much indeed.

'Hurry up, vixen,' I muttered. 'You're creating a problem.'

'What problem?' Vita asked.

My head snapped up and there she was, standing in front of me, wearing the first of three gowns. This one had a fitted bodice and frothy skirts, with a thousand crystals sewn everywhere, glittering like stardust.

And my heart did a strange thing. It felt like it… turned over.

She looked like a princess.

'What—' I had to stop and clear my throat, unable to speak. 'What do you think?'

Vita put the veil she was holding on her head then turned to the full-length mirror that I'd had brought in and set up opposite the couch.

'It's heavy.' She kicked at the skirts, frowning. 'All these crystals are a bit much.'

We both looked at her in the mirror.

'You look…lovely,' I said, unable to get rid of the husky edge to my voice.

Colour swept over her face and she gave me a smile that made my heart turn over yet again.

'Thank you.' She smoothed the skirts. 'But I feel like I'm wearing a suit of armour. I don't think it's really me.'

'It is you,' I said. 'You look like a princess.'

Again that smile. I could barely keep my hands to myself.

God, what the hell was wrong with me? It was only a wedding dress for a wedding that wasn't even real. It didn't mean anything.

'Try on the second one.' I kept my tone brusque, looking down at my phone so she couldn't see my face.

I heard her leave the room while I went over some work emails. Or tried to. Difficult when every sense I had was tuned to the sound of her in the bedroom, trying on the second gown.

I wasn't ready when I heard her come back in.

I wasn't ready when I lifted my head to look at her.

This gown was more fitting than the previous one,

the skirts slimmer. There were no crystals, but there was a long train that spilled out behind her like trailing foam from a wave.

If she'd looked like a princess in the first gown, in the second she looked like a queen.

Desperately, some part of me tried to find the angles and plain features of the woman I'd met in the nightclub a couple of weeks earlier. But I couldn't find her. She was gone.

All that was left was the goddess in front of me.

She seemed oblivious to me staring at her like a fucking idiot, turning around to look at herself in the mirror again.

'This one isn't as heavy. But the train is a pain in the neck. I won't be able to walk anywhere.'

'You look amazing.' I tried to be casual, yet the words were somehow difficult. 'But yes, I wouldn't want anything getting in the way. Especially not when the time comes for me to claim my wedding night.'

She glanced at me in the mirror and I realised what I'd said. And what it meant.

A wedding night. We hadn't talked about that. About what we would do in those few months of 'blissful wedlock' before I left the country. Initially, I'd assumed I'd leave her to her own devices, but now... Would our wedding really be our last night together? It made sense to end this affair between us there. Both for my own sanity and hers. Though, how ironic. A marriage was supposed to signify a beginning, not an end.

Vita said nothing, but the light had dimmed in

her dark eyes. As if she'd had the same thought and it had made her sad.

It makes you sad too.

I gritted my teeth, my jaw aching.

'Try on the last one,' I said roughly. 'That one doesn't have a train.'

She nodded and disappeared back down the hall-way again.

I got out my phone once more, gripping it tightly. Yet more emails and this time all wedding-related. Fuck, I didn't want to answer them. All I could think about was whether or not I'd insist on our wedding night as our last night together.

It had to be. Because afterwards I'd be leaving and never coming back.

You want to stay.

I scowled at my phone. No, I didn't want to stay. I couldn't. There was nothing for me here but my brothers, and they didn't need me. Xander had his numbers and Ajax his thirst for vengeance. While all I had were orders—and someone else's orders at that. I hadn't been my own man when Dad had been around and I still wasn't my own man now.

I had to go somewhere else. Start a new life where my past didn't matter. A life I chose, not one that was forced on me.

But that's not the life you want.

My chest constricted, an ache sitting just behind my breastbone, the dreams of long ago replaying in my head. Dreams of a normal family, with a husband and wife and their children. No violence. No blood. No crime.

You could have that with her.

I blinked, the ache inside me deepening.

Scones in the morning with coffee. And a lovely woman with auburn hair and flour on her cheek, wearing my shirt and smiling as she wiped cream from my lip. Blushing as I licked it from her finger then drew her close. Telling me that she trusted me…

No. It was a life I'd never had. A dream that wasn't meant for me.

Because to have it I'd have to care. I'd have to take my armour off, be vulnerable and give the power to someone else. And I couldn't. Caring was the end of you. The cut you couldn't heal from. The real torture.

All those cigarette burns, those knife wounds, they weren't the things that hurt. The agony came from knowing no one had come for me, not even my own father. I was expendable, unneeded. My life not even worth the ransom money they'd tried to extort from him.

I would never leave myself open to that again.

I heard her footfall as she came back and this time I waited before I looked, pretending I was more interested in what was on my phone to cover the beating of my heart and the rush of blood in my veins.

'Leon,' she said.

I had to force myself to look.

The third gown was the simplest of all. It was ivory satin that followed her every curve, the same way I followed them with my hands every night. The fabric gathered at one shoulder in a Grecian style before falling gracefully down her back.

In the first two gowns she'd looked like royalty, like a fairy tale.

But in this one, all simplicity and elegance, she looked like herself.

Bright. Passionate. Honest.

My heart didn't turn over this time. It stood still.

She'd taken her hair down and it curled over her shoulders in an auburn tumble, and I could see exactly how she should wear it for the wedding. Either loose or in a long braid, and there should be flowers woven through it, simple white flowers to accentuate the lovely colour.

'What about this one?' she asked, hesitant.

She wanted me to like it, I could see by the look on her face.

The reply I'd been going to make—something dismissive to hide my own reaction to her—died unsaid. I couldn't bring myself to say it.

It's too late to protect yourself. Too late to pretend you don't care.

I shut that voice off. Hard. Then I put my phone away and I got up from the couch. And I moved over to where she stood, letting my gaze roam over her, from the top of her red head down to her feet, lingering on my favourite places—her breasts, her hips, the swell of her thighs and her elegant calves and ankles.

Then I lifted my attention to her face, staring into her dark eyes, watching those stars twinkle brightly in the velvety blackness.

She could be yours. Your wife. You could have scones and coffee and her. You could have the family you always wanted.

My heart twisted painfully.

I'd met many dangerous people in my life, but suddenly I knew that the woman standing in front of me right now was the most dangerous of the lot.

She had the power to destroy me if I let her.

'Yes.' I fought to keep my expression neutral. 'That's the one.'

She blushed, giving me a smile that had my heart restarting, battering against my ribs like a prisoner trying to escape a cell.

'I think I like it.' She turned back to the mirror. 'It feels much lighter and it's easier to move around in.'

It was difficult to speak. Like someone had their hand around my throat and was squeezing.

To cover my reaction, I took the end of the length of fabric that fell down her back. 'I wonder what would happen if I pulled this...?'

'Don't you dare.' She moved away, then turned to give me a mock stern look. 'It's not our wedding night yet.'

All she was doing was standing there. With bare feet and her hair loose around her shoulders. Dressed in ivory satin.

I wanted her so badly I couldn't speak.

Lust, that was all it was. Nothing to do with her telling me how good I was for her or how she trusted me. Nothing to do with the way she looked at me, as if my past didn't matter. As if she saw a man worth looking at.

Nothing to do with that at all.

I grabbed her, pulling her up against me.

Her eyes went wide and she put her hands on my chest. 'What is it?'

I was breathing very fast, like I couldn't get enough air.

In a couple of weeks all this would be over. I'd be leaving the country a few months after that. I'd be giving her up and that was a good thing. A very good thing.

'Nothing.' I managed to force the words out. 'You're just really fucking sexy in that dress.'

But those bright eyes, they saw through me. 'Leon.' Her voice was quiet. 'Tell me.'

The satin of her gown felt slippery beneath my fingers, my grip on her tenuous. 'I don't want to let you go,' I heard myself say hoarsely. 'I don't want our wedding night to be the last night. I want to keep you.'

She blinked in shock and I thought for a moment I saw tears in her eyes. Then she blinked again and lifted her hands to my jaw, her fingers cool against my skin. 'So keep me.'

'I can't.'

'You can.' The words sounded husky, a fierce glow lighting her gaze. 'You don't have to let me go. I don't want you to.'

'But that's why I can't.' I stared down into her lovely face. 'You want more and I don't. So I have to let you go. I have to protect you.'

Her throat moved. 'Protect yourself, you mean.'

I didn't deny it. 'I have to, Vita.'

By rights she should have got angry, but it wasn't anger I saw in her gaze now. It was something softer, something almost tender. 'It wasn't your fault, you know,' she said quietly. 'That he didn't come for you. He should have fought for you, protected you. The way my father should have protected me.'

I wanted to tell her it didn't matter, that I didn't care, but the words wouldn't come. With a couple of simple sentences, she'd shattered my goddamn armour in two and I wasn't sure I could repair it.

So I did the only thing I could.

I turned around and walked away.

CHAPTER NINETEEN

Vita

THE DOOR OF the limo opened and I took a breath, trying not to fuss with the skirts of my gown, my fingers bunching the fabric.

A large male hand came over mine and gently pressed it down.

'You'll be fine,' Leon said calmly. 'Don't forget that your fiancé is the most dangerous man in the room and he'll punch anyone who dares to even look at you funny.'

The warmth of his hand was reassuring and I felt my nervousness ease.

I tried to be stern. 'No, you wouldn't.'

'I would.' There was a feral gleam in his golden eyes. A glimpse of the lieutenant he'd once been.

I shivered, and not because I didn't like the thought of a man offering to do violence on my behalf. I did like it. No one had stood up for me when that video went live. No one had defended me. I'd been sent away in disgrace instead. The thought of Leon protecting me gave me a delicious thrill, as if I'd some-how tamed a vicious predator.

'That appeals to you, doesn't it?' Leon observed lazily.

'Yes.' No reason to deny it. 'I feel like I've tamed a lion.'

Surprise flickered across his beautiful face. 'A lion?'

I looked at him lounging beside me, ridiculously handsome in the perfectly tailored tux he was wear-ing for tonight's function. 'You're all…' I gestured at him '…golden and commanding and dangerous.'

One of his rare genuine smiles curved his mouth. 'You better believe it, sweetheart. And all it took to tame me was scones, sex and chemistry. Maybe you should write a seduction "How to".'

I grinned, an odd excitement fizzing in my chest.

Then I remembered something I'd been trying hard not to over the past week.

Tonight was our last date before the wedding.

The excitement inside me died, leaving me feeling flat and stale, like a bottle of champagne that hadn't been corked properly.

A week had passed since that day I'd tried on wed-ding dresses in his apartment. I shouldn't have said anything then and I knew it. But the moment he'd said he wanted to keep me a stupid burst of hope had ignited inside me. And I'd opened my big fat mouth and told him that he could before I could stop myself.

I shouldn't have. I shouldn't have said a word, but I had. And then I'd made things worse when he'd refused me by handing him a truth he hadn't asked for and plainly didn't want to hear.

He'd walked out, leaving me standing there in the lovely wedding dress I'd felt so good in, knowing I'd made a huge mistake.

We'd told each other that sex was all it was, yet in that moment we'd both crossed over that boundary. Which couldn't happen.

I couldn't want more because he couldn't give it to me.

We were volatile compounds that shouldn't mix outside a controlled environment or else we'd destroy each other.

When he'd returned later that night with a bouquet of beautiful orchids and taken me to bed without a word I didn't push.

I pretended it hadn't happened.

We'd had other dates since then where we'd talked about everything else. Politics and art. Science and books. Our favourite movies and TV shows. Anything. Everything.

Everything but the chemistry between us. A chemistry that showed no signs of burning out, no matter how many dates we went on, no matter how many times he took me to bed.

And that made it so hard to pretend.

He made it so hard to pretend.

'Hey.' His fingers brushed my cheek in a light caress. 'You look sad. What's up?'

Damn. Why did he have to be so observant? Or, rather, why couldn't I be better at hiding my feelings?

I forced a smile. 'Nothing. Just nervous.'

'Like I said, nothing to be nervous about.' He grinned, the dangerous gleam in his eyes only enhancing his charisma. God, he was so hot I could hardly stand it. 'You look utterly lovely. The dress is perfect.'

I blushed.

He'd taken me shopping the day before to find me something to wear for this charity function of my father's. It was black tie all the way, and I had nothing suitable.

Dad had never invited me to his parties—before my video I'd been too young and after he hadn't wanted me anywhere near potential donors—but tonight he'd told me that my presence was required, as was Leon's. He was going to give his public blessing to our marriage, aka introducing Leon to some potential investors.

I hated parties but I couldn't refuse this one. It was required as part of my role as Leon's fiancée. The dress was sexy, wrapping around my figure while leaving one shoulder bare. The colour suited me and I was amazed at how good I felt in it.

'Thank you,' I said. 'For the dress.' And then, because I wanted him to know, I went on, 'For the dates too. Thank you for…' For making me feel good about myself. For making me feel beautiful. For making me feel special for the first time in my life. 'For everything.'

His smile was warm, real. The smile that was just mine.

It made my heart turn over in my chest.

'You're welcome.' He kissed my palm. 'Come on, vixen. Now that we're a few minutes late we can make a grand entrance.'

I grimaced. 'Not sure I want a grand entrance.'

His fingers closed around mine. 'Sweetheart, when you're with me all entrances are grand.'

The gleam in his eyes had turned from dangerous to wicked and my stupid heart turned over yet again.

You're falling for him.

The venue for the charity function was an old historic building that was in the process of being revitalised.

Outside, the building's elegant façade remained untouched and it wasn't until we got inside that I re-alised the whole thing had been gutted in prepara-tion for rebuilding.

It was an amazing space, brick walls soaring high right up to the roof, no ceilings in the way. A tempo-rary wooden floor had been put down for the night, the lighting lots of bare old-fashioned bulbs hang-ing down on industrial wires. They looked like tiny moons or planets, the light they gave off diffuse and warm.

At one end a chamber orchestra played while a bar had been set up at the other. Couches and chairs in various different configurations were scattered ev-erywhere, while on some of the walls big screens dis-played logos of the charity the function was in aid of.

The place was packed with the cream of Sydney

high society, all of them talking raucously, but if I'd hoped to slip in unnoticed I was disappointed.

The moment Leon walked in, his arm around my waist, there seemed to be a lull in the hum of voices. Heads turned in our direction, following our progress as we made our way through the press of people to where my father stood, ready to greet us.

I felt the weight of those stares but, unlike a couple of weeks ago, it didn't bother me the way it had on those first couple of dates.

In fact, I relished it. Because here I was, the 'I Love You Girl', in a spectacular dress with an incredibly handsome man on her arm. A man with a dangerous past who was clearly possessive and obviously besotted with her.

It was intoxicating, powerful.

As we approached my father, I lifted my chin and met his gaze, for once not afraid of the disapproval I saw in his eyes whenever he looked at me.

That disapproval was evident now but this time I let it slide off me, smiling instead.

'Tom,' Leon said expansively, stopping in front of my father and reaching out to shake his hand. 'Good to see you.'

My father's smile looked forced, his handshake stiff. 'King.'

'Oh, come now, you're my soon-to-be father-in-law. Don't you think it's time you called me Leon?' He grinned, not at all put off by Dad's wooden formality. 'We're almost family.'

Dad didn't reply, his smile remaining fixed. He

turned to me instead and for a second I thought I was going to get a handshake from him too, but at the last minute he stepped up and gave me a kiss on the cheek.

'Vita,' he murmured.

'Dad.' I didn't offer a hug. He wouldn't have wanted it anyway.

He stepped back, studying my face, though what he was looking for I had no idea. 'Are you…okay?' he asked tentatively.

The question surprised me since he'd never been interested in my well-being before.

'Of course,' I said. 'Why wouldn't I be?'

'He's worried I might be corrupting you,' Leon murmured, pulling me closer, his mouth brushing my ear. 'He's right. I am.'

Dad frowned, looking from Leon to me and then back again, noting how close we were and Leon's proprietorial arm around my waist.

The frown deepened.

He wouldn't have known that Leon and I had been sleeping together. But now he did. And he wasn't happy about it.

A bolt of satisfaction shot through me and I let myself lean against Leon's tall, muscular body, my hand coming down to rest over his on my stomach. I smiled at my father.

'Are you worried about me, Dad?' I met his gaze squarely. 'Because promising me to a complete stranger didn't seem to bother you before.'

I don't know why I said it because I wasn't here to fight. In fact, I thought I'd long since given up caring what Dad thought of me. Yet now the little dig was out I didn't want to take it back.

I was conscious of Leon beside me, his arm a reassuring weight around my waist. He didn't say a word; he knew this was my fight, not his.

Dad scowled. 'Of course I'm worried about you. The Kings are—' He stopped, his gaze flicking to Leon.

'The Kings are what?' Leon's voice held a dangerous undertone.

My father shifted on his feet, looking uncomfortable. 'It's nothing. Forget I said anything.'

'I can't speak for the King family,' I said, unwilling to let it go. 'But I can speak for Leon. And I can tell you he's been nothing but kind and respectful towards me.' I paused. 'Unlike some other people in this room.'

Dad flushed, a spark of anger in his gaze.

Good. I'd wanted to goad him and I had.

'If you're implying—'

'What? Am I implying that you haven't treated me with either kindness or respect? Yes. I am.'

It wasn't the right time and this wasn't the place for a family argument, but seeing him turn his habitual expression of disapproval on Leon and talk about the Kings in a disparaging tone made me angry. That Leon deserved it for blackmailing Dad into giving me to him didn't matter.

What mattered was that Leon had been good to me and I wasn't going to stand for anyone badmouthing him.

'Vita,' he began.

But I was on a roll and I didn't let him finish. 'Leon has been nothing but good to me, Dad. He's certainly treated me better than you or Mum ever did, and I won't hear a bad word spoken about him.'

'He blackmailed me,' Dad said through gritted teeth. 'He—'

'And you promised me to a complete stranger to save yourself from your own bad debts.' I kept my voice low so no one would overhear, but I didn't hide the ferocity I felt. 'You sacrificed me to save yourself, just like you did the last time.'

Dad didn't say a word this time, staring at me in stony silence.

I'd never confronted him about his behaviour towards me all those years ago, but now I had, I couldn't seem to stop.

'I should never have agreed,' I went on. 'But I did. Because I thought you'd finally see me as your daughter instead of a stain on the family name.'

'I didn't—'

'No. I don't want to hear your justifications. But you should know that I'm not marrying Leon for you. I'm marrying him for me. Understand?'

Utter silence fell.

Leon was silent beside me while Dad simply stared at me.

He wouldn't understand. He wouldn't know what Leon had said to me about rewriting my own story. But that was okay. I wasn't going to explain it to him. I'd said what I'd needed to say, let him know that what he'd done to me all those years ago had hurt. And that I wasn't going to let him emotionally blackmail me into doing anything for him again.

It was Leon who broke the silence in the end.

'In future, I think it's best if you don't cross my beautiful fiancée.' The smile he gave Dad was hard-edged and sharp. 'Now, isn't it time you introduced my brothers and me to some of your important friends?'

CHAPTER TWENTY

Leon

I'D SEEN AJAX and Xander enter the building as Vita gave her father the dressing-down he so richly deserved, and he swung round now to watch them approach.

But I didn't pay any attention to them.

I could only look at her.

The fierce expression on her face remained and her dark eyes were glowing with anger. But for once it wasn't aimed at me; it was aimed at her father. On her own behalf, yet also, strangely, on mine.

Ah, Christ, she shouldn't say things like that. She shouldn't come to my defence, making me admire the sheer guts of her, how she was calling her father out in the middle of his own function.

I'd thought she couldn't get under my skin any more than she had already.

I was wrong.

But I couldn't let it.

Over the past week or so, since the day she'd tried

on wedding dresses, I'd gone on as if I hadn't told her that I wanted to keep her.

As if she hadn't seen right through me and told me that it was myself I was protecting.

I'd simply gone on as if nothing had happened and that had worked. She hadn't mentioned it again. And the dates had continued and so had the nights, and I'd thought I was good. That I'd patched up my armour, that it was strong.

But her doing shit like this? Defending me against her father? It only made me aware that I had to be stronger. That I had to try harder.

That, no matter how well protected I thought I was, it wasn't enough.

If I'd had my way I would have ended the affair the day I'd seen her in that wedding dress, but I'd made a promise to my brother. And that promise meant keeping up this deception. Marrying her to legitimise the King name and get us into the luxury apartment market.

I couldn't let Ajax down, not after what he'd done for me.

What about her?

I ignored the question, turning instead to greet my brothers as they came through the crowd towards us.

They'd been sent invites to this little show, their presence required so Hamilton could introduce us to his high-flying friends.

Ajax was a huge hulking figure in jeans, a T-shirt and a leather jacket—the man had no goddamn sense of occasion—while Xander, not quite as tall but no less broad, had at least made an effort and put on a tux.

Both of them kept glancing at Vita, making me instinctively pull her closer.

Staking your claim?

Well, she was mine, at least for now, and I wanted to make sure my brothers knew it. Ajax, particularly, was rapacious in his tastes and, as for Xander… Though his interests lay with protecting his money, if he thought Vita was a threat to us he wouldn't hesitate to make that known. In ways that would be painful for all concerned.

'Ajax, Xander,' I said as they stopped in front of us. 'Meet your future sister-in-law, Vita Hamilton.'

Ajax turned his disturbing light blue stare from me to Vita, the look on his face unreadable. 'A pleasure.' His voice was neutral as he held out a hand to her.

Vita took it and instantly every instinct I had went on high alert.

I didn't like her touching him. I didn't like him touching her.

You're a fucking lost cause.

I crushed the thought. Since telling Vita not to shake my brother's hand would look strange, I didn't say a word but I kept a close eye on Ajax, resisting the urge to knock his hand away.

'Hello,' Vita said gravely. 'Nice to meet you too.'

Ajax nodded, holding on to her hand for a second too long, making me nearly growl my displeasure. His gaze flicked to mine and I swear I caught amusement there.

He was messing with me, the bastard.

I bared my teeth at him, in no mood for games.

Xander, meanwhile, shook Vita's hand while his dark gaze ran over her, coldly measuring and assessing. He didn't say a word, not even a hello.

'Your manners are beautiful as always, Xander.' My tone was acid as he dropped Vita's hand like it had burned him. I reached for it instead, threading my fingers through hers, and when I felt hers tighten around mine I felt warmth spread out in my chest.

I ignored the sensation as I turned to Hamilton. He was struggling to hide his disapproval—now I knew where Vita had got her bad acting skills from.

'You know my brothers, don't you?' I said pleasantly. 'Though, of course, they need no introduction.' I smiled. 'Now, you're going to introduce us around, aren't you? Let everyone know how happy you are that I'm going to be part of your family. So happy and excited that you're to share the plans King Enterprises has for a new luxury apartment complex, hmm?'

Hamilton hated that; I could see it in his eyes. And he hated me too, which was not surprising. Not when I held all the cards.

Too bad. Perhaps if he'd been a better father to Vita and less of an arrogant bastard, I might have felt more lenient towards him. But he wasn't, so I didn't.

'Yes, of course,' Hamilton said through gritted teeth. 'Please excuse us, Vita. I'll show the Kings around.'

We made the rounds of the room, Hamilton introducing us to his high society cronies, but I found myself unable to pay attention. I kept looking in Vita's direction, checking to make sure she was okay. I knew she hadn't been looking forward to this, not with all the people, and I wanted to check that no one was hassling her or giving her grief. But she was smiling, obviously enjoying the conversation she was having with some prick in an overly fancy tux.

I didn't like it.

I should have been focusing on Hamilton and the people he was introducing us to, on the conversations that were happening all around me. I should have been taking part, using my charm to get those potential investors on our side. But for some reason that didn't seem very important right now.

What was important was that some bastard was standing next to Vita and obviously flirting with her. My Vita.

So much for her being only a chemical reaction.

There was a pressure in my chest, a tightness I couldn't ignore. I'd never been jealous before and there was no reason for me to be so now. Maybe it was simply because we didn't have much longer together before the wedding and I wanted to spend that time with her.

Or maybe no one touches what's yours?

But she wasn't mine and I didn't want her to be.

Across the room, another man had joined the first standing next to Vita and she smiled at him too. Then, as I watched, that smile faded and her face went white, and it felt like a bomb had exploded in my chest.

'Excuse me,' I murmured to Ajax as Hamilton presented us to yet another rich bastard who looked at us as if we were dirt. 'I have something I need to attend to.'

Ajax frowned. 'What? You need to—'

But I'd already turned away, threading my way quickly through the crowd to where Vita stood. A bright stain of colour stood out on her white cheeks and there was a fixed smile on her face. She was trying to pretend she was okay, but she wasn't.

That fucking bastard had said something to hurt her, I was certain.

You're not supposed to care.

No, I wasn't. Not caring was how I got through my entire fucking life. And yet I couldn't seem to not care about Vita.

I headed straight towards her and she noticed me approaching. Her eyes widened, the tiny stars in them flaring with what looked like relief. And that hit me like a punch to the gut, made the pressure in my chest increase as if someone had dumped a large and heavy stone directly on it.

She needed me.

It made something deep inside me crack.

I slid an arm around her waist as I got to her, pulling her in tight against me before rounding on the two pricks standing near her.

I smiled at them with teeth and fury, giving them a glimpse of the lieutenant. And, much to my satisfaction, both of them went as white as Vita had.

'It appears my fiancée is in some distress.' My

voice was barely above a snarl. 'What did you say to her?'

Instantly, they began making excuses, falling over themselves to assure me they hadn't said a word, and besides, they'd only been joking.

'If either of you have hurt her,' I interrupted pleasantly, 'I will kill you. Understand?'

And I meant it. I meant every goddamn word.

'Leon,' Vita murmured.

I turned sharply, taking my arm from around her so I could cup her face between my palms. 'They hurt you. What did they say?' Fury ran hot in my veins, and along with it, the need for violent punishment. 'I meant it. I'll fucking kill them if they—'

'No,' she said quietly but firmly. 'It was nothing.'

'It wasn't nothing. I saw you go white.'

And she still was. But her gaze was very calm, very direct. 'He only made some comment about the video and I wasn't expecting it.'

I snarled, ready to let her go and turn on the assholes who'd hurt her, everything in me wanting to deal them back in kind. But her hands came over mine where they rested on her jaw, holding them there. 'Don't. You don't need to do anything. You came to support me and that's enough.'

'But you—'

'I thanked him for his comment and told him that if he liked the earlier video, he should see the one I made with you.'

My heart was beating fast, adrenaline pumping hard in my veins, and I wanted to do violence. Yet there was apparently room in me for admiration. Shit, this woman...

'Are you saying you didn't need me to defend your honour?' I tried to make it sound like a joke, except it didn't come out like one.

She smiled, a faint curl of her lovely mouth, as if she'd heard the desperate note in my voice. 'No, but I'm glad you came back anyway.'

Of course she didn't need me. She was strong— much stronger than she gave herself credit for.

The pressure on my chest felt suffocating all of a sudden, desire and an inexplicable desperation filling me. I wanted to be somewhere private, somewhere I could show her that she did need me. Somewhere I could make her as desperate as I was now.

I was supposed to be keeping distance between us, yet right now that felt impossible.

I leaned down so we were nose to nose. 'Come with me.'

She gave me a surprised look. 'Why? Where are we going?'

I gave her the only response I was able, bending to kiss her hungrily right there in the middle of the crowded party. In front of everyone.

She didn't protest. Didn't resist. Her mouth opened beneath mine immediately, the sweet taste of her filling me.

But it wasn't enough.

It's never going to be enough.

The whisper in my head was insidious and I ignored it. Releasing her, I stepped back then took her hand. 'Come on. Let's go.'

As I strode towards the exit with Vita I could see my brothers on the far side of the room, shaking hands and making nice. Or at least as nice as they'd ever get. They needed me to smooth the way since neither of them were exactly good with people. Ajax was too impatient and Xander was too cold.

I should be with them but Vita's hand was in mine and I couldn't let her go. I just…needed some time with her, to get rid of this desperation, and then maybe I'd come back and do what I was supposed to do.

Ajax was staring at me, frowning. But I didn't stop.

Later. I'd make this up to them later.

Outside, I texted the limo driver and within five minutes he had the limo waiting at the kerb.

'Are you okay?' Vita asked as I hustled her inside it. 'I'm not hurt, really.'

Fuck. What had I given away? And more importantly, how had she noticed? Not that I wasn't okay. Of course I was.

I put my hand behind her neck and pulled her forward, taking her mouth again, stopping any conversation.

Her taste filled me once again and I thought it would calm me, but it didn't. It only made me more desperate.

This was crazy. Fucking crazy. What was wrong with me?

I'd tried to protect her, but she hadn't needed it, and that should make me glad, not make me feel like

I was trying to hold on to something that kept slipping through my fingers.

I'd walked out on my brothers during an important function. And all because a woman was suddenly more important to me than the promise I'd made to Ajax. More important than the King name.

It was insane. I should tell her it was a mistake, get out of the car and go back to what I was supposed to be doing.

Yet I didn't.

I spread my fingers over the back of her neck, tightening my hold, pushing my tongue into her hot, sweet mouth. Kissing her hard and deep. Letting her know who she needed, no matter how much she told me she didn't.

Me.

'Leon,' she murmured against my lips, her hands coming to my chest and pushing. 'Not here.'

But I was rapidly passing the point of no return.

My cock ached. Everything ached. I needed to be inside her now.

Pulling away, I leaned forward to mutter some instructions to the driver, then I stabbed the button that raised the partition between us and the front seats.

I shouldn't give in to this feeling. I should try and master it, not let it master me. Not let it feel like it was breaking something inside me.

Or maybe I should find some other woman to help me deal with it, one who didn't get under my skin or leave me feeling like I couldn't breathe.

But even the thought of another woman left me cold.

It was Vita I wanted.

It was Vita I had to have any way I could.

My brain tried to insist that this was a dumb idea, but I was past caring what my stupid fucking brain thought.

You care and you know what happens when you care.

Caring was a weakness and when you became weak you became a target. Easy to manipulate. Easy to betray.

Hadn't I learned that? Hadn't Thompson used my hope that my dad would come for me against me? He'd tortured me with the fact that Dad wouldn't pay the ransom simply for his own amusement. Making me feel insignificant, expendable. And all because I'd cared that Dad wouldn't come.

Because I'd thought he loved me.

Christ, I needed to stop this. Get back to the function. Do the things I'd promised my brothers I'd do.

Instead, I put my arm around Vita and pulled her in close again, burying my fingers in her hair and pulling her head back. Bending to kiss her exposed throat, bite her. Taste her skin. Mark her. Get her flavour and her scent all over me and mine all over her.

She shuddered, gasping as I bit her, then I tensed as she raised her hands. But she didn't push me away again. One hand crept around the back of my neck, her thumb stroking my skin, while the other threaded into my hair, holding on as tight to me as I was to her.

I bit her again, not gently, relishing her tremble

and shiver. Then I pulled the golden gown from her shoulder.

She wasn't wearing a bra underneath so there was nothing to stop me from taking one small round breast in my palm. Her skin was hot and silky, her nipple hard.

'Leon,' she murmured, shuddering again as I circled the tip of her breast with my thumb. 'The driver...'

'The partition is up. We'll be stopping soon.'

Then I covered her mouth again before she could reply, licking my way inside, wanting her sweetness and heat. Kissing her deeply, completely. As if she was mine.

Because she was.

All of her was mine.

I didn't question the rightness of the thought, merely angling her head back to give me greater access to her mouth while I stroked and teased her hardened nipple. She panted, arching up into my hand, her hold on the back of my neck tightening.

The car had stopped moving, which meant the driver had done what I'd instructed and parked in the underground car park of my apartment building. The door slammed, indicating he'd got out.

Excellent.

I'd planned to whisk her upstairs and have her in my bed, but there wasn't time. I couldn't wait.

I sat back against the seat, pulling her into my lap so she was astride me, facing me. Then I tugged her skirts up around her waist, freeing her legs, urging her forward so her knees were spread wide and that hot little pussy of hers was positioned over my hard dick.

I looked into her eyes as I reached down and tugged aside the fabric of her underwear, and I kept on looking as I stroked through her silky folds, all hot and slick against my fingers.

Desire was in her eyes, but a crease had also appeared between her reddish brows. I knew that crease. I'd seen it whenever something puzzled her.

Too bad. If she wanted to know what was happening to me, I had no answer to give her. Because I didn't know myself.

I only knew that if I didn't get inside her right now I was going to explode.

'Leon.' Her voice caught as I slid a finger inside her. 'W-what's…wrong? Something is.'

'The only thing that's wrong is that I'm not in your pussy yet.' I slipped another finger into her damp heat and her head fell back, a groan escaping her. 'Are you ready, vixen?' I spread my fingers out, feeling her wetness and the tight clasp of her sex. 'Are you ready to take me?'

Her hands came to my shoulders, holding on tight. 'Yes.'

I didn't wait. I clawed at my trousers and got them undone. Then I took my cock out, gripping her hips and positioning myself.

I thrust up into her, hot and slick, feeling her grip on my shoulders tighten. Listening to her sharp gasp of pleasure. Watching her eyes, dark as midnight, get even darker.

I thought being inside her would help, would ease the ache in my chest and the desperation that had sunk its claws into me.

But it didn't. If anything it got worse.

She was so close to me, and I was inside her, the wet heat of her pussy wrapped like a glove around my dick.

Yet it felt like there was still a distance between us. A distance I should have been keeping and yet now couldn't stand. A distance I wanted to close.

I pulled at the gown, tugging the material down until she was bare to the waist, the gold fabric bunched around her hips. But I didn't care. I slid my arms around her, caressing her spine, urging her to lean back. She did so, her breasts firm and ripe near my mouth.

Bending, I flicked one stiff little nipple with my tongue, feeling her tremble, hearing her moan. Then I shifted, gripping her tight as I thrust up into her. I kept on teasing her nipple, sucking on it, biting it as I moved inside her, deep, slow strokes designed to drive us both mad.

Except I was the one going mad.

I was deep inside her, the pleasure of it intense. I couldn't get closer than this, yet why did it feel like I needed more?

Sliding my hands up her back, I buried them in her hair and held on tight as I moved, looking into her dark eyes as if the answer to that question was there for me to read.

Yet all I could see was desire and a rising concern that I knew would kill the mood if I let it. So I didn't let it.

I moved, taking her down onto the seat and pushing her onto her back. Then I began to drive myself into her, deep, hard, fast. As if I could fuck the hunger and desperation right out of my system, drown us both in pleasure.

She wrapped her legs around my waist, her fingers digging into my shoulders as she lifted her hips to match my movements. The air was full of the sound of our gasps and the thick, musky scents of sex and sweat. The windows were fogging, the car rocking as I fucked her harder, deeper, slamming her into the seat beneath me.

Pleasure was blinding me. She was too hot, too tight, too much of everything. Yet even this, even with her wrapped around me, half naked, her breasts bouncing and shivering every time I thrust into her, it wasn't enough.

Her eyes were black as they looked into mine, yet full of those bright stars. And I wanted to fall into that velvet darkness. It would be so soft, warm, welcoming.

'Vita.' Her name was magic on my tongue and I slid one hand between us, finding her clit and pressing down.

I felt the moment she came, her pussy clenching tight around me, saw it flash like a comet in her eyes.

She cried out, the sound echoing around the car, and it was only then I let myself go.

Getting in as deep as I could, I braced myself over her, watching her as I moved.

She was staring up at me as if she'd never seen me before in her life and I had no idea what she saw. But when she reached up and touched my cheek I felt something inside me crack right through.

'Lion,' she murmured, her voice a husky whisper. 'My lion.'

I had no idea what she meant, but then it didn't matter because the pleasure that licked up my spine was starting to take me apart piece by aching piece, stealing my awareness of everything but her beneath me and the silky wet velvet of her pussy holding me tight.

The orgasm swept over me, a tide of raw ecstasy that reached out and pulled me under.

And my last thought was that if this was simply a chemical reaction then why did it make me feel like I had a chest full of broken glass?

CHAPTER TWENTY-ONE

Vita

LEON'S BREATHING WAS fast and hard in the silence of
the car. He was lying heavily on me, but I didn't mind.
His weight covering me made me feel inexplicably
safe and cared for. Protected.

He'd turned his head into my neck and I could feel
his breath against my skin. It made me shiver. He
was still deep inside me and I had my legs wrapped
tightly around him as if I wanted to keep him there.

I'd told myself we had to stay separate from one
another—each compound safe in its own test tube—
but now… Something was wrong and I didn't know
what it was.

He'd told me he couldn't keep me, that he couldn't
care about me, and yet back there at the function
he'd stalked towards me radiating menace, a kind of
lethal intent that promised retribution of the worst
kind. He'd put himself between me and the two guys
as if he'd wanted to shield me and keep me safe.
Then he'd taken me out into the car, seeming half

feral, claiming me with an insistence that bordered on desperation.

It didn't make any sense.

If he didn't care, why had he wanted to protect me? And why had he then taken me so desperately?

I lifted my hands instead and touched his hair, pushing my fingers through the thick, soft tawny silk. He was still breathing very fast, golden lashes veiling his gaze.

Had it been because I'd dealt with those guys myself? That I'd told him I didn't need him to protect me? But, if so, why had that made him desperate? And what was he desperate about?

Perhaps it's you.

But I didn't want to go down that path, not when it didn't lead anywhere. And reading anything into his behaviour would be a mistake. This affair might feel real to me, but it wasn't. He'd told me so himself.

Something ached deep inside me, but I couldn't afford to pay any attention to it so I didn't.

I let my fingers play through his hair, focusing only on the moment, his body on mine and the feel of him still buried deep inside me. He was getting hard again.

He shifted all of a sudden, pushing himself up. 'No condom,' he said thickly. 'I forgot.'

'It's okay. I started on the Pill, remember?' I'd begun taking it when we'd first started sleeping together since condoms alone weren't fail-safe.

An expression I couldn't name flashed over his face then was gone. He turned away, pulling out of me before moving down one end of the car seat and carefully tucking himself away.

I sat up, conscious that my gown was a crumpled mess bunched around my waist and that I was just about naked, my breasts bare, my knickers pulled to one side.

He wasn't looking at me and that made me feel awkward. I began to set my clothing to rights. Usually he helped me with it, but he didn't now, running one hand through his hair then pulling at the sleeves of his jacket.

The silence in the car felt heavy. Thick.

Something was very, very wrong.

'Did…' I began, then my voice cracked and I had to start again. 'Did I…do something?'

He shot me a look. 'What do you mean?'

'You're very quiet. I wondered if I'd done something wrong.'

'No. You haven't.' He put his hand on the door handle. 'I'll get the driver to take you home.'

My stomach lurched. Normally he'd take me upstairs to his apartment.

'You're sending me away?' I couldn't mask the quiver that crept into my voice. 'I thought you wanted to be alone with me?'

'And I have been.' His expression was taut, his eyes glittering. 'But it would be better if you went home now.'

'Why?' Hurt bloomed inside me. 'Leon, you need to tell me if I did—'

'I can't.' He cut me off, his voice suddenly hard. 'I can't do this with you any more.'

It took a moment for my brain to process what he'd said.

The expression on his beautiful face was like granite and just as cold.

'I don't understand.' I tried to make the words sound as level as I could. 'Can't do what with me any more?'

'I can't continue sleeping with you. It's for the best anyway. The wedding will be in a couple of days and then eventually I'll be leaving for good.' He gave me a hideous forced smile. 'Better to end on a high note.'

'Sex in a limo is the high note?'

'Sex anywhere is a high note.' He pulled at his jacket again, paying special attention to the sleeves. 'I'm sorry, Vita. But I have a lot to do to get ready for leaving Sydney.'

I didn't know where I got my courage from. But maybe standing up to my father and that guy who'd made the rude comment had enabled me to find some backbone because a rush of anger filled me.

Ignoring my own fears, I reached out and grabbed Leon's chin, turning his face towards me.

'No,' I said furiously. 'You don't get to do this. You don't get to pull me away from Dad's party like you can't get enough of me, have me in the back seat of your limo because you can't wait, then tell me it's over. Like it meant nothing to you. Like I mean nothing to you.' I could feel the tension in his muscles but I didn't let go of him, staring into his hot golden eyes.

'Don't treat me like that, Leon. Don't treat me like Simon did. Don't make me feel like dirt. I deserve better than that from you.'

He stared at me, unmoving. Then suddenly he grabbed my wrist and held on to it, his fingers pressing against my skin.

'I can't care about you, Vita,' he said harshly and abruptly. 'I told you that already. I can't. I won't.'

The lurching sensation in my gut got worse, which was strange since I knew this.

'I'm not asking you to care about me,' I insisted. 'Sex only—that's what we agreed and I'm fine with it.'

His amber gaze was unreadable. 'Well, I'm not.'

'What do you mean you're not?' I struggled to understand. 'You mean you're not fine with it being sex only? But I thought that's what you wanted?'

'I thought it was what I wanted too. But you're right.' His gaze focused intently on me. 'You do deserve better than that.'

'But I don't—'

'You deserve more than just sex—far more. You're honest and scarily intelligent. You're bright, beautiful and brave. And you deserve someone who can match you. Someone who cares about you. Someone who can give you what you need.'

I stared at him, bewildered. 'But I never said anything about wanting more. Or needing more.'

Strangely, his gaze softened. As if he could see things inside me that I couldn't see myself. 'You might not think you do. But you deserve it all the same.'

There was a lump in my throat, making it feel sore and dry.

'What about you?' I shot back. 'Don't you need more than that too? Don't you deserve it?'

'Sweetheart. I'm the last person in the world who deserves anything at all.'

There was something bleak in the words and in the expression on his face. It made my heart ache.

He thought of himself as bad, I already knew that. Untrustworthy and irredeemable. But that hadn't been my experience of him. Sure, he was arrogant and manipulative and way too sure of himself. But there was also a kindness in him that he kept cleverly hidden. A kindness that in the past week had become more apparent as he'd taken me out on those dates, turning them from a stupid pretence into an experience he made sure I enjoyed.

He didn't have to do that, just like he didn't have to make me feel good about myself.

Yet he had.

'You're wrong,' I said thickly. 'You're worth more than you think you are. And I think you deserve a lot. In fact, I think you might need it.'

He gave a bitter laugh. 'I don't need anything.'

'You do. You need someone who cares about you.'

The look in his eyes glowed briefly. Then the glow faded, his expression hardening. 'It doesn't matter what we need or deserve. I can't care. That's the whole goddamn point.'

I couldn't concentrate. He'd said he couldn't care… Did that mean, on some level, he did?

My insides went into free fall, spinning around and around, full of that ridiculous wild hope I'd felt the day I'd tried on wedding dresses.

I shouldn't have asked, but I couldn't stop myself. 'You…care about me?'

'I'm trying not to.' His beautiful mouth twisted. 'It's a weakness. A vulnerability. And once you've given that to someone they'll exploit it, believe me. That's human nature.' His thumb pressed gently on the centre of my palm, his eyes gleaming. 'I won't be weak, Vita. Remember, I told you. I can't give that power to anyone else ever again.'

My insides stopped spinning, a chill settling in my heart.

So he did care. But he didn't want to and, hell, I could understand that, especially after what he'd gone through at fifteen.

I should have agreed then, let him drive me home, let our affair end. It would have been the dignified, mature way to go. But I wasn't ready and I didn't want it to end, and if there were only a couple of days to go then I wanted them. I wanted each and every damn one.

It might end up breaking me, but that I could deal with later. There were some things that only Leon could give me. Things I didn't want anyone else to give me but him. And I had a feeling that, after all of this was over, there would remain things that I would only ever give to him.

'Thanks for the heads-up,' I said, everything in me aching as the hope I hadn't even realised I'd been nurturing died. 'But, like I already told you, I don't need you to care and I don't want you to anyway.' I swallowed past the lump in my throat. 'You can give me this one thing, though. You promised the "I Love You Girl" her happy ending. And I want it. And that includes hot sex until the wedding day.'

He didn't say anything, and I wondered if he was going to refuse.

I didn't want to beg but I would. For this. For him.

His gaze focused, a laser of molten gold, making my breath catch. 'What can I give you that someone else couldn't?'

I could feel the atmosphere in the car change and I knew that somehow this question was important to him and that my answer was going to matter.

So I gave him the truth. Because he deserved that too.

'You understand me.' I let him see everything in my eyes. 'You know what happened to me and you understand what it did to me, and you wanted to make it better. And you did. You made me feel good about myself and you made me feel strong. I trust you, Leon. No one else can give me that. No one but you.'

He remained quiet a moment longer, his gaze on mine. Then he lifted my hand and pressed a kiss to my palm, his mouth warm. 'Another few days, until

the wedding then.' There was a warning in his eyes.
'But that's all, vixen. That's all I can give you.'

'I know,' I answered. 'I'm okay with that.'

And I tried to tell myself I would be.

CHAPTER TWENTY-TWO

Vita

'REMEMBER, YOU DON'T have to do anything but get out of the car, go up the church steps, walk down the aisle and say the vows.' Dad gave me a forced smile. 'Nothing to be nervous about.'

'I'm not nervous, Dad,' I said. 'But thank you.'

Maybe if I kept telling myself that I wouldn't be, though perhaps it was the unexpectedness of Dad being supportive that made me feel like I had a stomach full of butterflies.

Then again, I knew why he was being supportive. It was in his interest that the wedding went ahead considering Leon was going to pay off his debts the moment we were married.

Leon.

My mouth dried and I looked down at my hands, at the simple bouquet of calla lilies he'd chosen for the ceremony.

No, it wasn't Dad making me nervous. It was Leon. He'd been insatiable the night before, keeping me up virtually the whole night with his magic hands and wicked mouth. As if he couldn't get enough of me.

Yet when I'd woken up that morning I'd found myself alone.

He'd sent me a text a bit later, apologising for his absence—he had some business to tie up before the ceremony so he'd see me at the altar.

The groom not seeing his bride the morning of the wedding was tradition, but somehow I knew it wasn't that keeping him away. Or the business he had to attend to.

He was staying away deliberately.

I couldn't lie to myself any more. Couldn't tell myself it was only about sex now. It was more and had been ever since that night he'd held me in his arms and told me about the men who'd tortured him.

About the father who'd abandoned him.

He was damaged and, like the cliché I was, I wanted to help him. Heal him the way he'd healed me. But he wouldn't let me.

My heart ached like someone had kicked it.

A commotion came from outside the car and I looked up. There'd been some paparazzi waiting outside the church as we drew up and a couple of them had got into an argument. Were they still at it?

But there weren't any paparazzi there now—the church steps were empty—and the commotion turned out to be my father exclaiming as the limo door was pulled open.

'Get out,' Leon ordered Dad tersely.

I blinked in shock. What was he doing here? Wasn't he supposed to be waiting at the altar?

'Wait a goddamn minute, King,' my father protested. 'What the hell are you—?'

'Out,' Leon interrupted. 'I'm not going to ask again.'

Still protesting, Dad nevertheless did as he was told and, as soon as he'd got out, Leon got in, slamming the door behind him.

Even though I'd only seen him the night before, I still felt starved for the sight of him.

He looked so good—dressed to perfection, his black suit with a bronze tie that echoed my flowers, beautifully tailored, fitting his broad shoulders and chest like a glove. Except his hair looked like he'd raked his fingers through it one too many times and his eyes had gone dark, more brown now than gold.

My hands trembled. I wanted to touch him. But I didn't. I kept a tight hold on my bouquet instead.

'What are you doing here?' Great. At least my voice was level. 'Aren't you supposed to be inside?'

His expression remained hard and something dropped away inside me.

'You're…not going through with it, are you?'

His continued silence gave me his answer.

I don't know why it felt like he'd sunk a knife into my chest. I hadn't wanted this in the first place. So him not going through with it shouldn't have hurt.

But it did.

I lifted my chin, ignoring the pain. 'I see. So,

what? The "I Love You Girl" doesn't get her happy ending after all?'

The look on his face became a mask, his eyes darkening even further. There were dark circles beneath them, like he hadn't slept.

'I've paid your father's debts already, and as to getting those investors on board, my brothers can work that one out. But the proper happy ending for the "I Love You Girl" is to leave the man who loves her standing at the altar.'

'What?' I stared at him, uncomprehending. 'I don't…'

'It's perfect. Don't you see?' His gaze burned suddenly. 'That prick humiliated you, turned your confession into something that hurt you. But this way you get to turn it back on someone else. Me. And I'm happy to do it, vixen. I'm happy to be your fall guy.'

Something trembled way down deep inside me and I clutched my bouquet tight.

'And then what?' I couldn't mask the shake this time. 'You get to sail off into the sunset?'

'That was always my plan, you know that.' His expression softened. 'It was never real, Vita.'

No, of course it wasn't. And I'd always known it. So why did it hurt so much?

'But why can't it be?' The words came spilling out before I could stop them. 'Maybe not the marriage, but you don't have to leave. You can stay.'

'No.' His mouth hardened, the look on his face shutting down. 'There's nothing to stay here for.'

I shouldn't let him know how much that hurt. I should protect myself, act like I didn't feel the knife he was twisting in my chest.

But I'd never been very good at pretend.

'Not even your brothers? Not even me?' My voice cracked on the last word:

'Vita…'

Impulsively I reached out to put my hand on his, desperate to feel the warmth of his skin, to make a connection. 'Stay, Leon. We don't have to go through with the wedding if you don't want to. But stay. Stay with me.'

His tawny head was bent, the light through the window turning strands of it into gold. Carefully, as though it was made out of porcelain, he took my hand from his and laid it back in my lap.

'It's perfect,' he said, expressionless. 'This way you'll get everything you want.'

Anger and pain tangled in a ball in my chest and, just like that, I was done with hiding. This was important. More important than protecting myself. More important than my fear of being hurt again or of being humiliated and shamed.

He was more important.

'Yes, I'll get everything I want,' I said clearly. 'Everything except you.'

He looked up, his eyes dark. 'Vita, you can't—'

'That might be a happy ending for the "I Love You Girl",' I went on right over the top of him. 'But I'm not the "I Love You Girl" any more, and that's not the happy ending I want for me.' A helpless tear slid down my cheek, ruining my make-up, but I didn't care. I didn't wipe it away. 'Not when my happy ending has you in it.'

Gold flared in his eyes, bright and sharp.

Then it died.

'That's the one thing I can't give you, Vita. And you know why. It's a chemical reaction, that's what you told me and you're right. That's all it is.'

My heart squeezed tight in anguish. I'd thought I was so smart to tell him that, being the scientist and taking emotion out of it, reducing everything to a simple chemical reaction.

But it was so much more than that.

Suddenly I was angry—angrier than I'd ever been in my entire life. 'And I was wrong. You know what else I know? I know you're letting your past stop you from having what you really want. I know you think you don't deserve it. And I know you didn't listen when I told you that you do, that you deserve everything.' My knuckles were white where they clutched my bouquet and my chest was full of hot stones. 'I know you're nothing but a bloody coward.'

'Vita—'

But I'd had enough.

I leaned forward, looking him in the eye. 'I'm sick of men choosing my story for me. So today I'm choosing for myself. I'm not going home. I'm getting out of this car and I'm walking up that damn aisle. And if you decide not to be there too then that's fine. That's your choice. But if you don't come, you're not the man I thought you were.'

There were tears on my cheeks but I didn't care.

I turned and pushed open the door.

Then I got out and went up the church steps with-out looking back.

CHAPTER TWENTY-THREE

Leon

I WATCHED VITA walk up the steps to the church in her ivory gown with her hair full of flowers, feeling like she'd gouged a great hole in my chest.

She wasn't wrong. It was all chemicals and soon those would burn out and what would she be left with?

A coward. A weak, useless piece of shit.

I was lead, not gold, didn't she know that? Didn't she understand?

A few days earlier, the night I'd taken her so hard on the seat of the limo, I'd been certain that ending our affair would be the right thing to do. She was getting under my guard, becoming a weakness I couldn't afford, a crack in my already badly patched armour.

Then, to make matters worse, she'd told me that she wanted me. That she needed me. Only me, no one else. And I hadn't been able to refuse her. Even though every damn threat sense I had was going haywire, telling me I had to protect myself because she was stealing my control, sapping my power.

Xander had been right that night in the nightclub. Women were dangerous and Vita Hamilton was the most dangerous one of all.

But no one had needed me before. My brothers all had their own problems and my mother had died long ago. And Dad, well, he'd left me to Thompson, which showed you how much he cared.

So I'd given her those last few days before the wedding, but that was all.

I had nothing else to give her.

You're just protecting yourself.

Yeah, because who else would do it? The only person I could trust to look after myself was me. And if that made me a coward then, fuck, I'd be a coward.

I leaned back against the seat, ignoring the pain, knowing I was right and yet for some reason not feeling it.

I couldn't marry her because I knew myself too well. Once I put that ring on her finger I'd never let her go. And how could I do that when she hadn't wanted to marry me in the first place?

So I'd come up with an alternative, a way to get her everything she wanted. The perfect way for the 'I Love You Girl' to get her happy ending—her jilting me. Wasn't that the best revenge?

Except she hadn't wanted that after all.

'My happy ending has you in it.'

My jaw ached, every muscle in my body pulled tight.

How could that be true? How could a man who'd blackmailed her into marrying him then seduced her, then made her care only to shut her out, ever deserve a woman like her? A man whose own father hadn't thought him worth rescuing from torture?

No, she deserved better than that.

It felt like someone was standing on my chest and I had to open the window to get some goddamn air.

My phone buzzed and I fumbled in my pocket for it, looking down to see what it was. A text from Ajax.

Where the fuck are you?

I hadn't told my brothers that I wouldn't be at the wedding or that I'd be leaving. I hadn't told them anything at all.

'I know you're nothing but a bloody coward.'

She saw me. She saw right the fuck through me. Even from the first moment we'd met, she'd known what I'd always been.

I was a coward. I'd been terrified of the life I'd been born into and my father knew it. That was why he hadn't come for me. Because he'd always hated cowards.

Not bothering to reply to Ajax's text, I reflexively opened the video app to watch yet again the video she'd entrusted to me and that I hadn't deleted, because I was a prick.

The video of her on her knees in front of me, ready to blow me.

I'd watched it obsessively all morning without knowing why, because it wasn't that it got me hard, though it did.

It was because of the way she was looking at me. As if I was the only thing worth looking at in her entire world.

It had been that look in her eyes that had caught me the first time I'd watched her Internet video and it caught me now. And she was still looking at some prick who didn't deserve her.

Except now that prick was me.

'You're not the man I thought you were.'

I wasn't. I never had been.

But you could be.

The thought hit me like a bullet to the chest, an explosion of force and then a shattering pain. I couldn't be that man. Could I?

Depends on how much she matters to you, doesn't it?

I felt like I was balanced on the edge of a cliff and any movement would send me over into a chasm.

What kind of man did she think I was? She'd told me once that my father should have come for me, should have protected me and I'd ignored that. Then she'd said that I deserved to have what I wanted and I'd discounted that.

I hadn't listened to her. I hadn't believed her.

But she believed. She was inside that church, in front of all those people, waiting because she believed. Putting herself at risk of public shame and humiliation for the second time in her life. For me.

She was doing that for me.

For some insane reason, despite the betrayals she'd endured in her past, she believed in me.

It was her choice and one she hadn't been forced into. A choice she'd made for the woman she was now, the brave, passionate chemist. A choice for the future.

'I know you're letting your past stop you from having what you really want. I know you think you don't deserve it...'

She was right—I didn't deserve it. But she believed I was something more than my past and who was I to prove her wrong?

How could I let her stand up in front of that crowded church and face all those people alone?

It flooded through me then, through the hole in my armour, bursting that badly patched crack wide open, washing all my careful defences away.

She mattered. She mattered so fucking much it hurt.

No, I didn't deserve her. But I could try, couldn't I?

All I'd wanted was a fresh start. Well, maybe that fresh start was waiting in the church for me all dressed in white.

Maybe my fresh start was Vita.

My heart was beating like a drum, my palms sweaty, every danger sense I had telling me that this was a risk I couldn't afford to take.

I ignored it.

I put my phone away and I got out of the car.

I walked up those steps and into the church.

The whisper of restless people hit me immediately, shifting in their seats and murmuring to each other.

But it wasn't them I looked at. It was Vita, standing at the altar with her head high, clutching her bouquet.

Alone.

As I walked in she saw me and then she went very, very still.

I began to walk down the aisle, a shocked silence following in my wake and by the time I reached the altar you could have heard a pin drop.

Not that I was listening. There was only one person I was aware of.

She stared at me, her dark eyes liquid, stars glittering deep in them. 'You're here,' she whispered hoarsely. 'Why?'

'Why do you think?' I reached for her and pulled her into my arms. 'Because, Vita Hamilton, I love you.'

I kissed her then, in front of the crowd, in front of everyone, and afterwards she whispered into my ear, 'I thought you didn't care.'

'I was wrong,' I whispered back. 'And you were right. I was a coward. I was afraid I couldn't be who you wanted me to be. But I'm here to try, Vita. You believed in me and I want to be the man you believe in.'

She turned her head, brushing my jaw with her mouth. 'You don't need to try, idiot. You already are that man.'

My heart slammed hard against my breastbone and I wanted to be alone with her. No clothes. No defences. Just us. Together.

But we were in front of a whole crowd of people and there was a marriage ceremony to get through.

She pulled back and looked up at me. 'Is it real,

Leon?' she asked quietly. 'Or is this all for the "I Love You Girl"?'

I met her gaze and let her see the truth. 'This is real. You can have your happy ending if you want it.'

That crease between her brows appeared. 'But… do you want it?'

I gave her the honesty I should have weeks ago. And it wasn't spurious this time. 'I've never wanted anything more in all my life. You have my heart, vixen. Can I trust you with it?'

Her smile set me on fire. Then she took my hand and turned to the vicar, who was still waiting, and gave me my answer.

'You can marry us now,' she said.

And he did.

EPILOGUE

Leon

I BARELY GOT through the ceremony, let alone the reception, and I only lasted until we cut the cake then I dragged my new wife off to my Darling Point mansion and I didn't let her leave.

Two days later I left the country, taking her with me.

But not for good. We had a last-minute honeymoon to get to in Greece and I didn't want to miss a second.

'Some chemical reaction,' she said, holding my hand as we took off. 'I should have known that theory wouldn't stand up to any scientific testing.'

'There's more to life than chemicals, my little scientist.' I kissed her hand. 'For example, have you joined the mile-high club yet? I'd be happy to help you with your admission.'

Her smile was the private kind, the one that was mine and mine alone.

There was more to life than chemicals. There was love.

There was her.

Vita. It was Latin for life. And that too was appropriate because that was what she was. My beautiful new life.

* * * * *

LOOK AT ME

CARA LOCKWOOD

MILLS & BOON

For the love of my life, my husband, PJ.

CHAPTER ONE

CHLOE PARK STARED at her laptop as she sat at her kitchen table in her roomy north Chicago condo. She fanned her face, desperately trying to get a breeze from her open window. Outside, the June heat pushed the temperature up beyond eighty-five degrees and the noon sun beat mercilessly down on her brick building. Soon, she'd have to break down and call someone to repair her AC, but not yet. Not with her bank account hovering near zero until the end of the week when she expected the arrival of her next freelance check. Chloe tried once more to focus on a work email, but the high-pitched squeal of a truck's old brakes drifting in through her open window broke her concentration. She tried to ignore it, focusing on her screen and the last few sentences she'd need to write before she could hit Send. Then came the sound of metal clanging against metal.

'Really?' she asked her apartment, feeling as though everyone were conspiring against her to get no work done. She had at least five client social media accounts to update and a proposal to send out to a new corporate client who needed freelance social media updates *now*. But she couldn't focus on any of that. Chloe abandoned the email, frustrated, as she swiped a bit of sweat from her brow. This heat! Ugh. She hated it. And the noise outside didn't help, but she also knew if she closed that window her condo would turn into a brick oven. The clanging was replaced by the voices of men, made louder by the echo effect of the small alley.

She lived in a small building of just five units, each stacked on top of the other in an old factory renovated for condos but originally built in the 1920s. She lived at the top of their building, on floor four, in between an office building to the south and to the north a condo building that was being gutted and repurposed.

Unable to resist any longer, she grabbed the can of Coke from her table and went to her window, glancing out to see a small white moving truck in the alley beneath it, and one mover who struggled to slide a heavy metal ramp out from the open back.

New neighbor? she wondered, and immediately knew which one. Had to be the building across the street, the one she'd seen construction crews head in and out of as they gutted it and redesigned the three-flat. The building was made of solid brick with a faint Herron and Co. logo on the side. No windows faced her, except three on the top floor and a single lone window on the second. Those had been the old offices of the executives running the company. She heard it had once been a cold storage facility back in the early 1900s. This explained the garage doors below narrow enough to fit the horse-drawn carriages that came to pick up deliveries, and the first floor, which was entirely bricked in. Someone told her a condo owner decided to renovate the fourth floor back in the 1980s, adding in windows that looked out on the alley between them. Still, the old icehouse was one of many reasons she loved Chicago, where new lived beside old, modern beside antique and old buildings like this one found new life.

The neighboring building was big enough for three condos, but as far as she knew, the entire building had been empty since she'd moved in eight months ago. There'd been construction crews coming and going, and the rumor from her downstairs neighbor—a Realtor—was that the entire building was being converted into one massive home: no doubt for one very rich couple or a very rich family of ten, since the three-story brownstone could easily hold ten bedrooms and five bathrooms. From her floor, she could see straight into the top floor of the building, where she saw a spacious living room with dark-stained pine floors and had a full view of the expansive rooftop deck: covered in wood, complete with a built-in fire pit and benches. Last week, gardeners had arrived with potted plants, and so the entire deck was in bloom with white and yellow flowers.

Now she studied the movers. None of them looked up. Chloe had gotten used to not being seen from her vantage point. People just didn't glance up beyond the second floor of her building. Chloe sank into the little bench at her bay window, sipping her soda and watching the men work. Because it was so hot, Chloe could only bear to wear a tank top with thin straps and a pair of old gym shorts. She hadn't bothered putting on makeup, because she worked from home and the humidity would just melt it off anyway. She'd swept her dark, nearly black hair up in a hastily made ponytail, but didn't care. She doubted the movers would be looking up. She felt invisible on her perch. She took another sip, watching the burly workers below as they waited to unload their cargo. They seemed not able to get in.

Then a brand-new Maserati roared up to the back of the building, steered by a man in his early 30s. He parked in the alley, not caring about a proper parking space. She guessed a man with a Maserati could afford a parking ticket. He popped out of the driver's seat, dressed in a T-shirt and shorts. Hang on. *Hello.* Tall, built like a linebacker, with muscles she could see from where she sat. What was he—a boxer? A fitness trainer? No trainer she knew could afford a Maserati.

He ran a hand through a thick head of dirty-blond hair as he dropped his phone in his pocket. He instantly started directing the movers.

She glanced at his flat stomach hugged by his skintight shirt and thought: *Bet he's gay.* She didn't know any straight guys who worked that hard on their abs. And she knew next to no rich men who did. After all, why bother, when their wallets could speak for themselves?

But...if he is straight...mmm, mama. He had just

the right amount of blond goatee covering his chin. She saw no ring on his left hand. Then he grabbed keys from his pocket and opened the back door. Could he be…the new neighbor? He certainly acted like it. And the Maserati fit the profile of someone who'd just bought a whole building for himself.

She willed him to look up, to see her, but he didn't. Not that he would.

No one bothers to see me up here. The benefits of being invisible meant that she could spy with abandon.

The new neighbor was gorgeous, with a capital *G*. And had more money than God if he was going to live in that building all by himself. Lincoln Park real estate was anything but cheap. Just ask Chance the Rapper, who lived two streets over. Not that money alone really spoke to Chloe. Sure, she wouldn't mind having more of it, but her Korean dad and Irish mom raised her with Midwestern values. They told her to work hard, keep her head down and not be flashy.

A strand of her nearly black hair fell into her face. She blew it off her sticky forehead and fumbled with her tank-top spaghetti strap that kept falling off her shoulder. She watched as the new neighbor directed the movers, as they unloaded the truck—a big gray sectional coming first, as they maneuvered it into the open door across the way.

At least I'm not moving a couch wearing a jumpsuit in this heat, she thought, fanning herself and taking a sip of her now-lukewarm soda.

A few minutes later she saw them maneuver the

same couch into the third-floor living room. She realized then she could see the entire living room, the fireplace, a bit of the kitchen and even, when the bedroom door was open, a little of that as well. And now the shades were up and she saw movers walking about the space below. She watched the new neighbor in the alley pick up a few boxes himself, his biceps rippling beneath the weight. What kind of billionaire *lifts his own boxes*? Now Chloe's curiosity was piqued. Maybe she was wrong. Maybe that wall of muscle was the billionaire's personal assistant? Yet something told her no. It was the way he carried himself. This man was in charge, and not just of the move.

The intriguing man disappeared into the staircase. Chloe's phone dinged then, an incoming message, an email alert. She absently went to get her phone, and scrolled through her messages. Spam, actually. She dismissed it and returned to the window, noticing that the mystery neighbor popped up at the top floor and walked the boxes into the living room. *Doesn't hurt to watch, does it? Not that they'll see me anyway.*

He hadn't noticed her, and yet she was close enough to see his forehead start to glisten a little with sweat. For once, she was glad of her invisibility cloak. Now she could see his face a bit better as he stood at the window, looking down. He took off his sunglasses and wiped his forehead, and she could see his eyes weren't brown. Blue, maybe? Or green? Hard to tell. He swiped at the bead of sweat on his temple.

Wish I could wipe that off...with my tongue, she found herself thinking, and then giggled to herself at the ludicrous idea as she clutched her phone in her sweaty palm. Where did that come from? It had to be because she was newly single, she figured. Suddenly, everybody was a possibility. As she finished off her can of soda, she watched the new neighbor dump a box in the living room and then run an arm across his own sweaty brow. Then, to her utter surprise, he whipped off his tee.

Oh...my. Hello there, sexy. She hadn't seen such an amazing chest before except on the giant posters of her gym. He had abs, yes, and that amazing little vee stretching down into his low-slung khakis. His well-defined pecs and chiseled arms seemed like they should be wielding a hammer.

She also noticed this bad boy had tattoos. A big one across his right arm and shoulder. What was it? She couldn't make it out. She pulled up her phone's camera and then zoomed in, trying to get a better look. Was the tattoo part of a wing? She wasn't sure.

Okay, what bazillionaire lifted his own boxes *and* had tattoos? Chloe shook her head. The new neighbor was all kinds of mystery rolled into some serious eye candy. He patted his face with his own shirt, and Chloe felt like she'd suddenly been taken out of time. Everything she watched seemed to be on a slow-motion reel, even as her sexy new neighbor grabbed a bottle of water and took a deep swig. She watched his Adam's apple bob and suddenly wished he'd dump the whole bottle on his head.

What's wrong with you? This isn't a male revue, for goodness' sake. Chloe tried to mentally shake herself, but she still sat at the window anyway, transfixed. She clutched the phone in her hand. Should she take a picture? She was tempted. Then the dazzling neighbor moved away from the window and out of sight.

Dammit. Where did the bad boy with the abs go?

She pushed forward, trying to see, and her spaghetti strap slipped again from her shoulder. She wore no bra, since it was too hot for one in her opinion, and the fabric of her shirt slung dangerously low, but she didn't pay it any mind. She was too focused on getting one more glimpse of her Nordic god neighbor.

Where had he gone? She couldn't see him at the windows anymore. The door to the roof creaked open then, and she saw him head out on the slate tile of the patio. Now he was even closer, a perfect place to take a picture. Should she? Her friends would never believe such a hunky man had moved in. And what if he was famous? An actor, maybe? From *Chicago Fire* or one of the dozens of regular shows that filmed in downtown Chicago?

She held up her phone, debating whether to take a shot, when he suddenly glanced up and their eyes met. For a second, she froze from sheer shock. Surely he wasn't *actually seeing her.* Nobody saw her up here. But he gave a slight nod of his head, a little smile, and she realized he had seen her. He held his hand up in a wave.

Horrified, Chloe scrambled to hide her phone, but the sudden movement sent the smartphone slipping out of her sweaty grasp. She watched helplessly as her phone—brand-new—toppled out of her open window. She leaned out of the window, but it was too late. Her prized possession was taken by gravity. It flipped downward to the alley below, missing his shiny new Maserati by inches, landing between it and the moving truck with a sickening crack on the asphalt.

She glanced back up at the neighbor, who seemed surprised, but was watching her—not the phone. He was transfixed, frozen, and that was when she realized—too late—she was hanging out of her window, practically falling out of her tank top, the fabric so low she was flashing the man her nipples.

Chloe, mortified, pulled up her shirt, ducked away from her window and retreated to her kitchen, her heart pounding.

That's just great. Throw your phone out the window. Flash the neighbor. Maybe he'll throw you some Mardi Gras beads.

The heat of embarrassment burned her cheeks. *Maybe he's gay and doesn't care.* At least, she could hope for that. After a few minutes, Chloe felt like an idiot standing barefoot in her kitchen. She wondered if he was still there. Carefully, she tiptoed from her kitchen, and then kicked herself. *He can't hear me,* she scolded, and tried to catch a glimpse far from her window. But when she looked out, she didn't see the bad boy anymore. She slunk closer to the window, trying to hide herself behind a side curtain. Nope. The deck below her sat empty except for the potted plants.

Then she remembered her phone, dropped four

stories onto the ground below. She needed that—it was her lifeline!

She didn't have time to change. What if someone stepped on it? What if someone stole it? She roused herself out of her stupor and moved to her front door. She jammed her feet into flip-flops and headed for the staircase. She swung open the back door ready to jump into the alley and nearly collided with…her new neighbor.

He was holding her mangled and decidedly cracked phone in his hand. 'Uh… I think you dropped this?'

Standing in front of him, she realized now how very tall he was. His muscled shoulders were all power. And he still wasn't wearing a shirt. And she was more than aware of the fact that she wasn't wearing a bra.

'Uh… Yeah. I…' *I just flashed you a second ago. Sorry about that.* 'Uh… Thanks.' She grabbed the phone, with its shattered face and bent corner. It still lit up when she touched it. That was good, at least.

'I'm… Jackson Drake.' He extended a strong hand.

She took his hand dumbly and shook it. His palm was smooth and big. The man had big hands, bear paws almost. What was it that they said about big hands? His sharp blue eyes never left her.

'Looks like we'll be neighbors.' A slow smile curved his lips. He had nice teeth, too. Model-white.

So he *did* own that whole building. What was a billionaire doing…fetching her phone? She happened to glance at his wrist and saw the gleaming Rolex there. Yep, definitely rich.

'And you are…?'

Idiot. Didn't even tell him your name. 'Chloe… Chloe Park.'

'Nice to meet you, Chloe. Do you mind if I call you by your first name? I feel like after today, we need to be on a first-name basis.' He grinned a sly, wolfish smile.

Still, her face flamed at the reference of her spilling out of her shirt. 'I'm sorry. I'm not used to having neighbors. I'm not even in the habit of shutting my blinds. That building has been abandoned for so long.'

'Don't change on my account.' He took a slight step closer. His bare chest filled up most of her field of vision. She wondered if his skin felt as smooth as it looked. Something told her he wasn't gay. Gay men didn't flirt like this with her.

Chloe again lost the ability to speak. Pretty soon, he'd start thinking she was slow. Chloe felt a tingle at the back of her knees. 'Park…' he said, blue eyes never leaving hers. 'Is that Korean?'

'Dad's Korean. Mom's Irish. You know, a living representation of the melting pot. They live in Seattle, but I see them a couple of times a year…' What was she yammering on about? She always did that when she was nervous.

'Hey! Drake!' called one of the movers carrying a large box. 'This going to the first floor or…?'

Jackson hesitated, seeming to want to linger. Or maybe that was just because he didn't want to deal with moving. Moving day was always terrible, no matter how rich you were, Chloe supposed.

'Well, I see you're busy, but, uh…thanks for the phone. It's my lifeline.' She held up her battered phone. *If* her lifeline still worked, that is.

Jackson nodded. He couldn't be more confident in his own skin, standing at her back alley door. But then, why wouldn't he be? He was gorgeous and rich. He was probably used to women falling at his feet. *Or falling out of their tops*, she thought ruefully.

'Until…next time then. Chloe.' He nodded once at her, and she was held there, for a second, trapped in his ice-blue eyes. Eventually, she remembered she was a sweaty, unshowered mess and wasn't wearing a stitch of makeup—or a bra. Her girls were probably bouncing all over the place. Self-consciousness consumed her. She crossed her arms awkwardly across her chest.

'Till next time,' she squeaked, like a mouse, and retreated. Even as the alley door closed, she felt her heart pounding.

CHAPTER TWO

JACKSON DRAKE COULDN'T get his mind off the dark-haired beauty who'd given him a show as he drove his Maserati down North Avenue later that day. He grinned to himself. He remembered her shock and embarrassment when she'd realized she'd shown him her left breast and almost all of the right, her dark nipples puckered just the way he liked them. They came in the perfect size, natural, but not too heavy, much more than a handful. He wondered what they'd feel like against his palms. The idea of having a sexy new neighbor who often went braless was a perk he hadn't anticipated when he'd bought the old icehouse. Drake had made a fortune in real estate, in transforming old buildings into new condos and offices. He was one of the city's most successful large-scale flippers. A real estate magazine had labeled him a renegade, since he always bet on buildings and neighborhoods others wrote off, plus, his bad-boy look made him seem more biker gang than Fortune 500. But his facial hair grew so fast, he'd need to shave twice a day if he had even a fighting chance of being clean shaven, so he decided long ago not to fight it. Goatees and beards came easy to him.

But those who thought he looked more thug than businessman would be wrong. He prided himself on doing more research, knowing everything there was to know about a neighborhood, before he invested in it. But somehow he'd missed the intel on the sexy neighbor next door.

I would've finished the renovations earlier if I'd known, he mused, grinning. *And maybe added more windows.* He was already regretting only having one on the second floor facing the alley.

The light turned green and he gunned his car, beating the BMW in the lane next to him as he roared down the street.

He thought about her cracked phone and frowned. He made a mental note: he'd grab one of the many smartphones they kept at the office to hand out to new Realtors. It would be easy enough to replace, and besides, he was just being neighborly. He imagined what she'd do when she saw the new phone. Would her face light up with delight?

Then, almost instantly, his excitement faded a tad. He'd wondered, briefly, if it had all been an act. Most women saw the money before they saw him. He worked hard on his body, but he'd begun to think that didn't matter in the least. Hell, if some woman wanted him for his abs it would be a welcome change of pace. Most women saw the Maserati and Rolex, and then didn't care what he looked like. Jackson shook his head. It was why he'd all but given up hope on finding someone who actually cared about *him*. His last relationship had been a disaster from the get-go: she'd been a social climber disguised as a bartender—Laurie, a woman he'd caught in his bathroom, legs up on the bathroom counter, as she tried to tip the contents of a used condom inside her to impregnate herself. It was a calculated move to get child support, or 20 percent of his gross income per year until the baby turned eighteen.

Every time Jackson thought he'd become as cynical as you could be about women, he managed to find a new level. The experience had been enough to make him want to never date again. Lately, Jackson had been relying on old friends-with-benefits relationships, the kind that came with no strings, no commitments. Women who liked nice meals out, the occasional gift, and didn't mind that Jackson would disappear for months at a time. Having money wasn't all bad.

He'd been telling himself for years that this was exactly what he wanted: a rotation of gorgeous and willing women. Mostly, this worked just fine, until he spent Thanksgiving with his cousin and his wife and kids in the burbs and wondered what it would be like to have a family of his own: a house full of love and laughter and a little bit of chaos. It was really why Laurie's antics had hurt him so much. He worried that he'd never find genuine love, a woman who could see beyond the money and could love the man beneath.

He steered his car to the office bearing his name—Drake Properties—and pulled into the underground parking beneath the sleek skyscraper that housed his office in the Gold Coast near downtown Chicago, aptly named for its stunning multimillion-dollar condos and its proximity to the Magnificent Mile, home to the swankiest stores in the city. He was happy to see that most of the spaces dedicated to his office were empty. That was a good thing. That meant Realtors were out doing their jobs. After all, you couldn't sell property from inside an air-conditioned office. He headed to the elevator, texting his assistant to let him know he'd be arriving soon. In seconds he was inside the lobby of the building, which they shared with a few other businesses. He waved at the security guard up front and then headed to the bank of elevators that would take him to the top floor.

The elevator door barely opened before his assistant, Hailey, greeted him with a piping-hot cappuccino, foamed up just the way he liked it, an elaborate swirled pattern down the center.

'Good morning, sir,' Hailey said, beaming her million-dollar smile as she handed him the perfectly foamed cappuccino. Blond perfection in a steel-gray pencil skirt and blouse, Hailey was all business, just the way he liked it. Clients were stunned by her beauty, but he loved the fact that she never missed the smallest detail.

'Here are the dailies,' she said, handing him a folder with the highlights of the day as well, including the brewing deals in the office. 'And the Housing Network called again. They wanted to know if you'd given any more thought to their show.' Hailey paused at his door, waiting for his answer.

Jackson shook his head. 'Don't have time for reality TV discussions this week,' he said, even though he knew HN wouldn't give up. They'd been hounding him for months to come do a guest spot on their show that put experts in touch with amateur home flippers. While the possibility was intriguing, Jackson had his hands full with current projects, and fame had never really interested him much.

'Thank you, Hailey.'

'Yes, sir,' Hailey said. 'Oh, one more thing. Mr. Roberts is waiting for you. In the lobby.'

'Why?' Jackson frowned. Roberts was his major competition in Chicago, and the only other developer who flipped buildings as fast as Jackson did. But while Jackson believed in revamping the community and trying to keep housing reasonably affordable, caring about the city as a whole, Roberts was a typical slumlord: he'd been born wealthy, a trust fund baby who had gotten richer on the backs of the poor. He had a vast holding of decrepit properties on the South Side. The two never saw eye to eye on anything. So why was he waiting for a meeting?

'He would only tell me that you'd want to hear his proposition.'

'I'm not interested in any deal that man offers.' Jackson took a sip of his cappuccino and then headed into his spacious corner office, made almost completely of glass. His sleek glass-legged desk waited for him, as did his new laptop. From his vantage point, he could see Lake Michigan, dotted with small white sailboats, the beaches nearby filled with sunbathers, even on a weekday.

Hailey barely hid a smile. 'That's what I figured. Shall I tell him to leave?'

'No need, Miss Hailey,' came a baritone from Jackson's office door. The two turned to see Kent Roberts standing there. Jackson frowned. He glanced at the tall, fit, dark-haired real estate baron hanging in his office door and hated the look of him: the preppy blue blazer, crisp khakis, expensive loafers and gleaming designer aviators perched on top of his wavy dark hair. His preppy, too-buttoned-up style rubbed Jackson the wrong way. It was as if he'd never grown out of the exclusive prep school uniform look. Then again, he probably went to boarding schools as a kid, so maybe he didn't know how else to dress.

Jackson was a man who liked to get his hands dirty, who would be just as likely to pick up a hammer on a construction site as blueprints. Kent, however, had delicate, manicured hands that had never seen a day's hard work in his whole life. The two were polar opposites.

'Sir?' Hailey asked, her single word loaded with meaning.

'It's all right, Hailey. I'll handle this.'

With a swift nod, she backed out of his office, leaving him and Roberts alone.

Jackson ran a hand over his goatee, which was quickly on the border of turning into a full-fledged beard. He took smug satisfaction in Kent's baby-faced chin. The man couldn't grow anything, he was pretty sure. Jackson sneezed and had a moustache.

'What can I do for you?' Jackson braced himself. He'd learned long ago not to underestimate his adversary. He might look like he never got his hands dirty, but he wasn't afraid to stab anybody in the back.

'It's what I can do for *you*, friend.' Kent smiled, but the smile didn't quite reach his eyes. 'I heard you moved into your house on MacKenzie. We're neighbors.'

'Neighbors?' Jackson asked stiffly.

'Well, I just bought the property next door.'

Jackson frowned. How did he not know the building was for sale? He would've scooped it up, if only to protect his property values. Kent grinned, knowing he'd won that small victory.

'Which one?' Jackson asked.

'1209.'

That was when Jackson realized it was Chloe's building, his sexy new neighbor. Now it really didn't sit well with him. He didn't like the idea of Chloe having a new slumlord owning her lease, a man who'd no doubt raise her rent but then refuse to fix anything. He might not know Chloe well, but what he did know he liked, and besides, no one deserved that.

'What do you plan to do with it?' Jackson asked.

Kent grinned even bigger. 'Why, sell it to you, of course.'

Now Jackson was on full alert. Kent was not the kind of man to ever do him any favors. 'Why?'

'Because I know you'll make me the best offer. You've got all that *new* money lying around.' He tapped Jackson's desk to make sure he hadn't missed the dig. 'I'm sure you can afford it. Unless…you'd rather save your money for NASCAR, or whatever it is you like.'

Kent always made a point of referencing the fact that Jackson came from humble beginnings. Kent had inherited his wealth. Never really worked a day in his life. Jackson's father worked as a carpenter. He just happened to have a heart attack on the job when he was near retirement, and that gave Jackson the ability to buy his first office and flip it. Sure, they'd both inherited money, but Jackson's inheritance came with much fewer zeros.

'I earned my money,' he said. 'I'm not embarrassed about that.'

Kent frowned. 'Well, like I said, I think you should think long and hard about making me a good offer.' Jackson suddenly felt that if he didn't buy the building, Kent might turn it into something terrible, like a truck stop in the middle of the city. Or a strip club. Something that would make living next door impossible. 'How about I have my people get in touch with your people… I just know we can make a deal.'

Kent stood, arms crossed, a fixed grin on his face that said he was enjoying this little meeting a little too much. Kent loved lording this over Jackson. He had no doubt the developer would insist on the most unreasonable price for the building, just so Jackson would keep it out of his hands. Honestly, it was lazy and stalkerish of Kent. Was his plan just to follow Jackson around the city? Buy up anything next door?

Jackson sighed. 'Fine,' he said, hating this little game of cat and mouse. He'd rather just ignore Kent, pretend he didn't exist, but Kent had other ideas. He'd seemed obsessed lately with picking a fight, and it was in no small part due to the fact that Jackson was far more successful than Kent, had reality TV offers when Kent had none, and had outbid him on a recent parkland deal with the city, a lucrative project that would turn junkyards into public spaces. Jackson understood that Kent was a bad developer, that he'd lost out on a number of big deals recently because he hadn't had the vision or the courage to jump into new projects. Jackson had both. Of course, if Kent spent less time in strip clubs and more time reading up on real estate, he could be as successful, too.

Kent hung around, standing near the door, that smug grin on his face that Jackson hated. Jackson glanced back at his computer, dismissal obvious. When Kent didn't leave right away, Jackson reluctantly looked up. 'Is there anything else?'

'I'll have my people call your people,' he said, completely unaware of how pretentious and clichéd he sounded.

Jackson didn't respond, but stared at his computer screen until Kent had left.

Hailey rushed in when he was gone.

'Everything…okay?' she asked, tentative.

'Fine. He's just blowing hot air—as usual. The man has an endless supply.' Jackson shook his head.

'How bad is this rivalry going to get?' Hailey asked. 'Should I schedule a fight after school?' Her mouth quirked up in a teasing smile. Hailey, who just married her longtime partner, Kristi, last year, had little tolerance for testosterone-fueled fights.

'I would totally win that fight,' he felt the need to say, for the record.

'Oh, I know you would, sir.' Hailey grinned.

'You'll be hearing from him about a property near my house. I'm sure the first offer will be laughable. Just be on the lookout.'

'Will do,' Hailey said and ducked out of his office once more.

He took another sip of his now-lukewarm cappuccino and tapped on his keyboard, bringing his computer screen to life. After discussions with Kent, he needed to cleanse his palate. He thought about his new neighbor and her dark eyes and…exposed nipple. He loved her look, not quite Korean, not quite Irish, something in between. He was all kinds of mutt, mostly Celtic, a little bit Cherokee in there somewhere, German, and a spattering of Cajun, too. Curious about Chloe, he pulled up her building and saw it was a rental property, apartments, which he knew already. He saw old pictures of what must be her condo, a small efficiency. As he swiped through them, his phone lit up with an incoming message from his ex-girlfriend.

Miss you.

He stared at the message and shook his head. Laurie. Really? She missed him? He knew that was a lie. She missed his money, maybe. Him? No way. He deleted the message. Hearing from Laurie felt like a bucket of cold water over his head. Why was he thinking about the mystery girl next door? She was probably no different than Laurie.

Even Jackson realized he was slipping down into a dark place. He didn't like it, either. Didn't like his new morose attitude. He'd always been a go-getter. That was how he'd built his empire from nothing.

Then he got another message. How's the move going? Bed assembled yet? This from Annaliese, one of his friends with benefits, an Eastern European model who was more than happy to be kept in rotation.

Maybe, he said.

If it is, how about I come over and help you break it in tonight?

Jackson thought about Annaliese's curves, her sleek red hair and the way she had a knack for distracting him from problems, namely with her talented hands. And mouth.

He'd never fall in love Annaliese—she was far too single-minded for him, and it was purely just about the sex. She never wanted dinner or drinks. She'd made it clear from the start that she had no interest in any relationship, and even if she did, he'd be the last person she'd think about marrying. Annaliese had a theory that no one could be faithful, really, especially rich men. Not that she'd given him the chance. Still, he couldn't even imagine what it would be like to sit across from Annaliese at a dinner table. Most of the time when she showed up at his place, she wore a raincoat and nothing else. Occasionally, she'd wear garters. Or transparent lace. Or thongs. He found himself wondering what she'd choose tonight.

It's a date, he wrote.

You know I don't date, she wrote back, and he grinned.

CHAPTER THREE

'YOU SHOULD COME out with us tonight,' said Ryan on the phone as Chloe glanced down at her just-microwaved burrito. She had her hands-free set tucked in her ear as she sat in her warm kitchen, though it was cooling off now that the sun had set outside and a soothing breeze seeped into her open window. She glanced at her shattered screen. The phone still worked as a phone, but there was no way she'd be able to check text messages or Twitter. It would be one more expense she'd need to make when she got her next check. She'd just have to wait until then. It didn't help that most of her social media clients of late were nonprofits who took a long time paying their bills. She'd worked most of the afternoon with a nonprofit group called Our Home, which tried to help low-income families stay in neighborhoods that were slowly being gentrified.

She'd uploaded some photos of their work. Much of what they did resembled Habitat for Humanity projects, except they repaired damaged buildings and pressured local aldermen not to green-light commercial real estate that could threaten low-income housing. Of course, if Chloe didn't get paid soon, she'd have to move herself to the category of *low income*. Her laptop remained open on the dining room table, proof she had been working some today. She was still wearing the outfit she'd flashed her new neighbor in (her pajama tank and shorts, having not bothered to change since she'd been chained to her laptop most of the day). Owning her own consulting business meant she got to work from home, but it also meant that work never stopped, either. Not if she wanted her business to survive. She'd just gotten a notice in her mailbox, too, something about a new owner of the building. She hoped that didn't mean a rent hike when her lease was up in a few months, but she knew it might.

'Ryan, I don't know…' *I'd have to shower. Change. It seems like such a production.* Or she could sit and eat her burrito, binge-watch *Game of Thrones*, and call it a night. The latter seemed so much simpler.

'Brendan says if you don't get out of the house *once* this week, we're officially holding an intervention.' Chloe grinned. She loved Ryan and Brendan— she'd stood up in their wedding the summer before. She'd been friends with Ryan since college and had been thrilled when he'd met Brendan—the two were great together: both dark-haired and lean, both rabid outdoorsmen, with a bent toward mountain climbing. Whenever Chloe thought love might not be in the cards for her, she looked at them and thought that if they could find their soul mates, then probably so could she. She would've been nauseated by their sickly sweet Facebook posts, except that she loved them both to death.

'Seriously, Chlo, how many days in a row have you worn the outfit you're wearing *right now*?'

'One,' she said. Then she wondered if that was true. Had she changed yesterday? Now she couldn't quite remember, though she had to admit, the thought had crossed her mind to just head to bed in the same pajamas. Would that be a new low? Not showering and not changing two days in a row. Hell, but wasn't this one of the major perks of working at home?

'I think you're lying.'

Chloe had to laugh. 'I'll catch you guys next time, okay?'

Ryan sighed. 'Okay, but you're starting to turn into some weird hermit, you know that? You need to get out. Socialize with people. You do *social media* all day, but you *never talk to anyone anymore*. Like when was your last *human* interaction?'

'That's not necessary for my job,' she pointed out.

'No, but it is for your mental health. Since the breakup…'

'Don't even mention his name.' Kevin. The investment banker who'd made fun of her consulting business, who often told her she should 'get a real job' and endlessly made jokes about how work done in her pajamas was no work at all. But Chloe was proud of her accomplishments, proud of being her own boss. But because she didn't have a traditional job, Kevin thought she was somehow less important. He saw a girlfriend mostly as an accessory and not a person, which was why he called her by the wrong name in bed…a name she discovered from a series of lurid text messages on his phone belonged to his coworker, a woman he'd been sleeping with on the side.

'You've been hiding, Chlo. Time to break free and get out there,' Ryan said.

She knew he was right, but she didn't feel like getting out there. As awful as Kevin had been to her, she'd gotten to the point where she had really started to think they might get married. He'd told her as much. The fact that he'd been cheating was a blow she still felt six months later. It was because Chloe knew she wanted more. She was closing in on thirty, and her biological clock had kicked into overdrive. She wanted a baby, a family, a husband, and she was pretty sure she wasn't going to find any of those things going out to a bar with Ryan.

'I will—eventually,' she said, and glanced at her cooling burrito on her plate, thinking about how unappetizing it looked. 'I just need some time. Besides, I've got a new neighbor who just moved in. Totally ripped. And loaded, too.'

'Oh! A Christian Grey!'

'Uh…well, if Christian Grey wore shorts and had tattoos.' She took a bite of the burrito and nearly scalded her tongue. She dropped the too-hot microwaved dinner.

'Ooooh. A bad boy. A *rich* bad boy. I like it.'

Chloe laughed. 'Don't tell Brendan. He'll get jealous.'

'He might. You should go for that. Ride that *bike* if you know what I mean.'

'I think he might be gay. I mean, he's got a six-pack.' Chloe bit her lip as she wandered to her window and glanced at her new neighbor's darkened third floor. She'd watched all afternoon but hadn't seen Jackson again. Instead, an army of assistants had come and unpacked him entirely. She'd never seen such efficiency before, but in a matter of hours, they'd unpacked his kitchen, set up his bed, even hung art on the walls. It must be nice to be rich, she'd thought, as she'd watched his minions do all the grunt work.

Ryan considered this. 'You're right. Six-pack abs—they are rampant in the gay community,' he deadpanned.

Just then, the neighbor's light flickered on. Chloe backed away from her window. 'Uh…gotta go, okay? I'll call you later.'

'Just remember what I said. Don't be a hermit!'

'Love you!' she called, and then clicked off. She told herself she shouldn't spy on her neighbor, and besides, it was probably one of his assistants anyway. But as she hovered near the curtains, she watched Jackson enter the third floor from the open stairway at the back of the living room. He immediately tugged off his shirt.

Oh, my. That was a view she could get used to: well-toned pecs, rippled abs, broad, muscled shoulders. She wondered again what he did for a living. Model? Action hero? Jackson could be either. He disappeared into the far right room, his bedroom,

as she'd watched his home-decor minions set up his
bed, and carry in armful after armful of expensive
suits. She didn't see a kitchen, so it had to be on one
of the two floors below. She couldn't imagine what,
exactly, he was doing with all that space. For all she
knew, the first floor could be an indoor basketball
court. Or filled with trampolines. She had no idea
how the über-rich lived.

Maybe he was just going to bed, she thought, and
then went back to her burrito. She took a bite that
was still part frozen. How was one end on fire and
the other an ice cube? Ugh. She put it down, suddenly
not feeling like eating it. She clicked off the overhead
kitchen light, the oven light the only thing illuminating her small kitchen. She glanced up and saw Jackson emerging from his bedroom wearing only mesh
shorts, slung low on his hips, and still no shirt. He
sank down on his plush leather couch and put his feet
up. His phone must've sounded because he picked it
up and pressed it to his ear. Then, a second later, he
tapped the screen. He laid back on the couch, his eyes
on the staircase. Suddenly, a woman clad only in the
shortest silk jumper Chloe had ever seen appeared
on the stairwell in strappy stiletto heels and too much
makeup, her auburn bob cut at chin length. She was
gorgeous. She sauntered over to the couch, a pouty
expression on her face, and he sat there, watching her.

Was that his girlfriend? She felt a hardened pit at
the center of her stomach.

But she didn't greet him like a girlfriend. They
didn't hug or kiss. Instead, she began to slip out of

her little shorts romper, the silk sleeves fluttering downward, revealing the fact that she wore no bra. She was all business, this one. No warm fuzzies. He watched the show appreciatively as she kicked out of the one-piece, now wearing only stilettos, her bare, toned body in front of him.

Well, he's definitely not gay.

Chloe knew she needed to stop watching. But she couldn't. She clutched at the curtain, half-hidden, mesmerized by the action unfolding in front of her. It was a billion times more interesting than her abandoned burrito. Her bad-boy neighbor stood then, and the woman knelt in front of him. She jerked down his shorts as he grabbed a handful of her hair and gave it a playful tug.

I can't watch this, her mind screamed, and yet she couldn't look away. The woman freed him, and Chloe nearly gasped…he was bigger than Kevin. Much bigger. She didn't even know they *came* that big, even while the woman worked at it with both hands, and he stiffened beneath her touch. He watched her intently as she took part of him in her mouth, the tip. *God, did they not know the windows were wide-open? Did they not know she could see…everything?*

This was taking the invisible fourth floor to an *entirely* different level.

Yet part of her realized neither one of them cared. They were intent on sex, only on the sex. After a minute, he pulled her to her feet and whirled her around, completely in command as he bent her across the arm of his couch. Jackson reached his fingers down to her inner thigh, stroking her, then disappearing inside her. She moaned, throwing her head back. Then he had a condom package in his mouth and ripped it open, rolling the latex down his now-ready self. Then he entered her: strong, possessive, decisive.

I shouldn't watch this. Yet she couldn't turn away, either.

Chloe felt her whole body run hot. For a second, she imagined herself there, over that couch, him taking her from behind like an animal, him filling her up. She watched his abs tighten as he worked himself in and out, the woman's face showing joy and want, as she took the whole thick length of him again and again. Chloe watched, transfixed, unable to turn away. She'd never had a man that big before. What would that feel like? The strange woman in his living room gripped the sofa cushions, her knuckles white as she seemed to cry out. Was she climaxing? Her whole body vibrated…and Chloe shivered. God, she felt a stab of jealousy. She wanted to climax just like that, feeling Jackson deep inside her.

Instantly, her body came alive, her belly feeling warm and tingling, her pajama shorts suddenly sticky between her legs. *What am I doing? I'm a Peeping Tom. It's wrong...* And yet all she wanted to do was slip her hands down the waistband of her own shorts, to touch herself. She could feel a beat of a pulse between her legs, feel the want there, the need.

Wasn't this illegal? Snooping in people's windows?

I need to turn away. Close my blinds. But she kept watching, mesmerized and focusing on his magnificent body, his strong hands holding her hips, as he explored her deepest places. Her nipples stood at attention, her small, firm breasts bouncing with his every move. She rocked against him, too, grinding upward, arching her back, enjoying every inch of him.

Chloe bit her lip, feeling her nipples strain against her own shirt, and suddenly her body was overcome by want, like a fever. She wanted to be on the other side of that glass window. She wanted to feel the man's hands on her. Those thoughts consumed her as she stood half-hidden by her curtain.

She was almost tempted to touch herself then, scratch the itch building deep within her. But no. That would be wrong. Wouldn't it?

Chloe watched him, his eyes on the woman's body, his face serious. Then, as if he could sense her watching, he glanced up, and for a heart-stopping second, he saw her.

She froze. Ice-cold fear ran down her spine. He saw her! She'd been caught spying!

Yet she couldn't break his gaze, his blue-eyed stare. Her heart pounded in her chest. She was caught.

He's going to be mad. He could even call the police...

Then, the smallest hint of a smile quirked his lip. He almost looked...amused. He kept eye contact with her and he thrust even deeper into his prize.

Her mouth dropped open. His gaze felt like a tractor beam, holding her in place. He gave her the littlest of nods. *Go on*, his eyes seemed to dare her, *watch me*. The woman before him had her eyes closed, ob-

viously enjoying the feel of him inside her, but suddenly it didn't even matter he was having sex with
another woman. As Jackson watched Chloe, it felt like
the two of them were the only people in the world. It
felt strangely intimate, somehow. Chloe was watching the man at his most vulnerable, and Jackson was
letting her.

Something about that was so wrong…so naughty…
yet she couldn't break his gaze, couldn't turn from
the window. How could he watch her when he was
inside someone else? And yet, he seemed to…*want*
her to watch.

Could that be?

And was it her imagination or was he turned on
by it? Yes, she realized. He was. Excited by her. By
her watching. She felt strangely powerful then. She
wasn't a third wheel; she was *affecting* what she saw.

He leaned over, nuzzling the woman's neck and
cupping her firm breast, tweaking the woman's pink
nipple, but his eyes never left hers all the while, as
if somehow, he was offering to do this to her. Heat
burned in her belly.

Yes. Just like that. Touch her.

Touch me.

Instinctively, Chloe's hand covered her own breast
as she felt her desire grow. The weight of her own
hand against her chest felt like his then. She imagined
what it would feel like for him to nuzzle her neck,
even as he pushed ever deeper inside her.

Jackson straightened again, grabbing the woman's
hips, moving her slightly so she could see him from

the side, see the very thick length of him move in...
and out. God, he was huge, so hard for her. How did
she even take that much?

Yes, Jackson. Just like that, she thought. *That's
how I'd want it.*

Fast.

Hard.

Deep.

He picked up his pace, as if he could hear her own
thoughts. He was all animal, all want. Slickness ran
between her legs as she gawked, unable—and unwilling—to look away. All the while, he stared up at her,
sharp blue eyes never leaving her face.

She wanted to see him come, wanted to see him
pour himself into this woman, because that was what
she'd want. All of him. All that he could give her.

Then, after several furious thrusts, he came: his
face overcome with the pleasure of pure relief. Jackson briefly closed his eyes as he'd found his release.
She knew then she'd helped him. She'd excited him,
pushed him over the edge. She felt the thudding pulse
between her own legs and knew he'd had the same
effect on her. Her body had come alive with need
and want, as both flooded the blood in her veins,
pumped by her fast-beating heart. What she'd give
at that moment to be able to feel him inside her. God,
she wanted him.

Then the woman before him opened her eyes, and
the spell was broken. Suddenly, the intimate little
bubble she'd occupied with Jackson was burst. Chloe
ducked behind her curtains, fearful the woman would

see. She pressed her back against the brick wall, heart pounding in her ears.

What had just happened?

It was wrong what had just happened. So very wrong. How would she feel if someone had watched her and her…boyfriend? Yet she'd never been that brazen. She would've never done it with the blinds up like that. She remembered the confident smirk of the woman as she'd stepped out of her jumper. Chloe doubted the woman would even care if she'd been seen. Hell, she was the one who had sex in front of the windows at night, with the blinds up.

She clicked off her foyer light, her own apartment now dark. She felt the cloak of darkness like a cover of protection. Could she ever even look at Jackson again? She frantically shut her own curtains.

No. It had been wrong. She shouldn't have watched. Yet she liked it. She liked it even more when he'd caught her watching. When he'd shown her how much he'd enjoyed it. Those stark blue eyes watching her, excited by her watching… She'd never forget the look on his face when he'd come.

Heat built between her legs as she slipped her hand down the waistband of her shorts. She found herself so very wet, so very wanting. She touched her most delicate center and shivered, knowing this was what she'd badly wanted to do while she watched Jackson, and now she could hold back no longer. She thought about his hands, his eyes, how he'd feel inside her, filling her…and then, before she knew it, Chloe came in a heated rush, so fast, so hard, a quick explosion of need.

God, she'd never done that before: made herself come in just a matter of seconds. But she knew why this time had been different. It had been Jackson. All Jackson.

What would he do if he knew she'd...just done this? For him?

The thought danced in her mind. So wrong. Yet right.

She felt like she'd *been* there with him. And... her. Her heart settled a bit, her breathing slowed, and she wondered if her neighbor had gotten dressed. If he and that woman were cuddling, kissing now. The thought made her feel a flare of jealousy. Why? *I'm not his girlfriend. I'm just the neighbor who flashed him...and watched him come.* How she wished she could see that look of pure pleasure on his face again, but this time, with him deep, deep inside her.

She slumped down at her kitchen table and stared at her drawn curtains. Should she take another peek? Would she dare? No. She fought herself. *I've invaded the man's privacy enough. I've broken enough laws.*

What if Jackson called the police?

She shook her head. No. She remembered the pleasure on his face as he glanced up and saw her. No. He liked it. He liked it when she watched.

But who was that woman? Girlfriend? Escort? She wasn't sure which would be worse. She didn't like the idea of him having a girlfriend, an intimate, loving relationship, but she also didn't like the idea of him paying for sex, either. She heard a door slam in the alley and curiosity got the better of her. She jostled the curtain a centimeter and peered down. The woman he'd just had sex with slipped into an Uber waiting in the alley.

Definitely not a girlfriend, she thought. Then… what?

Chloe thought about the man in his big three-story building all by himself, sated now, maybe even still naked. Maybe rinsing off in the shower. For a split second, a crazy thought ran through her head…what if I went over? Rang his doorbell?

Instantly, she dismissed the thought. Really? She was going to…what? Tell him she was sorry for spying? Or ask him to do *exactly* what he'd just done to that woman to her?

Her inner thighs tingled at the thought. Heat rose in her abdomen again. She'd only just taken care of that. Hadn't she? Yet, was she wanting this again? So soon? Just the thought of seeing Jackson made her wet.

No. He'd think she was crazy. Wouldn't he?

After she watched the Uber drive away, she glanced back up at the new neighbor's windows. She didn't see him, and figured he'd moved to his room, though his blinds were still wide-open. Maybe he'd forget about the whole thing. Maybe he'd pretend it never happened. Maybe that was what she should do as well.

Then she saw him return with a bar of white soap in his hand and a small bowl of water. What was he…? She hid once more as he came to the windows. The idea of him seeing her spying *more* made her face flame with embarrassment. She waited for a few minutes, breathing hard.

Go to bed, Chloe, she told herself. *What are you even doing?*

She waited a few more moments that felt like hours. Should she look? Once more? What *was* he doing with that bar of soap?

Chloe peeked around the curtain, leaving just enough space for one eye. The living room was now empty. No sign of Jackson.

But he'd used the soap to write a message on his window. It was big enough for her to read.

Next time, want to do more than watch?

CHAPTER FOUR

CHLOE COULD BARELY sleep as she thought about what that message might mean. Did he want her to join him? Or join him *and* her? A threesome? Chloe thought about the woman's amazing body and instantly shelved that thought. No way could she get naked in the same room as that runway model. She wasn't about to let her muffin top compare to the skin-and-bones double-zero. Chloe had curves, and that meant that sometimes they jiggled when they weren't supposed to. Maybe Jackson hadn't really invited her over for sex. Maybe he was just calling her out on her snooping? She couldn't figure it out, no matter how hard she thought about it.

Part of her was embarrassed—after all, she'd watched her neighbor *have sex* and hadn't turned away. Granted, they'd left the windows open, but still. It violated basic rules of decency, and Chloe knew it, yet she couldn't help but feel even more intrigued by Jackson now that she knew he was so… endowed. Part of her wanted to tell him she *did* want to do more than watch. Ugh. Did that make her a raging slut? Probably. Or was she just looking after her own needs? Just *look* at the man! Gorgeous. Rich. Probably never intimidated in any locker room he ever entered. Chloe felt her face flush once more, the image of him naked flitting through her mind. Her running shoes pounded the pavement taking her east to the running trail on Lake Michigan.

After crossing a few intersections, she took the underground pedestrian tunnel to the lakefront and then wound her way north on the running trail, the sun rising above the pristine blue water, looking expansive across the horizon, so large it seemed impossible that it was fresh water and not the salty sea. The waves broke on the sandy beach as she ran, her heart thudding. The air got warmer while the sun rose in the sky and sweat broke out across her lower back. Just a few more feet, she thought to herself, and then she turned around, heading back to her apartment. This morning she'd shower. She'd put on something cute. Maybe even put on makeup.

Trying to impress Jackson? Hoping he gets a glimpse of you? Are you going to tell him he made you touch yourself last night?

Part of her wondered if he'd like to know.

She bit her lip. She'd taken the flirting to a new level when she'd watched him last night. She'd crossed a line. *And* that was probably his girlfriend. She couldn't get involved with a man who was so clearly involved and *deeply intimate with someone else*. She remembered just how deeply as she thought of his long, hard thrusts.

Though the woman hadn't stayed the night. That still didn't mean anything. There could be a million reasons for that. She was coveting her sexy neighbor, but he was in a relationship, and Chloe wasn't going to cross that line.

Was she? She bit her lip.

She ran back to her apartment, punching in the code to her place and trotting up the stairs and swiping the sweat off her forehead. She tried to catch her breath, convinced that the best thing to do was just ignore the message. Wasn't that the right thing? Yet, as she eyed the message—still in his window that morning—she felt a little shiver run down the back of her knees.

Next time, want to do more than watch?

Hell, yes, she thought to herself. She did. She wanted to do so much more than watch. Yet what was she thinking? Was she seriously going to *jump into bed with her neighbor*? What happened if she did and…the sex was terrible? Or worse, he broke things off? How would she feel living next door to an ex?

All rational thought told her that fooling around with her neighbor was a bad idea.

The cold water from the shower flushed a little of her desire down the drain, but her brain still buzzed with Jackson's invitation. She wanted to ask him a million questions, she needed to know exactly *what* he was offering.

She remembered the dark tattoos on his shoulder. Wings of some kind. She wanted to see them up close.

To touch them. Read the inscription, if there was one. Ask him why he got them.

But he lives next door. This could be a disaster.

She thought about Ryan. He'd be telling her to go for it, no doubt. She almost imagined his hearty congratulations if she told him she'd finally found a rebound from Kevin. Hadn't Ryan just told her she needed to put Kevin behind her…and be more social?

Still, was she really going to do this?

Chloe hesitated. She still hadn't decided what to do about his message. Ignore it? Reply?

She glanced out her window, seeing the words there as clear as day, his third floor dark. Was he still sleeping? Had he left for work while she was out running?

She suddenly imagined herself writing a message on her window and then his blinds popping up, and him catching her in the act. The idea was mortifying. She wasn't even sure she could bear to look him in the eye after last night.

Chloe decided to ignore the message and booted up her computer. Then, after answering a few emails, she glanced once more at her neighbor's darkened windows. He might be at work. She might be able to send him a message. But what?

No. That was crazy. Why would she write him a message? *Just let it go, Chloe*, she told herself. *Just pretend none of it ever happened.*

Except that she couldn't. Even as she tried to focus on work, her attention kept wandering back to Jackson's darkened windows, to the message he left for her there. She couldn't forget his amazingly chiseled body, his blue eyes watching her.

She didn't have a bar of soap to write on her window, so opted for a pad of sticky notes. Her window was large, and she began laying out her message, using the notes to form letters. Then she stopped and ripped them all down. She glanced at Jackson's darkened windows. She was crazy for replying to this, wasn't she? She had to be crazy.

She glanced at the pink sticky notes in her hand. Maybe she was crazy. She started again before she lost her nerve.

Jackson sat at his desk in his office at Drake Properties, flipping a pen around his fingers, thinking about the dream he'd had the night before. He'd dreamed of Chloe, standing on the other side of a full glass window, wearing nothing but cherry-red heels. He hadn't been able to pay attention to even a single email this morning, as he wondered what Chloe had done when she saw his message that morning.

He knew he'd taken a risk putting the message on his window, but a man like him didn't build an empire without taking risks. He had seen the want on her face, knew that if he pushed hard—but not too hard—she might just wind up in his bed. How he wanted to know what she was like. Did she just like to watch? Or would she perform, too?

What was she doing right then? He hoped crafting a response. The thought made him smile. He'd never been so aroused by a woman's eyes before. By her dark, sensual eyes. She'd watched him and An-naliese boldly, almost without fear. He couldn't wait to see what she'd be like in person, when there wasn't a window between them. He wanted to explore her darkest places.

'Mr. Drake? Call on line one. A Miss Smith?' his assistant asked through the intercom on his desk.

Jackson felt snapped back into reality. That was Laurie, his ex, on the line.

'Send her to voice mail, please,' Jackson called to the intercom.

Just then, a new message popped up on his phone. From Laurie.

I need to talk to you. Please. Call me.

He hit Delete again, and then he thought about blocking her. She wasn't taking no for an answer, and it irked him.

There's nothing to talk about. We're done.

She quickly wrote back, But I love you.
Please.

She didn't know what love was. She knew all about betrayal and deception and greed, but nothing about love. Jackson saw the flashing red light on his phone, indicating the voice mail left by Laurie, and quickly hit Delete without bothering to listen to it. He didn't have time for such nonsense. She was obsessed with his money, nothing more.

He finished the first offer letter to Kent for the 1209 property and sent it off, pretty certain that it would be flat-out rejected. It was below market value of the building, but Jackson had to start somewhere. He figured they'd eventually meet in the middle if Kent really was serious about selling to him and this wasn't just some elaborate game. It could be. Kent no doubt would love the idea of just toying with Jackson, making him believe he had a chance at a property that Kent had no intention of selling. Kent didn't care so much about wasting their time as he did about annoying Jackson. Honestly, the man should get a hobby. Or a wife to keep him busy. Something.

Still, he liked the idea of being Chloe's landlord. He knew he could take better care of her and her building than Kent ever would. He liked the thought of dropping in, asking her if anything in her apartment needed fixing. There were certain things he'd like to fix right now, like the fact that he wanted to see her naked. In his bed.

This made him wonder if she'd responded to his question yet. He glanced at his calendar, which was thin for the rest of the afternoon. Maybe he'd just pop home and see.

He walked out of his office and saw Hailey typing at her desk. Then he remembered Chloe's smashed phone and the devastated look on her face when he'd returned her mangled device.

'Oh, Hailey, do we have any extra smartphones? I need a backup,' he said.

Hailey didn't miss a beat as she turned to fetch a key from her drawer to unlock a cabinet near her knees. She pulled out a box and handed it to him.

'And a manila envelope, please?'

She handed it to him, no questions asked.

'Thanks, Hailey. I'll be back in an hour or so. Let me know if anything urgent comes in.'

'Will do, sir,' she said, and nodded at him, and then turned her attention back to her computer.

Jackson tucked the new phone into the envelope, and thought Chloe would be surprised when he showed up with a replacement for her smashed one. He remembered how absolutely brokenhearted she looked when she saw her phone fall from her window. She wouldn't have been sitting there if they hadn't been moving in, and so he figured the least he could do was replace it.

He liked the idea of getting her a gift, and whistled to himself as he took the elevator down to the parking garage. A quick drive home in his Maserati meant that he was pulling into the parking space near his condo a few minutes later. He glanced up, clearly seeing her message to him. It was spelled out in Post-it notes on her window.

Maybe.

He grinned. *Maybe* she wanted to do more than watch? Well, he'd have to get to work on convincing her he was worth the trouble. He carried the envelope holding the brand-new phone he'd taken from his office as a replacement for her cracked one. He scribbled a quick note there on the porch and slipped

the piece of paper into the manila envelope. He took
the package and laid it on top of her mailboxes and
then rang her buzzer.

Chloe heard the buzzer, but finished the posts she was
doing for her client on Instagram. She figured it was
just another package delivery, though she couldn't
remember what she'd ordered exactly. She finished
up the post and then headed downstairs, swinging
open her building's front door. A manila envelope
sat on her mailboxes, addressed to her. Except it had
no postage. Or mailing label. Just her name in thick
black marker: Chloe Park. There was a small note
inside. It read:

> Chloe,
> *'Maybe' sounds like you need more convincing
> that it's more fun to do than to watch. Call me
> if you need the reasons why.*
> *Jackson.*

Bewildered, she ripped open the package and
found a *brand-new smartphone.* What the…? Her
new, rich, tattoo-clad neighbor had just handed her
an eight-hundred-dollar phone. She glanced at the
mobile, shocked. Who did that? *Someone who owns
a Maserati and a whole building.*
    She fetched her cracked phone from her kitchen
table, and then compared it to the sleek new phone.
She couldn't believe this. Was he…for real? He didn't
even know her. She couldn't accept a gift like this.

Besides, what would his leggy, model girlfriend think? The one who showed up at his house not wearing a bra or underwear beneath that microjumper?

She glanced up at his building across the alleyway, but she couldn't see into his window from this angle, though she saw the blinds were open and it seemed like there might be a light on, but the daylight made it hard to tell. Should she march over there and give this back to him?

Or would he get the wrong idea and think she was there to do *more* than watch? But maybe that was exactly what she wanted to do.

She studied the phone. She couldn't keep it. It was too big a gift from someone she didn't even know.

You know what he looks like naked and you know how he can satisfy a woman. And not only is he up for a booty call, but he gave you the phone to do it.

Still, she told herself, tamping down her naughty thoughts. What if she took the phone and then he expected her to...*do* things in return?

Then again, that didn't sound bad. Not bad at all.

No. She had to give the phone back. She couldn't keep such an expensive gift. Right? It was crazy, wasn't it? Just as she debated what to do next, the new phone in her hand came to life with a standard ringtone.

What the...?

She glanced down at the phone and realized the thing was on. On and clearly activated, because a call was coming in from *Jackson Drake.*

Uh...should she answer? Should she ignore it?

Why did the man give her a phone with his *number* programmed into it? No better time than now to tell him she couldn't accept such a gift.

'Hello?' she said as she pressed the phone to her ear.

'Hey, neighbor.' Jackson's voice was like melted chocolate. Smooth, sexy, sweet.

'Oh…uh. Hi.' When she looked at her windows, she saw the back of her own blinds. She'd drawn them after the show the night before, not trusting herself not to glance out once more. Her window was still open, though, since she didn't want to call the AC repair person just yet—not until a few more freelance checks came in. The light in her studio apartment was dim, so she flicked on the kitchen light and went to retrieve some water from the tap.

'I see you got my gift.' His voice, warm, deep, made her own insides go gooey.

'Uh, right…about that… I mean, thank you so much. It's so generous of you, but… I don't think I can *accept* it.'

'You don't like it?' Now Jackson sounded concerned. She almost felt he might run out and buy her a different one if she'd asked.

'No. No! I love it. I mean it's an amazing phone.' And it was. The sound quality was so good, and the thing was so light, the screen so big, she knew from the commercials she'd seen that this was the brand-new, just out, must-have model.

'If you love it, then keep it.'

'It's so expensive, and… I mean…'

'Chloe.' He said her name as if he owned it. The determination in his voice sparked something inside her. Want? Or maybe more primal. Need. His voice rumbled through her chest and settled in her belly. 'I have many phones for the Realtors at my office, and so, seriously, I insist. Take one. Otherwise, it'll just sit in a drawer and not get used.'

'Well, if it's really no trouble, but I'll need to switch it to my plan and…'

'If you'd like,' he said. 'But even if you don't, that's fine as well. I'd insist you keep it. My gift to you. If the movers hadn't been such a distraction, you would've never dropped that phone.'

The movers weren't the distraction, she thought. *You were.*

'Well, thank you. I mean it. The phone is…well, amazing. Thank you. I'd been worried about how to get a new one.' Suddenly, she felt the weight of the gesture. It was nice of him, even if it wasn't any trouble for a man as wealthy as he was, and who else did she know who would give a brand-new phone to a perfect stranger?

'Well, then. Worry no more.' The way he said it made her laugh a little.

'So, how did you know I'd gotten the phone? Have you been calling it?'

'No. I saw you pick it up.'

Now she felt self-conscious, her face flushing hot. He was watching her door? That meant…

'Wait…you're home?'

'Why don't you open your blinds and see?'

Chloe's heart sped up, thumping like a caffeinated rabbit in her chest. He'd seen her? She leaped to the blinds and tugged on the string, even as she remembered that she hadn't had time to put on makeup since her shower. Still, she yanked up her blinds and there, across the alley, was Jackson, clad in a white undershirt that left nothing to the imagination, and shorts.

He grinned, a bright, shining smile, beneath that full, bad-boy goatee. He waved. Her heart leaped a little. God, the man was gorgeous. If he was a son of anarchy, then let the chaos begin.

'Hi,' she said, and waved back, her voice catching in her throat. Then she felt silly. He was all the way across the alley, but even from this distance, she could feel the attraction. His blue eyes studied her even from behind his window.

'Hi, back,' he said, in a tone that Chloe felt in the balls of her feet. The man's voice was so deep, so confident.

He grinned once more. She felt like an idiot, suddenly at a loss of what to say.

'Now my view just got a whole helluva lot better. Anyone ever tell you how gorgeous you are?'

'Me?' squeaked Chloe. She fanned her face, the air in the apartment close and thick suddenly. Sweat broke out on her lower back. The wind had all but died. She felt the benefits of her earlier shower evaporate in the warm air. 'But, I'm sweaty and...'

'I like sweaty.' Oh, she knew he did. She remembered just how he liked to work up a sweat after watching him the night before. Chloe felt her face flush hot, and it had nothing to do with the warm summer air.

'I know you do. You got quite a workout last night.' The words were out of her mouth before she even realized what she was saying. What on earth? Had she just brought up her peeping? There was something about that man's dangerous smile, the daring look on his face right now. She wanted to shock him.

Jackson chuckled. 'Did you like what you saw?'

Chloe bit her lip. If she admitted she did, she was probably a pervert, but if she said no, she'd be lying. So she just stared at him, hand on the window. She gave a slow nod. 'That was…*quite* a performance.'

Jackson laughed again, a deep rumble that she felt in the back of her knees.

'Good,' he said, his eyes never leaving hers.

'I—I never do that. I usually…'

'Close the blinds before you get to the good stuff?' Jackson slowly shook his head and wagged a disapproving finger. 'Why would you do that?'

Now Chloe did laugh, nervously. Why did he make her feel like it was totally okay to watch him? Why wasn't he more upset? The whole thing was just… crazy, but the way Jackson was looking at her right at that moment, through the window, made her think it was all somehow normal. No, not just normal… right. Was it right?

She remembered how turned on she'd been watching him. Wasn't that…wrong? I mean, how could she *like* watching him and his girlfriend? Also, what if she'd noticed her—the uninvited guest?

'Well… I shouldn't have. I promise next time, I'll let you have your privacy.'

Jackson cocked his head to one side. 'What if I don't want my privacy?' This sent a tingle down the back of her legs. 'What if I *like* you watching?'

Now Chloe was speechless. He *had* liked it. She knew on some level this was true, but now he'd admitted it. Her lips parted, and she realized she had no idea what to say.

'What if I want you to watch?' He moved closer to the window, pressing his palm against it, as he glanced up at her. 'What if I want you to do *more* than watch?'

Her throat went dry and she swallowed—hard.

'Well, I'm sure your girlfriend might feel differently.' There. She'd said it!

Jackson frowned and gave a single shoulder shrug. 'Oh, she's not my girlfriend.'

Suddenly, Chloe felt a hard pit in her stomach. Not his girlfriend? Oh, please not something more… She hoped not fiancée or…even worse, his wife!

'What is she?'

'Just a friend.' Jackson's tone was all business.

She remembered the night before, how he'd been so deep inside her, thrusting again and again, each time ever deeper. Longer. Harder. 'You didn't *look* like just friends.'

'We sometimes take advantage of certain benefits,' he added.

'Friends with benefits.'

'Actually, to be honest, more like just the benefits. Annaliese…prefers it that way. We rarely talk, except…well, about positions.' He chuckled a little. 'And speed.'

Chloe swallowed the excitement building in her. The woman didn't mean anything to him, not in any real way. She remembered how his eyes lit up when he saw her watching. Did that mean she excited him even more than Annaliese?

'Chloe, I was wondering…'

Was he going to invite her over? The thought sent a shiver of excitement down the back of her legs.

'Aren't you hot? I'm feeling a little bit warm.' Jackson pulled at the hem of his shirt and then whipped it over his head. Chloe sucked in a breath. The man was all brawn and tattoos, a dangerous combination that immediately sent her heart racing. Her attention lingered on the glorious vee that dipped into the waistband of his shorts. He glanced up at her, expression playful. 'Now, your turn.'

'Mine?' Oh, God. Was she going to take off her shirt? Was she seriously going to do this?

'Only if you want to.' He grinned. Part of her did want to—that was the crazy thing!

Then she remembered that beneath her tank was one of her newest sports bras. It had a sexy vee, a keyhole and lots of crisscrossing straps. At least she'd had the foresight to wear one today. It had full coverage and was hardly scandalous, but it did lift the girls, a hint of cleavage at the neckline. She could remove her shirt and be wearing more than she did on the beach.

'I don't want you to do anything you're not comfortable doing. And, besides, I'm over here. I can't even touch you.'

That's the only problem, she thought.

'Fine.' She tugged off her tank, revealing the low-cut push-up bra.

'You're beautiful,' he said, awe in his voice. 'I want to see more.'

'You first.'

He grinned, just the hint of a smile on his face. He didn't hesitate as he put his thumbs into the waistband of his shorts and tugged them down. In seconds, she saw his dark blue boxer briefs that left absolutely nothing to the imagination, the bulge in the front of them enormous. She hadn't imagined the size of him the night before. Even not standing at attention, his bulge was impressive. Everywhere she looked she saw tight, taut muscle, a man built for sex.

'Your turn.' He cocked his head to one side, anticipating her next move.

Well, I'm in this far, she thought. She cautiously slipped out of her yoga capris, revealing a low-cut black string bikini. She inwardly felt grateful she wasn't wearing an embarrassing print one—with red cherries or the ones covered in a Wonder Woman emblem.

'You're gorgeous,' Jackson breathed, a murmur in her ear, as he looked at her appreciatively. 'I wish I could touch you.'

'Me, too,' she barely whispered, not believing she could actually be this bold. Was it the alleyway that separated them? The glass? She felt like a different person somehow, and yet…very much herself at the same time.

'If I stare at you much longer, I'm going to need to take these off.' His hands skimmed the front of his underwear.

Her heart thudded like a bass drum beating in her chest. Yes. That's what she wanted. To see him naked again. To see his powerful self, fully and completely on display for her. She wanted to see all of him. And, she realized with a shock, she wanted him to see her, too.

Then she heard a high-pitched whistle. 'Nice undies!' shouted a garbageman from the alleyway. She'd been so engrossed in Jackson, she'd missed the city worker who was wheeling trash cans to his truck waiting near the curb by the sidewalk. Instinctively, she covered herself with one arm and backed away from the window, her face feeling like it was on fire. She wrapped the curtain around herself, toga-style.

'I'm going to demolish that jerk,' Jackson said, pecs flexing as he glared down at the garbageman. He was all mean brawn, and for a second, Chloe imagined he would literally destroy the out-of-shape city worker if given the chance.

'No, it's okay. I'm standing half-naked in front of my window!'

'I'm sorry about that,' Jackson said, frowning. 'I'll go down there and make sure he doesn't look in your window ever again.'

Chloe had visions of the city worker beaten to a pulp.

'No! That's okay. I'm fine. Really.'

'You sure?'

'Yeah.' Chloe grinned, still feeling self-conscious, her heart beating wildly. What did she expect? She was half-naked during the day in front of her own window!

'I feel responsible.' Jackson looked contrite. 'Let me make it up to you.'

'How?'

'Let me take you out to dinner.'

CHAPTER FIVE

CHLOE SPENT THE rest of the afternoon trying to figure out what to wear, even though part of her hoped that at the end of the night, she'd leave all her clothes on Jackson's floor. She imagined a dozen scenarios, all of which ended with him taking her on his couch, in full view of that window, just like he had Annaliese. Her stomach twisted into a knot when she thought of the gorgeous model-thin waif he'd had. It shouldn't turn her on so much and yet every time she thought about it, she felt a little tickle in her tummy. Friends with benefits, he'd said. Or, really, just benefits. But how many of those did he have? And was she going to fill yet another spot in his schedule?

She wondered.

She also wondered if she really cared.

It had been months since Kevin called her the wrong name in bed. Months since she'd broken it off with the man who failed to truly see her. Who didn't understand what she did for a living or why she did it, who forgot her very name in the most intimate of moments. She was ready to move on, she decided. She'd hidden in her apartment long enough.

Her buzzer rang promptly at seven, and Chloe gave a hasty check of her appearance in the mirror: short sundress, strappy, sexy heels, her hair up in a messy, thrown-together way that took her nearly an hour to perfect. Her stomach buzzed with nerves as she grabbed her small cross-body bag and headed for the door. The last thing she saw before she'd headed to the hallway was Jackson's darkened window, and with a thrill, she realized she might be there later that very night.

When she swung open her glass front door, Jackson stood on the stoop, dressed in a starched collared shirt, open to the third button, and jeans, looking every inch the billionaire…and the bad boy, a hint of his tattoo visible near the open collar of his shirt. His stark blue eyes lit up when he saw her as he gave a low, almost wolfish whistle.

'You're a knockout,' he said, and she felt a blush creep up her neck.

'So are you… I mean, even with clothes on.' She laughed an anxious laugh and he joined her. It was strange. She'd seen him completely naked, and yet with clothes, he seemed even sexier somehow.

'Did I mention you're gorgeous?' He leaned in to give her a hug. He pressed her to his chest, and she felt herself melt into him. 'I'll be staring at you all night,' he whispered in her ear, and she felt his hot breath on her neck.

'I hope so,' she blurted, before she knew she was

speaking her thoughts aloud, and the blush grew hotter. 'I mean, good.'

He pulled away and grinned. His blue eyes sparkled. 'You sure you want to go to dinner?' He nodded up at his apartment. 'We could order in.'

Yes. That's a fantastic idea, she was about to say before she caught herself. What was it about him that made her throw caution to the wind—and her clothes as well, if earlier was any indication? Then her stomach grumbled—loudly.

He frowned, ever so slightly. 'Nope, better get some food in you,' he said. 'Our car awaits.'

'Car?' she asked, thinking of the Maserati she saw the first day, but then he nodded to the sleek Bentley waiting at the curb. A driver in a jacket and dark pants waited for them, holding open the back door.

Chloe felt her mouth drop open. She'd never ridden in a limo before. In a *Bentley* limo. No wonder he had gorgeous women at his beck and call. Who wouldn't want this kind of luxury?

'I find it's easier this way. So I can drink and not worry.' He took her arm and led her to the car. She ducked into the plush leather seats that smelled new, and waited for him to walk around the car and join her in the back seat. He slid in next to her, and Chloe felt his body heat as his leg pressed into hers. She glanced around the car feeling a little bit uneasy. How could a man who had all of this ever settle for just one woman?

And why am I thinking about that, anyway? I'm supposed to be looking for a rebound, like Ryan sug-

*gested. Why am I even thinking this isn't going to be
anything but amazing sex? Superhot, naughty sex?*

'Where are we going?' she asked him.

'That depends. Do you feel like champagne and
caviar or whiskey and pork belly?'

Chloe didn't hesitate. 'I love whiskey, so that's
my vote.'

She'd had her share of craft whiskeys and bourbons,
something her light beer–drinking ex never quite understood. But Chloe liked what she liked, and she
wasn't going to make apologies for it.

Surprise flickered across Jackson's features as he
studied her in the darkened back seat of the Bentley.
Chicago slid by them, the city beginning to come to
life as the summer sun hit the horizon.

'A girl who loves whiskey? You're after my own
heart.'

Chloe felt a little glow of warmth in her chest.

'I've never been a frilly, white-wine-with-an-ice-
cube kind of girl.'

He laughed a little. 'Then you're my kind of girl.'
Jackson held her gaze for a beat, his blue eyes promising more.

'Ed,' Jackson said, addressing his driver, but never
moving his gaze from her face. 'Take us to Longman
in Logan Square.'

The sun had just set as they zoomed west, away
from sparkling Lake Michigan, and down Diversey,
the streetlights flickering on as they drove past bou-
tiques and little cafés on their way to Logan Square,

one of Chicago's eclectic, diverse neighborhoods west of downtown, known for attracting aspiring artists and musicians.

Chloe could feel Jackson's attention on her as they drove through the darkening summer dusk.

'What are you thinking about?' he asked her.

About you, naked, taking me every which way possible.

'Uh…what do you do for a living? To afford a Bentley?'

'Real estate.' Jackson shrugged. 'I used to be a bartender, actually, but then my dad died of a heart attack and left me insurance money. I bought up some bankrupt properties at the right time, fixed them up myself and made quite a profit. Now I've got a little company.'

The Bentley rolled past a billboard-sized ad painted across a nearby building that read *Drake Properties*.

'Wait—that's you? Drake Properties? I see those signs everywhere.'

'I get around.' He grinned as he stroked his goatee. She wanted to do the same.

'Must be weird.' She couldn't even begin to imagine what it would be like to be a real estate magnate. They drove past a bar advertising Chicago's local Goose Island brew as throngs of people crowded the sidewalks.

'Why?' He seemed puzzled.

'Because you go from just ordinary bartender to über-rich guy in a short amount of time. What's the best thing about being rich?'

Jackson glanced out the window. She got the impression that he didn't like to talk about money. 'I dunno. Not worrying, I guess.'

'And the worst?'

His attention snapped back to her, sharp blue eyes intelligent and calculating. 'You think there's something bad about being rich?'

'I'm sure there is. What do they say...mo' money, mo' problems?'

He focused on her intently. She felt the weight of his gaze.

'Nobody has ever asked me that before.'

Chloe grinned. 'Well, I guess I'm not like anybody else you've met.'

Jackson's eyes sparkled. 'No, you're not.'

'So what is the worst thing about being rich?'

'Being invisible,' Jackson answered quickly, without hesitation.

She glanced around the inside of their slick limo.

'That can't be,' she said. 'I mean, you've got this flashy car, and tons of cash, and isn't that the opposite of being invisible?'

Jackson shrugged. 'People start to see just the money. They don't care about the monkey in the monkey suit anymore, it's just the label on the suit that matters. My last girlfriend only saw me as walking dollar signs. She tried to get pregnant—on purpose behind my back. She used one of our...condoms, if you can believe it. To try to get child support.'

'That's awful!' How could a woman do that? Chloe couldn't imagine the cold calculations that would lead a woman to do something like that. Chloe would only ever want to have a baby for love, with a partner she'd trust to be a good father. Having one simply to get money was something that had never occurred to her.

'Well, it happens, more often than you'd think. People don't see me. They just see what I can buy.' He shrugged a beefy shoulder, as if he'd long ago become resigned to this fact.

'I know what it's like to be invisible,' Chloe said, thinking that she had more in common with her hunky neighbor than just attraction. 'My old boyfriend never saw me. He even called me by another woman's name. During…you know…'

'What?' Jackson sat straight up, his spine rigid. 'How could he do that?'

'He just never really saw me. I just fit a role in his life, but he never really cared about me.'

'He's an idiot. And he's blind. You're gorgeous.'

Chloe felt her insides grow warm at the compliment. Jackson reached over and took her hand, and she felt a little electric current run up her arm. His hand was so big and warm.

They arrived at the famous whiskey bar in Logan Square and Jackson breezed in, and after a few words to the hostess, managed to snag them a corner table in the crowded restaurant with the masculine decor, the wooden ceilings, the long dark bar, and the wood-and-metal bar stools that gave the bar an antique and rustic feel at the same time. The menu was anything but rustic, however, as Chloe saw foie gras among many of the small-plate offerings.

'How did we get a table so fast?' she asked him, noticing the crowd of patrons waiting for seats at the bar.

'They know me,' he said and shrugged.

Chloe let that sink in for a minute. She wondered how many other connections he had around the city. She could see why women would be impressed, dazzled by the man's money and his influence, but what about the man?

'So, a man like you, who seems to have everything.' She glanced out the front window at the Bentley that slid away from the curb outside, the driver who would be back for them later. 'You've got all your needs taken care of. So what is it that you still want?'

He hesitated, mulling over her question, as they both looked over the menu.

'Conversation, like we're having now,' he said, and grinned at her.

'You can't be serious. You have... Annaliese. And...'

He laughed a little sheepishly. 'I know it sounds crazy, but I want more than that. I always have. A family, a partner. Something long-term.'

'You want to give up the literal wet dream of every man I know. All the sex he can handle, but none of the responsibility.' Chloe rolled her eyes, and he laughed. She liked that he could take her ribbing, that he wasn't ultrasensitive. Guys with fragile egos were a major turnoff. Chloe thought about Kevin, about how he'd ultimately looked to other women to constantly validate himself. He didn't feel like a man unless he was cheating. It was sad, really.

The waiter materialized, and he ordered two of their finest whiskeys.

'I want a real relationship,' he said. 'I want a real connection. Someone special to share my success with, but I've almost given up on finding that person.'

'Why? Because of your ex?'

He nodded, looking a bit sad.

'It's just…hard to be put in a box,' he added now. 'Women see the money and then, well, they don't care about anything else. I'd dismiss the friends with benefits in a heartbeat if I found the real partner.'

'Really?'

'Really.' Jackson fixed her with a serious stare. His blue eyes flashed with honesty. A little bit of hope flared in her chest. Maybe he wasn't a hopeless playboy after all. Maybe she wasn't crazy in thinking the connection they had might go beyond the physical.

'So, am I here auditioning for the part of friend with benefits? Or…something else?'

A slow smile spread across his face. 'Which will get you into my bed faster?'

Chloe threw back her head and laughed. She loved flirting with this man, loved the raw, powerful energy she felt coming off him in waves. She dared not answer that question, because she was pretty sure she'd slip into his bed without any trouble at all.

Jackson grinned as the waiter delivered their drinks and the two clinked glasses. Chloe sipped at the cool amber liquid, amazed at its taste. This was far beyond Jack Daniel's.

'So, time for me to ask you, a beautiful, single and successful woman like yourself... What do you want?'

'I'm not as successful as you,' she conceded as she took a sip of her rich aged rye whiskey.

'You are renting an expensive apartment without a roommate. You work from home, and you've got your own little social media empire there and you're younger than thirty. I'd say you're pretty successful.'

Chloe put down the glass. The candle at the center of their table flickered in the dim light of the bar, as shadows danced across Jackson's handsome face.

'That's true,' Chloe said, but failed to add that sometimes paying bills was tight. She supposed she did all right in the balance. When her tax refund came in, then she paid down debt and even had extra to tuck away in an IRA. Still, she'd be lying if she said she didn't envy Jackson's independent wealth. Who wouldn't want to not worry about where the next car payment was coming from?

They shared a batch of delicious small plates and another round of drinks, and Chloe found her head spinning from the rich food, the good company and the amber whiskey in her glass. She found herself jumping ahead, wondering what it would be like to date someone like Jackson Drake. Or was this just how he treated all his 'friends with benefits'?

She watched as the waitress kept her eyes on Jackson, the way she took note of his Rolex watch.

'Why did you convert the building next door?' she asked him. 'Why did you want all that space?'

Jackson shrugged. 'I guess I wanted to be in the city, but I didn't want neighbors.'

Chloe cocked an eyebrow. 'You've got me.'

'You're a beautiful neighbor,' he said, correcting himself. 'I was more worried about disturbing them, actually, with some of the noise I make.'

'Having sex with beautiful girls?' Chloe quirked an eyebrow as she took a sip of her drink.

Jackson let out a bark of a laugh. 'Well, yes and no. I have a workshop. For woodwork. I like to work with my hands, always have,' he explained. 'Since I started my company, I do less of that, but I'd like to do more.'

Chloe felt a ripple of surprise. The man made things? Next, he'd tell her he was into other manly things: riding motorcycles, hunting, chopping down trees. She wouldn't be surprised. It would explain his bulging muscles.

'What do you make?'

'Furniture, mostly. Antique bar stools. Tables. That sort of thing.' Jackson nodded toward the bar with the old swivel bar stools: wooden on top, antique metal on the bottom. 'I made those.'

'You *made* those?' Chloe gaped at the stools lining the dark oak bar.

'I found the metal, those old pipes, in a building I bought in Printer's Row, an old pipe manufacturer that Al Capone once used to store some of his bootleg. The city is full of amazing antiques, some right in front of you, and with a little elbow grease, you can reuse them, repurpose them.'

'I love that. It's one of the things I love about Chicago, about how it's both an old city and a new one, all at once.' Chloe felt like in that moment they shared a brain. Her friends never quite understood her fascination with both old and new.

'It's what I love about the city, too,' he said. 'It's why I like to take old buildings and make them livable and usable again.

'It's a hobby.' Jackson took a drink. 'When I was first flipping properties, I'd go to stage them with furniture, but never really liked what I found. Sometimes, I'd end up making my own pieces. It's what my dad did for a living, actually. I'd probably be a carpenter like him if I hadn't made those real estate investments.'

'Which do you like doing more?'

'I like them both,' he admitted. 'The woodworking gives me something to do with my hands.'

Chloe remembered just how well he'd used his hands.

'I'd like to see your shop sometime.'

'Really?'

'Yeah, I would. I admire that you make things. All of my work is in the virtual world, so sometimes I feel like I've got nothing to show for all the hours I've put in.' Chloe shrugged.

'But today, social media is everything,' Jackson said. 'Maybe you could help with Drake Properties, too. If you're taking new clients.'

Would she! 'Uh, yeah, I—I'd love to work with you. I mean, what an honor! You'd be more than welcome as a client.' Chloe failed to mention he'd automatically be her biggest client. The second being a well-known consulting firm in town. But she had no client as high-profile as Drake Properties.

'Right now, we don't have a centralized media presence. I have an assistant who posts to my account and then, of course, we have individual agents.' Jackson pulled up an account and showed her the feed.

Chloe thumbed through the feed and nodded. 'This is typical of businesses with a lot of independent contractors,' she said. 'You've got a lot of individual posts, agents selling or flipping properties, but you don't have a cohesive social media message from the corporation itself. We can change that.'

'Can you?' Jackson looked at Chloe appreciatively. She felt a little blush creep up her cheeks.

'Yes, and you can leverage the followers your individual agents already have. I can work out a plan for you. We can make this happen.' Chloe felt confident she could get a lot of buzz going about Drake Properties, especially since it was already practically a household name in Chicago. Social media was all about understanding how to tap into the power of people.

'You seem to be a woman of many talents.' He studied her over his now-empty plate and Chloe felt rooted to the spot. She'd never felt so *visible* before, so fully and openly seen. There was something about the way Jackson studied her, the way he asked her questions, the way he listened, that made her feel he was fully present. She hadn't felt this valued since the last time she'd had dinner with her parents, who lived in Seattle and came to Chicago twice a year. It was always an interrogation fest, as her mom worked to make up for lost time. Chloe was their only child, but they also just retired and spent a fair amount of their time traveling.

She liked being the focus of Jackson's attention. She felt like she knew him, almost as if she'd known him much longer than just a couple of days. *Then again, I did see him...naked. And...intimate. Why wouldn't I feel intimacy?*

Chloe knew she was getting ahead of herself—again. She was a planner and liked to think three or four moves ahead, and she hadn't even slept with Jackson yet and she was already trying to figure out if they *worked*. Why couldn't she just turn her brain off and...enjoy this? Why did she have to analyze every angle?

It was what made her a good social media publicist, though, thinking through scenarios, predicting outcomes.

Chloe felt full, her head spinning with whiskey and with the proximity to Jackson's fit body. The longer the dinner wore on, the more Chloe was aware what might be coming after. She'd been keenly aware of the skin she could see: his strong forearms, his strong, thick neck, braided with muscle; and more than aware of the skin hidden beneath his clothes, and the very impressive bits of him that lay covered still. She was both eager and anxious all at the same time to see them once more.

What if he was actually too big for her? Then again, what if he were the very best sex of her life? Throughout dinner, she felt like she was walking a knife's blade of anticipation. It hadn't even occurred to her *not* to sleep with him.

The waiter set the bill on the table and they both reached for it.

'No,' Jackson said, shaking his head firmly. 'I said I'd buy.'

'But can I help?' She didn't want him to think she was one of those girls who was just after his money. And she did make her own. She could help pay her own way.

'Not this time,' he said. 'My treat.'

Reluctantly, she let him take the check. He paid for it with a luxury credit card, one of those heavy metal cards that could probably take a bullet in an emergency. It hit the table with a *thunk* and she eyed it, wondering if this was just one more way the rich were different. They carried around cards made of *literal* platinum.

'Are you in the mood for dessert?' he asked her.

'Are you?' she asked, uncertain about what he had in mind.

'I am interested in dessert.' He studied her, amusement in his eyes. 'But only the kind we have at my place.'

CHAPTER SIX

JACKSON FELT AN impatience welling in him as they left the restaurant and ducked into the back seat of his Bentley. He'd known from the second he saw Chloe watching him from her fourth-floor window that he wanted her, and having dinner together only increased his desire. Throughout dinner, he'd been mesmerized by her dark, knowing eyes, the same eyes that had watched him the night before when he'd been with Annaliese, those eyes that had driven him to heights he hadn't felt in years. She'd even offered to pay some of the bill.

Only after you'd admitted most women only want you for your money, a nagging little cynical voice in his head said. *She could still be playing you.*

Yet something told him she wasn't. She'd been genuinely interested in the furniture he made, which astounded him. Most women found it boring, because that was a hobby that didn't make him much money. For the time he put into each piece, they cost more to make than to sell, but he still enjoyed the work, and the feeling of making something useful. And he loved *talking* with her, loved the way her mind worked, loved her quirky sense of humor. It was the first time in a long time he'd found a woman's brain as sexy as her body, and he wondered if that played a part in fueling his desire.

He wasn't going to get ahead of himself. Not this time. If he really analyzed his feelings, which he had no intention of doing, he'd probably figure out that rushing into sex was his way of avoiding feeling at all. Desire and want—well, those things were easily solved. Love and intimacy? Those were complicated animals, best left alone, since pursuing them inevitably led to disappointment.

He held her hand as his driver, Ed, thumped the door shut and slipped behind the wheel. There was no partition between the back seat and the front, but Ed normally kept to himself, a man of few words but excellent driving skills, and was an ex-Beret. Jackson kept him purely on a part-time basis, but Ed was happy to be his exclusive driver, especially since he got to drive the Bentley.

'Home, please, Ed,' he told him, and he nodded, pulling away from the curb without another word. Chloe had grown quiet in the car, her face obscured by shadows, and the streetlights occasionally illuminating her big, dark eyes. He ran his finger up the soft skin of her bare arm, and she shivered beneath this touch. How he wanted her to watch him do all kinds of unspeakable things to her. Her lips parted, ever so slightly, as if she were about to say something, but then caught herself. He saw the outline of her full lips in the streetlights flickering by. How he wanted to taste them.

He glanced at Ed, in the front seat, his eyes fixed on the road. No, he wouldn't kiss her. Not yet. He moved his hand downward, toward the hem of her skirt, which hit just above the knee. He traced the amazing caramel-colored skin there with one finger, silently asking a question. When she glanced at him, dark eyes welcoming the touch, he continued his exploration. Ever so slightly, she shifted, moving her knees a little apart: an invitation.

She glanced down, watching his hands as they moved up to her inner thigh. He gave just a little squeeze there, and she sucked in a breath. God, her skin was so soft. His hand disappeared beneath the fabric of her short sundress and went farther up her leg. He saw her glance up at Ed, his back to them, his eyes fixed on the road. Her lips were slightly parted, pupils dark and wide. He stroked her inner thigh and felt the goose bumps rise there as he moved ever upward. She spread her knees even wider apart, an invitation. He gently, so softly, felt the edge of her lacy thong. He stroked her through the fine fabric and he could feel her heat, her want, there.

Her eyes flickered closed as she leaned backward into the leather seat, her chest rising. He could see her nipples rise against the thin lace of her halter bra, her back arching while her full breasts struggled against the thin fabric of her sundress. He teased her, rubbing her lightly and then softly, a caress that promised more to come. She welcomed him there, her legs stretching apart even more as he stoked the flame of her heat. Her breath deepened and a flush crept up the side of her face. She was primed for him. He could feel just how ready she was, her desire soaking the thin lace lining of her underwear. Unable to help himself, his finger slipped past the thin barrier and then he felt her bare: hot, willing and wet. God, she was so wet, so slick beneath his fingers. He wanted her. Wanted her now.

His own groin grew tight then, straining against the confines of his pants. Then, amazingly, she reached out for him, her hand covering the growing bulge, working her fingers across him, making him stiffen even more. Soon, he'd have to unzip himself just to relieve the pressure. She looked at him now, her dark eyes full of mischief and daring as they shared this dirty secret, Ed none the wiser as he slowed at a stoplight on Fullerton.

Now, with her hand on him, he couldn't wait. He pulled her to him with his free hand and kissed her, pressing his lips against hers, wanting to devour her. The kiss turned white-hot as he continued to explore her with his fingers. She opened her mouth to him and he tasted her with his tongue, his goatee brushing against her chin. Below, he felt her clench tightly around his fingers. God, so tight. How he wanted to explore the deepest, warmest part of her. She kept her hand on him as well, and he pressed against her hand, desperate for more of her touch. He strained against the confines of his pants.

Ed might have seen them by now, his green eyes

in the rearview mirror, but Jackson didn't care. He
was paid well for his discretion. Chloe didn't seem
to care they had an audience, either. Did she like to
be watched, almost as much as she liked to watch?
The naughty thought thrilled him. Yes, this is what
he wanted, a woman who was daring, who was bold,
who knew what she wanted and went for it. That was
what had turned him on so much when she'd watched
him through his window. This was a woman who
wasn't afraid.

He deepened the kiss and their tongues met in a
kind of heated, primal dance. Instinct took over as
he pushed his finger deeper inside her, finding the
delicious ridges that he knew would be her most sensitive spot. She groaned into his mouth. He felt her
delicious warm wetness. He wanted her. He wanted
her now. Then, the car came to a stop and Ed cleared
his throat, loudly, before opening and shutting his
door—a cue to him as he realized with a start they
now sat in the alley near his building. Had they kissed
the entire way home? Her delicious scent still clung
to his fingers when he pulled away from her and she
tugged down the hem of her skirt.

Ed opened the door and Chloe got out, face
flushed. Jackson watched her toned, tanned legs as
they moved from the car before he followed her out.

'Thanks, Ed. That'll be all tonight.'

Ed just gave a curt nod and ducked into the driver's
seat without a word. Once he backed away from the
door, Jackson slipped his hand around Chloe's lower

back and pushed a code into his back door keypad. The door swung open.

They kissed again once inside the door, passionate, urgent, the door still half-open, as he pressed her to the wall, his hand running up the outside of her leg. His tongue dived deeper into her mouth. She tasted so good, all he wanted to do was kiss her again and again. Finally, he broke away, panting. He saw her in the dim light of his staircase, lips swollen from kissing, dark hair ruffled and eyes fixed on him.

'Let's go upstairs,' she suggested. Before he could argue she was tugging him by the hand, up the two flights of dimly lit stairs to his living room. He strained against his pants the entire way, finding walking awkward since he wanted her so badly. He would've done her in the stairwell, hot, urgent, eager. But he soon realized she wanted to be in the room before his open windows. She flicked on the lamp, the same light he'd had on the night before. She walked to the window and glanced out, up at her own apartment, just across the alley. Her apartment was dark now, the alley deserted.

When she turned to face him, she slipped one spaghetti strap of her sundress down her shoulder. Then came the other one, and before he knew it, she'd shimmied out of it, letting it fall to the ground in a soft heap of cotton.

She stood before him in a lace halter bra and matching thong, her breasts large and heavy, yet seeming to defy gravity. Then she walked to him, all gorgeous curves. He wanted to memorize every one

of those delicious lines and taste every inch of that
soft skin. He bent down to kiss her, and he reached
around her back, undoing the halter bra fastener with
one hand, releasing her full breasts. He cupped them,
and she moaned, arching her back, filling his hands.
Then she found the hem of his shirt. She tugged it
up, and then he was out of it. She pulled away, tracing her pink nails down the front of his bare skin.
He shivered at her touch, straining against the strict
confines of his pants. He needed to be free, and she
sensed that as she found the zipper of his pants. She
released him, and he stepped out of his pants and
boxer briefs, standing bare before her. She dived in,
working him hard with both her hands. Now it was
his turn to groan.

'You're even bigger than I thought, and I thought
you were big,' she murmured into his mouth.

'It's all for you,' he said, and meant it. He wanted
every inch of himself inside her. Her hands worked
the length of him as his need grew. She pulled back
and their eyes met, an electric current zapping between them. Her dark gaze drove him wild. Even
as she stared at him now, topless, her nipples puckering, he grew harder in her hands. This is what he
wanted: her eyes watching him. Watching every move
he made.

She released him and then tugged down her thong
so it fell to the floor.

'Do me…like you did her,' she commanded, voice
low.

Yes, he thought, he would take her just like he'd

had Annaliese the night before. Wrong on some level, maybe. Yet on another, ever so right. He flipped her over, kneading the firm skin of her rounded backside, now all of her inner pinkness in full view. He reached down and grabbed a Magnum condom from the pocket of his pants on the floor, anticipation running through him. The moment he'd been waiting for, he'd fantasized about, was here.

CHAPTER SEVEN

CHLOE WAITED, HER body an electric current of want as she bent over the couch, Jackson behind her. Could she take all of him? He was…so big. All of her lovers had been pretty much adequate to average, or even the small side of average.

Chloe felt Jackson rub his thick tip against her thighs. So big. So monstrously big.

She remembered Annaliese's face from the night before, pure ecstasy as she took him. All of him. Now it was her turn. But first, Jackson teased her. He rubbed himself against her. She didn't think she could be more turned on, and yet as he touched her, she grew hotter, the need burning inside her like a flame. She glanced out his windows and saw a light come on in her building, a single yellow square across the alley.

For a second, she worried her neighbor would see her, just as she'd seen Annaliese and Jackson the night before.

But then he slipped the massive knob of his tip inside her and all worry about modesty fled her mind.

He pushed in an inch, maybe more, parting her, testing her wetness. God, so big. So hard. Just the first part. He worked himself slowly, gently, teasing her, making her want even more. Now it was all she could do not to cry out. He wasn't even all the way in yet, and she was parted in a way she'd never been. *Yes*, she thought. *Yes. I want you. All you can give me.*

She glanced at another square of light across the alley beneath closed blinds. Did she care if she was seen? She didn't care. Let them watch.

This is what I needed. What I've always needed.

'Do you want more?' he asked her, voice a low rumble.

'Yes,' she croaked, a slave to her own desire, her own need to have him. All of him. In full view of her neighbors. She didn't care. Couldn't care. All she thought about was him behind her as he pushed forward a little deeper. She cried out in pleasure as he stretched her even more. She was so full, so deliciously full.

'More?'

'More!' she cried out, wondering how much more she could take. Then again, she was so very wet, her body willing to take all of him. He slid in the full length of himself, and she nearly came right then as he pressed her limits, finding the deepest, virgin parts of her. Only he had been this deep. Only he had parted her like this.

'Oh, God…' he murmured, voice catching in his throat. 'You're so…tight. So very tight.'

She burned with need, with want, with overwhelming desire. Then he slid out, ever so slowly, before moving right back in. Chloe barely noticed the windows now, her thoughts focused on the sensations running through her body. Oh, God. She was going to come right now. She'd never felt like this before, never realized how primal sex could be. She was a slave to his power, to his pure physical domination as he took her, harder now, from behind, reaching deeper inside her, setting her on fire as he made her burn for him again and again. She was going to come, and she'd never come this way before, never come with a man taking her from behind. Yet now she knew exactly how Annaliese felt, bent over the couch, dominated by a man who was born to pleasure a woman. No wonder she'd come so quickly. How could she resist? How could she *not* come, not when every inch of her cried out to come, to shout for mercy? Watching him had been amazing, but nothing compared to being with him, to having him inside her, so very deep.

A light across the alley flickered off. Another, on the second floor, came on, and a man walked across it, yawning, not having seen them. If he looked up… he'd see everything. But he didn't, and instead, sauntered out of view.

So dangerous. So deliciously wrong. They should shut the blinds.

Yet part of Chloe liked being wild, liked feeling like a primal animal in a city where laws were supposed to rein in desire, pin people in. Yes, this was what she wanted. To be on display, just like Annaliese the night before, to let everybody see that Jackson desired her, wanted her, was so very hard for her. *He wants me*, the open windows shouted to the world. *He's having me. He's making me come.*

Jackson thrust harder and she vaulted over the edge, hitting a peak of pleasure she'd never felt before. She cried out his name then, hoarse, raw, as he gripped her hips hard, riding her as she came, pushing inside her, deeper, for every wave of pleasure, making every ripple of her climax last longer than she thought possible. Her whole body contracted and shuddered in wave after wave of pure pleasure she'd never felt before. As the last bit of her shocking climax ebbed away, he slowed, and she wondered how she could continue. Her knees had grown weak, her legs shaking from spent passion. He withdrew, and she collapsed atop his couch.

'I want to see you,' he said, and turned her over. She saw him then, his impressive physical prowess, and still couldn't believe his size. She'd taken that. She'd taken it all. He moved her so that she was lying on her back on the couch and moved to take her once more. Could she do this? She felt so spent, so worn, and yet, as she gazed up at his sharp blue eyes, her body came alive again. Those eyes, she thought. Her heart pumped harder, just like it had when she'd met his gaze through the window. Could it be she wasn't yet satisfied? It was true. She wanted him once more.

He pushed into her again, stretching her to her limits.

She wondered if he could even move inside her,

and yet somehow he did. He was above her now, his eyes watching her as she touched his chest, slipping down his shoulder tattoo now visible to her. It was the wing of a dragon. Big, strong, powerful.

'Chloe,' he moaned. His breath came sharply. 'I don't know if I can...if I can hold it.' She could see the strain in his face. She felt his need for her as he picked up the pace, as he slid in and out, as he seemed to amazingly grow harder, bigger, inside her. Every nerve ending in her body came alive as she once again began a steady climb to another climax. She felt the need building in her, the red-hot desire. She saw a dim reflection of herself in his steely blue eyes, she saw how much he wanted her as well, and that knowledge drove her wild.

'I can't hold it. I can't...' He fought, but lost the battle, though it didn't matter, because after a few more deep thrusts, she once again found herself swept up in a tidal wave of uncontrollable pleasure. She shut her eyes against the rush of pure release, a shout ripped from her throat as she was powerless to stop it. He cried out, too, and then he collapsed on top of her, their sweat-slicked bodies sliding together in delicious harmony. Chloe felt the weight of him on her, the delicious weight, her chest pressed against his taut muscles. The man was all muscle. All raw power.

'I'm sorry. I usually, uh, last longer than that.' Jackson looked sheepish as he pulled himself up on his elbows.

'I came twice,' Chloe breathed. 'I think you lasted long enough.'

He chuckled, a rumble she could feel with his belly pressed against hers, him slowly softening inside her.

'You were...' His blue eyes sparkled. 'So deliciously tight. I couldn't help it. You made me come so fast.'

A blush crept up her cheek. 'I'd never had someone so big, uh, before.'

'Good,' he said, eyes never leaving her face. She glanced at the open windows.

'I've never—' She nodded to the open windows. 'I mean—' She paused. 'Do you always...'

'Leave the blinds open?' He grinned. 'Sometimes. Sometimes not, but there's something about being on display that's hot. Don't you agree?'

Chloe nodded vigorously. 'I just never thought I'd do something like this.'

'I wonder what else we can try next time.' He shot her a wolfish grin and Chloe felt anticipation tickle her toes. *Next time*—that implied there'd be one.

Jackson shifted a little, holding the condom so he could carefully withdraw, but he didn't move from the couch right away, and neither did Chloe. Now that the fury of sex was over, she could truly take him in, his amazing body, his tight muscles and intriguing tattoos.

'What does this mean?' she asked, as she traced the dark looped design around his shoulder. It held the hint of a head of a dragon.

'It's a Celtic symbol for dragon,' he said. 'My father was part Irish and English, and Drake, our family name, means dragon...or snake, depending.'

Chloe giggled a little. 'You certainly have an impressive snake,' she joked.

He laughed as well. 'I don't think that's what the ancestors necessarily had in mind.'

'Well, an apt name anyway.'

'Dad had a dragon tattoo as well, a small one, on his upper biceps. Got it when he joined the navy. I got mine when I turned eighteen. You could say it's a Drake family tradition.' He hugged her a little closer and she snuggled in, their body a tangle of limbs on his couch. 'Someday maybe my son will have one, too. Or daughter.'

'So you want a family?'

'If I find the right girl,' he said. But the way he looked at her now with his sharp blue eyes, she thought he might mean she had a fighting chance. 'Do you want a family?'

'It's all I've ever really wanted, but…' She thought of Kevin. 'It has to be the right person. Someone who'll be a good dad.' *Someone who loves me.*

'Fair enough.' Jackson glanced down at his belly and his now-sleeping member. 'Well, let me take care of this.'

He rolled off the condom and headed to the bathroom. Seconds later, she heard a telltale flush. She remembered his ex, the girlfriend who tried to impregnate herself. She wondered if he now flushed all his condoms for fear of it happening again.

Chloe bit her lip. He didn't trust her. But why would he? They'd only known each other a short time. Still, it bothered her slightly. She wondered why. With him gone, she felt exposed on the couch, more naked than naked. She glanced at the open windows that stared up to her building and saw another light behind mostly closed blinds flicker off. She couldn't see any faces at the windows, and the blinds seemed drawn. Maybe no one had seen them. Maybe everyone had. Who knew?

Still, she realized how reckless she'd been. Now, without Jackson here, she felt a bit vulnerable and scrambled to put on her clothes. She laughed a little to herself. *When have I ever been that bold? Never.* But with Jackson, sex was just…different. Jackson could take her anytime, anyplace, she thought. A body like that. A man who knew what he wanted and wasn't afraid to get it. A man who seemed to be born to pleasure a woman. Why wouldn't she want people to see? Yes, she'd do it all over again, open windows and all. She realized that most of the other men she'd been with had been shier than she was about sex, more conservative, definitely. Jackson wasn't that. He was liberated, out in the open, bold. She liked that. She liked that quite a lot. She remembered how reserved Kevin had been, how he'd insisted on the lights being dim before going at it. She wasn't sure if that was because he was really timid or if it was because he wanted to imagine he was having sex with someone else. Either way, she realized how insecure Kevin had been in all ways. How truly confident Jackson was.

As she stared at the closed bathroom door, his phone, sitting on the end table, dinged. She hadn't meant to look, but then, it was *right* there. Staring her in the face: a message from Annaliese.

Need your glorious cock. Tonight.

Chloe's stomach tightened. Gorgeous Annaliese, from last night. Texting him at nearly midnight. Booty call. Would he take it? She almost wanted to lunge at his phone, delete the message. She glanced at the closed bathroom door. Would he catch her if she did? No, she couldn't do that. It was an invasion of his privacy, and besides, she'd come into this with her eyes open—literally. She'd seen him fuck Annaliese the night before. But two nights in a row? That seemed like an awful lot of benefits for just friends. She shoved the nagging doubt away.

No, she didn't think he'd lied to her.

Then his phone binged again.

I won't look, Chloe told herself. *I won't*...

'Want to take a shower with me?' Jackson called from the closed door of the bathroom. She nearly jumped out of her skin, her heart thudding.

'One sec,' she shouted back.

She couldn't help it. She had to look. The text would disappear soon, behind the pass code of his phone. She glanced at the screen. His phone now showed a text from someone else. Someone named Laurie.

I miss you. Can I come over?

Her whole body ran cold. Who was Laurie?

Remember, he told you: friends...with benefits.
Chloe knew he had more than one, so why did it
bother her to see the evidence?

Then a picture arrived, a headless shot of...bare
breasts, nipples puckered, standing at attention. Followed by a full-frontal shot, showing her hairless
mound, pink lips spread ever so slightly, an invitation.

She stood up, mind whirling. She *knew* this about
Jackson. He'd been more than up-front with her. Hell,
she'd *seen* him with another woman, and yet all the
women on his phone just made her feel dizzy. A little
bit sick. Was she going to be another willing *friend*,
another benefit? Another in a long line of women
desperate for his attention?

And why did she care? Then again, she thought
how amazing the sex had been. She could already
feel herself growing attached, wanting Jackson in a
way she shouldn't. Because he wasn't hers. Probably
would never be hers.

'Chloe?' Jackson asked, from the door of the bathroom.

Chloe jumped back from the end table, terrified
to be caught looking at his phone. 'Actually, I've got
an early-morning meeting tomorrow,' she lied. 'Probably should go.'

*This is best. Get out before you're in too deep. Be-
fore you get too attached.*

'Are you sure?' Jackson hesitated.

Chloe hated lying to him. *Just tell him you saw*

that stuff on his phone. Just freakin' tell him. But she froze. Why wouldn't the words come?

'Chloe,' Jackson said, moving so he stood between her and the door, 'I want you to stay.'

Her head shot up, and she met his blue gaze, serious, unwavering.

'I—I can't,' she said, and went around him, heading for the staircase.

'Why?'

'I thought I could do this. The friends and benefits thing,' she said to him. 'But I don't think I can. I think I'm… I'm looking for something more serious.' There, she'd said it. This was what made the phone messages so hard to take. Sure, she'd fallen into Jackson's arms easily, but she also knew herself well enough to know she wanted more of a connection with him. She wanted something deeper. She couldn't just be one of the rotating faces on his phone. She never wanted to feel like she felt with Kevin: as an afterthought.

'Chloe…'

'No.' She shook her head and gave him a weak smile. 'No, I mean, don't change you, okay? I'm not going to ask you to give up something you don't want to give up. We had a nice time tonight. I just don't want to go on if it's not…well, something more.'

'Let me walk you home,' he said, reaching for his pants.

'No. That's okay,' she said. She hurriedly grabbed her bag, skipped down the stairs and out the alley, terrified he'd come after her. Terrified that he wouldn't.

She glanced up and saw Jackson standing up in his living room, staring down at her through the open window.

Better this way, she thought. Yet why didn't it feel like the right thing to do?

CHAPTER EIGHT

JACKSON DIDN'T KNOW what happened. One minute, he was having the best sex of his life and the next minute, Chloe was running out of his place like it was on fire. He watched as she ducked inside her building on the other side of the lit alley and then he waited, staring at her windows. Eventually, a light came on, but her blinds never came up. At least she was home safe. But what had happened?

He yanked on some shorts and grabbed a beer from his fridge just as his phone dinged.

That was when he realized he had a ton of messages. In an instant, he knew what had happened. Annaliese and Laurie had happened.

Dammit.

Now he got it. Her speech about the friends and benefits. Did he want her as just one more woman in his phone? He wasn't sure. Maybe. Maybe not.

But what he did know was that she'd be at the top of his list. He'd never answer their invitations, not with Chloe in his bed. He found it ironic that usually he was the one shooing women out the door. Now the one he finally wanted to stay fled before he had a chance to convince her she should sleep over. Chloe just felt… different from the others. And he felt differently about her. He'd meant what he'd said about ditching the other women if the right one came into his life, and there was a chance Chloe was the one. She intrigued him in a way he hadn't been intrigued…maybe ever. He also had to admit he liked the fire of her standing up for her convictions, her needs. She'd told him that she wanted more. Like him, she wasn't going to be pushed around. He respected that.

He glanced at Laurie's X-rated texts and deleted them. Honestly, what did his ex think? He'd see her naked and forget all the betrayal? Men were simple creatures, but not *that* simple. He decided to ignore her as he usually did. He still couldn't get the image of her trying to impregnate herself out of his head. She'd said she'd loved him, but really, all she wanted was a paycheck. He watched Chloe's light click off. Was she going to bed? She should be beside him, sleeping.

I'm outside your place.

This made him back away from his window, dread dragging at him. Was she here? Jackson went inside, to his buzzer, where he could also see all views of the outside of his building through closed-circuit TV. He checked all the entrances, but saw no sign of Laurie. Then he remembered: she only knew his old address, the one on North Avenue.

I'm buzzing. Why aren't you answering? I need to talk to you.

This had to stop. He imagined her waking up his neighbors. Or the lawyer who'd bought his new place.

We're done, Laurie. I told you. We're over.

He waited, but didn't get a response. Thank goodness. He thought of Chloe once more. Would she end up just like Laurie? Crazed by all the extra zeros in his bank account? This was why it was just simpler to keep it about sex, he thought. And if everybody knew up-front it was just about sex, then nobody got too attached—either to him *or* to his money.

Honestly, he'd never truly been comfortable with the wealth he'd accumulated in a relatively short time.

He texted Chloe, hoping to smooth the waters.

Had a great time with you. Mean it. Would like to see you again.

She didn't respond. He felt a little disappointment in his stomach, but then that was replaced by determination. He wasn't done with Chloe Park. Not yet.

Now wide-awake, he headed to his laptop to check in on work and found an email from Hailey. Kent had countered his offer with another for Chloe's building. It was as outrageous as he thought it would be, with at least one more zero on the end than it merited. He instructed Hailey to send the man a counteroffer: his price, minus two zeros. After that, still feeling awake, he headed to his wood workshop downstairs and decided to work a little more on his new project, an ornate bar for his house. Even as he put his hands to work, his mind whirled with thoughts of Chloe. For the first time in a long time, a woman occupied his thoughts. Usually he didn't give Annaliese, or any of his other friends with benefits, another thought after a tryst, but now his head was full of images of Chloe's dark eyes. The way she'd come with such an unbridled passion. The way she'd stood in his living room and demanded respect. He might even love that even more. He wanted to see her again. He needed to see her again.

As he molded the wood in his hands, he thought about her soft body, about her tight center. Getting a taste only made him want her more. He'd have to find a way to satisfy that need. He'd figure out a way to see her.

'Well, I'm proud of you, pumpkin, for getting out there.' Ryan sat opposite Chloe in one of their favorite lunch spots in Old Town two days later. He wore a crisp plaid button-down short-sleeved shirt and khakis, his standard business-casual fare. He worked as a buyer for a retail chain and was on his lunch hour. Chloe pushed around the kale salad on her plate, feeling a bit despondent. Ryan had ordered a BLT, which he'd mostly devoured.

'Yeah, I guess.' Chloe wasn't so sure. Jackson had sent her a sweet text, but she hadn't responded. Not

yet. She wasn't certain what she wanted to say. Sometimes she felt completely in control, adult about it,
and philosophical. Jackson had broken no promises.
He'd offered her white-hot, commitment-free sex, and
that was what he'd delivered, and yet at other times
she felt like a middle-schooler who'd been let down
by a crush. 'I don't usually jump into a man's bed on
the *first* date.'

'Oh. Right. You have your three-date rule.' Ryan
rolled his eyes to show what he thought of that. He
was clean shaven, and wore his perfectly coiffed hair
long on top and short on the sides. His dark eyes
studied Chloe.

'Hey! I've got *standards.*'

'I know! I'm kidding. So he must've been hot if
you junked your three-date rule.' Ryan popped a
small french fry in his mouth.

'Beyond hot.' That was the understatement of the
year. Their sex might just fuel her alone-time fantasies for weeks to come. Even now, thinking about
Jackson's strong hands and…massive self made her
belly grow warm.

'So, I get you want more. But how about just be
Buddhist about it. Live in the moment, you know?
He said he *might* be into something more serious.'

'But the women on his phone… I just don't know
if I can hang in there, compete with them.'

'You don't know until you try.' He dipped a french
fry in ketchup, swirling it around at the edge of his
plate.

'You think I should see him again.' Chloe had her

doubts. To her, he seemed like the poster child of a toxic bachelor, the kind that would just toy with her and then eventually break her heart. Like Kevin.

'I think you want to see him again.' Ryan quirked an eyebrow, and even she couldn't argue with truth.

Chloe glanced down at her plate. 'Yes, of course I do, but I think that's a mistake. Not if he doesn't want what I want.'

Ryan's eyes grew wide. 'Tell me again how seeing a gorgeous rich man is a mistake? This I have to hear.'

'Because I'm just a number, one more willing woman in his phone. It feels…not so good. It's Kevin all over again. And I *swore* I'd never do Kevin.' Chloe pushed around the remains of her salad, her appetite whittling even further as her stomach tightened when she remembered the missives on the phone, the gorgeous pictures of naked women. How could she compete with a torrent of willing women? And he'd told her he preferred no strings. That's not what she wanted. Not at all.

'First of all, he's not like Kevin,' Ryan said, taking a drink of water. 'Kevin was a rich poser, but this guy really is rich.'

Chloe laughed a little. 'Not funny,' she protested. 'I didn't care about Kevin's money. It was the fact that he couldn't keep his dick in his pants.'

'Right, and about that. Jackson was up-front with you about the other women. He also told you he'd tell them all to take a hike for the right woman, didn't he?'

'I don't want to put pressure on him to do that. Either he does it or not, but I shouldn't have to ask him.' Chloe felt like the man ought to volunteer.

'It's your job to elbow the competition out of the way, girl!' Ryan took a small bite of his sandwich. Sunlight filtered through their sidewalk-side window as pedestrians streamed by. Chloe absently watched a woman walk her tiny dog down the sidewalk and sighed.

'Roller-derby dating isn't my style, and I know myself well enough to know that I don't want to be in a catfight over a man who doesn't even *want* what I want.' Chloe shrugged one shoulder. 'It's just a recipe for disaster. So, I see him again, and we have more awesome sex, and then what? I'm just going to have my heart destroyed—again.' She thought about him flushing the condom. One day she wanted a baby, didn't she? Marriage and the whole nine yards. He wasn't in a position to trust anyone, he'd said so, and maybe he'd never be. 'Besides, you should've seen those women. They're gorgeous.'

Ryan fixed her with a steady, brown-eyed gaze. 'So are you, sweetheart.'

'Pffft. You have to say that because you're my friend.' Chloe exhaled a frustrated breath. She glanced down at her slouchy tee and gym shorts. She wasn't even wearing any makeup today.

'No, actually, if you weren't gorgeous, I'd simply change the subject—awkwardly, and talk about how the Cubs are doing.' Ryan grinned. 'Besides, you told me that he got all hot and bothered when you saw him with what's-her-name?'

'Annaliese.'

'Right. Her. So maybe what's making you so jeal-ous is also making you *attracted* to the man at the same time. Sex is complicated, and often contradic-tory. We want what we don't want most of the time.' Ryan popped a french fry in his mouth. 'But I think you're wise. You know what it is you want. But you're assuming you also know what he wants. You don't know for sure. Maybe you ought to let it play out a bit, see how you feel.'

'You mean sleep with him some more and then see if he commits? But how can I compete with all those other women?'

Ryan nodded, slowly. 'Because you're amazing. Besides, think of all that amazing man meat you get to enjoy until then. Oh, and maybe he'll take you to Girl & the Goat. Or—even better—Alinea.'

Those were Chicago's swankiest restaurants, where a tab for two might easily cost hundreds of dollars.

Chloe barked a laugh, and a few of the other pa-trons turned to stare. 'You're awful.'

'I'm just honest.'

Her cell phone lit up then. It was an incoming mes-sage from Jackson.

I want to see you. You free tomorrow?

At the mere sight of his name on her screen, Chloe felt her body react. Yes, how she did want to ride—er, see—him again. There was no question of that.

'Who is it? Is it him?' Ryan leaned forward, eager. She showed him the screen.

'Looks like someone is getting lucky,' exclaimed Ryan, reading her phone from across their small table. 'Oh…*my*.' He raised his eyebrows, meaning clear. 'What are you going to do?'

'I don't think I should see him.'

'Why?'

'Because I'll get naked again, *that's* why.' Chloe knew her self-control was nil when she was with him.

'And that's wrong how?'

'Because I'll get naked, and then I'll fall in love. It only takes two times. Maybe three for me.' Chloe shrugged. She knew herself. She wished she could have tons of amazing sex and not get involved, but her emotions just wouldn't be kept at bay. And she was already too far along in falling for Jackson, anyhow.

Ryan shook his head. 'You straight girls are a trip.'

Chloe laughed. 'Please. You're worse than me. You were picking out wedding invitations for Brendan two days after you met him.'

Ryan barked a laugh. 'I hate that you remember things. Correctly. It's one of your worst qualities.' Ryan gave her an exaggerated eye roll. 'Okay, fine, so I'm a romantic at heart. You got me. But for the record, Brendan and I had done it *at least* five times by then. Maybe six.'

Chloe laughed. 'Fair enough.'

Ryan chewed thoughtfully. 'You told him you want something more serious, and he's asking you out, so why not wait and see if he offers it?'

'You think?' Chloe wasn't sure. She thought about all those pictures on his phone. Yes, attraction was complicated, but what about her own self-respect?

I don't think that's a good idea, she responded.

'I can't believe you just turned him down!' Ryan cried, looking at the phone. 'How do you know how serious he is—or isn't—until you give him a try?'

'That's the problem. I already tried him. And I like him. Too much.'

Another message came through.

I think we should talk.

'Talk?' Chloe echoed. 'About…?'

'Maybe the man is going to give you what you want.' Ryan took a sip of water, swallowing down a bite of sandwich.

Chloe scoffed. 'You think he's going to want an exclusive relationship with me?'

'Maybe. He said he wants to talk. You know how much guys hate to talk.' Ryan bit into another fry. Chloe studied the phone in her hand.

'But I literally already gave the milk away for free…'

'Maybe he *really* likes your milk, honey.' Ryan laughed a little at his own joke.

I want to talk. I also need a date today. I'm throwing a party for my employees. Wanted to know if you'd be my plus-one? We can talk after. I promise.

'Well, now,' Ryan said, reading the screen. 'Bring-ing you as a plus-one to anything doesn't sound like a man who's planning to relegate you to the role of friends with benefits.'

A little bit of hope sprang up in Chloe's chest. 'Do you think so?'

'Definitely.'

The party was held at the horse track, in the elite pri-vate club rooms far above the race. For an invitation to Arlington Park, Chloe figured a sundress would do, but Ryan had warned her that Drake Properties threw fancy parties. She pulled on strappy stilettos to make the easy sundress more formal.

She wondered what it meant that he was bringing her as his date. Was Ryan right? Was he more serious about her than the other women? Then again, she also told herself, what did *she* even know about Jackson Drake? He had money and he had abs and…a mem-ber that wouldn't quit. But shouldn't *she* slow down and get to know *him*, too? She'd go on this date, hear what he had to say, and then make up her mind. If he wasn't prepared to give her what she needed, she'd walk. She wasn't about to start up a relationship with another Kevin.

She took a deep breath as she touched up her makeup, wondering if her sleeveless, halter-like sun-dress was too revealing. It was a lower-cut neckline than she usually wore, but Jackson was making her braver than her normal self. Maybe that's one of the reasons she was drawn to him. He was bold and he made her feel bolder, too. Dangerous, that's exactly what he was. Part of her couldn't resist playing with fire. After all, she'd never felt so brazen before, never felt so exposed *and* so seen.

Looking in the mirror, at her dark hair up in a low ponytail, she felt passable, maybe more than that, now that she was wearing dark eyeliner that highlighted her nearly black eyes. Plus, she couldn't help think they did have a connection somehow. The passion she'd felt wasn't something that came along every day, and part of her thought Jackson must feel it, too.

Jackson's car roared in the alley, the amazing engine a burst of just-bridled power. Chloe went to the window and saw him behind his familiar Maserati. The hood gleamed in the sunlight, all expensive lines, chrome and brand-new leather seats. The afternoon was a rare seventy-five degrees, a perfect Chicago summer's day, with a breeze off Lake Michigan that dropped the temperature a few degrees. Jackson wore a collared shirt and a tight mesh fedora, which somehow he made look slightly dangerous.

'Nice hat,' she said, nodding her approval.

'It's the thing to wear to the racetrack, so I hear.' She was barely paying attention to what he said as she was too busy following the lines of his tattoo, just visible from the open collar of his shirt. God, the man was all sex and danger.

He left the car and sauntered over to her as his eyes swept her outfit. 'Hey, sexy,' he purred, and then pulled her close. She bent her head, and he laid a soft kiss on her lips. His blond goatee brushed her chin and she felt a shiver of pure pleasure run down her back. Her body responded to him so instinctively. Warning bells went off in the back of her mind. If she wasn't careful, she'd wind up falling for him. Hard.

If she hadn't already.

'Hey,' she said, pulling back, his ice-blue eyes studying her. God, did she love those eyes. She could stare at them forever. No—the talk. Remember! They needed to talk first.

'So...you wanted to talk?' Chloe was proud of bringing it up right away. She wasn't going to let him off the hook.

'After the party, okay?' he said.

'Okay,' she agreed, reluctantly.

Jackson pulled the passenger-side door open, and she slid into the low-set caramel-colored leather.

'How many cars do you have?' she teased as he rounded the car and headed to the driver's side.

'Not enough,' he said, and grinned. He slid into the driver's seat, and the car roared to life, and soon, he'd swung them out of the alley and into traffic.

She'd never been to Arlington Park before, and about forty minutes later, as they pulled into the special parking near the track, she could hear the sounds of fans cheering the races that had only just begun. Jackson took Chloe by the hand and led her to a private elevator, where nearby, men and women casually stood in groups talking, all of them dressed elegantly, the women wearing expensive hats. She was beginning to think this was more Kentucky Derby than casual outing, and suddenly even her long sundress and strappy stilettos didn't seem dressy enough.

'Should I have worn a hat?' she asked as they stepped inside the elevator.

'You're perfect just the way you are,' Jackson growled, knocking his own fedora down a little so it covered his blue eyes. With his goatee and sharp, rugged good looks, he seemed too primal for the dark suit jacket he'd slung over the oxford button-down he wore, the expensive wing tips on his feet.

As the elevator doors shut, Jackson pulled her into his arms and kissed the life out of her, his tongue mingling with hers. He tasted like peppermint, the gum he'd been chewing, yet it was the firmness of his chest and abs pressed against hers that reminded her that kissing wasn't the only thing he did well. She had a sudden urge to explore the front of his pants but then stopped herself. The elevator was opening any minute. That was when Jackson's hands moved downward and he possessively cupped her backside, pulling her to him so their groins met. She felt the stirrings of his massive size there and instantly felt dampness between her legs. Suddenly, she didn't much want to watch the horses race. She'd much rather hit Stop on this elevator and see where the next moments took them.

The elevator doors slid open then, and cool air-conditioning hit them.

'Welcome to the Governor's Room,' he said, and held the doors open as she walked off the elevator onto thick blue carpet. A wall of windows met her, and she realized she was at the top of the racetrack, looking down on the dirt circle where horses gathered at the starting gate for the next race.

Waiters in suits carried champagne on trays, and already people milled about the expansive private room, painted a pristine white, with large, expensive light fixtures hanging from the ceiling, and a long granite-topped counter filled with every kind of fine food imaginable. A waiter offered her a glass of champagne, but Jackson smoothly intervened.

'Get the lady and me some of my private select bourbon on the rocks, please,' he said, and grinned at Chloe. 'I remembered you weren't a bubbles kind of girl.'

'You get points.'

'I hope so.' The way he was looking at her now, Chloe felt like the only woman in the world. She wished she always felt that way, and then immediately tried to banish the negative thought. *You're here with an amazing man, on an amazing date. Do what Ryan said. Live in the moment.*

The waiter returned with two amber-colored drinks and handed them to Chloe and Jackson. Jackson clinked his glass against hers. 'To the most beautiful woman in this room,' he said, and she felt red-hot heat creep around her ears. She certainly wasn't the most beautiful woman in the room, that was for sure. The room was crawling with what Chloe could only guess were the prettiest women in Chicago. Some looked familiar, like they might be from *Chicago*

Fire. Anything was possible. As Chloe sipped on her delicious bourbon, she watched Jackson as he took in the crowd. It wasn't long before a beautiful, statuesque blonde approached them.

'So glad you could make it, sir,' she said, bending her head slightly in formality. 'And who's your lovely date?'

Chloe stared at the woman, amazed at the fact that she could literally see no pores on the woman's face. Her skin was perfection itself, and she was thin, tall and striking. She felt her gut tighten in jealousy. She was short, curvy and dark, not tall, lithe and model-like.

'Hailey, this is Chloe. Chloe, Hailey. She's my right brain at work. The world's best executive assistant.'

'Pleasure to meet you,' Hailey said, sounding genuine as she shook Chloe's hand. Chloe wondered if the two slept together. She also wondered if she'd *always* suspect that when Jackson introduced her to a good-looking woman. Looking around at the Drake Properties party, she realized there were desperately few ugly people in the room. She wondered if Jackson did that on purpose. Or maybe beautiful people just sold more real estate. Whatever the case, it was hard not to feel intimidated.

'You, too,' Chloe said, inspecting Hailey's amazing, British-royalty-wedding-worthy hat. 'I should've worn a hat.'

'Hats optional, don't worry,' Hailey said, giving her a genuinely affectionate grin. Chloe warmed to the gorgeous blonde, suddenly grateful for her friendly smile. 'But if you really want one, I have a few stashed away, just in case. We've got clients coming as well as agents, and my motto is always be prepared.'

'That's why she's the best assistant in the world.' Jackson said it as a matter of fact, and Chloe noticed there wasn't any flirting in his tone. No, the two didn't have benefits, she decided. Would she be worried about every woman he knew?

'You don't mind if I borrow one?' Chloe was feeling decidedly underdressed. It's not like she had fancy hats lying around her closet at home. Clearly, she wasn't used to private box parties at horse racetracks. But then, why would she be?

This is how the other half lives, she thought. *Or scratch that, the other 1 percent.*

Chloe followed Hailey into a large walk-in coat closet, and Hailey reached up for a fabric crate. 'I think I know the perfect one. It'll match your dress perfectly. By the way, lovely dress. Where did you get it?'

'On sale. Nordstrom Rack,' Chloe said, and then immediately cringed as she glanced at Hailey's Christian Louboutin pumps that cost more than her whole outfit, times three.

'I love bargains,' Hailey said, being kind. Chloe had no idea what Hailey made as Jackson's assistant, but judging by her clothes, her salary had more zeros than Chloe's. Hailey pulled out a floppy felt camel-colored hat that did manage to go perfectly with her strawberry-and-cream-striped dress.

'What's it like? Working for Jackson?' Chloe

asked, curious, as she took the hat, studying it and trying to figure out which was the front and which end was the back.

'Oh, he's an amazing boss. Fair, generous and so very smart. I've learned so much from him. He's caring, too. He stood up at my wedding to my wife last summer.' She emphasized the word *wife*, and realization dawned on Chloe.

'Your wife?' Well then, there was *definitely* nothing going on between her and Jackson. She felt a rush of relief flood her. 'Congratulations!'

Hailey smiled. 'Thank you. We're very happy.' She beamed, and Chloe perched the hat on her head and glanced at the long mirror hanging on the back of the door. She had to admit, the hat did complete the ensemble. She almost looked as sophisticated, and rich, as the rest of the party.

'You look…great!' Hailey chirped. She studied Chloe a beat. 'You know, it's none of my business, but…'

Chloe paused, wondering if this was when Hailey told her that she didn't stand a chance against his legions of adoring naked fans, all the willing women in his phone.

'Well, I think you two must be serious because Jackson never brings a date to these things.' Hailey stared at Chloe. 'How long have you two been…'

Uh, two days.

'Not long,' Chloe said, trying to process the fact that Jackson's assistant was telling her that despite the many women she knew were waiting in his phone, he usually preferred to go stag to company events.

'Well, I'm very glad to meet you, because we always say Jackson needs to date more. We never see any serious girlfriends.'

'Never?' Chloe thought about all his friends with benefits, and realized how he must keep those secret from work. Or maybe, there weren't as many women as she thought. Either way, she couldn't help feeling a bit special. He was taking her to a work event. Maybe she was *not* just another friend with benefits?

'Seriously, we never get to meet anyone he dates, so he must think you're special. He wouldn't bring you here if he didn't.' Hailey beamed at Chloe, and Chloe couldn't help but beam back. Was that true?

Hailey straightened Chloe's hat a bit. 'I've known him for years,' she continued. 'If he's letting *me* meet you, and all his other employees, then that is something. Trust me.'

Chloe's heart ticked up. She liked that revelation a little too much. *Could just be gossip from an assistant, nothing more*, she warned herself.

'Knock, knock.' Jackson stood at the coat closet door, resting against the doorjamb, all six foot two inches of him. His own straw fedora was tilted dangerously down over his sharp blue eyes. He held both their drinks in his hands. 'I like the hat,' he said, handing her the drink he'd been holding for her. He glanced at Hailey, a subtle exchange between boss and employee.

'My work is done here,' Hailey exclaimed. 'I'll see

you two out there.' She scooted past Jackson, leaving the two alone in the coatroom. Jackson put his drink down on one of the open cubbies in the closet.

Jackson took a step closer, moving the brim of Chloe's hat back a bit. She craned her neck as his blue eyes fixed on hers, the oversize ice cube clinking the side of her glass.

'You look good enough to eat,' he said, voice a low hum in her ears.

Chloe heard the chatter from the party outside, the coatroom door ajar, but all that didn't seem to matter as Jackson took another step closer. He trailed a single finger down the neckline of her dress, his finger caressing the hint of cleavage there. She sucked in a breath and held it. She'd promised herself that she'd keep her clothes on until they talked, but now, standing before Jackson, she realized the temptation might be too great for her to resist. Could she tell this amazing man no? Her body sure as hell didn't want to.

'I want you,' Jackson said, gaze never leaving her face.

'Right now?' Chloe squeaked, glancing back at the open door.

A daring smile crossed his face. 'Right now, right here.'

CHAPTER NINE

JACKSON LEANED IN and took her drink from her hand. The fact was, he wanted her, badly, and was tired of fighting the urge to keep his hands off her. Yes, they were at a work function, but that didn't curb his libido at all. There was something about Chloe that just got under his skin, bypassed all logic circuitry of his brain. He wasn't sure what it was, or how it had come over him so quickly, but she was different. Maybe it was her boldness? He stepped closer, his lips close to touching hers, when his phone rang, interrupting the moment. He pulled it out of his pocket and saw Laurie's name there. Damn that woman! He silenced his phone and put it back in his pocket.

'You sure you don't need to get that?' she asked him, dark eyes wide.

'I'm sure.' More than sure.

Then Chloe's own phone dinged. She dug it out of her bag, glanced at the screen and then quickly put the phone away. Did she have suitors, too? His stomach knotted a little. What if she had an untold number of men on her phone, pinging her all the time?

He should've guessed she had. After all, she was gorgeous, whip smart and funny. Why wouldn't she be pursued? If he was interested, others would be, too.

Somehow, the thought made him want her even more. He took a step forward, keeping his back to the door as he leaned in and kissed her, a feather-soft kiss. Even with that light touch, he felt his own body respond to hers, stiffening with want. He almost didn't care about the party outside the open door. He knew he shouldn't take this any further, and yet part of him wanted to.

Then he heard the distinct sound of a man clearing his throat. Chloe jumped a mile, but Jackson just slowly drew back, a ripple of frustration running through him as he turned to address the intruder, a man wearing a polo and khakis, a cocktail in hand.

Kent.

What was he doing here? He wasn't a Drake Properties employee.

'Jackson! Been looking all over for you... Sorry, didn't mean to interrupt.'

Jackson knew Kent absolutely intended to interrupt. The man had the worst timing. Also, he didn't like the way Kent was looking at Chloe. Correction: looking at her chest.

'Kent,' Jackson said, voice slightly strained. 'I wasn't aware...you were coming.' *Or that you were invited. Actually, I know you weren't.*

'Oh, I just happened to be in the suite next door with friends, and saw the Drake Properties party sign. Figured I'd drop in and say hello.'

Jackson wished the man would drop himself off the balcony.

'You've said it, and now…'

'Aren't you going to introduce me to this gorgeous little lady?' Kent grinned, but he still stared at Chloe's chest. If he kept doing that, Jackson would have to do something about it.

'Kent Roberts, this is Chloe Park. My *date*.' He said the word emphatically, so Kent would have no misconceptions. Chloe was *his* date. Not up for flirting with the likes of him.

'Yes! Wanted to let you know I got your offer. Maybe we could meet in the middle?'

'Let's talk about it—Monday,' Jackson said, cutting him off and not really caring if he sounded rude. Kent was overstepping his bounds. The last thing he needed at the moment was an open discussion of how he planned to buy Chloe's building.

He turned to Chloe. 'Are you feeling hungry? Maybe you'd like a bit to eat?'

She nodded, and he led her past Kent into the party, where dozens of his own agents and workers were already mingling, cocktails in hand. Kent trailed behind them, annoyingly close, and Jackson made a mental note to try to lose him as soon as possible. Then he saw Hailey talking with the head of security, frowning. He knew something was up even before she made eye contact with him across the room and gave him a subtle head nod.

He squeezed Chloe's elbow as they reached the

buffet and she grabbed a golden-rimmed plate. 'I'll be right back,' he said, voice low.

Chloe glanced up at him.

'Everything okay?' she asked.

'I just need to check on something,' he added, and retreated, meeting Hailey across the room with three long strides.

'What's the matter?' he asked, knowing by the look on her face something wasn't quite right. He kept his voice low enough that it didn't rise above the general hum of conversation around them.

Hailey looked uncharacteristically uncomfortable. Whatever she had to tell him, she didn't want to deliver bad news. 'Do you know a woman named Laurie?'

Instantly, Jackson felt a weight on his shoulders.

'Unfortunately. We dated. Briefly.' He never should've started dating her at all, he thought.

'Well, she's at the main gate. Demanding to see you.' Hailey bit her lip, looking extremely uncomfortable as she shifted from one foot to the other, her own gaze hesitant to meet his.

Jackson shook his head. 'I broke things off with her, but she's not taking no for an answer.' He sighed. 'Please have security escort her off the premises. She is not welcome here.'

Hailey nodded quickly. 'Yes, sir.'

Jackson hated that Laurie had made his personal life public, especially since he'd made it more than clear that they were done. He wondered briefly if he ought to get his attorney involved, get a restraining order.

'Oh, and Hailey,' Jackson said, almost as an afterthought. 'Call my attorney on Monday, would you? I'd like to talk to her.' Best to nip this in the bud. He couldn't have a crazy, money-obsessed ex showing up at his home and business. He needed advice on what to do, maybe even the steps to getting a restraining order.

Hailey nodded quickly. 'Yes, sir.'

Jackson turned then and saw that Kent had maneuvered Chloe into a corner. She was holding on to an appetizer plate like a shield, the tiny sliver of china only thing between her and him. He was talking emphatically about something, and clearly invading her personal space. He frowned. He didn't like Kent making a move on his date. He had his hand on her *elbow*. She wasn't entirely resisting him, either. It was true Kent was a decent-looking guy, and his money made him even more attractive. He felt a flare of jealousy even as his rational mind told him that Chloe wasn't doing anything more than being polite.

He crossed the room in quick, purposeful strides and caught the tail end of their conversation, which had something to do with Kent's yacht.

'Sorry about that,' Jackson told Chloe. 'Just a little work emergency.' He was glad to see that Chloe looked happy—and relieved—to see him.

'No worries,' Kent said, grinning like a cat who'd eaten a canary. 'I was just telling Chloe that she was welcome aboard my yacht anytime. We're sailing to Greece this year.'

'Oh?' Jackson wished the man would set sail *right now*. 'Is that because you raised rents in Pilsen this year?' Pilsen was one of Chicago's eclectic neighborhoods, part hipster, with a heavy Latino influence, and a mix of housing. Kent owned condos near the Thalia concert hall, but he was notorious for his high rents and his lack of fixing real problems, like a back staircase that collapsed last summer.

Kent frowned at the reference.

'Well, it was good to see you, Kent, but if you'll excuse us?' Jackson put his hand on the small of Chloe's back and led her away from the slumlord. Jackson maneuvered Chloe to the other end of the private room, closer to the windows facing out to the racetrack. 'Tell me you aren't going to go on his yacht.'

'Him? I don't think I'd want to be anywhere near him,' Chloe declared. 'I only talked to him five minutes, and all he wanted to talk about was himself.'

Jackson chuckled a little. 'It's his favorite subject.'

'But he did say he had a private chef,' Chloe teased, meeting his gaze.

'I'll cook for you as long as you stay away from him.' Jackson glanced at Kent across the room. The man lacked a moral compass, and it was all about greed for him. How much he could make, and how hard he could screw others out of a hard-earned dollar. That was what he liked the most about the real estate business.

'Is that a promise?' Chloe lifted her face, her

floppy hat falling back a bit, so that her dark eyes shone in the sunlight, making them look a lighter brown, almost golden. Jackson felt his need for her rise again.

'Yes,' he said, voice a little huskier than usual. 'I want to kiss you again.'

Chloe's lips parted. 'Here?' She glanced around at the crowded party, and Jackson realized she had a point. Making out with his date in front of his employees probably wasn't the smartest idea. He glanced over at the nearby coatroom, but saw a few people hanging by the door. That venue was out. He gently took her hand.

'Feel like exploring?' he asked.

A slow grin broke out across her face. 'Sure,' she said, as if she'd been made his partner in crime.

He led her out of the party room. Several of the suites were taken, but at the end of the long carpeted hallway, they found an empty room. He pulled her inside and slid the lock into place behind them. He turned to find her studying him with her dark eyes. He glanced at her in her floppy hat and her sexy sundress, which now, in the sunlight, seemed slightly transparent. He could see the outline of her sexy legs as she stood before the sun-drenched windows.

The room was empty, nothing but large blue carpet, a single empty table in the center, and a wall of windows facing the races. Outside, someone fired a starting gun and the horses took off in one of many scheduled races. But Jackson cared only about Chloe at that moment.

'I missed you,' he said, realizing that since their one night together, just days ago, he *had* missed her. Ached for her, actually. Since having her in his living room, he wanted nothing more than to get her naked again. He wasn't used to feeling so exposed, so needy. It wasn't like him.

'You've been with me all day.'

'Not the way I want to be.' He took a step closer and claimed her mouth with his, this time, his hands roving freely down her back as he grabbed her hips and pulled her to him. She arched into him, her mouth opening for him, eager, wet, delicious.

As his tongue explored her mouth, his need grew. He wondered if he'd ever have his fill of her. He was so busy tasting her, pushing his body into hers, that eventually they hit something solid: the glass wall. Her back against it, he trailed kisses down her neck, making her moan with want. God, he loved to make her moan. He wanted to make her do it all day. All night. He could feel her rapid intake of breath as he kissed her neckline, softly licking the delicious vee where her breasts met. He cupped one, felt its heavy weight in his hand. Perfect.

He claimed her mouth once more, and she ran her nails through the back of his hair, laying perfect trails across his scalp. She raised one knee, opening herself to him, as he ran his hand up her thigh, pushing away the fabric until his palm hit bare skin. She was so soft, so perfect there as he held her outer leg and pressed himself against her warmth at her very center. His body screamed with need as the blood rushed to his groin. He wanted her. Now. Here. He didn't care that the room was open, that the wall of windows had no shades. He didn't care if anyone saw them. He reached up and touched the edge of her G-string. The woman wore the sexiest underwear.

It was then he realized that if he moved his hand much farther, he'd show the entire world her G-string since she was pressed against the windows. Not that she seemed to care, but still, he pulled her away from them, retreating back into the empty suite. The closest people were sixty feet down, anyway, in the rows of spectators beneath them. And most of them had their attention fixed on the track. A roar of cheers went up as the horses neared the final turn and the announcer called the lead horses out by name.

Something about the daylight streaming in through the clear windows, the muted roar of the crowd outside, made his heart pound harder.

He pushed her up on the table against the far wall, keeping his back to the windows, his tongue deep in her mouth. He broke free, breathing ragged.

'Want me to stop?' he asked.

'No,' she said, need in her voice. Want.

'I don't have a condom,' he managed, realizing that he hadn't planned on ravishing her here, in this suite. Hard disappointment hit him like a fist.

'I don't care,' she said, pulling his hands up to her inner thigh. He brushed the thin fabric of the lace there, the only thing between him and her sweet, wet center. It was drenched with her desire, and feeling her white-hot heat for him only made his own groin tighten painfully. He needed to release himself. He needed her. Now. 'I… I'm on the Pill,' she managed.

'And… I don't have anything,' he said, to address the other concern. Safety. 'I get checked for STDs every year, and I'm clean.'

'Me, too,' Chloe murmured, voice low. 'I got checked after…my breakup with my ex. All clear.'

Was he going to do this? Trust a woman he barely knew? Laurie had said she was on the Pill, too, and then he'd caught her trying to get herself pregnant. Never before in his life had he set cold calculation aside, and he'd certainly never been this careless before. Once again, Chloe seemed to change all the rules. He didn't know how, but she did. For the first time in his life, he felt he could truly trust a woman. He believed her.

She was undoing his pants, freeing him, and he felt the cool air-conditioning on his groin, but it did nothing to drench his pulsating need for her. His mind went blank about anything but her. She wiggled free of her underwear, sliding it down one leg. Her pupils had grown so big her eyes looked nearly black. Yes, she wanted him. Her lips were red and raw from his kisses. How could he say no to this? He couldn't care less about the distant windows behind them, about who might see them together, about the lack of protection. He needed her. He couldn't wait any longer.

He plunged into her, her tight wet center grasping him, and he nearly came inside her right then. God, it had been years since he'd felt a woman like this, bare, no condom, just skin on skin. He'd always been so careful, the first to put up barriers, to prevent pregnancy, to prevent entanglement and other consequences. He'd forgotten how wonderful this was, how much better sex really could be. Or it might be that with Chloe, it just *was* better. And in this moment, he found he didn't care at all about that. Not now. Not when she felt so wonderfully perfect, not when it almost seemed like every second of his life was for this one moment. Inside her. Bare. This was what he was meant to do.

To hell with consequences. He needed her. He needed her just like this.

She clutched at him, muffling her cries. Her face was flushed, and her panting grew. She glanced at him, eyes dilated with pure pleasure.

'Oh, God. I'm going to come,' she told him, the news rippling through him, driving him to grow even harder, his need a throbbing tower. She grabbed his shoulders, and her grip on him grew so tight he thought he would lose it. She came in a rushing spasm that nearly toppled him over the edge. That was what he wanted to do, he realized. He wanted to come in her. He was meant to come in her. This was where he belonged.

He was going to do it. Gush inside her. Deep inside.

Then a sliver of rational thought caught him at the end. What if…she wasn't on the Pill? Or, what if the Pill failed? The frigid thought choked him and at the very last second, he pulled out, spilling himself across her belly in an almost never-ending river. God, so much come, so much come that was meant for her. This was how badly he wanted her, the evidence glistening on her lower abdomen in a shocking streak. He sucked in air, his heart pounding from his climax and from the notion that he'd almost *come inside her.* No condom. Nothing. Never had he been so reckless. It was what the woman did to him.

'I'm...sorry. We shouldn't have done that,' he murmured now, feeling contrite. The dangers of that made his mind whirl. Sure, they'd both said they were clean, but he also knew there were still risks. But what scared him most was the hollow disappointment in his chest about not coming inside her. He felt a strange emptiness.

'No. It's okay,' she murmured, cheeks flushed with her own come. 'I wanted it.'

And he did, too. He knew that. Part of him even realized that it had all been worth it: to feel her, all of her eager for him, needing him. Even now, he wanted to feel her again, without barriers, skin on skin. He wanted to be as close as was physically possible. He wondered if his feelings for her bordered on manic.

He took his shirttail and gently wiped his evidence from her stomach.

He felt his groin shiver with renewed life. Did he want to feel her again? Did he want to come in her this time? Yes, he realized with a shock. He did. He'd thought she drained him, and yet now, he almost wanted to see if she could draw more out of him. He knew he wanted to feel her clench him as he came. All of him. At the very deepest point inside her. He imagined all that come inside her, filling her up…and he felt himself begin to harden once more.

He pulled away from her and tucked himself back in, zipping himself up to keep from trying once more. He couldn't afford thoughts like these. Dangerous thoughts. Coming in her? Was he crazy? Was he really ready to trust her so much?

She pulled down her dress and laid a cautious hand on her hair, her attention flickering to the bare windows behind them. Then she shrugged.

'Looks like I've crossed over from voyeur to exhibitionist,' she said, and grinned. God, he loved her free spirit, her devil-may-care attitude. She was bold, like he was. He admired that. And it made him think they'd have brave, adventurous children…if they chose to.

'Whatever you are, it's perfect. You're perfect,' he said, and meant it. He'd never come that hard for a woman—that much before—that he knew of. He'd never been with a woman who made him feel so on edge, so dangerously close to giving up everything. He felt like he was walking on a tightrope without a net below him, and it felt exhilarating.

Was this what love, true love, felt like?

CHAPTER TEN

CHLOE AND JACKSON returned to the party, and Chloe felt like everyone there knew the two had just had the most incredible sex. She almost thought they should be able to sense it somehow, maybe even smell it on her, as she mingled in the crowd. She felt dirty, but in the best possible way. He put a cocktail in her hand and she sipped at it, feeling the cool orange sweetness of the old-fashioned slide down her throat. She felt jittery, unnerved. She couldn't believe she'd just had sex *in public*, but that she'd also done so without a condom, or even having the talk about whether they were exclusive or not. She almost cursed herself. She'd promised not to get naked, and yet…that's exactly what she'd just done. The man was like walking heroin, though. How could she resist him? Gorgeous, strong and endowed. Oh so endowed.

She glanced at him at her elbow, easily making small talk with a few of his agents, and wondered if he thought she was *that kind of girl*. Honestly, she was never so careless. She'd always used condoms, always did it with the shades (mostly) down, but something about Jackson just invited her to be…naughty. She found she liked it. The thrill of it all, the risk. She felt daring and bold, like the bad girl she maybe always secretly hoped to be.

It was worse than she had feared when she told Ryan. Hadn't she said this would happen? That she would get naked? God, she didn't even wait until they'd gotten *home* from the party. Inwardly, she laughed at that. Of course, it's not like she'd ever really been into vanilla sex, but she'd never pushed the boundaries like this, either. Chloe wondered briefly what Kevin would think of her now. If *this* bold, daring version of Chloe had been in his bed, maybe he never would've accidentally called her by a different name.

Was that why she was so determined to take such risks? Was she proving something to Kevin? To herself? Or was it the allure of Jackson's desire for her? She'd never felt so wanted, so desired by a man before. The feeling made all her nerve endings come alive.

Maybe her attraction to him was so strong, she'd do anything he asked. Strip naked right here in the middle of this cocktail party and fuck him while everybody watched. The idea sent a chill down her spine, and she felt a warmth pool between her legs. She'd just come with Jackson inside her and now here she was imagining sex with him again?

She took another slug of her drink. No, she would have this talk with him, he promised. He said after the party, and so she'd wait. Just because she'd had

sex with him—again—that didn't change her feelings. She wanted more from him, and if he couldn't
give it to her, she'd leave.

Leave the best sex you've ever had?

Chloe had to shore up her resolve. She had to walk
away if there was no future with Jackson.

Jackson made a joke and the circle around them
laughed. Chloe only half remembered their names,
and it was probably because with Jackson at her
elbow, all she could think of was him: the feel of his
bare skin against hers just seconds ago; him, all of
him, inside her. Was there such a thing as being addicted to a man? Because she might need rehab. Soon.

She mentally shook herself. At this rate, she was
going to get naked—again—before they got home.
She tried to focus on Jackson, on the conversation at
hand. He was so good to his employees and seemed
to truly care about them. She liked that he wasn't a
standoffish billionaire boss. Everyone felt like they
could approach him and did. She got more than a few
curious stares, and she realized that Hailey had been
right: Jackson didn't bring around many women to
work functions. She made a mental note to ask him
why he'd made an exception.

Then again, after what they'd just done down the
hall, maybe she had her answer.

'We don't have to stay,' he said in her ear. 'Do you
want to go?'

The last race was about to begin, though the crowd
had thinned out a bit.

'Let's stay for the last race,' she said, nodding out to the track. 'I haven't even bet yet!'

'Then let's do that.' Jackson grinned at her and led her to their own electronic teller near the corner and pulled out ten hundred-dollar bills.

'That's too much!' she cried.

'Which horse do you like?' Jackson asked, making no room for argument. She looked at the various names: Jefferson's Dog, Henry's Folly, Neck and Neck, Recon Elite, Panda Art, Miya Sophia, Sarina Jon.

'I don't know anything about horses,' she protested, not sure how this all worked.

'Just pick by the name. That's what I'd do.' Jackson grinned.

'Okay…if you're sure…' She studied the list of horses. 'I'm going with Miya Sophia. That has a nice ring to it.'

'How about for second place and third place?'

'Sarina Jon, and… Panda Art. Why not?' Chloe giggled.

He punched a few options on the touch screen and the computer spit out betting tickets, which he took. 'Okay, bets are laid. Now let's go watch.' Jackson led her to an open spot near one of the windows, which also had a view of the television coverage. The horses neighed and shook their heads in the race stalls, as their jockeys climbed atop their backs and worked to settle the big beasts. Nearby, women and men crowded the glass, wearing suits and fine dresses and straw hats. Jackson gently clasped her hand as they watched the screens, as the jockeys settled in, readying for the starting gun. She loved the feel of his big, smooth palm pressed against hers, and standing so close to him, she got a whiff of his aftershave, something spicy and sweet all at once. Boy, he smelled good. She found herself leaning into his shoulder, inhaling deeply.

The pop of the starting gun grabbed her attention, and she watched the TV as the horses catapulted out of their pens. Far below them, she couldn't see the actual horses. They were on the other side of the giant stadium, blocked by tents in the middle of the field. Their box had a straight view to the finish. She watched the television as the horses galloped down the dirt track, flinging up bits of mud as the small jockeys steered them around the first bend. Jackson let out a whoop as Miya Sophia burst ahead of the bunch, followed closely by Panda Art and Roblox Elite. Sarina Jon and Neck and Neck lagged in the thick of the pack.

'Go, Panda Art!' Chloe shouted, and had to laugh at how ridiculous that sounded. Still, she squeezed Jackson's hand as she watched Miya Sophia widen her lead, and Sarina Jon broke free of the crowd, inching closer to the front. Neck and Neck was neck and neck with Panda Art. 'Come on!' Chloe shouted once more, but Neck and Neck looked like he was losing steam in the last stretch. The horses came thundering down the pass, and now Chloe could see them in real time down the stretch of track beneath their box. The jockeys urged the horses on, but in the end, Miya

Sophia won, followed by Sarina Jon and… Neck and Neck. Panda Art couldn't pull out the third-place finish after all.

But Jackson cheered and hugged Chloe. 'Two out of three isn't bad. We won a little money,' he said.

'Did you win?' Hailey asked them both.

'We won part of our bet,' he said. 'You?'

'Nope. Lost another dollar!' Hailey said. 'Oh, well. It's just not my lucky day. I haven't won any of these races.'

Jackson reached in his pocket and handed her a ticket. 'We have more than one winning ticket on this race. Here, this is yours.' He handed it to her. Chloe wasn't sure what it had won, but Hailey seemed to know since her eyes lit up.

'Sir! Are you sure…?'

'Positive. You take that one.'

She clutched the ticket and beamed. 'Oh, thank you, sir. Thank you.'

'I'll see you on Monday,' he said, and took Chloe gently by the crook of her elbow and led her out the door.

'What was that ticket worth?' she asked him.

'It was the marginal winner. So, two thousand dollars?'

Chloe felt her throat go dry. 'That's a *marginal* winner? What did *we* win, then?'

'Ten thousand dollars. Give or take. Those were long odds on Miya Sophia. And I happened to add in a ticket that included Neck and Neck in third, too. To hedge our bets. So we got a trifecta.'

Chloe felt her head spin. Ten *thousand* dollars? They'd just won…more than two months of her salary. He was so blasé about it, too, but then again, she realized he was flush with cash. He didn't have to worry about which utility bill he'd pay first, not like her. She was suddenly aware of how very different their lifestyles truly were. He thought a five-hundred-dollar bet was nothing more than buying a single lotto ticket, and the prize winnings didn't even faze him.

'Let's go claim our prize,' he said as he led her into the now-open elevator.

Chloe looked at Jackson: the handsome, dirty-blond with the tattoos, the goatee and the straw fedora, and wondered if she'd ever get used to the easy way he treated money. Is this why women fell for him? Was it the endless supply of cash? The allure of being taken care of?

The elevator doors dinged open and Jackson went to the cashier, to claim their $10,000 prize. The man ducked into a locked back room, and then he emerged with two thick stacks of hundred-dollar bills tucked in a manila envelope. Jackson thanked him and handed the envelope to her.

'Oh, no. I can't accept this!' She tried to give the money back.

'You picked the horses,' he pointed out.

'So? It was your money. I'm not taking this.' She stuffed the envelope back into the pocket of his suit jacket. She felt wrong taking the money, even as she knew it would mean unlimited air-conditioning for the summer and she'd completely pay off her Visa, maybe even pay her student loans *ahead* of time. But still. It was too much.

'You should take it,' Jackson said, holding out the envelope as they stood in the lobby of the racetrack.

'No.' She shook her head firmly. 'I'm with you for the *sex*, not your money,' she joked.

Jackson threw back his head and laughed at that, and Chloe laughed, too.

'Fine,' he said, and tucked the cash back in his jacket pocket. 'Then let's get naked again if you're just after me for my body.'

She looped her arm through his. 'What are we waiting for?'

Back at his apartment, he led her into his dark foyer as he flipped on a light. She'd barely paid attention to the lower two levels the first time at his place, since she'd been in such a rush to get to his living room, the room with the windows that faced her apartment. As they passed the second floor, he flipped the switch and she now saw his workshop clearly. Almost the entire floor was dedicated to his woodworking hobby. He had pieces of unfinished wood, a saw on a table, and a dozen shelves filled with tools, screws, nails and everything he'd need to build and sculpt furniture. A set of half-finished bar stools sat stacked neatly in the corner.

'Are these all yours?' she asked, momentarily distracted by his work, amazed at how *much* of it there truly was.

'Yep,' he said, moving into the space. 'It's what I do when I can't sleep—which is a lot, really.'

'You have trouble sleeping?' she asked him.

'Sometimes. During stressful times. Working with my hands feels more natural to me, really. More natural than real estate, if I'm honest. I like working with my hands. Like my dad. He liked working with his hands, too.'

He leaned against the wall of his workshop, focused on her.

She could feel his gaze on her, watching her every move. She loved it, him studying her. She felt powerful beneath his gaze, sexy. She moved slowly, deliberately, aware of the gentle sway of her short sundress, the way it tickled the back of her thigh.

Chloe let her fingers trail down a finished but unvarnished table. 'This is beautiful. I can't believe you made this.' She looked at an ornate dining room chair, which had just been varnished a deep stain, one of four that would eventually go around the table. She admired the workmanship on the arms of the chair, which curved inward. He had a modern yet classic sensibility when it came to woodworking. She admired his taste.

'Why don't you try it out? You can sit on it. It's dry.' He nodded toward the chair, and she sat down. 'It's comfortable,' she said, feeling the warm curves of the wood that seemed to be made to fit her body. She put her hands around the smooth edges of the arms of the chair. 'And sturdy. You do nice work.'

'Do I?' he asked, his voice sinking a little bit lower

as he crossed the room. 'You look so damn sexy sitting in my chair. It makes me think I need to do some more work.'

'You promised me we'd talk.' She wasn't going to let him get her naked again. Not without at least a serious conversation.

'Yes, I did.' He uncrossed his arms, his gaze never leaving her. She stood, uncertain. 'I thought about what you said, about wanting more.'

She sucked in a breath.

'And?'

He crossed the room to her. 'And… I want that, too.'

'You do?' Could this be true? She glanced up, confused, as he knelt down in front of her, his stark blue eyes never leaving hers. She could stare at them forever, she thought. Just like this. Then the man was on his knees in front of her, a slow grin spreading across his face. 'Yes, I do. You intrigue me, Chloe Park. I want to see more of you, much more. I want more than friends and benefits.'

Slowly, he put his hands on her bare knees, and she could feel the weight and heat in his palms. Then, ever so slowly, he spread her knees apart. She sucked in a breath, amazed at how quickly they'd gone from conversation to this…yet, on the other hand, part of her had expected this. Had hoped for it. The electric current that flowed between them seemed ever present, always ready to ignite from the smallest spark.

He gazed at her, focused, as his hands moved

up her skirt. He found the edges of her lacy underwear and slipped it down. She lifted her butt to help him get it off, feeling a delicious rush of the cool wood of the seat against her bare bottom. She felt frozen now, staring at this gorgeous man, sitting in the chair he made. He dipped his head and kissed her inner knee, his eyes never leaving hers as he moved slowly, ever slowly upward to her center, waxed nearly bare.

'I want you to know how special I think you are.'

God, this was what she wanted. To be chosen, and yet… She wondered, what did he mean she was special? Did this mean she would be dating him exclusively?

'Of all the women I know, you're my favorite.'

She felt thrilled at beating out the competition, and yet at the same time, distantly worried there still *was* competition. If she were the favorite in the harem, didn't that mean there was still a harem?

He moved upward, and she felt her body anticipate his touch, his warm, insistent lips on her delicate skin, and the questions evaporated from her mind.

He might be using sex to distract her. Might for sure be doing that. Jackson parted her inner folds with his fingers and then, gently, ever so gently, teased her with his tongue, a gentle, determined lick.

'You taste…so good,' he murmured into her thigh, as his tongue sent electric bolts of desire up her spine. He lapped at her with an enthusiasm she'd never had before, and she felt her body arch to meet each swipe of his amazing tongue. Her eyes flickered closed against the rush of sensation. God, she was going to come. She was going to come…*soon*, if he kept that up.

She opened her eyes once more and found Jackson staring at her from between her legs, his eyes telling her how much he enjoyed driving her wild, how much he loved his tongue exploring her, worshipping her. Chloe couldn't look away from his face. She sucked in a breath as she watched his tongue come for her again and again, tasting her, so intimate, so…amazing. He reached up with one hand and cupped her breast through her dress, making her moan even louder.

He was so good, so very good at this. He was driving her insane with want. His words had already driven her mad, and now this…it was so good.

He hummed into her innermost depths. A hum that sent all the nerve endings in her body tingling, near exploding with pure pleasure. He picked up his pace, and she felt her pulse pound between her legs, as he nipped at skin, driving her to greater heights. She wrapped her hands in his hair just to hang on to something. Her body seemed as if it might fly off the chair, off the very ground. Suddenly, every muscle in her body stiffened, and she hit the peak of passion. Just then as he plunged his tongue into her, she came, a river of pleasure so forceful she cried out, loud, a shout of pure satisfaction, as wave after wave of an amazing climax shuddered through her, shaking her shoulders, raking her entire body.

He lifted his head, a big, accomplished grin on his face.

'Do you feel special now?' he asked her, humor dancing in his eyes.

'Uh-huh,' she managed, completely spent, her legs feeling like jelly. Then he raised her up, lifting her, and moved her to his unfinished table. She went without protest, watching, amazed, as he unzipped his pants. He was ready for her, more than ready, as if making her come aroused him.

'Now it's my turn,' he said, teasing her swollen folds with his oversize tip. How could she take him now, when she was so completely spent? Yet part of her wanted to, wanted to see how his massive width would feel inside her swollen, newly climaxed self. If anyone could make her come again and again, it was Jackson. *Yes*, she thought. *In me. Again. And again.* She spread her legs for him wider on the table as he teased her with his tip, his smooth knob spreading the wetness of her come across its tip. Yes. More. She wanted more. And he did, too.

Then she heard a noise. A footstep on the stair?

'Can I join in?' The strange voice startled them both and Chloe whirled in time to see a woman coming down the stairs, clad only in a trench coat she left gaping open to reveal her breasts and bare stomach.

'Laurie!' cried Jackson. 'What the hell are you doing here?'

CHAPTER ELEVEN

CHLOE SCRAMBLED OFF the table, and Jackson pulled her behind him as he quickly zipped up. She glanced at the woman's blond hair and perky, bare breasts, her light pink nipples hard in the cool air-conditioning of the studio. She wore red heels, and she looked familiar, and then she remembered: this was one of the women from his phone. The one with the hourglass figure who'd sent him nude photos.

'What the hell are you doing here?' he repeated, voice low, a warning. He wasn't exactly glad to see her. Chloe was glad of that, but still confused, her heart beating madly in her chest. She felt violated. Exposed. She pressed her knees together, fiddling self-consciously with the edges of her sundress, keenly aware her G-string was on the floor near her feet.

'You always *insisted* on condoms with me, but I see *with her* it's different.' Laurie frowned at Chloe, sending her a look that could cut glass. Chloe shivered, feeling the hostility radiating from the woman. Jealousy. Just-pent-up rage.

Something was off about the woman. Other than

the fact that she let the trench coat come open entirely to reveal she wasn't wearing underwear, either. Her pink waxed-bare skin shone in the low light of the work studio. She was heavier in person than her pictures suggested, but more like Chloe in body type than she wanted to admit. Curvy, just like Chloe. Chloe crossed her arms in front of her, an unconscious gesture of protection.

'Laurie, you need to leave,' Jackson said, a note of warning in his voice. 'We're over. I told you.'

Laure frowned. 'Come on. I can join in. You two and...*me*. It'll be fun.'

Chloe tightened her grip on Jackson's arm. No way would that be fun. No way would she...do that. Seeing him with Annaliese might have been naughty, tantalizing, but now that they'd had sex...well, she didn't want to share him. She knew that right away, the realization feeling like a frigid wind across her face. Well, at least she had boundaries. She had been wondering if, with Jackson, she'd actually had any. But here, she felt, was a full, hard stop. No threesomes. Not now. Not ever.

'How did you get in here?' Jackson kept Chloe behind him, his shoulders rigid, every one of his muscles seeming to tense.

She ignored the question. 'Please. Give me a chance. I'll play—with you *and* her. I don't need you all to myself. Not at all. Just so long as I get a little taste of that magical cock of yours. Don't you want me? Don't you want both of us—at the same time?'

The idea of sharing him right now made Chloe's

heart beat faster. No, she didn't want to do that. Not with this stranger. She glanced at Jackson's face, worried he wanted it.

'No, I don't.' Jackson squeezed Chloe's hand in reassurance.

'I'm going to ask *one* more time. How did you get in here?'

The woman hesitated, but then came clean.

'Window. You shouldn't leave it unlocked like that.' She laughed, a weird, off laugh. Suddenly, Chloe's blood ran cold. She'd *broken in*? This woman was a stalker, or deranged, or both.

'Laurie, I'm going to give you two minutes. Then I'm calling the police.'

'But how can I go out like this?' She rubbed one of her own bare nipples.

Chloe glanced up at Jackson's face, seeing a look of revulsion pass across it. She was so glad to see that. This woman didn't turn him on.

'God, cover yourself,' he murmured, looking away from her. Disappointed rejection crumpled her features, and she quickly wrapped the coat around her.

'Jackson…' she pleaded, all sultriness gone and in its place a crazy kind of desperation. 'Please, Jackson. We need to talk. I…'

'No more talking!' Jackson snapped. 'I told you, we're done.'

'But I need to talk with you.' She glared at Chloe. 'Alone.'

'No. There's nothing you have to say that I want to hear. You're going. Now.' Jackson pointed to the staircase, but she didn't budge. Then he grabbed his phone from his pocket. 'I'm calling the police.'

Laurie's lip trembled then, and fresh tears glistened in her eyes. 'No! Don't. I'm… I'm going.' She cinched the belt of her coat tightly around her waist, her heels clicking on the stairs as she climbed upward.

She paused at the doorway of the studio.

'You're going to regret this,' she promised, eyes on Jackson. Then she focused on Chloe, her gaze flickering up and down her curves, clearly finding her wanting. 'I'd watch out if I were you. He gets bored. Easily.'

'Get out.' Jackson ground the words between clenched teeth.

A little ripple of fear passed over Laurie, but then she hurried out the door.

'Stay here,' Jackson whispered to Chloe as he followed Laurie down the stairs. Chloe heard the door open and slam and then the *click* of the lock. Chloe's heart thudded hard in her chest as she glanced around the empty studio. She didn't know what to think, or how to feel, even as she heard Jackson moving through the first floor, hopefully to find that unlocked window and lock it. She heard him on his phone as well, giving out terse instructions to someone on the other end. All kinds of thoughts bounced around Chloe's head: Who was Laurie? Had she broken into his house before? And perhaps the most burning question of all: If Chloe *hadn't* been here, would Jackson have taken that crazy naked woman into his bed?

She wondered, was the show of kicking her out

just that? Would he have acted differently had she not been there? She couldn't answer the question for herself, and doubt plagued her. She bit her lip as she remembered how he'd opened the door to Annaliese that first night, how she'd shown up wearing a jumper but nothing beneath. Surely she had to figure that half-naked and fully naked women showed up at his place all the time. Rich, gorgeous, eternally available. Why wouldn't they?

She wrestled with jealousy even as she struggled with the cold vulnerability of feeling so exposed. She shivered and hugged herself, not sure if she'd be able to get the woman's eyes out of her head, the smugness in her expression as she'd caught them. *Maybe I'm not such an exhibitionist after all*, she thought, *not if getting caught makes me feel a little bit sick to my stomach.* Or maybe the nausea was just the fact that a crazy woman had *broken in* and demanded a threesome.

'Chloe.' Jackson stood at the studio door. 'Are you okay?'

Chloe bit her lip, a surprising rush of emotion overtaking her: fear, jealousy, worry, embarrassment and, distantly, a sour disappointment. The woman had ruined an intimate moment, robbed her of sex with Jackson. No, she wasn't all right.

She shook her head. He crossed the room, pulling her into his arms. Reluctantly, she went, not knowing if he could provide the comfort she needed, fearing that if she really shared her feelings with him, she'd come off as too needy, too emotional. *I know other women want him. He said he wanted to date me, but did I really think the other women would go away so easily? Yet I came back for more. That makes me culpable, too.*

'I'm so very sorry,' he murmured in her hair, squeezing her tight, even as she kept her arms deliberately crossed in front of her. She wasn't ready to hug him back. She felt anger and resentment, too, but she wasn't sure if she ought to be angry just at Laurie, or Jackson, or even herself. Had he been encouraging Laurie, she wondered? Had he only just made a split-second decision tonight to date her exclusively and hadn't bothered to tell anyone else? Or was it something he might just tell her and never really get rid of the other women? Did he reply to her naked picture on his phone? Praise her perky breasts so much she felt the need to come over and show them to him in person? And she also felt like kicking herself.

'Laurie is the ex I told you about,' Jackson continued. 'The one who tried to get pregnant without my consent.'

Something hard in the pit of her stomach loosened a bit. 'She was?'

'She's the last person I ever want to be with, and I've told her that, but she's not letting go.' Jackson sighed. 'She's sent me unwanted messages on my phone and has kept calling, and even showed up at the work party tonight. You can ask Hailey. She had to ask security to escort her from the premises.'

The realization that Jackson was the victim here slowly began to sink in. 'She's been stalking you?'

'Yes. I thought she might eventually stop on her own. I didn't want to get the police involved, but now…' He squeezed her tighter. 'I never thought she'd do something so extreme as break in. But I'll have to get a restraining order now.'

Chloe uncrossed her arms and hugged Jackson's trim waist as he squeezed her harder. He rested his chin on the top of her head.

'Why didn't you tell me she was bothering you?' Chloe asked. 'I think I saw her message on your phone. I just assumed she was one of your arranged relationships, your regulars.' Chloe sucked in a breath.

'You thought I wanted her?'

Chloe nodded into Jackson's chest.

'No,' he said, sounding resolute. He pulled away then and stroked her cheek. 'Don't you know? The only woman I truly want is you.'

CHAPTER TWELVE

CHLOE COULDN'T BELIEVE her ears. Jackson was asking her to be exclusive. He'd hinted about it before, but now…now, she knew for sure: he wanted only her.

'You do?' she blurted, standing in front of him in his studio, feeling the cool wooden floor beneath her bare feet. Her head bursting with questions, her heart daring to hope it was true.

'Yes.' His blue eyes shone as he traced the lines of her chin with his finger. 'I just want you.'

'But the women. On your phone.' Not just Laurie, but the others. Annaliese, and probably many more.

Jackson looked amused. 'I'll delete them, now.' He took out his phone from his back pocket then and showed her his messages. There were indeed several from interested women, friends with benefits as he'd called them. One by one, he began deleting all of their contact information. He even blocked Laurie, to make a point that he truly was done with her. Chloe watched, amazed, as the women disappeared, one by one, before her eyes.

'See? I don't care about any of them, Chloe. Not since I met you. I only want to sleep with you.'

'I... I don't know what to say.' Chloe felt like it was all too good to be true.

'Say you'll do the same. Say you want to be with me.' Jackson took both her hands. 'Tell me I don't have to worry about you slipping *your* number to Kent, or anybody else.'

'Kent?' Chloe echoed, and then remembered the egotistical man at the racetrack, the one who talked her ear off about himself the entire time and never asked her a single question. 'Oh, no chance of that, don't worry.'

'He was interested in you,' Jackson pointed out.

'He can be interested all he wants. The feeling isn't mutual.' Chloe was shocked to discover that Jackson, too, could be jealous. Did that mean he was really sincere? He wanted to be with her, and he wanted her to want him, too.

Jackson grinned. 'I'm glad to hear that.' His gaze grew serious again. 'I mean it, Chloe. You're the woman I want. You're gorgeous, fun-loving, free of all inhibitions. You want to devour the world, just like I do.'

She wanted to devour him, that's what she knew.

'You're the woman for me.' He pulled her close then and kissed her, gently, a promise in the gesture. She kissed him back, sealing the pact. When she pulled away, she was suddenly aware of the dark corners of the studio and the fact that Laurie might be back. What if she did more than climb through an unlocked window? What if she broke in?

Chloe shivered. 'Why don't we go to my place?' she offered. 'Laurie doesn't know where I live. You know, just in case.' She paused. 'Unless you *want* another shot at Laurie and a threesome.'

Jackson chuckled. 'No, thanks. I don't want to share you,' he said. 'Not with Laurie, or anybody else.'

He kissed her once more, a reassuring kiss, and she felt the knot of worry loosen in her stomach. He *picked* her. He wanted her. And she knew she wanted him just as much.

Jackson liked Chloe's apartment. It wasn't as spacious as his, but it was tastefully decorated, with clean, modern furniture. She also kept her place relatively neat, a relief for him since he liked things orderly, and clearly, so did she. They were so alike, he felt, from their sexual adventurousness to the way they approached business. He knew she worked hard from how she spoke about her job and the little he'd seen when he'd Googled her online, and she, like him, was a self-starter, someone who preferred making her own way in the world rather than accepting a traditional job with a traditional boss.

Chloe glanced at her phone and frowned.

'Do you mind if I check email really quick? I've got a client who needs an update,' she said, booting up her laptop. As he watched her work, despite all that had happened that evening, he felt a surge of appreciation.

'I admire you,' Jackson said as he glanced at the tidy apartment, with her laptop open on her table.

'Why?' Chloe sounded taken aback, surprised even as she paused at the keyboard.

'Well, you've made a decent living on your own.' He nodded to the laptop. 'I had my father's insurance money to work with, but you've built a business from scratch.'

Chloe grinned, looking a little embarrassed, but also a little proud. 'I guess so.'

'I mean it. You're on your own, freelancing, making ends meet. You're paying your bills. You're a go-getter. I'm impressed.' Of late, Jackson's dates either had no ambition, or their ambition revolved solely around getting him to propose or getting pregnant with his baby. He liked a woman who had her own life, who had goals that had nothing to do with him or his bank account.

'I love what I do, and I love setting my own hours,' she said.

'Working for yourself is hard,' he said. 'It requires a lot of discipline.' He leaned against her breakfast bar. 'Like replying to an email on a Saturday night.'

'Well, my clients don't sleep.' She shrugged. She typed a response quickly and then sent it off. 'There, I'm off the clock now.'

'Good,' he said as she stood. He studied her, her beautiful curves, the way her dark hair shone beneath the lights of her kitchen. So dark, so glossy. 'So, I am curious about something. Why didn't you take the prize money today?'

He patted his jacket pocket, where he'd been carry-ing the $10,000. He realized it had been a little care-less to keep that much money on him, and yet truly, the amount was pretty small for him. His own bank account had many more zeros attached.

'It wasn't mine,' she said. 'That money is yours.'

'Every other woman I've ever dated would've taken that envelope,' he said. 'They wouldn't wait to be asked twice.'

'It's not my money,' she reiterated, sounding more resolute this time. 'I earn what I keep.' She nodded at her laptop. 'That's what my parents taught me, and I believe it.'

She swept her shining, reed-straight hair off one shoulder. He wanted to touch her, feel the softness of her skin.

'So you won't take the money, but I want to hire you, remember? As a social media consultant? Con-sider this a retainer.' He pulled the packet out of his pocket and handed her the thick manila envelope.

She glanced at him, mouth agape. 'I usually charge by the hour *after* I do the work,' she said.

'Well, consider this an advance.' He grinned. 'Come on. Take it.'

She hesitated, then eventually, tentatively, took it. 'I'll make an accounting of *all* my work for you, and I'll account for every penny of this.'

'I know you will.' Jackson glanced at the kitchen counter, and that's when he noticed a letter from Kent Realty. He frowned and picked up the already-opened letter.

'You read this?' he asked her, holding up the envelope. 'This is from Kent's company. The man you met tonight.'

'It is?' She looked surprised. 'So *he's* the one I'm sending rent checks to now? If I'd known, I would've asked him to knock off a hundred dollars.' She laughed a little at her own joke, but Jackson wasn't in the mood for laughing.

'Mind if I look?'

'Help yourself,' she said, and he skimmed the letter. Kent planned to up rents by nearly 30 percent when she renewed, which was highway robbery. No doubt he wanted the rent value on paper so that he could try to gouge Jackson in the negotiations. Underhanded tricks.

'This isn't right,' he said.

'I know,' Chloe said. 'But, I was already thinking about moving.'

The thought made Jackson snap to attention. 'You can't move.'

Chloe grinned. 'I can't?'

'No! Not unless you move into my bed.'

Chloe quirked a playful eyebrow. 'Is that an official invitation?'

'A standing invitation,' Jackson offered, and pulled Chloe into his arms for a kiss.

CHAPTER THIRTEEN

CHLOE WOKE IN her own bed with Jackson spooning her from behind, both of them naked, though, she remembered, they'd fallen asleep almost as soon as they'd lain down the night before—each of them exhausted from their long day and from the stress of the break-in. Somehow, wrapped up in Jackson's arms, waking with him, felt more intimate than even their hot sex at the racetrack yesterday. He stirred behind her, shifting slightly against her back.

'Morning, gorgeous,' he whispered in her ear, squeezing her tightly. She turned, rolling around in his arms so she could face him. His eyes were so starkly blue.

'Morning,' she echoed, snuggling up to his thick, muscular chest. The man was all hard ridges, all muscle, and she felt protected in his arms.

'I think *he* also wanted to say good morning.' Jackson pushed against her, and she could feel his thick hardness resting against her belly.

'Well, good *morning*.' She reached down and wrapped her hand around him, and he groaned in appreciation as she worked the length of him, her hand steady, knowledgeable, sure.

'At that rate, we're never going to get to brunch,' he said.

'Brunch can wait.' She ducked down beneath the sheets, determined to drive him just as wild as he'd done her the day before in his wood workshop.

She flicked her tongue across his wide tip. He rolled over on his back.

'Oh, Chloe,' he murmured, and she felt a little jolt of delight. She remembered Annaliese that first night taking him in her mouth. She knew he liked that, and she wanted to please him. She wanted to be better than Annaliese, better than Laurie, better than any other woman he'd ever had. She wanted to give him everything. The rush of competitiveness surprised her, and yet she wanted to erase all other women from his mind. She wanted to make sure he didn't regret his choice.

She took his tip in her mouth, working her tongue around it, amazed at how little of him filled up her entire mouth. Chloe used both hands to work his shaft and celebrated as he grew harder with each movement.

'You're so good at that,' he said, running his fingers through her thick hair, grabbing it up into a ponytail and giving it a little tug. He urged her to go faster, and she did, taking what she could. 'Yes, Chloe. Oh, God, yes.'

She worked to take more of him, not sure she could, but then, in a burst of white-hot heat, he came, so deep down her throat she couldn't help but swallow. She rolled off him, panting, but he took her in his arms and kissed her.

'That's one helluva good morning,' he declared, and she laughed.

They spent a lazy Sunday together, first walking to brunch at a nearby café, and then strolling through a farmers' market, with Jackson warmly holding her hand. Laurie's intrusion receded to the back of Jackson's mind. He'd instructed his lawyer to look into a restraining order, which she'd promised to do, and now he was able to just enjoy time with Chloe. The more time he spent with her, the more he was convinced that she was *the one*. She'd even taken one of her pills from her pack in front of him. He felt reassured: she was on the Pill. Unless she was going much further than Laurie ever did to trap him. His gut told him that Chloe was nothing at all like Laurie.

He felt comfortable with her, more so than he had with any other woman. She was one of the first women he'd ever met who felt like his true equal. Of course, part of him still felt guarded. He wasn't used to trusting anyone, especially not women, and the feeling didn't come naturally. The warm summer's day cooled toward the evening as a breeze rolled in from Lake Michigan, and the two moved their marathon date to his rooftop deck, where he grilled up some chicken skewers and roasted vegetables as they both sipped wine.

'This has been the perfect date,' Jackson said.

'And the longest,' Chloe pointed out. They'd been

together for most of a weekend, and yet it had felt like no time had passed at all. Jackson wasn't the least bit edgy or tired of Chloe's company, and the more time he spent with her, the more he wanted to spend.

'True. This might be the longest date I've ever been on,' Jackson admitted.

'I figured, since I think the Annaliese date was under an hour,' she joked, and Jackson had to laugh. He loved her humor, her playful teasing. He deserved it, all the grief she could give him.

As he turned over the roasted veggies wrapped tightly in tinfoil on the grill, his phone pinged with an incoming message. He glanced over and saw Chloe lighting a citronella candle, as he checked his phone.

You up for a little naked time?

He frowned at the message, not sure who it came from since he deleted his contacts.

Sorry. No can do. In a relationship now.

Oh—good luck, then. If it doesn't work out, ping me.

Jackson had no intention of it not working out. He slipped the phone into his pocket. It would be quite a change, he realized, slowly weeding out the women he'd been using in his life as fillers, and yet it didn't feel like a sacrifice. He wanted Chloe to know she was the woman for him, and he didn't want women who didn't mean much to him to scare her off. For the first time in a long time, he was beginning to feel hopeful that maybe he'd found his match. Jackson had never considered himself a romantic, but as he glanced at Chloe's profile in the warm light of the summer sunset, he wondered if he'd been wrong about himself. Maybe he'd just never met the right woman.

'What is it?' asked Chloe, seeming to feel suddenly self-conscious beneath his gaze.

'You,' he said. 'You're so beautiful. So perfect.'

'I'm not perfect. Not by a long shot.' Chloe laughed uneasily. 'My ex-boyfriend used to say that I was lazy, which was why I worked from home. He thought I didn't have the competitive edge or the know-how to work for a 'real' company.'

'Your ex was an idiot,' Jackson said, feeling anger welling up in him. 'It's far harder to work for yourself. And scarier, too.' Jackson studied her a second. 'Was that the reason the relationship didn't work out?'

'Kevin was cheating on me,' she said, simply. 'He felt entitled to, I guess.'

'Forget me saying he's an idiot. He's also a fool.'

Chloe took a step closer to Jackson, and he folded her into a side hug, pulling her into him. He wanted to protect her suddenly from everything that could possibly hurt her. He wanted to make sure she was safe.

'He never really knew you, it sounds like,' Jackson said as he took the food off the grill, onto waiting serving platters. Chloe helped him carry it to the table they'd already set, with a candle flickering in the middle. 'Like my exes never really knew me.'

Chloe nodded. 'I think you're right.' Chloe bit her lip, the slightest hint of a worry line etched into her forehead as she slid into her seat across from Jackson.

'What's wrong?'

'Speaking of exes, do you think Laurie will be back? It was so…weird. Yesterday.'

'I'm sorry about that,' Jackson said. 'Truly. If I'd known she was that unhinged… Well, I would've acted sooner.'

Chloe glanced at Jackson, the candlelight warming her features as the sky above them turned a cool purple as the sun dipped below the horizon.

'And…how do I ask this…' Chloe pushed the spaghetti strap of her sundress up one shoulder. Then she took a big breath. 'Had you… I mean, been leading her on at all?'

His sharp blue eyes met hers.

'No, I hadn't.'

'She wasn't a…friend with benefits?' Jackson could see how much Chloe had been thinking about this. It concerned her, and all he wanted to do was reassure her.

'No, absolutely not. The last time I saw her in any kind of romantic way was three months ago, when I caught her in the bathroom, pouring our used condom into her…well, you know.'

Chloe looked relieved. 'Good,' she said.

Jackson reached out and grabbed her hand. 'I've told everyone else on my phone that I'm in a relationship now. If you want to look at my phone, here.' He offered it up to her. 'I mean it, I have nothing to hide.'

'I believe you,' she said, and squeezed his hand. He squeezed hers back as they dug into the warm meal in front of them. Jackson was already thinking about the next day, a busy workday in another busy workweek, wondering how he'd manage to squeeze Chloe into his schedule, but already determined to find a way. Dinner flew by, and the sky darkened around them. Above them, stars shone in the cloudless sky. He poured them more wine, and then they moved over to the cushioned outdoor love seat in the far corner of his roof. The air held a slight chill as the moon rose in the sky. Jackson lit the small fire pit, and the warming smell of a small campfire filled the night air. Despite the fact that they sat on a city rooftop, surrounded by other buildings, it felt solitary, as if they were the only two people in the world.

'Now all we need are s'mores,' Chloe said, snuggling into the crook of Jackson's arm as they both stared at the small orange flames.

'I think all I have are protein bars,' he said, and they both laughed.

'Somehow, I don't think that would be the same.'

Jackson agreed, hugging her close as the two finished their wine. Chloe looked up at Jackson and he felt, once more, awed by her beauty. He took her now-empty wineglass from her hand and put it on the table with his.

'Do you think we're moving too fast?' Chloe asked him, a note of anxiousness in her voice. He realized they had moved quickly, but he also thought of himself as a man who knew what he wanted. And right now, that was Chloe.

'When you know, you know,' Jackson said, tracing her delicate chin with his finger.

He dipped down to kiss her lips, and she met him halfway. Her lips, warm and willing, parted for him, and he tasted her once more, the hint of the blackberry in the residue of wine on her tongue. The instant their lips met, he felt the rise of his desire for her, as he deepened the kiss. His want for her knew no bounds, and he wondered distantly if a fire that burned this hot would burn itself out…or if it would continue to blaze. Still, all he knew was that he wanted her again, right here, beneath the stars.

The fire pit began to die down, and the shadows grew larger on the patio, and it felt oddly safe there.

He glanced at her and grinned. 'What do you say to a little exhibitionism?'

She laughed a little. 'I'd say…hell, yes.'

He moved closer to her. He ran his hand up the edge of her skirt as she straddled him. One of her straps fell down one shoulder, and he kissed her bare skin where it had once been. He inhaled her scent, with a hint of honey vanilla, and put his hands on her hips as she pushed her warm center against him, the heat there unmistakable. Just the small business of his gym shorts and her underwear worked as a barrier between them.

She broke free of the kiss, gasping. 'We're going to get arrested if we keep this up. For public indecency.'

'Not if we're quick,' he murmured back, determined not to wait a second longer for her.

Her lips found his again as her nails raked his scalp, and his whole body came alive. He felt her soft breasts against him and couldn't help himself. He tugged down the front of her elastic sundress and found her braless, his mouth claiming her nipple. She moaned, arching her back, and he sucked her as her whole body became taut with need. Yes, he thought. This woman, every day. Every night. She was so responsive, so full of fire. It would take years and maybe even decades before he'd tire of this magnificent body. The stars above them twinkled as her bare breasts were now both exposed to the night. She didn't seem to care, and that thrilled him. He wanted her and wanted the whole city to know.

Let someone call the police. He'd be long finished before they arrived.

He moved her slightly so that he could nudge the elastic waistband of his shorts down, revealing that he was more than ready. Beneath the cover of her skirt, he gently rubbed against her, against the thin barrier of her thong. He almost felt like he might come just like that.

He hesitated a moment, remembering how perfect she'd felt when he'd been bare, remembering his sour disappointment when he'd come on her belly. Would he come inside her this time? Would he feel her around him when he came? The idea almost made him climax right then, and he wasn't even inside her yet. *This woman*, he thought, *this woman drives me mad.* Chloe straddled him once more, moving her thong aside with one finger, letting him past the last remaining barrier. So easy. So right. Their passion was shielded by her skirt, her bare nipples puckering in the moonlight. In the dying light of the fire pit, he saw desire in her eyes as she took him deeper inside her slick, warm center. She was ready for him, oh so ready. Chloe rode him slowly at first, teasing him, every little movement like agony. He wanted hard and fast, but she was going to put that off for as long as possible. A small smile spread across her pink lips, and in that moment, deep inside her, Jackson had never loved a woman more.

CHAPTER FOURTEEN

THE NIGHT BELONGED to them, Chloe thought, as she
sat astride Jackson, not caring about who might see
them. She'd never felt as primal, as animalistic, as
she did now, with Jackson, beneath the stars. Growing impatient with the pace, Jackson lifted her off,
flipping her around so she was on her knees, back to
him on the cushy outdoor sofa. Distantly, below on
the street, a cab honked at a car cutting into his lane,
but neither cared about the sounds of traffic below.
The drivers couldn't see them. He moved behind her
and she grasped the back cushions, feeling suddenly
vulnerable as he grabbed the hem of her skirt and
flung it upward, the night air whisking across her
bare back, her thighs exposed to the slight chill. He
tugged off her thong, tired, she thought, of moving
around it, and it hit his wooden deck with a tiny whisper of the elastic fabric on wood. Now she was completely bare in the night air. Her knees shook as she
anticipated him, and he delivered, thrusting into her
with shocking determination. She gasped as she took
the whole length and width of him, completely bare,

clutching the back of the couch for support. So big, she thought. So very big. Her knuckles went white.

'I've never felt like this with anybody,' Jackson whispered in her ear. 'Do you feel that?' He pushed harder inside her, deeper. 'I'm home here. I'm meant to be here.'

'Yes,' she murmured. *In me. Always in me.*

'You're the woman for me,' he murmured, sending her heart racing, the pulse between her legs ticking upward, even as he stretched her, filled her. She was going to come right then, come a thousand times more, too. She burned for him, even as she felt her swollen clit protest, begging for attention.

'Touch me,' she asked him, voice husky and low.

He obliged, reaching around with his right hand, finding her ready for him, as he gently caressed her bundle of nerves with the pad of his finger. The sensation blinded her. Yes, this was what she needed. Him inside her. Him touching her. He picked up the pace instinctively, and she came with a violent shudder, losing every last ounce of control as the spasms took her. He didn't last much longer after that, coming with a primal grunt. She realized with a shock that he came inside her. He didn't withdraw this time, and it made her feel as if this moment were something special. He was trusting her in a way he'd told her he never trusted before.

She hoped his climax was as amazing as hers, even as she replayed his words in her mind: *I'm home here.* Yes, that's what she felt like, too. *I'm home with you.*

He slowly withdrew with a shuddering sigh, and

she felt what he'd left for her, his thick, wet want between her legs, and she felt an animalistic kind of satisfaction with that, too. She realized she wanted his come; she'd always wanted his come. He said nothing about the fact that he'd come inside her, about what this meant. Instead, he pulled his shorts up, and instantly she missed the warmth of his body. She tugged her skirt down, her legs feeling the wet combination of their primal need mingling together on her inner thigh. It made her feel both naughty and fearless all at once. She pulled up her neckline, tucking herself back into the top of her dress.

Chloe gazed about the roof, noticing a few lit windows nearby with shades drawn. She hoped nobody had seen, and yet at the same time, she knew she'd do it again in a heartbeat. She liked the feeling Jackson fueled in her, a recklessness. And now she knew he trusted her. He'd told her he felt at home with her. It's more than she could've ever imagined. The cool summer wind picked up, and she shivered, acutely missing the lack of Jackson's body heat.

'Let's go inside,' he offered, leading her back in his house, his hand laid protectively on the small of her back.

When she offered to head back to her apartment for the night, he wouldn't hear of it, instead insisting she stay in his bed. They slept, limbs entwined, and Chloe felt her heart fill with love.

Jackson slept the night, but woke early, loving seeing Chloe in his bed. She slept hard, her long dark hair spreading across her bare back as she lay on her stomach, naked beneath his thick cotton sheets. This was what he wanted, he realized, her in his bed every morning and every night. She belonged here, next to him. He watched her sleep, her thick dark lashes against her rosy cheeks, her thick lips slightly parted. She was so vulnerable there, so childlike. He wondered if their children would have her dark hair or his dirty-blond waves.

Their children. What was happening to him? Already he was imagining babies! Yet the thought wasn't scary in the least. Chloe just felt…right. They belonged together, and so babies, marriage, they just came with the territory. Sure, they'd only been dating a short time, but every fiber of his being told him *she* was the one. The only one.

Jackson traced her bare shoulder with one finger, amazed at the softness of her skin. She stirred then, her eyes flickering open.

'Good morning,' she murmured sleepily as she rolled over, demurely covering herself with a sheet. 'What time is it?'

'Seven,' he said.

She yawned and stretched. 'Do you need to head to work? I've got a phone conference at nine, but I'm free till then.'

'I have to be in the office at eight. But I have time to make you a quick breakfast.'

'You don't have to,' she said.

'I know I don't, but I want to.' He grinned and kissed her on the nose.

Chloe tucked the covers around her and seemed suddenly shy. 'Do you have…a, uh…shirt I can borrow?'

He tossed her a concert tee, and she pulled it over her head. She stood and it fell to her midthigh, and he'd never seen one of his shirts look sexier. He kissed her then at the foot of his bed. Their tongues met, and all he wanted to do was throw the shirt over her head and get her right back into bed.

'Wait…' she said. 'Work. Breakfast. We can't…'

He glanced at the clock. No, they didn't really have time. Not for what he wanted to do to her. That would have to wait.

Ten minutes later he served up a plate full of scrambled eggs and toast, as well as a steaming cup of coffee. Chloe dug in and so did he, just glad to spend a little extra time with her before they went their separate ways. He watched her eat a mouthful of scrambled eggs.

'You're beautiful, you know that?'

'You can't be serious,' she mumbled, mouth full. She pointed to her bedhead and her lack of makeup. 'I can't look anywhere *near* beautiful.'

'You do to me.'

Chloe swallowed as he studied her. God, she was beautiful. She didn't need makeup or, hell, even combed hair. She was the most beautiful woman on earth, even as she self-consciously swiped at her mouth with a napkin.

'I love you, Chloe,' he said then, the feeling welling up in him.

'You…what?' Chloe stared at him, shocked.

'I love you.'

'That's what I thought you said.' He could see the confusion on her face as she struggled with what to say. He knew she wasn't ready. Not yet. That was okay.

'You don't have to love me back, at least not now,' he said. 'But I promise you, you will.' He dipped down and kissed her then, and she kissed him back.

Eventually, the lovers parted—Chloe to head back to her apartment to work, and Jackson to go into his office for a set of meetings he couldn't avoid. Jackson promised to call her later, already trying to work her into his busy schedule. When he arrived to work he was humming, in the best mood he'd been in months, maybe even years. For the first time since his business really took off, he felt the pieces of his life falling into place. He'd found a woman who might truly be a real partner, and for the first time he allowed himself to think of what that might mean: settling down, maybe having a family. The idea intrigued him. He'd always wanted to get married someday, but after all his disappointments he had worried he wouldn't ever find a woman who loved him for *him*, not his money.

He greeted Hailey outside his office, but she looked withdrawn, even a little pale.

'Morning, Hailey. Something wrong?'

'Well, sir…' Hailey looked uncharacteristically flustered. She wouldn't make eye contact with him. 'Laurie is here to see you.'

Jackson felt his blood boil. He glanced through the

glass doors of his office and saw Laurie there, sitting in *his* desk chair, moving pens around his desk. 'Why didn't you show her out? We're working on a restraining order and…'

'I think you should talk to her, sir. She said…'

'I don't care what she said. She's not welcome here or at any of my other properties. I'm disappointed in you, Hailey. I'll show her out myself.' He headed to his office door, determined to give Laurie a piece of his mind, and maybe even have her arrested.

'But…sir…' Hailey seemed so very uncomfortable. There was something his assistant wasn't telling him.

'What?' Annoyance laced his voice. The last person he wanted to deal with this morning was Laurie. The fact that Hailey had failed at her job as gatekeeper irked him. Normally, she was so on top of things. He wondered what had made her hesitate.

Hailey moved closer, her voice barely above a whisper. 'The woman said she's pregnant, sir. With your baby.'

CHAPTER FIFTEEN

JACKSON FELT LIKE he'd been slammed in the chest with a truckload of bricks. This couldn't be true. Laurie couldn't be pregnant with his baby. He hadn't even been with her for three months, and then he'd caught her before she'd successfully poured the contents of the condom inside her...hadn't he?

'Uh. I'll take care of this. Thank you, Hailey.' His assistant looked up at him with a pained expression. He wanted to tell her it wasn't true, but first he had to find out what the hell was going on. 'I'll talk to her.'

'I thought you would, sir. It's why I didn't see her out.' Hailey's face flushed.

'You did the right thing. Thank you.'

Hailey nodded, but looked sad as she returned to her desk, still not meeting his eyes. She knew as well as he did that he didn't love Laurie. That she was the last woman on earth he'd pick for a biological tie.

'Hello, Jackson,' Laurie purred as he swung open the door, looking a tad bit contrite. 'I tried to tell you. I said I wanted to talk to you alone. When I came to your place.'

She had, he guessed, not that it mattered now. Laurie spoke in a heated rush, as if the way she delivered the news somehow was what she got wrong, and not deceiving him in the worst possible way for the worst possible reason: greed.

'Look, I know this isn't what you want, but now that I'm pregnant…well.' She took a deep breath. 'Let's try to work together. For the baby's sake.'

She gently placed a manicured hand on her abdomen.

'Drop the act, please. I know you don't care about that baby other than what the child support will buy you.'

'That is the worst thing I ever heard!' she cried. 'You don't really think I'm that horrible, do you?' She blinked fast. It would've been convincing, except he knew it was a lie. Deep down, he knew. She twisted her hands together. 'I love you, Jackson. That's why I want to have your baby.'

'No, you don't.' He shook his head fiercely. 'Would you love me if I were poor?'

'Of course.'

'Good,' he said. 'Then I'll give away all my money tomorrow. Your child support will be 20 percent of nothing.'

For a split second, Laurie blanched. 'See?' he said, reading her expression. 'It's the money you care about.'

Laurie sat down. 'No, it's just that I'm feeling light-headed. With the baby.'

Jackson laughed a little. Even now, she was pretending. 'How did this happen?'

Laurie giggled, as she swung his swiveling chair back and forth.

'Well, you don't think I only did that trick with the condom *that one time*, did you?'

Now Jackson's blood ran cold. 'You told me that was the first and only time you did that. When I caught you.'

Laurie laughed and then arranged her features into a girlish pout. 'Oops! I lied.'

Jackson mouth was dry. Anger and panic welled up in him.

Jackson felt blindsided and betrayed—again—and yet he had only himself to blame. Why had he believed her when she told him it was just the one time with the condom? Why would he be so trusting of a woman who'd been out to trick him from the start? He knew why. Because he desperately wanted that lie to be true. He didn't want to think about what would've happened if she'd been doing that *every* time they had sex. Now, of course, he remembered her quick escapes to the bathroom regularly, the same bathroom he'd used to dispose of the condoms, before he got into the habit of flushing them. He'd chosen to turn a blind eye to those facts. And now…now… His head whirled with a dark future: a baby with a woman he didn't love and who was just after child support. And what about Chloe? How would she react if she found out Laurie was pregnant?

Jackson felt light-headed. He stumbled to a chair and sat down.

'Are you sure you're…pregnant?'

Laurie reached into her bag and pulled out a Ziploc filled with two used pregnancy tests. They both had positive pink plus signs.

'I could take another one, here, if you want me to.' She pulled out a brand-new boxed test.

'N-no. Not necessary.' This was a nightmare, a nightmare from which he badly wanted to wake up.

Laurie stood and came around the desk, approaching Jackson. She trailed a bright pink nail up the arm of his chair. She was wearing a too-short sundress that barely covered her backside. She was all curves. He'd been attracted to her softness, her big breasts and bigger backside, when they first met at the bar where she worked, but now being so close to her just made him feel sick to his stomach.

'I'm so happy I'll be having your baby,' she said. 'You've made me so happy.'

Jackson couldn't think. Couldn't do anything but stare at her fake eyelashes, at everything about her that was fake, a lie. She played with the hem of her skirt, raising it a little higher. She stood with her back to the glass office door, and she pulled up the hem of her skirt high enough to show him she wasn't wearing any underwear.

'You can come in me now. Won't make any difference. We could close those blinds so that slut of an assistant won't see us, and you could do me right here. You should at least get to bareback me, officially.'

She grinned at him, and he felt like he was going to throw up.

'Get out,' he said finally, the idea of having sex with her ever again making him feel disgusted.

'What? I thought you liked ditching condoms now. Like with that new girl of yours. She's a little whore, isn't she? I saw you two. I remember.'

Jackson felt raw repulsion creep up the back of his neck. She was still a stalker, still imbalanced. Capable of anything. And now, pregnant.

She took a small step closer. 'I can be your little whore, too. If that's what you want.'

With her back to the door, Laurie reached down and slipped her own hand down between her legs, beneath the hem of her skirt. It was obvious she was touching herself. He felt anger surge in him and disgust.

'Come on. It won't hurt the baby. Come inside me, Jackson.'

'I mean it, Laurie. You need to leave.' He stood up. She shrank back a bit. He felt a rush of emotions: anger, resentment…even hate. This woman was ruining his life. He couldn't look at her anymore. He couldn't even be in the same room with her.

'Is this how you treat the mother of your child?'

'Just go.' Jackson glared at the floor. Thankfully, she took the cue and grabbed her purse, slinking to the doorway.

'Jackson. I need money. Say, five hundred dollars? Just to get me by…'

'Get *out*,' he ground out.

'Well… I'll let you think about all this and then maybe you'll come to your senses and do the right thing…before I have to get a lawyer involved. I'll be

in touch,' she promised as she walked out the door.
Unfortunately, Jackson knew that was no idle threat.
Thoughts of a restraining order disappeared from his
mind. If she was pregnant with his child, could he
still ask the courts to keep her away?

He watched her head to the elevator bank, and
as soon as she disappeared behind sliding doors, he
picked up his phone and dialed Hailey's extension.
'Thanks…uh, Hailey, for…uh…your discretion,' he
said, realizing how awkward that must have been for
his poor assistant to hear his ex-girlfriend announce
she's pregnant. 'Can you set up a meeting with my
lawyer? As soon as possible, please.'

Jackson's lawyer, Diane Corley, a heavyset woman
in her fifties who wore her salt-and-pepper hair cut
short, listened to his story and then shook her head
slowly as she sat across from him in his office, the
door closed behind her.

'Well, the problem is, there's no law against what
she's done,' she said, pushing up her tortoiseshell
glasses. She took the news that a woman had tricked
Jackson into a pregnancy without blinking an eye.
She was tough as nails and wasn't easily rattled. 'And
even if there were, it would be your word against hers.
She'd say you wanted her to be pregnant, or at the
very least you engaged in reckless sex.'

'I wore a condom every time!' he declared, ball-
ing up his fists.

'Yes, but condoms fail. There's a known risk with
intercourse.' Diane shook her head. 'I mean, you've

had sex ed. You must know this. Even if she hadn't…
done what she did, the condom could've still failed.
Sex is always a calculated risk.'

'I know.' Jackson sighed. He'd made the biggest
mistake of his life ever having sex with Laurie. How
he wished he could take it back. But he also knew he
had taken the risks. Condoms do break. *Or they're
used in ways I never condoned.*

'It just feels like a violation. There was no consent here.' He stood and paced behind his desk. 'Is
there anything we can do? Can we have her arrested
for the break-in?'

'Maybe. I'll look into it,' she said.

He shook his head. He hated that Laurie had made
another mess. He rubbed his eyes. 'What *can* we do?'

Diane thought about this a moment. She tapped
her pen on his desk as she sat across from him in his
realty office, the door tightly shut behind him. She'd
rearranged her afternoon schedule to come see him,
and for that, he was grateful. 'Well, first of all, we
have to make sure the baby is yours.'

'You think she was sleeping with someone else?
She was *trying* to get pregnant by me.' He paced behind his desk, feeling like a caged lion.

'Someone like that, who knows? She's clearly disturbed, so who knows what she was doing? In any
case, we can use the courts to ask her to get a nonin-
vasive paternity test, especially since she's liable to be
coming after you for half the pregnancy care costs.'

Jackson nodded. 'Good. Well then, that's a start.
But what if it's mine?'

Diane slowly shook her head. 'Then she'll get 20 percent of your income, and probably all the kid's healthcare and college taken care of.' She quirked an eyebrow over her glasses. 'Would you want to see the kid?'

Jackson thought about this. It wasn't the baby's fault he'd been too trusting of his gold-digging mother. Yet he also despised Laurie. How could that all work? But what about Chloe? How would she feel if he had a relationship with a child who wasn't hers? The thought of even *telling* Chloe about this made him feel sick.

'I don't know.' Then he thought about an innocent child, about how it wouldn't be his or her fault who his mother was, or how she'd come to be. 'Yes, I think I would. I couldn't abandon the child. It's not his fault.'

'Even if it means alienating your new girl. What's her name?'

'Chloe. Her name is Chloe.'

'Right, Chloe. Does she know yet?'

'No.' Jackson hadn't wanted to alarm her. It was bad enough they'd been interrupted by a crazy half-naked Laurie who'd broken into his house. No, Jackson didn't want her to know. Didn't want her to know as long as it was possible not to know. 'Like you said, what if the baby's not mine?'

'What if it is?' Diane asked him.

CHAPTER SIXTEEN

A COUPLE OF weeks passed, and Chloe noticed that Jackson seemed distant and distracted. He still texted Chloe often, and they dined together a few times, but work seemed to keep him away from her, and she felt a distance creeping between them and wondered why. Chloe thought things might be turning around when he invited her to Untitled, a bustling restaurant downtown in the basement of a building in River North, modeled after an old Al Capone speakeasy, built in the days of Prohibition. On the outside, the door was a simple black; on the inside, there was a thriving bar and restaurant, with a giant portrait of Capone sitting near the stairs.

It felt odd almost, being hidden away in the restaurant without a storefront or sign. They were surrounded by people in the dining room, and yet the place felt secretive. Dark. On the drive over, Chloe already felt Jackson's distance from her. He seemed disengaged as he stared out the window of the limo driven by his driver. His mood hadn't changed when they'd sat down in the restaurant and ordered wine and their meal. Making conversation felt like pulling teeth, and Chloe wanted to know why everything felt so heavy. She'd asked him at least twice what was bothering him, but both times he'd told her nothing. She knew he was lying.

'Something wrong?' she asked him—for the third time—seeing he'd barely touched his steak, a meal that Chloe realized wouldn't be cheap. In addition to the steak, he'd ordered one of the most expensive bottles of red wine on the menu.

'Nothing,' he said, and she got the feeling he might be lying. His phone pinged, and he grabbed it, glancing at it with interest.

'Who's that?' Chloe's inner insecurities popped up. Was that one of the women on his phone? She knew they occasionally still texted, even though he'd deleted their contact information. Should she ask him to block them? Or should she just trust that he'd say no every time?

'Just…work stuff.' Jackson frowned as he glanced at the screen.

She knew he wasn't telling her the truth. It was the same gut feeling she had about Kevin when he'd made excuses about working late in the weeks leading up to their breakup. If it was one thing Chloe knew, it was that her instincts were rarely wrong. Jackson was hiding something. The question was: What?

Maybe he's not ready to be faithful, a little voice told her. *Maybe he's chafing at being in a relationship with one woman. Maybe he doesn't actually like telling all those other women no. Or hell, maybe he's* not *telling them no.*

Chloe mentally shook herself as she reminded herself not to jump to conclusions or find Jackson guilty in the court of her own mind without any proof at all.

'Hey, you know you can talk to me,' she said. 'About…anything.' *Share with me. Whatever it is, we can work out. Just don't shut me out.*

'I know I can.' Jackson glanced up at her, as she'd temporarily diverted his attention away from his phone's screen. 'Sorry. I just need to…' He tapped out a response on his phone.

Jealousy flared in her mind. Was he texting an old girlfriend? A friend with benefits? Had he gotten another naked photo—this one he couldn't resist? Her mind was one runaway train, careering down the tracks, no brakes and no engineer at the helm. She needed to get a grip on herself. He'd promised he wasn't going to see anyone else, but what if he was growing tired of her? What if he was finding his promise harder to keep than he thought? Chloe put down her fork.

'You seem distracted tonight. Off,' she said.

'I know. I'm sorry. It's just… I'll finish here, one second.' He tapped more on his phone.

'If you're having doubts…' Chloe began.

'Doubts? About what?' Jackson kept his eyes on his phone. *Look at me*, she wanted to shout. She took a big gulp of their expensive wine. The complex bouquet of tastes was nearly lost on her as she was so fixated on Jackson.

'If you're having doubts about us, then just tell me.' Chloe exhaled. She had to mentally prepare herself for what might be coming next. She was giving him an out.

Jackson's head bounced up, surprise on his face. 'Why would I have doubts about us?' Now he looked confused. He set his phone down and reached for her hand across the table. 'Chloe, you're the most amazing woman I've ever met. I don't have any doubts about you.'

He squeezed her hand, and she felt a flood of relief. He seemed completely sincere. He still felt the same way. Whatever was going on with his phone didn't interfere with his feelings for her.

'Has Laurie been bothering you?' she asked.

'Why do you ask that?' He seemed a little defensive. Did the mystery texts on his phone have to do with his stalker? He eyed her warily. *What was he hiding?*

'Well, for one, she broke into your house.' Chloe cocked her head, and he sent her a rueful smile. 'And I wanted to know if the restraining order worked.'

Jackson withdrew his hand and took a sip of his wine. He seemed uncomfortable about even the mention of Laurie at all. 'Let's not talk about Laurie tonight. Let's not let her ruin our dinner.'

'Okay, but… I want to help.' *And I can't help if you don't tell me what the problems are, like when you didn't tell me about Laurie stalking you in the first place.* She remembered how he'd kept that detail secret until Laurie had burst in on them. Would she have ever known he had a stalker ex if that hadn't happened?

It was one thing to ask her to be exclusive, but it was another thing to treat her like a real partner, and that meant letting her in, letting her all the way in. Yet looking at Jackson's face, Chloe felt reluctant to push it. He'd told her his off mood had nothing to do with her, but was he telling her the whole truth?

Jackson's phone dinged again, and Chloe fought the urge to snatch it from his hands and toss it across the restaurant. Jackson glanced at his screen and his eyes bulged, a flush creeping into his face. Then he tossed down his napkin on the table.

'I—I need to… I'll be right back,' he stammered in a rush as he left Chloe sitting at the table, fork in hand, wondering what had just happened.

Jackson's heart pounded like the rat-a-tat-tat of a tommy gun in his chest. Laurie had sent him a picture, and not just any picture—one of Chloe and Jackson on his rooftop patio. Chloe, breasts exposed, straddled him. Her skirt covered their lower halves, but it was pretty obvious to anyone what was happening.

I was deep inside her right then, and her face, eyes closed, head back, implies it, too. The picture was taken from Chloe's building, he realized. Must have been, as the angle was from above and to the right. Had she broken into Chloe's apartment two weeks ago? The thought made Jackson's heart race even faster.

He stood beneath the bar's large open staircase as he looked at the picture once more. Laurie had sent it to him with a single message:

I need money for vitamins and a doctor's appointment for the DNA test. Send me $5,000 today or I'll tell your little whore about the baby you made inside me.

Blackmail. Of course she'd resorted to that. He'd expected nothing less of Laurie. And what kind of prenatal vitamins cost five thousand dollars? He was no fool. He knew she'd use the money on herself. Of course, five thousand dollars was nothing to him. He'd bet more on a single blackjack hand in Vegas before. At the same time, he also knew if he paid her, she'd keep asking for more. And then what?

He decided to stall.

I already paid for the DNA test. We're waiting for results, remember? No need for extra money for that.

She responded almost immediately.

I think we should do more than one DNA test, so I need $$. And your baby needs vitamins.

As he stood there pondering what to do, another message came through. There was another photo, this one showing all of Chloe's bare backside as Jackson readied to enter her.

Better decide quick, or I'll make this photo public.
Maybe everybody should see how she takes you.
Like the whore she is.

White-hot rage pulsed in Jackson's temples. All
he wanted to do was protect Chloe from this…crazy
woman. But the more he tried, the deeper the nightmare.

Don't do this, he texted back instantly.

His phone dinged again, and this time, there was a
close-up shot of Chloe—all of her down below. Laurie
was unstable, crazy. This nightmare needed to stop.

'What is that?' Chloe's voice behind him made
him whirl. With the hum of patrons in the bar, he
hadn't heard her approach, and now she was staring
at his phone. Had she seen?

'Nothing,' he said.

'That's a lie.' Chloe's mouth twitched. 'I saw it.
Someone sent you a naked picture.' The hurt in her
eyes was real, and in that instant, Jackson realized
the horrible conclusions Chloe was jumping to right
then.

'It's not what you think.' Jackson desperately
wanted her to believe him, but not ask any more questions. What was worse? Having her believe he wanted
to have sex with other women, or having her know
that he might have impregnated one of them?

'Then you'd better explain.' Chloe folded her arms
across her chest. Her dark eyes flashed fire, but he
was amazed at her calmness, her clarity. She wasn't
going ballistic, or shouting and screaming, like an-

other woman might. She was calmly waiting for an explanation even as fury burned just beneath the surface. Jackson realized he had one shot and one shot only at getting through to her before she made up her own mind. He felt like choking right then. What did he say? Anything he could think to say, even the truth, seemed like the wrong answer.

When he hesitated, Chloe tried once more. 'Now is the time for you to come clean, because there won't be another chance.' Jackson glanced at her, as she stood, clutch in hand, ready to flee. 'Just tell me the truth, okay? Whatever it is. The truth is better than a lie.'

'You might not be so sure about that when you hear it.'

'Just be honest with me.' Chloe swallowed hard as she took a step closer to him. Her dark eyes shone with unshed tears and the hint of pain. 'If you don't want to be with me exclusively, you can tell me.'

'No! That's not it. Not it at all.' Jackson ran a frustrated hand through his hair. The thrum of the noise from the bar felt like nails on a chalkboard. He grabbed her elbow and moved her to the hallway to the bathroom, where the noise was a bit more muffled.

She looked at him expectantly. Pain still in her eyes.

'It's not you. It's Laurie.' He took a deep breath. God, how was he going to tell her this? 'The picture you saw. She took it. Of us.' He showed her the picture on his phone. Starting with the close-up one and then flipping to the two of them together on his rooftop deck.

'What?' Chloe cried in shock as she studied the images. 'But...how?'

'I don't know. I think she was in your building.'

Chloe tried to take Jackson's phone, but he held it tightly. She pressed her face close to the photo. 'I think you're right. Has to be. From that angle.' Chloe glanced up at Jackson, fear on her face. 'Did she break into my building?'

'I don't know. But...there's more.' Jackson swallowed. 'She's threatening to make the photos public.'

Chloe's hands fell to her sides. 'What?' Her voice sounded hollow and empty, and the color drained from her face. 'But if she did that... I could lose clients. And—God! My parents might see!'

'I'm going to do everything I can to make sure the pictures don't get out.'

Chloe hugged herself. 'Can we have her arrested? For blackmail? Or...what's it called...revenge porn? Isn't that against the law?'

'I'll ask my lawyer about it.' *You've got to tell her the rest.*

'I can't believe this. I can't believe...' Chloe shook her head. 'This is a nightmare.'

A nightmare that's about to get worse.

'There's something else.' Chloe looked up at him, and he could see her steel herself for another blow. How he wanted to protect her from this. He wondered, briefly, if after she knew she'd even speak to him again. It was a lot to ask anybody to take. 'Remember when I told you that Laurie tried to get pregnant behind my back?'

Chloe nodded, a single stiff nod. How he wished he didn't have to tell her this.

'Well, that wasn't the only time she tried. Apparently.' Suddenly, Jackson couldn't look Chloe in the eye. God, how he wanted not to tell her this. 'She says she's pregnant. She says she's pregnant with my baby.'

CHAPTER SEVENTEEN

THE WHOLE WORLD seemed to shrink then, as Chloe watched Jackson's lips move but didn't hear anything else coming out. Laurie, crazy Laurie, was pregnant with Jackson's baby? No. God, no. Suddenly Chloe couldn't breathe. She felt like the walls of the small hallway were going to close in on her. A woman bustled out of a nearby bathroom then, brushing past them, and Chloe felt like she'd fall.

'Chloe. Say something.' Jackson gripped her by her elbows, blue eyes on her, pleading for something. His thick blond hair was a little long, a little ruffled.

She felt numb. Worse than numb, empty. She wasn't even angry, although she assumed that would come later. Now she didn't feel anything.

'The baby might not be mine.'

'But it might be,' Chloe choked out.

'Yes.' Jackson glanced at the floor. He didn't have to say more. Laurie was trying for this, on purpose, so what were the odds she was sleeping around? Panic, white-hot panic, began to rise in her throat. She'd asked Jackson to be honest with her, yet now that he had, she wasn't sure she could handle it. All the ramifications flooded her: a baby in their lives, a reminder of her, a mentally unstable stalker, who now had the important title of *mother of his child.* She remembered the crazy look in Laurie's eyes when she'd broken into his house, the twisted way she'd invited herself into their bed. She'd gotten off on it, too, somehow.

Just like you did? Watching Jackson and Annaliese? Now she felt sick to her stomach. Did she have anything in common with that crazy, horrible woman? Surely not. Yet the tiny voice wouldn't be silenced, either. *I was different,* her mind wanted to shout. *Jackson loves me. Doesn't he? He said he did. He wanted me. Not her.*

But with the baby, did that change anything? What if he decided to marry her? The thought made her feel like she couldn't breathe.

'What are you going to do?' she asked, cursing herself for lacking the courage to ask the question on her mind. Would he marry her?

'I don't know. Wait for the results of the DNA test next Tuesday,' he said.

'And then? If it's yours?' Bile pooled in her throat.

'I don't know, Chloe. I really don't.'

Chloe stepped away from him, and his hands fell away from her elbows.

'I... I need some time. To process all this.' She glanced away from his handsome face, the hurt obvious in his eyes.

He covered his goatee with one hand, agitated, upset.

'Please. Chloe. Don't leave me.' The pleading tone made tears spring to her eyes. He needed her, and yet she couldn't help him. Not like this. But what could she do? She couldn't breathe. Couldn't think. She needed to regroup. To figure out what she would do next. How she felt about all this. She'd been the one imagining having a baby with Jackson. Not helping to raise a baby that wasn't hers. That was *if* he didn't marry Laurie.

'I just… I can't right now. I need to think.' Tears choked her voice. She needed space from him. Jackson let her go.

'I guess I understand.' But his eyes told a different story. They looked betrayed, abandoned. 'Let me and my driver drop you home.'

'No!' Chloe shook her head. 'No. I want to go. Alone.'

Chloe left Jackson then, running up the staircase and into the warm summer's night. She felt a surge of guilt for leaving Jackson when he needed her most, and yet she just couldn't stay. Not when her heart was breaking. Not when she didn't know if she could accept this. Tears streaked down her face as she hugged herself, jogging past a couple on the street holding hands and laughing.

Chloe stood in her empty apartment, staring out her window at Jackson's darkened living room. He hadn't come home yet, or if he had, he hadn't turned on any lights. She sat in her dark apartment, too, still feeling stunned. She just couldn't handle it. She still wasn't sure what she was going to do. Never in a million years had she imagined being faced with a choice like this.

What if he lied about her tricking him? What if he'd gone inside her, like he's been inside me?

No, she reasoned. Laurie had even *mentioned* the fact that he insisted on condoms when she'd broken into his house. Also, she'd broken into his *house.* An unstable person like that would be the kind of person who thought trapping a man with a baby was a good idea.

What if he marries her? What if he feels it's the right thing to do?

The traitorous thoughts came fast and furious, like Hydra heads. As soon as she swatted down one, two more took its place.

Even now, as she struggled with how to feel about Laurie's pregnancy, she found herself missing Jackson. Even now, her body ached for him, for his touch, for his solid arms around her shoulders. But what if she never felt them again?

Talk to him, her mind screamed. But she wasn't ready. She just couldn't face it if he told her he planned to do the right thing, if that even applied in this situation. Was the right thing marrying Laurie?

She watched as the light flickered on in Jackson's second floor, his workshop. There was just a single small window there, but through it she caught a glimpse of his shadow, and then part of his back as he sat nearby and worked on finishing one of his bar stools.

How can he work at a time like this? she wondered, but then realized he probably was trying to calm down, maybe refocus his mind. He'd told her that woodworking was soothing. He was good at it, too, working with his hands. Chloe tried not to think about what else his hands were good at doing. She got up and moved away from the window. She was going to drive herself crazy. Maybe she ought to just go over there. Talk to him.

But I still don't know how I feel about this. Any of it.

She wanted to be okay with it, but deep down, she wasn't sure she could be. She'd never imagined being a stepmom, and especially not to a child conceived like this, not in love, but greed. And then having Laurie in their lives, potentially forever. It made her sick. The whole situation made her sick to her stomach. Could she get over it? Could she somehow learn to live with it?

Maybe she could. She wanted to, for Jackson's sake. *He told me he loves me. And I think I love him, too. But was that enough?*

She wasn't sure. She truly wasn't. And if there *was* a baby involved, then she felt on some level she had to be sure. She owed it to the baby, who'd done nothing wrong here. Chloe wasn't going to commit unless she was sure she could go the distance.

She glanced at Jackson's lit window across the alley. She needed some time to think.

Tuesday morning, Jackson sat at his desk in his office overlooking Lake Michigan barely taking note of anything around him. The whole world seemed to be drained of color now that Chloe had left him. He wanted to believe she just needed time to adjust to the news, but when he didn't hear from her Saturday or Sunday or Monday, he began to worry the split wasn't temporary.

How can I blame her, really? How would I handle the news if she told me she were carrying another man's baby?

He didn't know, couldn't know, but he felt jealousy burn in his gut at the very thought. She'd no doubt feel the same.

'Knock, knock.' Hailey stood at his office door, a look of pity on her face. She'd been extra nice to him recently—offering to get his dry-cleaning and other tasks he normally handled himself. He appreciated her effort. 'Want another coffee? I was going to run to Starbucks.'

'No, Hailey. But thank you.'

Hailey hesitated. 'How are you…holding up, sir?'

'Terribly,' he admitted, and she smiled. 'Chloe didn't take the news well.'

Hailey's features softened. 'Give her some time,' she said. 'I don't know Chloe well, but what I do know of her, I really like. She might come around.'

'Thanks, Hailey.' His assistant nodded once and then retreated from the doorway. Thankfully, Hailey had kept the news of the pregnancy to herself. Nobody yet was gossiping about it at work, and for that he was grateful he had such a loyal assistant. He made a mental note to up her bonus this year for a job well done.

Hailey made her way to the elevator for the coffee break and disappeared behind the sliding steel doors. Jackson tried to focus on his email, but he found his mind wandering. He couldn't focus on anything. He wondered what Chloe was doing. *How* she was doing. He picked up his cell phone and texted her. Just a quick message. How are you?

Her replies over the last two days had been curt and to the point, which he expected again. But before he could mull over that much more, he heard a knock at his door.

Kent stood there, looking predatory as usual, his blazer-and-khaki prep look solidified for yet another day. Jackson wondered if the man owned any other clothes. He frowned, not at all happy to see him.

'Ever hear of making an appointment?' Jackson felt his fingers clutch his phone as annoyance thrummed in his veins.

'You haven't been returning my calls,' Kent said, grinning. 'I *was* asking for a meeting, so I figured I'd take the bull by the horns.' He made himself at home by sitting in one of the chairs in front of Jackson's desk and crossing his legs at the knee. 'You not interested in 1209 anymore?'

Jackson sighed. Chloe's building. 'Yes, I'm interested. I'm just…busy with other things at the moment.'

The triumphant look on Kent's face made Jackson want to punch him square in the nose. 'So I've heard.'

'What do you mean, you've heard?' Now Jackson's guard was fully up.

'People talk.' He put his fingers together and

made a steeple. It was as if he was trying to imitate a James Bond villain. 'Let's just say I heard you... weren't careful.'

'What do you know?' *And who told you? Not Hailey. Not Chloe. Then who? Laurie.*

'Enough.' Kent grinned. 'I actually understand it. Laurie's a piece of ass. Tapped that myself.'

'Wait...what?' Jackson's head spun.

'You didn't think you were the only rich guy she was trying to reel in? But I'm too smart for that, friend. I got snipped so women couldn't trap me. Then the joke's on them. You know...when they are trying for it, but all they're getting are blanks.' Kent seemed proud of his little scheme, obnoxiously proud. The look on his face made Jackson disgusted. 'You've got to think ahead, man. And the best part is, they beg you *not* to wear a condom.'

'You're a lowlife, you know that? And why would you get that kind of serious surgery just...'

'Because I like to win, and this way, *I win.*' God, even sex was some kind of sick competition with him. 'I'm just playing the players.' He shrugged. 'They're trying to use me, but I use them instead. It works out nicely.'

Jackson felt sick to his stomach. 'When did you sleep with Laurie?'

'Right before you. She'd been trying to snag a whale forever. You just happened to be the whale of the month.'

'So you took advantage of her.'

'Something like that.' Kent crossed his legs and

studied his nails absently. 'Actually, you should thank me. She was so brokenhearted when I told her I'd been snipped. I told her all about you, how much you were worth and everything. She couldn't wait to meet you then. She even got a job at your favorite bar for the privilege.'

Jackson felt stunned. The whole thing was a... setup? He felt like he'd been hit with a sledgehammer.

Kent was still gloating. 'But I get it, it's rotten timing for you. Just when things were heating up with that sexy little number of yours. What was her name? Chloe?'

'Keep Chloe out of this.' Jackson's voice was a low growl.

'Those pictures of you two on the roof...'

'Wait. You saw the pictures? That Laurie sent?'

'Saw them?' Kent laughed a little, high-pitched, and clapped his hands in glee. 'I *took* them. I own that building next door. I just forwarded them on to Laurie. I knew she'd be interested. And she was.'

Jackson stood up and clutched the edge of his desk. 'Give me one reason why I don't throw you out of here right now.'

'Because I still have the building you want. You need me.'

Jackson fumed, staring at his longtime adversary. 'What I want to know is why? Why even tell me all this?'

'That's easy: to gloat, New Money. Like I said, I like to *win*, and I can't win if you don't even know we were playing a game. That you lost.'

'Get out,' Jackson ground out, barely restraining his temper.

'You're making a mistake, New Money.'

'Get the *hell* out.' Jackson banged his desk with his fist and Kent stood.

'I'll chalk this up to *paternal* stress, amigo.' Kent left the office, whistling. Jackson wanted to run after him and tackle the son of a bitch. Jackson shook his head. He should be glad that Laurie hadn't been crazy enough to break into Chloe's building. Kent owned it and had the common door key, so it wouldn't be hard for him to get on the roof and snap a few shots. Once again, Jackson was baffled by Kent's seeming obsession with him. Telling Laurie to go seek him out? Stalking his rooftop patio? Jackson shook his head. Seemed that Kent had nothing better to do than follow him around. Pathetic.

His temper cooled, and he found himself regaining a bit of his composure. Then his phone rang. He glanced at it and saw Chloe's name flash across the screen.

'Hey,' she said, voice sounding soft, contrite even. 'Do you have time for a break? I know it's not quite lunchtime, but…'

'Yes, I'll make time,' he said, hope welling in his chest for the first time that morning. 'Where do you want to meet?'

CHAPTER EIGHTEEN

THEY MET AT Navy Pier, where tourists thronged the pathway and the oversize Ferris wheel anchored the land side. Restaurants and little shops lined the pier, as did vendors offering boat rides to the lake. Every Saturday in the summer, the pier offered up fireworks and boat rides, but today all Jackson wanted was to see Chloe. She was sitting on a bench when he arrived. She stood, happy to see him. When Jackson opened his arms, she rushed into them, giving him a big hug. His heart swelled then. He'd missed her in the short time they'd been apart, and the worry that she was leaving him, forever, was almost too much to bear. God, she smelled so good. Her hair like lavender and vanilla. He suddenly wished they were alone.

'I'm sorry,' she said into his chest.

'Why?' he asked her, perplexed as he pulled away, the two of them surrounded by people and yet very much alone at the same time.

'For…freaking out on you.'

'You have every reason to freak out,' he said.

'Want to sit?' She offered a place next to her on

the bench, facing out to Lake Michigan. He took a seat there, the shadow of the Ferris wheel behind them. He took her hand, still worried she might be here to deliver bad news. *I never want to see you again* bad news.

'How have you been?' he asked, feeling as stiff as his words sounded.

'Bad,' she admitted. 'But I've thought things through.'

He took a deep breath. 'And?'

'And I just wanted you to know that...' Chloe swallowed. 'Whatever happens, I'm with you.'

For the first time since Laurie came to his office with the horrible news, Jackson felt a tiny sprig of hope bloom in his chest.

'You're with me,' he echoed. 'Even if the baby is mine?'

Chloe nodded. He stared at her dark eyes, full of emotion, and felt tears welling in his own. 'You're sure?' he asked, squeezing her hand.

'I'm positive. Whatever happens, we'll face it together.'

Jackson pulled Chloe into his arms and kissed her deeply. 'I love you,' he murmured.

'I love you, too.' Those words made his heart feel like it would explode. He hugged her even harder, not wanting to let her go.

'I'm sorry I took so long,' she mumbled into his chest. 'I just wanted to be sure.'

He released her. 'No, I'm glad you took some time to think it over. I know it's not an easy decision. Not at all.' He glanced back at the huge white wheel turning slowly behind them. 'Why don't we take a ride? We deserve a break, a little fun, I think.'

'You want to?' she asked, uncertain.

'I do.'

The line was short, and in minutes, they'd gotten their own car, sealed from the elements by glass windows on all sides. Jackson and Chloe sat across from each other, gazing into each other's eyes. There was a bit of sadness about her, but at the same time, Chloe was the kind of woman who'd be the partner he needed: fearless. Most women would've run away and kept running after they'd heard the news of the pregnancy. Not Chloe. Jackson knew beyond a doubt this woman was the one. If he had a ring in his pocket, he would get down on one knee right there in the Ferris wheel car and propose. As the car moved higher and higher into the sky, giving them a breathtaking view of the city skyline and the glistening blue lake, Jackson allowed himself to actually feel hopeful about the future.

'You've changed my life for the better, you know that?' he told Chloe. 'Standing by me, it's brave. And I'll never forget that. I've never trusted anyone like I trust you, and I hope you know that you're my partner. Now and always.'

'I trust you, too,' Chloe said. 'Thank you for telling me about Laurie. About what was going on. You could've kept it all from me, and… I mean, I was mad at first that you didn't tell me right away, but I also get you were hoping the DNA test proves it's not yours.' Chloe glanced at Jackson. 'Do you think it's possible it's not yours?'

'Well, Kent had been sleeping with her before me, and he's had a vasectomy. Told me all about it.' Jackson rolled his eyes.

'He—what?' Chloe frowned.

'Oh, yeah, and actually Kent is the one who told Laurie she ought to date me. So, small world.'

Chloe's mouth dropped open. 'You can't be serious.'

'Unfortunately, I am. Kent hates me, always has, and has had this chip on his shoulder ever since I outmaneuvered him on a parkland deal. He's been after me ever since, and looks like he finally got me.' Jackson glanced at the tiny white sailboats dotting the water of the massive lake far below them.

'No,' Chloe said, grabbing Jackson's hand. 'He hasn't won. Because you have me, and we'll get through this together. One way or another. I know we will.'

Jackson squeezed Chloe's hand, feeling his heart swell up with love and admiration for her. She was a good woman, through and through. 'Come over here,' he said, grinning. He patted the seat next to him.

'Can I?' She glanced around, clearly worrying about the balance of the car.

'Then I'm coming over there.' He made a quick move and then was beside her, pulling her into his arms. The car swung a bit, but righted itself soon enough. He kissed her long and hard, their tongues meeting in a promise of more kisses to come.

He felt her hand wander down to the front of his pants.

'Looks like you might need to open that zipper,' she purred in his ear, and he felt a shiver run down his spine. She was like a drug, a powerful aphrodisiac, one he was powerless to resist. He wanted her.

'Naughty girl! We're in a bubble. The *whole* city can see us.'

'You were the one who turned me on to exhibitionism,' she pointed out. He had to laugh.

'True. But then we were photographed and blackmailed.' He quirked an eyebrow. 'See how well that turned out?'

'That does put a damper on the mood,' Chloe agreed.

'Then again,' Jackson said, squeezing her bare knee, 'maybe I should take you right here. Right now.' Somehow, he knew he'd find her wet and ready.

The phone in his back pocket rang. Reluctantly, he glanced at it and saw Diane was calling.

'It's my lawyer,' he told Chloe. She nodded. 'Hello?' he said, and put the call on speakerphone. 'Diane? I've got you on speaker. Chloe is here with me, and anything you say to me, you can say to her.'

'Good. Because I've got news. The DNA test results came back.'

'And?' Jackson braced himself for bad news. He felt like he'd been zapped into a Maury Povich episode. Chloe squeezed his hand.

'And you're *not* the father.'

Jackson stared at Chloe, feeling a mix of emotions: relief, joy, shock. Chloe clutched at his arm.

'He's not?' Chloe could barely contain her glee. 'For certain?'

'Nope. One hundred percent not Jackson's. Actually, we ran two DNA tests, since she admitted to sleeping with another person around the same time, and *that* test came up positive, so you're off the hook.'

'Wait…was that other person Kent Roberts?' Jackson asked. Chloe's mouth dropped open in shock.

'I'm not technically supposed to know his name,' Diane replied, 'but I happened to look at the file, and the other DNA sample was labeled Roberts, so it's fairly likely.'

'Well, I'll be damned.' Jackson barked a bitter laugh. 'Looks like he has a malpractice suit on his hands.'

'A…what?' Diane asked, sounding confused.

'He had a vasectomy, but clearly it didn't take. He thought the surgery would mean he could sleep with whoever he wanted without protection. He didn't care about disease, apparently, or anything else.'

'Oh, I had a case once like that,' Diane said. 'It's rare, but it happens. One in one thousand men regrow the tube or whatever, and then…well, the highway is open for business again, I guess.' She coughed uncomfortably on the line, but Jackson didn't care. He laughed, a full-bodied laugh. Nobody deserved that nightmare more than Kent. Looked like the player got played, by his own body. Instant karma.

He felt a bubble of excitement and relief grow in his chest. He wasn't the father. He still couldn't believe it.

Jackson shook his head. 'So this means I don't owe Laurie anything?'

'That's right. And if she tries to release any photos of you, we'll hit her with everything we've got. I've already served her a cease-and-desist on the photos she has, and if she releases them, we'll take her for every penny she has. So you *and* Chloe should rest easy. Plus, I've got Chicago PD looking into filing burglary and trespassing charges as well.'

'Good,' Chloe said.

'Thank you, Diane. Really,' Jackson said.

'Anytime.' Diane clicked off the line, and Jackson hugged Chloe.

'God, can you believe that?' Jackson said, shaking his head. 'It's Kent's!'

'Well, looks like she's got her rich daddy after all,' Chloe said, laughing a little. Her face shone with happiness and relief, and she looked so beautiful. 'I can't believe he did that just so he could…you know…go without a condom. What if he decided one day he wanted kids?'

Jackson shrugged. 'I guess he doesn't have to worry about that now.'

The two of them laughed a little.

'They kind of deserve each other,' she said.

'Hell, yes, they do,' Jackson said slapping the cushioned armrest.

Chloe laced her fingers between his. 'I'm not going to lie, this makes me very, very happy. Does that make me a bad person?'

'Not at all,' he said. 'I love you. So much.' Jackson

drew Chloe into his arms for a kiss. 'You're the only woman I want, now and forever.'

'You're sure?'

'Beyond positive.' Jackson lifted Chloe up so she was sitting in his lap. He kissed her gently, and she returned the kiss. The Ferris wheel spun back by the platform slowly and then began its ascent once more to the top of the wheel. He broke the kiss and stared into her dark eyes.

'Now, where were we before we were interrupted?'

'About to break about a dozen public indecency statutes?' Chloe ran her long nails through his thick hair. He closed his eyes, loving her touch, eager to have it for many months and years to come.

'Oh, yes, that's right.' Jackson slipped his hand up the side of her skirt, feeling her soft skin, thrilled with the knowledge that one day, maybe she'd be the one to carry his baby.

'I love you,' she murmured, even as he worked his hand up higher, rubbing her outer thigh and squeezing.

'I love you,' he said, nuzzling her neck as she turned, straddling him in his seat. He could feel her warmth, her readiness, even through the fabric of his pants. This was exactly where he was meant to be.

Yes, he thought, *I'm coming home*.

* * * * *

COMING SOON!

We really hope you enjoyed reading this book. If you're looking for more romance, be sure to head to the shops when new books are available on

Thursday
1st November

LET'S TALK
Romance

For exclusive extracts, competitions
and special offers, find us online:

f facebook.com/millsandboon

◎ @millsandboonuk

𝕏 @millsandboon

Or get in touch on 0844 844 1351*

For all the latest titles coming soon, visit
millsandboon.co.uk/nextmonth